I0743107

PAPER ROSES
on
STONY MOUNTAIN

ALSO BY DIANA STEVAN

LILACS in the DUST BOWL

SUNFLOWERS UNDER FIRE

THE RUBBER FENCE

A CRY FROM THE DEEP

THE BLUE NIGHTGOWN

PAPER ROSES
on
STONY MOUNTAIN

A NOVEL

Diana Stevan

Island House
Publishing

Library and Archives Canada Cataloguing in Publication

Island House
Publishing

ISBN: 978-1-988180-21-2 (Large Print)
ISBN: 978-1-988180-12-0 (hardback)
ISBN: 978-1-988180-09-0 (paperback)
ISBN: 978-1-988180-10-6 (Kindle)
ISBN: 978-1-988180-11-3 (other eBooks)

"Oh, You Beautiful Doll" is a ragtime love song published in 1911 with words by Seymour Brown and music by Nat B. Ayer
"Let Me Call You Sweetheart", love song published 1910, Harold Rossiter Music Co. Chicago; composer, Leo Friedman; lyrics by Beth Slater Wilson.
"I Wandered Lonely as a Cloud", poem by William Wordsworth, written in 1804.
"She Walks in Beauty", poem by Lord Byron, written in 1814.

Cover design by Ares Jun
Formatting and layout by Polgarus Studio

Printed and bound in the United States

For my father,
Peter Klewchuk
a prince of a man

*Do not watch the petals fall from the rose
with sadness,
know that, like life, things sometimes
must fade,
before they can bloom again.*

Unknown Author

A Curious Incident

Lukia believed there was nothing like the sun's glow to dispel the darkest of moods, but despite the warm rays on her skin, she could not shake the feeling of foreboding that had come over her. She stopped weeding the vegetable garden to push some loose strands of hair off her forehead, then stretched her aching back and leaned on her hoe. Her daughter, Dunya, and daughter-in-law, Elena, had their heads down as they hoed the rows nearby. Their laughter over some shared joke punctuated the air, as did the honking of the geese flying overhead. Lukia wished she could share their joy. She should have been working, like them, with renewed vigor. From what she understood from the news reports on the radio, the Depression was nearing its end. A Depression that had given her nothing but grief ever since she'd immigrated with her family to Manitoba in 1929—eight years ago. The hard times weren't over yet, but rising grain prices meant hope on the horizon. That should have been enough to get Lukia dancing the kolomeyka up and down the rows, but her thoughts were elsewhere.

Her sons continued to quarrel. Egnat's frustration had grown over Mike's irresponsibility and his flirting with Elena. His wife had done nothing to encourage Mike, but her gentle nature had charmed the younger brother, who would often make excuses to help her with the children or some domestic chore rather than work alongside his brother in the fields. And then, when he returned drunk from the city with less cash than expected from the sale of their grain or dairy products, there was bound to be a fight. Lukia had lost count of how many times she'd pulled Mike aside to tell him to stop aggravating Egnat, to stop visiting the beer parlour or the bootlegger, to stop entertaining his friends and strangers, and to stop pestering Elena. No matter what she said or how she said it, he didn't listen.

Lukia stared into the distance, where Egnat sat on the horse-drawn mower, cutting the pasture. He had tolerated so much, and yet he never complained. Even when he had to build his father's coffin on his thirteenth birthday and help his mother raise his siblings. The problem was Mike was simply too close in age to allow his older brother to be his guide. His horns of envy threatened to tear her family apart.

As if she didn't have enough grey hairs, there was also the problem of Dunya, who was in love with a poor man. He'd stopped coming around a year ago over some silly argument, but when her daughter ran into him the other day in Winnipeg, she realized she still loved him and broke off her engagement to a Russian fellow, a man of means who worked at the Winnipeg Stock Exchange. Why did Dunya push Sergei aside and give up a chance for a good life? She hoped Dunya would come to her senses. Immersed in thought, Lukia nearly tripped over Puppy, who surprised her by charging out of the cornstalks, kicking up the dust and making her cough.

"Puppy! What's got you so excited? If you had my worries, you wouldn't be jumping like that." She leaned down to pet the collie before watching him scamper off to greet Dunya and Elena. Thrusting the hoe into the soil again, she hacked away at the weeds as if they were hiding the answers to all her problems.

Brooding over her lost love, Dunya brushed her long hair, then sat on her bed in the room she shared with her mother and her niece, Genya. She tried to make sense of what had happened in Winnipeg. Peter should've been standing there on the sidewalk when she came out of the jewellery shop. She could have sworn he had been staring at her through the window as she was picking out rings with Sergei. But when she ran out of the shop to talk to him, there was no Peter in sight in any direction.

Confused, she wondered if Peter's image had been a mirage. Or a sign from God saying it was Peter she should marry, not Sergei, even though Peter had broken up with her six months before. And who was she to argue with God? She told Sergei their engagement was off and left him standing on the sidewalk.

When she returned to the farm, she related this curious incident to her mother. But instead of being understanding, her mother scolded her. First, for breaking off her engagement to a successful man and then, for thinking of eloping without her mother's or priest's blessing.

Unabashed, Dunya had shrugged and said, "Why are you so upset? I didn't get married."

"Oy," her mother said. "That's all you have to say? My God, how have I raised you?"

"I'm sorry, Mama." Dunya knew better than to argue with her mother.

She said good night to her mother, donned her nightgown, and got down on her knees. After saying the Lord's Prayer, she asked God for another sign. "If Peter's the one I'm supposed to marry, have him come back to me." Satisfied with her request, she climbed into bed and fell asleep thinking of Peter.

A week later, Dunya decided she couldn't leave her future up to God alone. Though the day promised to be hot, the kind the English called a *scorcher*, she went with

Egnat in their wagon to Stony Mountain to get some flour and other staples. It was usually her mother who went, but this time Dunya offered to go, as she was hoping to run into Peter, who lived in the village which had a federal penitentiary on the hill leading up to it.

About a mile before the village, they passed the farm where the prisoners toiled. A large work gang in coveralls, their feet bound by chains, were weeding and thinning the crop while a guard on horseback stood watch. A few appeared younger than her. She thought their lives must have been awful if they had to resort to crime to get ahead. She guessed some were dangerous, or else why would they be bound like that and forced to do labour in such a humiliating fashion?

As her brother drove the horses up the hill, past the limestone prison—a massive structure that loomed forbiddingly over the highway and the prairies—Dunya shifted in her seat uncomfortably. There was no escape from the sun beating down on them. Her thighs stuck together in the unbearable heat. She flapped her arms, hoping perspiration wouldn't stain her dress and spoil her appearance. She thought about what she would say if she ran into Peter. Maybe he would be at Dan Balacko's General Store, one of two stores in the village. Dan's was popular with the Ukrainian farmers; the other was William McGimpsey's, popular with the English. General stores were where locals gossiped and discussed news and politics. She wondered what she should do if she saw Peter there. Should she apologize for her part in their breakup? Should she tell him she thought she saw him looking in the jewellery shop window? Should she say she never really loved her Russian boyfriend and was no longer engaged?

"You're awfully quiet," said Egnat as he drove past the penitentiary. "Are you sick?"

If she were being honest, she might

have said, *sick in love with Peter*, but she replied, "No, I'm just thinking. You always complain I talk too much. You should be happy I'm quiet."

He snorted as he flicked the reins. "You're right. It's a nice change when you're quiet."

She jutted her chin and looked ahead.

Outside Dan's store, a couple of farmers stood around an old truck, having a smoke. Egnat stopped to talk to them, while Dunya peered up and down the gravel road, hoping to catch a glimpse of Peter. But all she saw were two cars driving down the main street, which contained the Masonic Lodge, the Canadian Legion, a modern school, and three churches.

She found some shade under the store's eaves and stood in back of the farmers, who didn't seem to mind the sun.

Egnat pulled a hand-rolled cigarette from his shirt pocket and lit it. He said to the stout farmer in baggy overalls, "It's going to be another hot one. I heard on the radio, it's a record heat wave. How are your crops doing?"

"You know how it is. It looked promising this spring. I thought for sure the hell of the last eight years was past. One good thing, though. We fought the grasshoppers off this time."

Egnat's forehead furrowed. "I thought they'd never leave."

"At least grain prices have gone up," the elderly farmer said, taking off his battered straw hat to wipe his brow.

"A lot of good that will do," Egnat said, "if we don't have any grain worth harvesting."

The men nodded and took another puff.

The stout farmer nudged the old-timer. "How are you making out with that lady friend of yours?"

"There may be snow on top, but there's still fire in the old furnace."

The men laughed. Egnat flicked the

ash off his cigarette with his thumbnail, and after ensuring his rollup was no longer lit, put it back in his shirt pocket. The men smiled at Dunya, who took one last look down the street before following her brother into the store.

As usual, the storekeeper, Dan Balacko—a husky young man with dashing features—flirted with her. "Dunya, you're a sight to behold. You better watch all the fellas." Dan's eyes roamed over her figure, stopping at her breasts.

Egnat, always protective, said, "Dunya, I need some help in the back."

"I'm low on butter. Can you bring some in soon?" Dan asked Egnat.

"In a day or so," he replied, before walking away with Dunya. Together, they picked up fifty-pound bags of flour and sugar and carried them out to the wagon. Checking the list she got from her mother, Dunya browsed the store aisles and picked up a box of salt, a cylinder of pepper, a tin of black tea, and a large spool of black cotton thread.

They waited at the counter while Dan recorded their purchases under their family name in his ledger. So far, they were good on their credit. Dan wrote the total on a slip of paper and gave it to Egnat.

Dunya said to Dan, "If you see Peter Klewchuk, tell him Dolly Mazurec was asking about him. You can also tell him she's no longer engaged."

"Is that right?" said Dan, grinning. "It's Dolly now, is it? Damn, if I wasn't already married ..."

"Yeah, yeah, yeah," Dunya said jokingly. Even if Dan was unattached, she had no interest in him as a potential suitor. He was known as the town wolf. How much of that was true, she didn't know. But she believed, where there's smoke, there's fire. A girl couldn't be too careful.

The Poor Fellow

Oy, he's here again, thought Lukia, as she looked up from the chickens scurrying to eat the grain she tossed. A hen squawked in protest as a more aggressive bird pushed her out of the way.

Across the barnyard, Dunya was welcoming Peter with a hug. He'd ridden over on his bicycle from Stony Mountain to see her. And she had been anxiously waiting for him to visit. Lukia had never imagined he'd come back into her daughter's life. She threw more chicken feed, then glanced at the young couple. Their faces shone brightly, as if lit from within. Lukia exhaled sharply. She guessed he was staying for lunch. She rubbed her palms to release the feed stuck to her hand and waved at him, before hurrying to the house to check the borscht simmering on the stove.

Lukia pondered the young man while she seasoned the soup with salt and pepper. She knew nothing about his family. He wasn't a farmer. He did odd jobs. What kind of future could he promise her daughter?

The sound of the front door opening interrupted her rumination.

"Good day, Panye Mazurec," said Peter in perfect Ukrainian, as he entered the house with Dunya. "It's nice to see you again."

Lukia smiled. He must've been practising, she thought. His Ukrainian had improved. Dunya had mentioned he'd immigrated with his mother when he was two, so that could account for his poor Ukrainian speech. "Welcome," Lukia said.

"Please, sit down. I have some nice borscht."

While Dunya set another bowl on the table, her brothers came in from the field. Mike embraced Peter, as was the custom, while Egnat stood back to wait his turn. They were happy to see him; the young man was an enjoyable drinking companion.

Elena finished buttoning up the bodice of her dress as she entered the kitchen with her two children—Vera, who toddled on wobbly legs behind her, and Genya, a slender young girl. Seeing Peter at the table, Elena threw a quizzical look at Dunya, who puckered her lips and looked as if she was harbouring some secret.

Lukia put a plate of rye bread on the table and whispered to Elena, "What can you do? She likes him."

"Genya," Peter said amicably, "you've sprouted. How old are you now?"

"Eight." Genya smiled and ducked her head, then took her place at the other end of the table with her mother and sister.

Egnat poured the adults a shot of horilka while Dunya ladled the borscht into the bowls and put the pot back on the stove. Elena passed the sour cream to Peter.

"Eat, eat already," said Lukia. "The food is getting cold." She sat down at the table and raised her glass of horilka. They all clinked glasses and said, "Daye Bozhe," before taking a drink.

Lukia savoured the taste of the liquor. "Good," she said, then looked at Dunya's young man. He was as handsome as ever, with his raven hair, tanned oval face, and gentle hazel eyes. Her daughter was right; he looked like a movie star, or one of those male models in the Eaton's catalogue. Lukia could see the appeal, but good looks didn't put bread on the table.

"Delicious borscht, Panye Mazurec." Peter smacked his lips, underlining his compliment.

"I have more in the pot." Lukia

exchanged looks with her daughter. She was tempted to admit that besides his pleasing looks, he had excellent manners. And he had shown her respect by addressing her properly, as Panye, a married woman. Even so, as far as she knew, he was still poor. "Dunya said she bumped into you in Winnipeg."

Peter smiled at Dunya. "Yes, I was lucky to see her on the street. We both had something to buy at Eaton's, so we walked to the department store together."

Lukia said, "You know she was getting engaged that day—to a man who works at the stock exchange."

Peter's smile fell.

"After shopping at Eaton's," Dunya said to her brothers and Elena, "I met Sergei at the jewellery store across from City Hall to look at rings. While we were deciding which ones to pick, I turned to look out the window. I don't know why I turned. It was like something was calling me. I saw Peter looking in. My mouth fell open. He must've followed me back from Eaton's. I ran outside, but he was gone. I couldn't see him anywhere. I thought he was a mirage."

Egnat said, "What did Sergei do? He must've thought some madness had gripped you."

Dunya swallowed a spoonful of borscht and said, "He came outside and took my arm and started to pull me back into the store. I resisted. But just then a policeman walked by and said, 'What seems to be the trouble?' Sergei said, 'I'm escorting my fiancée back into the shop.' The policeman then asked me if that was true." Dunya chortled. "I said, 'I've never seen this man before in my life.'"

Mike laughed. "Dunya, Dunya. Did he believe you?"

Dunya shrugged. "I don't know. I walked away and took the streetcar home."

"Oy," Lukia said. Her daughter had told her the story before. It sounded just as dramatic hearing it again. Lukia didn't know what to believe. Her daughter could always tell a good story.

Dunya smiled. "Peter said he ran away when he saw me with another man."

"I did," said Peter, nodding.

Egnat buttered his slice of rye bread. "I don't know what kind of engagement that was. You never brought the Russian home."

"He was busy working. The stock exchange people work long hours."

Lukia said sourly, "He was always too busy to meet us. Maybe it's good you broke up. What kind of man wants to marry a woman outside of a church?"

"Mama," Dunya said, ready to change the subject. "Peter won another whist competition."

Lukia looked sideways at Peter.

"Congratulations," Egnat said. "It must be nice. We don't have time to play cards."

"He won five dollars."

Egnat looked at Peter with some interest. "Well, that's something."

Mike shook his head. "Don't mind him, Peter. He doesn't know how to have fun."

Egnat glared at Mike.

"Who has time for fun," Lukia said, "when there are crops to take care of?"

The table fell silent as they continued to eat. Peter kept stealing looks at Dunya, as if needing reassurance he was back in her life.

Peter left in the early evening when it was time for Dunya to milk the cows. Lukia watched him depart as she walked to the barn. She chuckled as he struggled a little to get on his bicycle. A few drinks had reddened his face and made him unsteady.

He was certainly different from her sons, Lukia thought as she opened the barn doors. The light was already dim, so she lit the coal oil lantern she kept on a shelf by the entrance and carried it to the stalls, where the cows were waiting.

Lukia had barely sat down on a stool when Dunya walked in singing, "Oh, you beautiful doll, you great big beautiful doll ..."

"Yeah, yeah, yeah," Lukia said. "Is that what he sings to you?" When her daughter didn't answer, Lukia added, "Oy, what a life we'd have, if all we needed to do was sing."

"Mama, you don't understand," Dunya mumbled, and began milking a cow one stall over.

Over the sound of the milk hitting the tin pails, Lukia said, "Nu Dunya, did Peter tell you he's working?"

"Why do you keep asking me? You know it's bad everywhere."

Lukia pulled on the cow's teats. "I know. That's why I'm asking. You told me he's twenty-eight years old. He's not that young anymore. What does he have to show for those years?"

"He's trying, Mama. He's trying to find work."

Lukia raised her eyebrows and turned to Elena, who was milking in the stall across from her. "What do you think, Elena?"

Her daughter-in-law shrugged. Of course, Elena had no worries like that. Egnat was a hard worker. He'd worked almost from the time he could walk. But Peter? What did he know about hard work growing up in Stony Mountain? And he'd quit school in Grade 9. Foolish boy. Sure, he had worked in the stone quarries, lifting rock for a while, like his father, lifting and loading stones on the skip car, but now he was taking odd jobs that paid little. He hadn't worked hard like farmers, who were up at dawn and didn't stop until the stars were out. *Oy, what is my daughter getting into again?*

After milking the cows, Dunya settled on the bench by the house and unfolded the long white tablecloth she was embroidering for her hope chest. Mike had made a smudge fire nearby to keep the mosquitoes away. She loved summer evenings, when it was cool enough to be outdoors without sweating. She poked red thread through her needle and began embroidering the petals of a flower. As the flower took shape, she considered her future. She hated the morning-to-night labour on the farm, and her work as a domestic for the well-to-do in Winnipeg in the late fall and winter. And yet she'd rejected the possibility of a life of comfort. Well, she didn't love Sergei. Why didn't her mother understand that? Hollywood movies were all about women rejecting a monied gentleman after they fell in love with a man who had far less.

Was it fate that had stood in her way? Peter was tall, dark, and handsome, like the man she'd dreamt of on St. Andrew's Day. But when he'd left her in a huff over that silly brooch, she accepted their union wasn't meant to be. And yet her heart had leapt at the sight of him peeking through the jewellery shop window. That's when she realized her feelings for Sergei were nothing like what she felt for Peter.

And now he was back, still in love with her. At least, that's what she assumed. Especially when he said he wanted her to meet his family.

So why was she still wondering what to do? She had to admit his situation bothered her. Her mother was right; good looks didn't put food on the table. Sure, Dunya had defended him to her mother, saying he was like hundreds of thousands of unemployed, but there *were* men who were working; there *were* men who were supporting their families. Though Peter seemed to be the one for her, she'd have to talk to him about his future plans. There had to be something he could do.

A Second Chance

Peter swung the golf bag over his shoulder. This was a job he didn't mind. Being a caddy for one of the Stony Mountain penitentiary guards in the annual tournament at the Assinawa Country Club gave him the opportunity to make a dollar and compete in a caddy contest at the end of the summer. Not able to afford the club fees or even golf clubs, he looked forward to the event, even if the fairways and greens were far from easy. The guard he caddied for said he'd loan him the clubs to play in that contest.

The guard and his nephew teed off on the first fairway. Peter watched their balls sail through the air; the guard's ball landed on the green. "Nice shot," he said. He had developed some know-how from observing the talented players on the course. A warden had had the idea for a nine-hole course back in the late nineteenth century and set the convicts to building it with a series of bunkers, boulders, badger holes, and downhill slopes—enough challenge for the locals who could afford to play.

Between holes, the guard and his nephew chatted, leaving Peter to his own thoughts. Normally, Peter would have continued to observe the players, but this day, the fresh air and slow pace took his mind in another direction. He thought of Dolly. Her family called her Dunya, but Dolly was the name he preferred. She'd been given the English name in school, and it suited her. Her round cheeks, sparkling eyes, and wavy dark brown hair reminded him of the dolls popular with girls.

He'd told her he wanted her to meet his parents. He expected they'd welcome her, but he wasn't so sure about his brother Bill, who was only a few years younger. His face had fallen when Peter told him Dolly was back in his life. Peter wasn't sure if Bill was jealous or unhappy that his brother was courting a farm girl. Bill could be uppity, thinking Ukrainian girls who couldn't speak proper English weren't worth pursuing.

Peter had told his brother that breaking up with Dolly had been a mistake and his own damn fault. He should never have gotten so upset over her not liking the brooch he'd given her. He'd ordered it from the Eaton's catalogue; it had cost several days' wages—money he'd earned as a hired hand for a local farmer. Admittedly, it was an unusual design, but that was why he liked it. But rather than appreciate its beauty, Dolly said the almond shape was all wrong. It had to do with some superstition her mother had.

That was bad enough, but when Dolly let her cousin take it, that was the last straw. He never called after that. What a fool he'd been!

And then, half a year later, he'd seen her again. He'd had no intention of going to Eaton's, but when he met Dolly on the sidewalk and learned where she was going, he made up a story about needing to buy some socks so they could walk together. And what a pleasant walk that was. She talked about some party she'd gone to, and without pausing, continued about her mother and brothers on the farm and how they hoped, with rising wheat prices, they'd be able to make their rent payments and even save for a farm of their own. She said this coming year might be the last year she'd be working as a housekeeper in the city. As she talked, her eyes danced and her hands moved like a bird's wings in flight. He listened, though his eyes kept darting to her lips. He wanted to kiss her, right there on the sidewalk.

While she went to the bargain basement in Eaton's, he took the escalator to the second floor. That was when he felt foolish. He didn't have money for socks, but how could he explain that to Dolly? How could he meet her afterwards if he wasn't carrying a bag? Though he saw her waiting at the Timothy Eaton statue by the elevator, he stayed out of sight, working up his nerve to meet her as they'd planned. But he waited too long. When she began walking towards the exit, he realized he couldn't leave it at that.

He followed her at a distance and rehearsed in his mind what he might say. But he never got the chance. His dream of reigniting their relationship shattered the moment he stared through the shop window and saw Dolly admiring gold rings with a well-dressed man. Then she glanced toward the window and caught him looking in. Their eyes met briefly. Embarrassed, he turned and left.

"Peter?" the guard said. "What club do

you think would be best?" Jarred out of his thoughts, Peter put his hand above his eyes to shield them from the sun and gazed down the fairway. He assessed the yardage, pointed out the downward slope of the putting green, and handed a nine iron to the guard. After hitting the ball, the guard handed his club back to Peter.

As they began their walk to the next hole, Peter resumed his daydreaming. He recalled how happy he'd been when Dan Balacko told him that Dolly wanted him to know she was no longer engaged. Clapping his hands, he said, "What do you know." He got on his bike that very day and rode over to her home to see her.

He was crazy about her. He hoped his family would be crazy about her, too.

A Tiny House

Dolly hitchhiked to Stony Mountain on a Saturday to meet Peter's parents. He'd offered to come and get her, but she'd said, "How are you going to do that? You don't have a car, truck, or even a wagon."

"I'll carry you on my handlebars."

She laughed. "Up the hill?"

Undeterred, he said, "Maybe I can get my friend, Gerald, to take me. He has a car."

"It's okay. I'll get there on my own."

Peter met her in front of Dan Balacko's store. His face lit up when he saw her, letting her know her efforts had paid off. She wore a jersey dress with a flower print that hugged her curves and polished white lace-up shoes with a wedge heel that added an inch to her height. Peter, at six foot two, was still a head taller, so she had to look up at him whenever they talked.

He was also excited he'd won the caddy championship; his prize was a golf club. When she congratulated him and said she wanted to see it, he said, "My friend Mike Slep borrowed it and broke it."

"How? Those clubs are strong."

"He made a bad shot and was so angry, he broke it over his knee."

"I hope he broke his knee, too. You should make him pay for it."

Peter put his hands in his pockets. "He was jealous."

"That's no excuse."

"What am I gonna do? He doesn't have the money."

She regarded his fallen face. "It's not fair, Peter."

"I know. But what's it matter if I have

a club or not? It's a rich man's game."

Peter took her hand, and she marvelled at the smoothness of his skin, unlike the rough hands of the farmers she knew. Though smooth, his hands were strong, giving her a sense of security. They walked north six blocks to a tiny two-room house on a dirt road surrounded by other small houses on the edge of town. Birch, oak, and elm trees lined the road, enhancing the modest exteriors.

He said, "The locals call this side of town Little Galicia. Lots of Ukrainians here—not all from Galicia, many from Bukovina, where I was born. The guards' families live on the other side of town."

Just ahead, a lanky boy with sandy brown hair waved, and Peter waved back. The boy rode his old bicycle towards them. His dungarees and shirt were well worn, like hand-me-downs.

"You want to throw a ball later?" the boy asked.

"That'd be nice, but we'll see, okay?

Dolly, this is my youngest brother, Johnny."

"Hello," Dolly said.

"Are you the farm girl?" His blue eyes were direct.

Dolly knitted her brows. "Yes."

Johnny nodded, as if to confirm she'd been the topic of conversation at home. He followed them to the gate of a grey one-storey wood home in need of another coat of paint, then said, "See you later," and sped away.

Peter pointed to a weathered wood enclosure across the street. "That's the hand water pump used by all the residents on our street." Rather than enter through the front door, he took her along the side of the house to the back. On the left side of the path was a tall rain barrel, and on the right, bees buzzed and cabbage butterflies flitted over a large garden of bright pink cosmos, brown-eyed Susans, yellow snapdragons, and mounds of white baby's breath.

"My father loves his plants," said Peter. "I think he loves them more than his children." There was a hint of sadness in his voice. She wanted to ask him what he meant, but they'd already arrived at the back door. Near it was a chopping block, stained red from chicken kills, and across from that, a weathered grey lean-to in danger of collapsing. Farther on lay a vegetable garden, well on its way to maturity, and another well-worn path stretching at least a hundred yards and backing onto another farm. Dolly could see an old barn and the neighbour's cows grazing on grass.

Peter opened the screen door to a young man on his way out. Dressed in dungarees and a cotton shirt, he was in his late teens and held a baseball mitt and ball in his hands. Behind him stood a stout woman in a print housedress, covered partly by an apron. "Dolly," Peter said, "this is my brother, George. He's third in line."

George's eyes crinkled. "Nice to meet you, Dolly," he said, shaking her hand. "Sorry I can't stay. I'm late for baseball practice."

"Nice to meet you, too." She liked him immediately; he spoke softly and had black-brown hair and hazel eyes like Peter's.

"See you then," he said as he ran off.

"And this is my mother."

Dolly smiled and said in Ukrainian, "Good day, Panye Klewchuk."

"Good day," she replied. "Come in, please."

Panye Klewchuk's brown hair streaked with grey was pulled back in a bun, and her serious hazel eyes and lined face showed a woman who'd had much to worry about. Peter's father, a fine-looking man with a greying handlebar moustache and thick, silky hair—which Peter later said was washed with rain water—stood hunched over a silver-horned gramophone set on a metal stand by the kitchen counter. He was listening to a classical record.

Peter said to Dolly, "That's one of Father's favourites. Czardas played by a Hungarian violinist."

The volume was so loud that Peter's mother raised her voice to be heard. "Tony, please," she said in Ukrainian. "Play it later."

Pan Klewchuk grumbled but took the needle off the record. He then stepped up and shook Dolly's hand. "You have a firm grip," he said in Ukrainian.

"Yeah, yeah, yeah," Dolly said, smiling. She liked to impress men with her strength. When she let go, Pan Klewchuk rubbed his hands.

"What did you expect?" Peter's mother said to her husband. "She's a farm girl."

While Panye Klewchuk prepared tea and her husband fussed with his plants, Dolly and Peter sat down at the wooden table covered by a faded oilcloth. Dolly wondered how the family ate together, as there were seven of them but only four chairs. The kitchen occupied half the main room; the other half was the living room, with a single sofa next to the wood stove. The two windowsills overflowed with small pots of various plants and on the walls hung a couple of family photos and two icons: the Lord's Supper and the Virgin Mary. At the other end of the room was an open door, through which Dolly could see a bed pushed against the front door of the house. She now understood why Peter had taken her around to the back. It would be impossible to open the door with a bed pushed against it.

His mother poured Dolly and Peter a cup of tea and placed the teapot and a plate of poppy seed rolls on the table.

Dolly took a bite of the roll. "This is delicious."

"Good," Peter's mother said as she tucked a loose hair into her bun.

Dolly said, "Peter told me he's the eldest of your children."

"Yes. I lost four before he came along. First two were boys, the last two were girls."

Peter said, "There was no doctor, no medicine, nothing you could do."

"You lost four? That's a tragedy."

Panye Klewchuk cleared her throat. "You know, it's not so easy in the old country. Kasha died when she was three. She had typhus. I took her to the market to buy her a bun, and she kept asking me for another. I said, 'Enough.'" Peter's mother shook her head. "She walked barefoot behind me, kicking up the dust. She didn't eat after that, just drank water. I should've given her another bun to eat."

"Mama," Peter said, his eyes welling. "You didn't know."

Silence filled the air as his mother gazed out the window, lost in her thoughts. Peter's father removed some dead leaves from a begonia before watering the plant.

After a few moments, Peter said,

"When I was born, my mother noticed I had a soft spot on top of my head."

"I was afraid I'd lose him, too." She leaned back. "I took him to a gypsy fortune teller. She knocked on his head and said, 'You can't kill this one. He'll live.'"

Dolly chuckled. "You must've been so relieved."

"Yes. I keep telling him he was born with a golden spoon in his mouth. He was plump-cheeked, with dimples, like a rich man's baby." She looked at Peter fondly. "He hasn't given me any trouble." Peter grinned and stretched his long legs.

Dolly noticed a violin case propped up on the floor by the gramophone. "Who plays the violin?"

"Peter does," said Pan Klewchuk, sitting down at the table. "You should play something for her, son."

Peter needed little prodding. He took the violin out of the case, then tightened and rosined his bow. "I'll play 'Danny Boy.' It's an Irish song." He tuned the strings, and after placing a folded cloth on his shoulder, he raised the violin and began to play the soulful tune.

His father closed his eyes and his mother, her hands resting in her lap, watched Peter's fingers changing position on the strings. Dolly had heard a fiddler play the song before at a country picnic. It had brought tears to one listener's eyes. Peter played it even more tenderly than that musician.

When he finished, Dolly clapped. "That's beautiful!"

His mother said. "He plays by ear."

"You should hear him play the banjo," his father said. "His friend, Nick Meronek, accompanies him on the violin."

Peter's cheeks flushed as he looked at Dolly sheepishly. His father stood, put on his hat, and left the house. Though Dolly thought his leaving without saying a word was peculiar, Peter and his mother accepted his abrupt exit as if this was a common occurrence.

While Peter put his violin back in the case, Dolly said to his mother, "Peter said you came from Bukovina when he was only two."

"Peter and I emigrated from Stavchan, Bukovina, in 1912. His father was already here."

Dolly waited for Peter's mother to say more, but she started fidgeting with her apron. Between his mother's unease and his father's departure, Dolly got the hint. "I guess we should go, Peter." Standing, she said, "Panye Klewchuk, thank you for the tea and sweets."

"It's nothing," said his mother, picking up the teapot and empty plate and carrying them to the kitchen counter. She'd barely put the dishes down when Dolly attempted to hug her.

Feeling his mother stiffen in her arms, Dolly moved back and said, "Until we see each other again."

His mother half-smiled. "Yes, until the next time."

Upon leaving the house, Peter put his cap on and grabbed his bicycle, where it was resting against the lean-to. With Dolly following, he pushed it out of the yard and onto the dirt street. "Where did your tato go?" she asked.

"I don't know. He might've gone to fix someone's watch."

"I didn't say goodbye to him."

"It's fine."

They hadn't walked far from his house when she said, "Your mother wasn't comfortable with me hugging her."

A pained expression crossed Peter's face. "Your family's different from mine. You show your love to each other. Mine isn't like that."

"Your mother loves you, no?"

"She's a wonderful mother, but she's not a hugger." He paused. "It's hard for her. With all us kids, she's in the house all the time. She goes nowhere."

"You came alone with her to Canada?"

"Tato was here, but he didn't come to

greet us when we arrived in Winnipeg. We found out later he was playing cards somewhere. It took a while for us to find him." Peter said, pushing his bicycle around a stone in the road.

Dolly couldn't imagine that kind of arrival. She missed her father, who'd died when she was five. Since her mother never disparaged him, Dolly assumed he had met her needs. But from the exchange Dolly had observed between Peter's parents, she suspected there was a divide between them as deep as a canyon carved over many years.

"We lived in a shanty on Jarvis Avenue until I was nine. That's when we moved to Stony Mountain."

"I wish I could've met your other brother and sister. Where do you all sleep?"

"It's crowded, all right. My brothers and I sleep horizontally on one bed."

"All four of you?"

"Yeah."

"Where does your sister sleep?"

His forehead creased. "Boy, you ask a lot of questions."

Dolly shrugged. "I want to know about your family."

He hesitated, then said, "Well, Mary, ...when she was home, she slept on four chairs put together. But later, when we had the second room, she slept on the couch you saw. It pulls out to make a bed."

"She doesn't live with you anymore?"

"No, she's working in Cypress River, a couple of hours west of here." He looked straight ahead as he talked about his sister.

"Oh." Dolly wanted to ask him why Mary was working there, but she hesitated. She'd heard rumours about Peter's sister, but decided now wasn't the time to pry. She didn't want to dampen his mood by bringing up what she sensed was another touchy subject.

It was enough that she'd asked him

earlier if he'd had any luck finding work. He said that without a car or money to get to the city, the only work he could get was odd jobs in the village. He still helped the Perrys in their boarding house: washing dishes, cleaning up, peeling potatoes and running the odd errand. And nothing had changed at the penitentiary. They only hired guards' sons and other relatives, men from English or Scottish backgrounds, not men from Ukrainian immigrant families. He'd considered applying again for work in the limestone quarry where his father continued to toil, but because of his near-fatal accident years back, he hesitated. At least for now, he said.

"What does your dad do there?"

"He's got the hardest job in the quarry. He packs dynamite in amongst the rocks; he has to know how much to put in and how deep, and then he goes into the bush on the edge of the stone pit and pulls the lever. Other days, he loads stones on the skip car. It's a helluva hard job in the hot summer. Twelve-hour days."

She couldn't blame Peter for not wanting to work there. He'd told her about almost being buried alive when he was only sixteen. He'd been working on top of the heap of rock with a shovel, trying to dislodge the jam of quarry stones, when someone opened the chute and he slid in. The limestone covered him completely except for his hands, which stuck out of the pile. Oddly, his mother'd had a premonition that something was going to happen. Had the crushed limestone continued to pour in, he would have suffocated within three more minutes. Fortunately, a fellow worker saw him go under and stopped the machine, then handed him a rope and pulled him to safety. Two men had died in a similar accident. His height was ultimately what saved him.

"I was just thinking about what you

told me, the accident you had."

"Yeah?" He turned to her. "I still shudder when I think of it. The limestone dust remained on my face for two days. It was quite fine and got into my lungs." He chuckled. "I was white as a ghost from the shock and the powder coating my skin."

They turned the corner and headed to Main Street.

A woman in a fashionable dress was walking towards them, carrying a lovely leather bag and a bag of groceries. Peter tipped his cap to her. "Hello, Mrs. Pritchard."

"Lovely day, Peter," she said, smiling.

When they'd passed by, Dolly craned her neck for another look. "Who was that?"

"One of the guard's wives."

There was something about the way the English walked, thought Dolly. Full of confidence and composure. And why wouldn't they be confident and content? They faced no discrimination. She wondered if she would ever be as comfortable in this country. Maybe with a man like Peter by her side, she would be.

When they got to the main street, just before the hill that would take her back to the highway, Peter insisted on giving her a ride on his handlebars. She laughed at first. "What, me climb on?"

"Sure. Even though you're a pullet."

"Ha! You think I'm a pullet," she said, impressed he knew something about chickens. "You're a leghorn. No meat on you."

He hooted and said, "C'mon. It won't be bad. You can sit on the handlebars. It'll beat walking to the highway to catch a ride."

She hesitated, then accepted because they'd be going down the hill and that would be fun. Once he dropped her off, he'd be able to make the uphill climb back on his own.

She climbed onto the handlebars, her back to him. She held on tight as they gathered speed on the fine gravel road. They passed the stone penitentiary on their left and some cows grazing in a pasture on the right. She felt his chest against her back; it made her feel safe in an uncertain world. And yet, after seeing Peter's poor family home, she knew any future with him would be a rocky one. Troubled by conflicting thoughts, she decided that right now, perched on his bike, she would let those doubts scatter like tufts of dandelion in a light breeze. She turned her face to the sun and savoured the wind frolicking in her hair, his warm breath on her cheek, and the skirt of her dress lifting and cooling her bare legs as they flew down the hill.

Parched

Lukia rose earlier than usual the next day, so that by the time the sun was up, she had bread baking in the oven. The smell of the loaves baking wafted through the house. Their aroma would stay for hours, giving her some relief from the barnyard odour, which was particularly pungent on a hot day.

Egnat and Mike, along with three local farmers, were already in the fields harvesting. The co-op threshing crew had showed up early in the morning with a tractor connected to a threshing machine. Since Lukia couldn't afford to buy such equipment on her own, Egnat had made the arrangement years back. The co-op members used the same equipment and helped one another bring in the harvest.

Despite the parched conditions of summer, their wheat had thrived, unlike the crops on the farms west of Manitoba. The announcer on the radio said the cool Manitoba nights, coupled with the poor rainfall in the early months of the growing season, had produced a hard spring wheat. Stony Mountain, Lilyfield, Stonewall and parts of Rosser were well represented in the shipments of top-grade wheat from their province. Grain was being hauled out at a fast rate, an encouraging sign for local farmers. It was so promising that new farming families, hoping for the same result from their labours, had moved to their district from Saskatchewan and Alberta.

While the men toiled in the fields, the women toiled in the kitchen, preparing mid-morning and mid-afternoon snacks as well as lunch and supper—the men were always hungry. After feeding the men in the fields, they went back to the kitchen to cook another meal.

When Lukia delivered food to the men, she stayed for a bit to watch them work. It was heartwarming to see the efficient assembly line they'd set up. Egnat took the rack and a team of horses to pick up the sheaves of wheat, then drove them back to the threshing machine. There, two men, using their forks, lifted the grain from the rack and tossed it into the machine, which beat the wheat and separated it. One spout spewed the straw onto the ground; the other spewed grain onto the bed of their truck. Mike supervised the process. When the truck bed was full, he hauled the load away to the granary, then came back to oversee another load.

These were the days they had been waiting for. Harvesting a decent crop was the payoff for all their sweat and tears and anxious nights. As Lukia prepared more nourishment, she thought of what her family had been through and how rosy the future looked by comparison. They'd been in Canada seven long, dry years. A lifetime of heartache behind them. Now, when she observed Egnat across the kitchen table at the end of a day, she saw fewer lines in his face, and sometimes even a smile.

Egnat's mood had improved because Mike was finally buckling down. He hadn't run into the city for a while, looking for trouble. He showed no interest in settling down, even though two lovely Ukrainian girls were currently throwing themselves at him. Times had changed, or maybe it was just the way young women were in Canada. They had no trouble batting their eyes and thrusting their breasts out. How they flirted! Her daughter did as well. In Lukia's day, the girls were not so forward. She clicked her tongue, thinking about it.

So far that week, there'd been no need to question Mike. With no need, there were no squabbles. Mike, at least, knew

Egnat couldn't complete the harvest without his help. The sight of her two sons working together lifted her spirits; it gave her hope that their conflicts would soon be behind them.

Lukia took off her apron and headed to the barn to join Elena and Dunya. With the sun low in the cloudless sky, it promised to be a fine day.

She entered the barn to the pleasant sounds of milk hitting tin pails and Elena and Dunya's laughter. "You're both cackling like hens laying eggs."

Elena smiled. "Dunya was just telling me about her bike ride with Peter down the hill."

"What hill?" Lukia asked her daughter as she sat down on a milking stool.

"By Stony Mountain. Peter gave me a ride to the highway. I sat on his handlebars. I think he got excited. His face was red when he got off his bike."

"Of course," Lukia said, setting her pail under the cow. "He's a young man. What do you expect?" She leaned in and inhaled the fresh hay smell on the animal's skin. She grabbed the cow's teats and began to pull rhythmically. "What are his parents like? Do they go to church?"

"I don't know. They don't have a car."

"They could take the streetcar to Winnipeg."

"Panye Klewchuk has an icon hanging in her kitchen. Peter told me she goes to church to bless the basket every Easter."

"Hmm. That's good. At least there's that. What church do they go to?"

"St. Michael's, on Disraeli."

Lukia said, "That's where some people from Bukovina go. Did she give you anything to eat?"

"Cookies and tea."

"That's it?"

"They don't have much."

"Even when we had nothing, we still found something substantial to put on the table." Lukia paused while her cow swished her tail. "Have you heard from

Olga? Every time I hear about polio, I think about her. Her back will never be the same. Hunched for life."

"I should go see her," Dunya said. "Maybe after harvesting. Maybe she'll be in church the next time we go."

Elena stood and picked up her full pail of milk. "I heard two babies became paralyzed after they got polio. Children seem to catch it easier than adults. We have to watch Vera and Genya, make sure they stay away from dirty water."

Lukia said, "We'd better tell the men to watch out for them, too. Especially when the girls are outside playing. You know how they like to make mud cakes and pretend they're baking. The water lying around could be contaminated."

Picking up her pail, Dunya followed Elena out of the barn, leaving Lukia with her thoughts. Polio had affected so many.

The months following harvesting flew by. There was much to do to prepare for another wicked winter. Fields were readied for the following year and food for the livestock was stored. The women canned stewed rhubarb, vegetables from the garden, and mushrooms that had been foraged from the forests not far from their farm. They made sauerkraut, pickled cucumbers, and gathered potatoes and cabbage for the winter.

In November, Egnat, who regularly listened to the crop report on the radio, told his mother that Manitoba wheat was selling better on international markets than the wheat from Argentina. Rust had affected the grain in the South American country. With improved grain sales, the Winnipeg Wheat Board could afford to pay more to local farmers. Though encouraged by the news, Lukia's throat tightened at the mention of Argentina and its struggles. It was where her grandson, Kolya, lived. A few years after her sweet daughter Hania's death, Damien remarried and left with Kolya and his new wife for

Argentina. That was the same year Lukia and her family had immigrated to Canada. Her last memory of Kolya was when he left Kivertsi, dressed in the sailor suit Lukia had sewn for him. Her grandson had always loved the sea.

She was thankful Damien wrote from time to time. And now that Kolya was older, he wrote as well. He said he wanted to join the Polish navy so he could come and visit her in Halifax. She laughed. He was only ten. If he could dream of their meeting again, so could she.

New Fears

With higher grain prices, 1938 promised to be a better year, but only if crop yields continued to improve. Lukia prayed for sorely needed rain. But new fears arose in early March that temporarily displaced her worries about another dry season.

News of a dramatic escape from the penitentiary prompted everyone in Stony Mountain and the surrounding districts to bar their doors. A heavy fog the previous morning had provided the perfect cover for three gangsters to escape the prison from its kitchen. Radio and newspaper reports said the thugs wore white kitchen uniforms, good camouflage for the snow-covered grounds. The guards found a few footprints, but the blowing snow quickly swept away further traces on the icy landscape. Some said a getaway car had been waiting, which led many to stop worrying that the criminals could end up on their doorstep. One escapee, Jack Hilderman, who was caught hiding behind a bush, initially confirmed there had been a car outside the jail but later changed his story.

Lukia said a quiet prayer of thanks when Mike returned safely from the city, where he'd gone to get the family truck serviced.

"Armed guards are everywhere," he said. "They stopped my truck and checked the back to make sure there was no one hiding there."

Surmising the other two convicts hadn't made it to Winnipeg after all, but were still hiding out somewhere in their district, Lukia said, "My God. Who knows what these crooks are capable of. You corner anyone, and they'd fight like hell to escape."

"Don't worry, Mama," Mike said. "I'm a pretty good shot." He went to the rifle by the door and checked the bullets in the chamber.

"Just make sure you're not drinking when they come around," Egnat said. "I don't want you shooting up the side of the barn."

"As if you could do better."

Egnat muttered something as he glared at Mike.

"Enough," Lukia interjected. "The last thing I need is you two fighting over who's the better shot. For now, we should all stay close to home and only go out when necessary. With both the convicts and guards running around, they could make a mistake and shoot the wrong person."

In the evening, Lukia and her family huddled around the radio for news updates. Their ears perked up when they heard that John Templeton, a farmer who lived close by, had reported seeing someone moving among his cornstalks. Again, she cautioned her family to keep their eyes open when they went outside.

At nightfall, Lukia found herself peering out the window at the moonlit barnyard, listening intently for any sounds from their livestock that would alert them if a stranger was in their midst. Puppy, who slept in the open doorway of the lean-to, could also be counted on to let them know if any prowlers showed up. Her heart pounded whenever she heard a sound she couldn't identify.

Even a floor creak made Elena—who'd been darning socks in the living room— jump and raise her head to look around. Startled at first, she laughed when she noticed it was just Dunya coming down the stairs. "I thought a prisoner had come in the house."

Dunya laughed, too, but understood her sister-in-law's anxiety. Normally fearless in the dark, Dunya welcomed Mike's offer when he said he'd stand outside the outhouse when she needed to use it.

His face stern, Egnat told Genya and Vera, "You can't play outside unless Baba, or Chocha Dunya or Dyadko Mike is with you. Do you understand?"

The wide-eyed children nodded solemnly.

It wasn't long before the prison guards showed up at their farm. The family stayed out of their way but watched warily from the yard as the guards searched the outbuildings. When they had finished looking in every corner, they assured the Mazurecs they'd found no sign of the prisoners. That was some relief, but as long as the escapees' whereabouts remained unknown, Lukia and her family couldn't relax. They kept the kerosene lamp in the living room burning all night. And Egnat kept the rifle close to his bed. To leave the house in the dark was not a choice when criminals were on the loose.

The next day, Dunya went with Egnat to Stony Mountain to buy chicken feed and flour. As she stepped down from the wagon by Dan Balacko's store, she heard three men talking over the latest news in excited voices. Egnat lit up a cigarette and joined them while she leaned against their wagon and listened.

"Two are still at large," said one farmer. "One stole a loaf of bread from Hector French's farm."

"That's all?" Egnat asked.

"Yes," said another. "That was yesterday. Since then, they got to Winnipeg. Some guy spotted them on Manitoba Avenue. They won't be able to hide from the cops too long."

"Don't be too sure about that," said the third. "They escaped, didn't they? Shows they're not stupid. If they could outwit the guards at the penitentiary, they can outwit the cops on the street."

When Dunya came home, she told her mother what she'd heard. "To think they were at French's farm. That's so close to us. Thank God they didn't come here."

Though relieved, her mother said, "You have to be careful in the city. Manitoba Avenue is only two blocks from Selkirk Avenue."

"I will, Mama."

Dunya considered her mother's warning and frowned. She still worked for Michelina, the dressmaker, during the winter months, close to where the convicts were last seen. As long as the criminals were on the loose, she would have to miss her weekly trip to see a movie at the Palace Theatre. It was on Selkirk Avenue.

This wasn't the only prison escape Lukia and her family had dealt with since they'd moved to the Lilyfield farm, but it was definitely the scariest. Such a wide manhunt had put everyone on edge. Knowing her sons wouldn't think twice about picking up a rifle, Lukia thanked

God the criminals were now in Winnipeg and the danger of a shooting on her farm had passed. When fearful men held guns, accidents happened.

Talk about the criminal prowlers and their whereabouts had declined, but they were still on Lukia's mind when the family gathered in the living room after they'd had supper and milked the cows. Seated on the chesterfield, Elena was securing a few loose buttons on Vera's cotton flannel dress. Beside her, Dunya embroidered a border of blue, red, and yellow flowers with green leaves on the long white tablecloth for her hope chest. Vera, stretched out on the carpet, watched Genya draw ball gowns on the back pages of her scribbler, copying the style of the dresses in the Eaton's catalogue beside her.

With her back to them, Lukia sat down at her Singer treadle machine to sew a navy-blue velveteen dress for Genya. As her feet rocked the treadle, the fabric moved easily under the presser foot. She loved creating new garments for her grandchildren. She still sewed for herself and Dunya, but she was slowing down. Right now, her pleasure in creating was dampened by her thoughts of the escapees from the penitentiary. They still hadn't been caught. She stopped sewing when she felt a burst of cold air from the front door opening. Egnat had entered the house with wood for the cookstove.

"Did you see Mike?" she asked.

"He's not back yet," Egnat said, carrying the wood into the kitchen.

"Oy. I hope he stays away from Selkirk Avenue." The bootleggers ran their business around that street. She looked at her wristwatch. "Put the radio on. I want to hear the news. I want to know if the police caught them yet."

Egnat raised his eyebrows.

"One time won't hurt," she said to reassure him. He hated using the radio for anything other than the weather and crop reports. Batteries were expensive.

He did as she asked, turning the dial to find the right station. Static crackled in the air. Vera put her hands over her ears. Elena said to her, "It'll stop soon."

When the station announced the hour and the news program began, Lukia stopped pushing the treadle. The family listened, but the announcer's quick, staccato presentation left everyone confused.

"What did he say?" Lukia asked. "Are the police still looking for the criminals?"

Egnat said, "Yes. They're still combing Winnipeg for the escaped convicts."

"I heard that, too," Dunya said, giggling. "I thought *combed* was just for hair."

Egnat smirked. "That means they're still looking for them."

"I know," Dunya said with irritation.

"Did you hear the news at the beginning?" Egnat asked. "Germany seized Austria. It's a Nazi state now."

"What?" Lukia said.

He turned off the radio. "It doesn't sound good. Hitler says one thing and does another. He's not to be trusted."

"Write to Pavlo," Lukia said. "Maybe he knows more." She hadn't heard from her brother in a while, not since their mother had died. He was still living under Russian rule in the Carpathian Mountains, hundreds of miles from Volhynia. Because Stalin appeared to have no quarrel with Hitler, maybe Pavlo and his family would be safe if the Fuhrer moved further east. But how long would the two leaders remain friendly? In war, alliances could change overnight.

"I'll write him," Egnat said.

Lukia straightened the velveteen fabric over the feed dog and pushed the treadle again. She was grateful she didn't have to worry about war in Canada. Despite the harsh years, she was glad she'd immigrated. No soldiers forcing her to abandon her home because the enemy was approaching. No one burning her home to the ground or marching her sons off to war. And no need to escape to a refugee camp, like the one she and her children fled to during the Great War. She prayed her family in the old country stayed safe.

In Stony Mountain, Peter was listening to the same broadcast. Because his brother had mentioned there was talk about the armed forces being shipped overseas, Peter paid close attention to what the news announcer was saying. The reception wasn't the best, with scratchy sounds intruding on the broadcast, so he pulled his chair closer to the radio on the kitchen counter. His mother had been complaining of abdominal pain and had gone to bed early, so only his father sat beside him at the kitchen table, the parts of a silver pocket watch—which a guard had dropped off earlier—spread out in front of him.

The announcer said in a grave voice, "Since the Treaty of Versailles was signed in 1919, there have been some momentous days in Europe: Mussolini marching on Rome, Stalin launching his first five-year plan, Hitler breaking the terms of the Versailles treaty, one by one. Today becomes another such mighty moment as Hitler carries his Nazi expansion across the borders of Germany into the land of his birth." Then the station played what sounded like a triumphant marching band with horns, cymbals and drums, as if what Hitler was doing had to be celebrated. Peter and his father exchanged glances. A shiver ran down Peter's back. Then the announcer continued speaking over the band's music. "As the Germans march in, schoolchildren salute the armoured cars. Along the road, the iron cross and the eagle wave in the breeze. Hitler himself drives into the city. This is the hour of his triumph, the hour when his dream of annexing Austria is realized." Having heard enough, Peter turned the radio off.

"Ha," Peter's father said with a sigh. "Austria. Hard to believe it fell. If a man of conviction like Kaiser Wilhelm II was in command, he wouldn't have surrendered like that. What's to become of them now?" He played with the watch chain on the table, fingering each link. "The Kaiser regretted getting into the Great War. And now this? ..." His voice drifted off as if some memory had intruded.

"It is hard to believe," Peter said.

His father put the chain down and replaced the glass on the watch's face. "You know, I met the Kaiser in Vienna when I was in the Austrian army. He was really something. Muscular, handlebar moustache. They wanted to make me a colonel, but I got fed up with that life." He grinned. "They found a mirror I kept in my cap. The buggers handcuffed my arm and leg to a table, and I had to lie on my side for hours. Just because I had a mirror.

What's wrong with wanting to look good?"

"Nothing," Peter said. "Nothing at all." He wanted to look good, too, but he knew if there had been a rule against it, he would have followed that rule.

The news had been jarring. Austria, once an empire, had yielded its power to what appeared to be an army of thugs. The country was now under the Fuhrer's control. The German leader's march eastward appeared to be unchallenged. Neville Chamberlain, England's prime minister, had reassured the world that Hitler would stop his march eastward and now had been proven wrong. Just like Canada's prime minister, Mackenzie King. He had gone to meet Hitler the year before and thought of him as Germany's Joan of Arc. How ludicrous! But then again, King had made disparaging remarks about Jews. He'd seen no problem with the way Hitler treated Jews in his country. To revere someone like that meant Canada had a leader who had no heart. If Hitler continued to bully his way forward, what would England do? If England declared war, Canada would surely follow. And then Bill would be shipped over, too. He couldn't imagine his brother going over to kill the Krauts, or kill anyone. Shooting tin cans and rabbits for dinner was one thing, but a human being?

Peter left his father at the table and went outside to shovel the walk. The fresh snow sparkled in the evening light and the crisp air flowed over him, as if to reassure him that Stony Mountain was too far away from what was ailing Europe for him to worry. But worry he did. He'd learned the history of the Great War in school. He knew what had happened after the war, how the Allies had forced Germany to its knees. As a result, inflation in that country was running wild. Their money had become practically worthless. The Germans were anxious to improve their economy. Hitler promised them a way out of their troubles. To them, he was a saviour. What non-German could convince them otherwise?

When Peter was alone, he often fiddled with his crystal set, the one he'd built years ago so that he could listen to shortwave radio broadcasts from England, introduced by the announcer saying, "This is London calling." He also heard the Fuhrer's voice. Peter couldn't understand German, but he recognized the power of Hitler's speech. His magnetism was remarkable. It explained why so many of his countrymen hung on to his every word.

The events in Europe seemed far away, but so were the events that had led to the Great War. Back then, most Canadians had never imagined they'd have to fight overseas until England declared war on Germany.

Peter kicked a stone into the pile of snow near the back door. What was he going to do about Dolly? He had such strong feelings about her, but the ongoing Depression, coupled with his inability to find a steady job, had kept him from proposing. Now a major war was looming in Europe. He walked back into the house with his forehead lined, his mind tormented by the news overseas.

Striking Out

March was supposed to go out like a lamb, but the flurry of snow hitting Peter's face said otherwise. He shivered in his shirt and trousers as he dashed from the outhouse back to the house. He ran inside and grabbed his jacket and cap off the hook by the door. His mother was at the stove making kapusnyak. The smell of the cabbage soup soothed him, but he knew there'd be none left by the time he returned.

His mother, sensing his longing, said, "I'll try to save some for you."

"Don't worry, Mama. The Perrys will give me supper." The Perrys, who managed a large boarding house just beyond the lime kiln by the stone quarry, needed his help to peel potatoes and wash the pots and trays used for cooking and baking.

As he tramped down the snow-covered dirt road, he thought of Dolly. He'd seen her every chance he had over the fall and winter months, which wasn't nearly as often as he would've liked. Dolly was working as a housekeeper in Winnipeg and was home only for the odd weekend. Even then, he had difficulty getting to see her because of the blizzards, especially the last one that had piled the snow several feet high and brought all traffic to a standstill. When it became possible to travel again, neither had a vehicle at their disposal. Occasionally, friends gave him a lift to her farm, and they got together when she and Egnat came to the village in their sleigh to buy supplies. He'd also taken the electric streetcar with her to Winnipeg to see a movie at the Palace Theatre. It was after the police had captured the last escapees from the penitentiary in that area and returned them to prison. It seemed all of Selkirk Avenue had breathed a sigh of relief.

Dolly couldn't seem to get enough of those Hollywood films. Especially the romantic ones. He had to admit he was a sucker for them, too. But she surprised him when she showed no interest in seeing the movie everyone was buzzing about. The papers said *Snow White and the Seven Dwarfs* was a miracle in filmmaking. She wasn't impressed because there were no movie stars in it. She said she didn't want to see a comic book on the screen. When he thought about it more, he recalled how she reacted to the cartoons that appeared before feature films in the movie houses. He'd laugh out loud in spots and she'd stare blankly at the screen, trying to figure out what was funny. He assumed she had trouble because her first language wasn't English and the dialogue was quick and snappy. It was hard for her to keep up. He tried to explain the jokes to her, but she got mad when she didn't understand the humour. She accused him of criticizing her.

"You don't think I speak good English."

"It's not that," he said. "I know they talk fast, and it's hard to pick it all up."

"I don't think it's funny," she said and refused to talk about it further.

Disappointed, he let it go. It would have been comforting to share the jokes with her. But somehow, despite their differences and the challenges of travelling to see each other during inclement weather, they'd kept the sparks between them alive.

As he trudged down the street, he bent his head, letting his cap take the brunt of the snowfall hitting his face. He didn't mind working for the Perrys. They were decent folk and treated him with more respect than his father did. There were days they didn't need the extra help but hired him anyway, just to help him out. But despite his having some work, Dolly hounded him about getting a decent job. She couldn't understand how someone with his brains found satisfaction working for the English, who called him on short notice and didn't give him full-time employment. It's not that he was satisfied, he tried to explain; it was just that there weren't many options. Even some of the rich folk in town found it hard to find work and had to go on relief after their business failed.

In fact, just yesterday, Bennett—who had lost the election and was now the Conservative leader—predicted there was going to be another recession. Hell, they hadn't left the one they were in. Bennett said exports were diminishing and workers in factories were being laid off.

Peter wished he could have joined the armed forces like his brother Bill, who'd signed up two years ago. But Bill had his high school education, and the armed forces weren't taking men with less than Grade 10 schooling. Peter thought of how Bill called the armed forces "brass button relief." The last time he came home to visit the folks, he said he was getting enough pay to save a little if he didn't throw it away on women and booze. "You should see the girls," Bill said. "They go crazy when they see a man in uniform."

Bill's training took place in Tuxedo, a ritzy suburb of Winnipeg, where there were nannies and housekeepers galore. These were young women who liked a good time after their work ended for the day. They'd meet the soldiers in City Park, which wasn't far from where they worked. Bill said all kinds of shenanigans went on behind the bushes on the grounds. Peter chuckled at that, knowing full well what his brother was referring to. Yes siree, his brother was having a good time.

Peter missed Bill. His brother was four years younger, but smart as a whip. He'd skipped an early grade and stayed at the top of his class every year afterwards, just like Peter had. Bill had even come second for an Isbister scholarship, which was given to the brightest student in the province. But he and Bill had more than brains in common. They were both athletic and showed their skills skiing on barrel staves on the hills in Stony Mountain or playing baseball. They both loved poetry and liked to quote it. And they were both curious types and could talk about anything, even politics.

Funny, though, how Bill didn't care for Dolly. He'd made fun of the fact she was a farm girl. Peter figured he was probably jealous because he hadn't found the girl of his dreams yet. Peter told his brother that once he met Dolly, he'd change his mind. She was really something; Peter was sure of that.

When Dolly came to meet his parents, she'd wanted to meet his whole family, but two of his siblings weren't home. Discussing Mary with Dolly was another story altogether. He didn't tell her his sister had moved out when she was seventeen. Five years ago, but it might as well have been yesterday. The pain of it lingered in his gut when he remembered his father's beet-red face as he yelled at Mary to get out. Peter couldn't forget the anguish on his mother's face, how she cried afterwards. Peter felt a lump in his throat just thinking of how much his mother had suffered over his sister being kicked out of the house.

He'd always had a soft spot for Mary, and not just because she was a girl. It hadn't been easy for her, growing up with four boys in the house and a mother who didn't speak English or associate with any of the other women in the village—except for Mrs. Adamovich, who lived across the street and spoke Ukrainian, too. He wished he had protected Mary to keep her from getting hurt. But no one in the family had seen it coming. When he and Bill found out she was in the family way, they planned to find the fellow and beat him up. But Mary wouldn't tell them his name. Perhaps she wanted to put it all behind her, or perhaps she was afraid her brothers would make it worse. That they'd actually kill the guy and go to jail for it afterwards. Peter suspected his sister was trying to save them from a life in hell. That's how caring she was. It was just like her to think of others before herself. Instead of letting her brothers throttle him for having his way with her, she was paying a price she should never have had to pay.

He wondered how she'd weathered those years, growing up in their small home and sleeping on chairs put together in the living room. He knew it couldn't have been easy, and yet she never complained. She had the sweetest disposition, now coloured by her sadness, a feeling that what she had was all she was going to get in life. Their mother had tried her best. She got Mary a new dress every year, but how could Mary possibly compete with the guards' daughters in town, who had more than one frock and the accessories that went with them? He had walked with his sister home from school one day and saw her darting glances of envy at another girl's delicately strapped shoes. It wasn't fair. It just wasn't fair.

"Well, Peter, you're right on time, as usual," said Mrs. Perry, who was on the porch, shaking out a hallway rug.

"Can I take that in for you?"

"That would be lovely."

Peter took the heavy cotton rug from Mrs. Perry and followed her indoors. He tried to put aside his thoughts about Mary. He didn't know how he was going to talk to Dolly about her. His girlfriend had definite ideas about what was proper and what wasn't. Peter understood the social mores of the day, but some matters weren't as black and white as Dolly made them out to be. Sometimes in life, there were situations you couldn't control. Things happened you couldn't take back. If you could change the course of history, that would be something.

He put on the full apron the Perrys provided and began peeling potatoes. The slivers piled up in the ceramic sink as he peeled one potato after the other from the burlap bag by his feet. They piled up like the years of his life since he'd quit Grade 9. If he'd had the presence of mind to look down the road to his future, he would have stayed in school. He would have swallowed his pride and gone back, even after his teacher, Mr. Blackwell, had strapped him hard for throwing a ball with his friend Lesley Woods in the school basement. What had he been trying to prove by quitting? Was he trying to teach Mr. Blackwell a lesson? That he shouldn't strap students if they broke a rule?

After the strapping, Mr. Blackwell had come to Peter's house and begged him to return to class. By then, his teacher's face had softened, no longer red with fury. Maybe if his dad hadn't been standing there, encouraging him to take a stand, to come to work with him in the quarry, Peter would have gone back to school. His friend Lesley had to return. His father said he'd kick him out if he didn't.

Stubborn is what Dolly had called Peter for standing fast, even when the teacher begged him to change his mind. So what if he was? There were worse things than that.

Peter rummaged around the bottom of the burlap bag for another potato, but there was none left. He cut the peeled ones into quarters and put them in the pot of water set on the stove. When the pot was full, he looked through the window at the snow-covered garden. There was a reason things turned out the way they did. Dolly would have to understand that sometimes life threw you a curveball. Even the best batters struck out.

The Errant Son

The crocuses had come and gone, and the air after a light rain smelled as fresh as laundry hung in the sun. It was cool, though, and Lukia had to pull her sweater tighter over her housedress as she followed her nephew Ted to the old black sedan parked in the barnyard.

Peering in the side windows of the car, she said, "Nice upholstery. You must be doing well."

"I paint a lot of houses," he said, stroking his black goatee.

"Are you painting any more pictures?"

"No, Auntie. No time. I can't make much money doing that."

"I understand. How's your tato doing?"

She hadn't spoken to her brother since he moved with his family to Toronto over two years ago.

A grave expression crossed Ted's face. "He's thinking of taking a trip back to Volhynia."

"Why? Is someone sick?"

"He hasn't received one kopek from that agent he hired to collect the rents from the apartment building he owns. Can you imagine? It's been nine years since we left. Not one kopek." Ted shook his head. "Tato says he's going to kill him. You know him. When he gets mad about something, watch out."

"I know. That's how our trouble started." She gnashed her teeth at the memory of the incident that had started the family fight. Her brother must have been jealous of her son's youth, his resourcefulness, and his lovely wife. Petro couldn't stop berating Egnat about this and that, and then one day he hit Elena because she had dared to reprimand him for using Egnat's hayrack without permission. Well, that did it. That was the end of any possibility of Egnat and his uncle working things out. After the court case, Lukia and her brother stopped talking to one another. Lukia would wake up at night thinking of how she could've avoided the family rift, how she could have prevented her brother from leaving the farm with his family. Perhaps if they had resolved their differences, the Karpinskys would still be living on the farm, too. They had left before Petro and his family did. Lukia was sure the Karpinskys had grown tired of the endless bickering.

"It's good on gas, too," Ted said, as he patted the black hood gleaming in the sunlight. The sound of his hand striking the metal of the car jarred her out of her reverie. He picked the brown paper shopping bag off the ground, opened the passenger door, and set it on the floor in front of the seat. He closed the door and embraced Lukia. "Thank you for the borscht."

"It's nothing. I'm happy you came to visit."

As he walked to the driver's side, Lukia said, "At least you and Alex come around." Two of Petro's sons had stayed behind in Winnipeg. They didn't get along with their father, either. Alex didn't drink and his father did, and, like many of his countrymen, Petro didn't trust those who didn't raise a shot glass with him at the table. Ted's relationship with his father was also strained. Petro couldn't understand Ted's dream of wanting to be an artist. He wanted his children to go into business or invest in real estate as he had done.

Ted rolled down his window. "Stay healthy, Auntie."

"You, too. Please tell your tato I wish him well."

"I will."

She watched his car wheels kick up

the dirt, creating clouds of dust over the road. She wondered if her brother would ever forgive her. As she walked back to the house, she mumbled to herself, "Aagh! He should worry about me forgiving him."

The rain they had been hoping for finally came. By the first week in May, they'd received about twenty-five percent of the moisture needed for a good crop. Thankfully, their seed was already in the ground, which gave them renewed hope that this year would be even better than the last.

Now Lukia dreamed again about owning her own farm. Renting was no way to get ahead. The landlord could take over at a moment's notice, and what would they have then? If they could harvest a stellar crop, they could save enough to buy in their district.

At night, Lukia got down on her knees and gazed at the icon of the Virgin Mary over her bed. She thanked God first for the rains and then asked when her trial would end. Hadn't she suffered enough? She curled her lips as she thought of Orest Parochnyk, the farmer who'd asked her to be his wife. If she'd accepted his proposal, she wouldn't be stewing about the survival of her crops, nor worrying about how her children would fare in the future. Had she made a mistake? She moaned, which made Genya, who slept with her, stir in bed. Lukia pulled the perina up to cover her granddaughter's shoulders. Orest had married someone else and seemed happy with his new wife. But she didn't have grown children. She didn't have to worry about their future. That was what had kept Lukia from accepting his proposal. He'd promised to take care of her and her family, but there was no guarantee. If he died, his sons might not be so generous. She'd heard too many sad stories about widows who had become destitute when their second husbands died and everything went to their children.

She'd elected to remain a widow and stay on her farm. But what hope was there in farming? Perhaps that was why Mike skipped out of his chores as much as he did. And yet, Egnat never veered from his responsibilities. He couldn't understand why Mike didn't help more. It irked him to shoulder not only the work but also the worries.

Her youngest, Harry, had rejected a life on the farm and had accepted an apprenticeship at a fellow parishioner's service station. His work at an auto garage on William Avenue had paid off. John Slipchenko, the owner, had trained Harry to become a mechanic, proficient at fixing whatever ailed cars and trucks. He'd been her quiet boy, the one who had overcome being bullied because of a speech impediment, the one who'd stayed out of the way of his older brothers. Perhaps he realized he'd always be in their shadow if he didn't take a step outside the family farm. She'd never told him how proud she was that he found his own way. She hadn't told him because she missed his help on the farm. But, being a responsible son, he helped by giving some of his pay to his mother. The rest went for his room and board in the city.

As for her daughter, she prayed God would give her wisdom, which Lukia wasn't sure she had. Dunya had rejected a secure future with one man and had chosen another whose future was uncertain.

And Lukia prayed for Mike, the most unstable of her three sons.

And lastly, she prayed for peace in the old country.

After the Divine Liturgy on Sunday, Lukia stood in the yard of St. Mary the Protectress Ukrainian Greek Orthodox church. She looked at the unfinished building. Because of the Depression, the parishioners hadn't been able to raise funds to finish the construction, and *Sobor,* as they called it, remained nothing more than an elaborate basement. She then searched the departing crowd for her friend Maria Karpinsky. Lukia missed the easy camaraderie she'd shared with Maria when her family lived with them on the farm in Rosser. When the fertile land the government had promised was nowhere to be seen, three families—the Mazurecs, the Korneluks, and the Karpinskys—had banded together to buy a farm. The Karpinskys now lived in the city. Lukia was thankful she could at least see her old friend in church. She strained to see over the heads of the congregants huddling in pairs, catching up on each other's lives.

Lukia spotted Maria talking to Walter Swystun, the choir director, but waited until he left before approaching her friend.

Maria took Lukia's hand. "Have you heard from Petro?"

"No. Oy, Maria, I never should've

taken Petro to court."

"What could you do? You had to do something. If you hadn't, your son would've left."

"It's true what you say. My brother has a bad temper. I thought they were going to kill each other."

"I thought so, too." She paused, then said, "Did Petro get the rents from his apartment building in Lutsk?"

Lukia shook her head. "His son, Ted, dropped by to see me. He said his father didn't get one kopek. Nothing. Now Petro is thinking of going back to collect the money."

"At least it isn't Stalin who's ruling Volhynia," Maria said. "Petro would surely have lost everything, including his life, if he had stayed."

"So much has changed since we left. Ukrainian farmers in the east have experienced such terrible hunger and death. I hear they had to give up their farms to the state. At least here, our farms are finally producing well, and people who work hard have a chance to buy their own."

Maria nodded. "It's true what you say."

"Thanks be to God."

"Say hello to your family for me."

"And you to Arkadi and your sons and daughter."

Lukia found Mike in the churchyard talking to one of the prettiest girls in the congregation. She wondered how much of the church service he had missed. He was a reluctant churchgoer, as were all her sons. Egnat had stayed on the farm that morning. He said he needed to check for rust damage to the crops. And Harry had stayed in the city after working late Saturday at the gas station. Their absence bothered her, but what could she do? They were just like their father, who had avoided church at every opportunity.

Lukia crooked her head to get Mike's attention, signalling they had to leave. Her son laughed at something the girl said before joining his mother. Dunya, who'd been talking with Olga Chimiuk, blurted goodbye to her friend when she saw her brother and mother heading for the truck parked around the corner on Burrows Avenue. Olga had the kindest soul, and yet she'd suffered so much.

Where was God when polio struck? These were the times Lukia questioned His actions. He hadn't answered her prayers when Hania and Ivan were dying, nor had He answered her prayers when Gregory lay dying. He also ignored her pleas for rain. What must Olga think of God's mercy? Lukia crossed herself. She reminded herself it wasn't up to her to question God's motives.

A Little Diamond

Dolly opened the barn doors. Two black and white Holsteins flicked their tails to ward off the flies pestering them before ambling outside.

She patted one on the rump. "You know there's no rush, don't you, Bossie?" She was the oldest cow and had been with the family since they'd set up the farm in Rosser. She was the one who kept the others calm whenever the family was late milking them or getting them to pasture.

It didn't take long before all ten cows were ambling down the path to the ditch by the road, where the grass hadn't shrivelled up in the dry conditions that had plagued the prairies. Puppy jumped around the cows' feet, keeping the herd together. Dolly had just reached the spot where the cows liked to graze when she saw Peter cycling towards her.

She brushed some dirt off her slacks, straightened her shirt, and smoothed her hair with her hand. She wished she had put a dress on. *Well*, she thought, *if he's going to judge me by what I wear, he'll have to find another girl.*

He greeted her with a big smile. "I was hoping I'd find you here," he said as he laid his bike on the side of the ditch near her. He put his arms around her and kissed her tenderly. She breathed in the pleasant musk and cedarwood scent of the Old Spice cologne he'd splashed on.

"I've missed you," he said.

"I missed you, too."

"Did you?" he said, his eyes questioning as well.

"Of course, you leghorn."

"Pullet."

She laughed.

He kissed her again, lingering longer. A cow looked over, then resumed chewing her cud. Peter's hands wandered over her breasts and his breathing quickened.

"You don't know what you do to me," he said.

She giggled. "You know we have to wait."

He grinned. "I know, but…."

She smiled. "No buts."

"Oh, Dolly." He said wistfully, his warm gaze fastened on her face. Taking her hand, he led her to a grassy slope, where they sat down and watched the cows graze near a patch of wild daffodils. He stretched his long legs out and rested his elbows on the ground. Gazing at the flowers, he said, "I wandered lonely as a cloud, that floats on high o'er vales and hills, when all at once I saw a crowd, a host of golden daffodils, beside the lake, beneath the trees fluttering and dancing in the breeze."

"You could be a schoolteacher."

He laughed. "We memorized poems in school and recited them to the class. The part I quoted is from a poem called 'The Daffodils,' by William Wordsworth."

"Pretty." She gazed at the flowers as well, admiring their beauty. She wished she understood poetry and was sorry she didn't. In her native land, citizens revered poets. The poet Taras Shevchenko, born a serf, was a national hero. His words had inspired many to fight for Ukraine's independence.

Peter played with the grass by his leg. "I haven't got anything steady yet, but the economy is bound to turn. We've had our bad years, and anyway, even if there's another bad one, I know we can figure things out."

"What do you mean?"

"If I go haying this summer, I could save enough for a ring and we can get married in the fall."

"Married? You want to get married?"

"I love you. I'm crazy about you, and I want you to be my wife."

She met his eyes; his sincerity was undeniable. Though she had been waiting for his proposal, his words surprised her. She was thrilled, but then her practical side kicked in. "Oy, Peter. How will we manage?"

"Like I said, we'll figure it out. I'm sure something will open up. If it doesn't, I can always get work in the quarry."

"You'd do that?"

"Sure, if I have to."

"I don't know, Peter."

His brow creased. "We could get a piece of land in Stony Mountain and build a house."

She murmured, "How would we do that? We have no money."

"Like other folks." He regarded his shoes as if there he could find the solution. His black oxfords were dusty, and the soles worn. She watched Bossie move to another patch of grass.

"There isn't anyone else, is there?" he asked.

She couldn't help teasing him. "I've had offers …" She smiled. "But I turned them all down."

"That's good." He leaned back again and sang, "Be my life's companion, and you'll never grow old, you'll never grow old, no, you'll never grow old."

"Yeah, yeah."

He spun back to her. "So is that a yes? You'll marry me?"

She nodded. "Yes, I'll marry you." He kissed her with such passion that desire shot through her body, like fireworks scattering light in the sky. Though tempted to lie down on the grass with him, she resisted the urge. She stayed seated, her legs curled under her.

Bossie mooed, as if she wanted a kiss, too. Peter and Dolly laughed, then stood up and followed the cows to a new grazing spot.

At first, Dolly kept Peter's proposal a secret. Though excited about getting married, she was superstitious about announcing their wedding plans until she had a ring on her finger. However, it didn't stop her from asking Mike his opinion of Peter. Of her brothers, he was the one she could talk to about matters of the heart. She found him throwing handfuls of sawdust on the floor of the pigpen, a cigarette dangling from his lips. When he saw her approach, he threw more sawdust down and came out of the enclosure.

"Have you come to help?" he asked, grinning.

"And what, take away the glory you get from finishing a job on your own?"

"Ha ha. What's twisting in your mind now?"

Dolly heaved a heavy sigh. "Peter. What else?"

Mike narrowed his eyes. "Has he broken up with you again?"

"No, no …"

Mike blew a circle of smoke over his head.

"I was wondering what you thought of him."

Her brother cocked his head. "Is he the one?"

"I hope so."

"He doesn't have anything, but he'll be good to you."

"Thank you, Mike. I think so, too. I just wish he wasn't so poor."

Peter took the haying job, but when Mike told his sister he could use Peter's help and would pay him a dollar a day to hoe their crops, he quit. Dolly enjoyed seeing him work on their farm, but she disliked hearing Egnat complain about his hoeing. He said Peter wasn't much of a worker because he weeded slower than Dolly and Elena.

She tolerated Egnat's grumbling, but also wondered about Peter's manner of working. He was unlike the farmers she knew, who tackled chores with great energy and completed them quickly. Even

Mike, who slacked off when he could, was a faster worker. Peter toiled with his mind, seemingly elsewhere. Though he didn't accomplish as much as the others, he worked steadily, hoeing each spot as if it had to be pristine before he moved on to the next. She kept her thoughts to herself. She didn't want to massage the complaints her family had about him.

Still, she was pleased that, after twenty-five days of weeding, Peter had made enough money to buy her an engagement ring. He told her while they were cooling themselves in the shade of an old oak tree at the end of a day's work. "How about we go to Winnipeg to buy your ring?"

"I'd like that," she said, planting a kiss on his lips.

He held her face in his hands and gave her another kiss. He said huskily, "I can't wait until we're married."

She couldn't wait, either. She couldn't wait to be the mistress of her own home, but, given how grim prospects were for steady work, that seemed as far away as the moon.

Peter and Dolly hitchhiked to the city in mid-July, then took the streetcar to Ben Moss Jewellers on Main Street. Because all he could afford was a tiny diamond, she selected a simple solitaire setting in white gold and a plain wedding band to match. Dolly admired the precious gem under the ceiling light. When the light shone on the ring, the bevelled sides resembled minuscule diamonds on each side of the centre stone.

With the decision made, Peter took his money out of a threadbare billfold, one he must have had since he was a boy, and counted out the cash on the jewellery store counter—twenty-five dollars for the engagement ring and five dollars for the wedding band. He then passed the money to the clerk, who counted the bills again.

"Excellent," the clerk said. "We'll have

them sized and ready for you next week."

"Thank you, sir," Peter said.

Grinning broadly, like kids in a candy shop buying their first treats, Dolly and Peter left the shop hand in hand, and danced their way down the street.

They returned to the jewellery store two weeks later on a Saturday, dressed in their Sunday best. As soon as they entered, the clerk went in the back to get their rings, and when he returned, he placed them in a velvet, satin-lined box with a hinged top.

Peter carried the bag as they left the store and crossed Main Street to a streetcar stop in the middle. Since it was such a beautiful day, they took the streetcar to Assiniboine Park, about seven miles away. Expecting he would give her the ring there, Dolly bubbled with excitement as they turned down Portage Avenue and rode past Eaton's and Hudson's Bay department stores. Women paraded down the sidewalk, outfitted in the latest style of dresses, hats, and white gloves. The ladies flitted from store to store, stopping at smaller ones in between or popping into the Metropolitan store, with its soda fountain, to get a hot dog and Coke. With any luck, she thought, she could be one of those smartly dressed women walking along the avenue one day, deciding where to shop for the latest fashions.

Scanning the interior of the trolley, she noticed both young and old women craning their necks to sneak a peek at her fiancé. The pleasure their admiring looks gave her ran through her body like a rushing river and she squeezed his hand. Maybe getting married to Peter would bring her luck.

The streetcar stopped near the entrance to the park on Portage Avenue. Peter and Dolly disembarked and crossed a stone footbridge over the Assiniboine River. They walked leisurely past other pedestrians towards the pavilion, a grand stucco and wood building with small-paned windows, two wings with gable roofs and, in its centre, an ornamental tower with the Union Jack flag flying from its peak. With every step, she wondered when he would give her the ring.

They bought ice cream cones inside the building, and, savouring their treats, they carried on down a vine-covered walkway to the English Garden. There, among the roses, Peter took the engagement ring out of the box and put it on her finger. "I love you, Dolly."

"I love you, too." Dolly raised her hand, allowing the sun's rays to bounce off the diamond, its tiny facets sparkling in the light. "It's so pretty."

"Like you." He gazed into her eyes. "She walks in beauty, like the night. Of cloudless climes and starry skies; And all that's best of dark and bright."

"Oh, Peter." He kissed her then, and

her whole being responded to his warm, sensual kiss. They stopped kissing only when an older woman came up the walk.

Giggling like little children caught in a naughty act, they held hands and walked to the Conservatory, near the Pavilion, to see the indoor garden. Much as Dolly appreciated seeing palm trees and other plants from warmer climates, she couldn't wait to show her mother and Elena the proof of her engagement. Her mother would have to be impressed. Yes, Peter was poor, but to land such a handsome and intelligent man had to be admirable. But the more she thought about it, the more she fretted. Although higher grain prices had improved prospects for farmers, they hadn't fully climbed out of the Depression yet. The weather continued to be unpredictable. Besides, Peter wasn't a farmer, nor was he interested in becoming one. She sighed so loudly that he turned to her with a puzzled glance. She smiled weakly and hugged his arm as they headed out the door of the conservatory.

It was late afternoon when they left the city. A couple they'd hitched a ride with dropped Dolly off on the road to her farm, and Peter continued the rest of the way to Stony Mountain with the driver and his wife.

When Dolly entered the house, her mother was plucking feathers off a headless chicken; its neck drooped over the edge of the table. Feathers covered half the tabletop, and the smell of raw poultry meat filled the room.

Lukia said, "Nu, did you get what you wanted in Winnipeg?"

"Where's Elena?"

"She went with Mike to sell dairy and cheese." Dolly had forgotten that this was the day they delivered sour cream, cottage cheese, butter, and eggs to several customers who attended their church.

Lukia plucked a few feathers.

Dolly raised her hand to show off her ring. "We got engaged."

"Oy." Lukia stared at her daughter for a moment, then said, "Come closer, so I can see."

Her mother's reaction wasn't what she'd expected. With shoulders slumped, she walked over and put her hand in front of her mother's eyes.

Her mother peered at the ring through her smudged glasses. "Hmm." She pulled more feathers off the bird's chest.

"Mama, is that all you can say?"

"What can I say? He's got nothing but the shirt on his back. How are you going to live?"

"He'll get something. He's smart and kind. I couldn't find a better man."

"He should've at least asked me first. He should've brought a bottle of horilka. In the old country, a young man comes with elders and a bottle of horilka and he asks the girl's parents for her hand in marriage."

"We're not in the old country anymore."

"But he's Ukrainian. He comes from a Ukrainian home. Didn't they teach him anything?"

Dolly admired her ring again. "Well, I like it." Though she said it with authority, her mother's cool response had diminished her joy. She recalled the time her mother had criticized the brooch Peter had bought for her birthday. Dolly had accepted there was something wrong with the decorative pin, and one thing led to another and they'd broken up when she repeated her mother's remarks. Well, she wasn't going to let her mother's disapproval put a wedge between her and Peter again.

Lukia filled an empty flour sack with feathers and began cutting up the chicken. Neither spoke. A curtain had fallen between them; one Dolly knew her mother would raise again to grumble about Peter's proposal and how he'd skirted old-country customs as if he knew nothing. Dolly rubbed her thumb against her forefinger, much like her mother did when she was stewing about something. Her mother had to understand they were living in Canada now.

Second Thoughts

olly should have been floating on air as she prepared for her wedding, but her mother's disapproval created doubts in her mind. It didn't help when she ran into Doug Lawson, the son of one of their neighbours, whose family owned a profitable mink ranch. He had courted her a few years ago. He found her walking on the road after she'd been let off by the bus on the highway. She was returning from visiting her friend Olga in the city. When Doug offered her a ride home, she hopped into the cab of his truck.

"Nice to see you again, Dolly."

"How have you been? Olga told me you married a schoolteacher."

He smiled. "That I did. And we have a little one on the way. How about you?"

"I'm getting married in October."

"No kidding. To who?"

"Peter Klewchuk from Stony Mountain."

"That lazy bugger?"

Startled, she said, "What did you call him?" It was bad enough she had to weather her mother's frowns, but to hear criticism from a friend she respected made her stomach sink.

"Dolly, you can do better. You work hard. You deserve someone who'll work alongside you."

"He's a good man. It's not his fault there's no work. You're lucky your father has a business. If it wasn't for him—"

"We've had our ups and downs," he said, interrupting.

She twisted her lips. "Not like the farmers around here. Tell me, honest-to-God, have you and your family suffered?"

"No, but—"

"Peter wasn't born into a well-to-do family."

"Listen, Dolly. I was just thinking of you. No hard feelings, eh?"

Dolly pressed her lips. "No hard feelings."

But when he dropped her off, Dolly couldn't get his words out of her head. *Lazy bugger* is what he'd called Peter. Was that how others saw him? Was love blinding her from seeing Peter's weaknesses? Was she so wrapped up in wanting to leave home that she was willing to throw her life away on a man who would never measure up? She kicked at the pebbles on the road as she walked towards the house. She should've told Doug off. He had no right to criticize her fiancé like that. He had ruined a lovely day.

It wasn't long after their engagement that Peter's work life changed once more. He and Dolly were hoeing the fields on her family's farm when his brother rode up on his bicycle.

"Peter," Johnny yelled, as he threw his bike down on the side of the road. Tall for his age, he was all arms and legs as he ran towards Peter.

"What are you doing here?" Peter asked, resting on his hoe.

"Dan Balacko's brother-in-law said he's got a job for you," Johnny said, pushing his sun-bleached hair off his forehead and breathing hard from the ride. "The city's repairing tracks to Stony Mountain and they're hiring men. They're going to pay twenty-five cents an hour. Two dollars and fifty cents for the day. You better get over there quick if you want to land the job."

"It's for a train?"

"No, a streetcar."

"Well, how about that."

When Peter hesitated, Dolly said, "What are you waiting for? That's more than what my brother pays you."

"But Mike—"

"Never mind Mike. I'll tell him you had to go. You can't say no to good money."

"You're right." Peter gave her a quick kiss and ran back to the house to get his bike.

When he pedalled past their field, heading to Stony Mountain, Dolly waved, then said to Elena, who was working nearby, "I have to push him."

Elena stretched and massaged her back. "Some men are like that. Once he gets going, he's a steady worker."

"Yeah, yeah, yeah … when he gets going." Dolly hit the ground with her hoe, sending a weed flying.

Peter got the job laying tracks for the streetcar route between Winnipeg and Stony Mountain, but the work they wanted him for was at the city's end. That meant a fifteen-mile bike ride there and back, which was arduous enough without tacking on a long day of lifting iron. When he told Dolly, she said she'd ask the

Karpinskys if he could stay at their place in Winnipeg until he completed the job. She used a neighbour's phone to call them, and they said they'd be glad to have him if he didn't mind sleeping on the couch. Dolly could barely contain her excitement. Peter had secured a decent job. He wasn't a lazy bugger, like Doug said.

Then There Was Bill

Dolly and Peter had set their wedding date for October 29th, well after harvesting time, and two months after Nick Meronek's wedding. Nick was Peter's friend from Stony Mountain, and he and his family were also from Bukovina, where Peter was born. Since she hadn't attended a Ukrainian wedding in Canada, Dolly wanted to see if any familiar old-country customs were going to be followed at the bridal couple's church ceremony and at the reception afterwards. Thankfully gone was the business of hanging the bride's blood-stained nightdress after the wedding night on the roof for all the neighbours to see. She was sure her mother would agree this was a ritual that deserved to be buried for good.

To Nick's wedding, Dolly wore a flowered jersey dress, rhinestone combs to hold the waves in her hair in place, and on her feet, polished white sandals. Peter wore the navy-striped suit he always wore, over a starched white shirt and tie. Standing in a back pew at St. Michael's Ukrainian Greek Orthodox church in Winnipeg, they watched the priest bless Nick and his bride by making a sign of the cross over their heads. After placing gold crowns on the couple's heads, the priest led them around the altar in front of the iconostasis three times. The church ceremony was nearly identical to what she remembered of her brother's marriage in the old country. Encouraged, Dolly couldn't wait to plan her wedding.

While the Meronek bridal party went off for photographs, Dolly and Peter headed to the community hall, where Victor

Karpinsky's trio—a violinist, accordionist and tambourine player—greeted guests with traditional wedding music at the door. Inside the hall, two men walked around the floor, offering each guest a shot of horilka from a bottle one carried. Several women bustled back and forth, carrying platters of food from the kitchen to a long table covered with a white damask tablecloth in front of the stage. Earlier, they had set the table with stacks of plates and piles of cutlery at one end and a large glass vase of late summer flowers in the centre.

After the bride and groom, their attendants, and their family had finished their duties in the receiving line, the leader of the band announced they could fill their plates first. Then Dolly and Peter lined up with the other guests for the buffet. With plates piled high, they sat down at a cloth-covered card table, joining Peter's brother Bill and a stout young man with a square face, wiry brown hair, and a ruddy complexion from too much drink or too much sun, it was hard to tell.

"Dolly," Peter said, "this is my brother Bill and my friend, Wally Slep."

Wally nodded.

Bill was shorter than Peter, with black-brown hair and hazel eyes that bulged, giving the impression he had little patience for fools.

"We finally meet," Bill said, giving her an appraising look. "You're getting a good fellow here. He could've had any girl in town, but he was too shy."

Peter's face reddened at his brother's remark.

"Is that so?" she said, amused by Bill's comment and tone. As if he was trying to bait her somehow. She also wondered why Bill didn't get up and give her a hug, especially now that she was engaged to Peter. But then she recalled how cold their father was and Peter's comment that his family wasn't the hugging kind. She also got the distinct impression Wally was judging her, and she took an immediate dislike to him. He was the one who had broken Peter's golf club and hadn't replaced it.

Bill cut a holupchi on his plate with a fork. "He's my favourite brother."

"You don't say," Peter said, smiling. "Is that the liquor talking?"

"Ha ha," Bill said, and swallowed a portion of the cabbage roll. "We sure had fun growing up. Did he tell you how we rode the rails together? We couldn't keep sponging on our parents, so we went west for work. First to Saskatchewan, then to Alberta to help with the harvesting. We also worked in those damn lumber camps." He snorted. "I ate more goddamn sawdust than food."

Peter said, "I was twenty-two, and you were—"

"Eighteen." Bill paused as a man came around and poured more horilka into each glass on the table. "Cheers," he said as he raised his glass and clinked it against Dolly's and Peter's glasses.

"Daye Bozhe," Dolly said, and drank along with the men.

After Bill drained his glass, he said to Peter, "Remember how dirty it was, riding on top of the boxcar? The train smoke was full of grit. It stuck in your teeth and turned our clothes grey. Good thing we packed clean clothes in a knapsack. When we got off the train, we had to change in a public washroom. We didn't complain because the price was right."

Peter laughed. "You can say that again." He ate a slice of kybassa and washed it down with the whiskey left in his glass.

Bill leaned back. "There were hundreds of us sitting high on the cars, all of us filled with wonder and curiosity. Food was cheap at the stops. You could get a full meal of soup, meat, dessert, and coffee for fifteen cents."

"That's cheap," Dolly said, picking up

some mashed potatoes with her fork.

Bill looked at her as if she'd said something profound. "You're damn right it was."

Peter said, "Most towns we stopped at had a hobo jungle. We stayed the night and got information about where to go next. Learned the best places to go."

"We met all types. Most of the men were decent. No one tried to get the best of us, which was good, because we were real green. Boy, were we green, eh?"

"You were still wet behind the ears," Peter said, chuckling.

"Ha ha," Bill said, wiping his mouth with a napkin. "The hardest part was climbing on and off those cars. When we went through the cities, we got off as the train slowed down, then picked up another train when it was leaving and not going too fast. Some of the railway cops were mean buggers, but most of them were on our side."

Peter dipped a varenyka in sour

cream. "We did two trips like that."

Wally said, "It's a wonder you weren't killed. I heard of a guy who was."

"It was dangerous, all right," Bill said. "If you were running to catch a moving car, you had to use your outside hand to grab the steel ladders. If you used your inside one, you could flip like a door and get flung under the wheels. We saw a few go down like that."

"Yes," Peter said, his face contorting. "Never knew if they made it out alive."

"And if you were on top of the car and wanted to walk down to another one, you had to be careful and not move too fast, 'cause if the train took a curve, you could sail right off."

Peter leaned in. "One time it was so cold, we were half-freezing on top and one of the crew in the caboose invited us in to warm ourselves."

"It was colder than a witch's tit."

Peter held his stomach and laughed. Wally laughed, too.

Holding a forkful of peas and carrots, Bill said, "That cherry red stove in the caboose did the trick. In less than sixty seconds, we fell fast asleep."

"And boy oh boy, the following spring, we hit the rails again."

"Yeah, this time east to Ontario. The feds had started relief camps, building airports across the country."

Wally said, "What were those camps like? I heard stories—"

"Like the army," Bill said, pushing his empty plate aside. "The camps were like the army. We lived in huts of about twenty men, and basically our job was to clear trees and stumps to make way for an airfield."

Peter chortled. "That khaki clothing they gave us to wear. I have to laugh about it now."

Bill guffawed. "A few guys washed it in a chloride of lime solution and they came out a real pretty yellow. That was really something. We only lasted three months and came home. Peter went to work in the quarry."

"You went back after your accident?" Dolly asked.

"Not right away. But there were no other jobs, so I worked there for a while."

As a few women put the dishes away and two men dismantled the tables, Dolly mulled over what she'd heard. Peter hadn't shied away from work. He'd taken tough steps to find jobs, rough ones across the country. She shouldn't have let Doug's remark bother her so much.

Once the floor space was cleared, the band began to play a waltz. Bill clicked his heels twice in front of Dolly and bowed. "Would you like to dance?"

Dolly hesitated, then said, "I'm sorry, Bill, but I came with Peter and he gets the first dance. You can have the second dance."

Bill's eyes grew dark. "Suit yourself." He abruptly walked away without another word.

"Bill!" Peter said, but his brother kept walking and didn't look back.

"Oy." Dolly threw her hands in the air.

Peter frowned. "I wouldn't have minded if you danced with him first."

"It's not right. He should know that. Didn't he tell you that a farmer's daughter knows nothing? I wanted to show him I know what's right."

Wally exchanged looks with Peter.

"Did I do right?" she asked pointedly.

"Yes," Peter said with a tense look, and took her hand to dance.

As they waltzed around the floor, Dolly searched the room for Bill, but he was nowhere to be found. He showed up later but never asked her to dance again. Though convinced she had done the proper thing, she sensed Peter had wanted her to accept his brother's invitation. Little did she know Bill could hold a grudge for a long time. Perhaps if she had known, she wouldn't have been so quick to reject him.

A Fist or Two

Lukia kneaded the bread dough and tossed it on the board as if it had committed some crime and she was in charge of meting out punishment. What was Dunya thinking? After all they'd been through. To marry a man with no steady job was not what she wanted for her daughter. And who were his people, not to even give Dunya a meal when she met them? She couldn't understand that kind of hospitality. Even those who had little in the old country would go without a meal to feed their guests.

She tossed the dough again. Her daughter was too stubborn for her own good. She wouldn't listen to reason. When she had her heart set on something, she went after it, and there was no talking to her.

Lukia sighed heavily; she wasn't the only one concerned. The other day, her old neighbour from Rosser, Natasha Chimiuk, dropped by for a cup of tea. Their friendship had continued because Natasha also attended church services at St. Mary the Protectress cathedral. Despite being middle-aged, she had the cherubic-looking face of a much younger woman. But she, like many women her age, complained about an expanding waistline and greying hair. She and Lukia often commiserated over their inability to watch their weight. But this visit, it wasn't dieting that filled their talk.

"I heard your daughter is engaged to Peter Klewchuk of Stony Mountain," Natasha said as she stirred a drop of milk and a spoonful of sugar into her black tea.

"Yes," said Lukia. "They plan to marry after harvest time."

"In Sobor?"

"Of course, Sobor." Lukia pushed the plate of oatmeal cookies towards Natasha. "Have one. I baked them this morning."

"They look delicious," Natasha said, as she took one. "Where are they going to live?"

Feeling a need to defend her daughter and her young man, Lukia said in a matter-of-fact tone, "My Dunya's smart. Together, they'll figure it out. Look around. What young man has anything these days?"

Natasha listed a few young men in the farming community who were showing some success.

Before she got to the fourth one, Lukia interrupted. "She doesn't want a farmer. Not after what we went through."

Natasha sighed. "It's true what you say. Young people have their own minds. Nothing you can do."

Well, thought Lukia as she sipped her tea, that was something they both agreed on.

They next talked about her daughter Olga's physical struggles. Natasha teared up when she spoke of her daughter's deformity. "Lukia, what hope does my poor Olga have of finding a good man?"

"We have to pray. Pray to God for his mercy."

After she left, Lukia crossed herself and thanked God that He had spared her children the disease that had affected so many families.

God had spared her children the plague of polio, but hadn't spared them the agony of conflict. The latest fight between Egnat and Mike happened when Peter was over for supper. The Mazurecs and Peter were halfway through their meal when Mike arrived home drunk, wobbling as he came in the door.

Lukia took one look at her son, who was struggling to stay upright, and said in a strained voice, "Oy. Again?"

Egnat shook his head and muttered.

Elena sat tight-lipped. Vera and Genya stiffened, their eyes glancing at their father, then their uncle.

"You're so late," Lukia said to Mike. When he stayed silent, she added, "Are you hungry?"

"I could eat," he said, slurring his words.

Lukia stood, but quickly sat down when Dunya said, "Sit, Mama. I'll get Mike supper."

While Dunya went to the stove to fill a plate with food, Egnat asked Mike, "How much did you get this time?"

Mike put his hands in his pockets and pulled out a roll of bills and some change, and put it on the table. Egnat counted it. After adding up the money, he said, his voice rising, "You're short. You must've gone to the bootleggers again."

Lukia glanced at her sons as Dunya carried Mike's plate to the table, then put her arm around her brother and tried to coax him to his seat.

Mike jerked his arm away from his sister. Unsteady, he stood with his face scowling and his fists clenched.

"Sit, Mike, and eat," Lukia said.

Vera's and Genya's eyes grew with the tension in the house. Peter's face blanched. He fidgeted in his seat as if he was considering leaving the table.

"Mike," Dunya said firmly, "sit down and eat."

Clenching and unclenching his fists, Mike stared at Dunya as if he hadn't heard her.

"You're nothing but a piyak," Egnat said.

Lukia tightened her lips. "Egnat, don't start."

"Me, start?" Egnat glowered at his mother.

"Who's calling me a drunk?" Mike said. His eyes bulged as he stared at his older brother, his fists at his side.

Egnat shook his head in disgust. "I'm calling you a drunk."

Though unsteady on his feet, he barked, "Take back those words!"

"Mike, sit down," Lukia said. "You're scaring the children."

Egnat stood up. "I'll take them back when you start pulling your weight."

"C'mon," Mike said, putting up his fists as he wavered from side to side.

Lukia rose and put her hands on the back of an empty chair. "Michalko," she said, "enough already. You're in no condition to fight. Sit down and eat. The food is getting cold."

"Let it get cold," Mike snarled.

Egnat said, "I don't know what's the matter with your head. You think I'm working here for nothing? Just so you can drink it away?"

Mike lunged at Egnat and threw the first punch. They were both short and roughly the same weight, but Egnat, being more muscular, easily pushed his brother off of him.

Elena ushered her children away from

the commotion and yelled from the doorway to their bedroom. "Egnat, stop!"

Undeterred, Mike attacked again, pummelling Egnat, only to be thwarted by a punch on the chin. Mike stumbled backwards and fell, landing on his rear. Dazed, he slowly got up and was about to return the blow when Peter stepped in between the two men.

Facing Mike, Peter said in Ukrainian, "Nothing is going to be solved this way."

Mike stared at Peter, his eyes glassy, his mouth agape. With Peter's tall frame blocking Mike's view of his brother, the two men calmed down. Mike lowered his arms.

"Egnat," Lukia said, "go to the barn. Let your brother be. Talk later, when he's sober."

Grumbling, Egnat left the house. Although Lukia breathed a sigh of relief, her stomach churned as it always did when her sons fought. Mike sat down to eat at the table. With Dunya and Peter keeping him company, Lukia followed Egnat out the door.

As Lukia marched across the barnyard, she vaguely noticed the air was still warm after a hot day. Her mind whirled. Images of her sons' red faces occupied her thoughts, disrupted only by a mosquito landing on her arm. She killed it too late. It had already left its mark of blood. Life, she thought, how precious and how short. What a shame Mike was wasting his life chasing she didn't know what.

She found Egnat smoking by the horses. She caught him mumbling to Dan, his favourite horse, the wild one he'd tamed when they moved to Lilyfield.

He looked over at her and said, "If you've come to tell me to go easy on him, I don't want to hear it. "

"Nu, what are we going to do? He has a weakness. You know how gentle he is. It's the liquor that makes him that way."

"Mama, you can't keep making excuses. He can't keep taking money from us. I'm not a fool. I'm not going to work, day in and day out, so he can go to Selkirk Avenue and buy booze for himself and his friends."

"I know."

"No, you don't. I have Elena, Genya and Vera to worry about. Did you know Selkirk Avenue is the meanest street in Canada?"

"What are you saying? I used to work there."

"It was in the papers. A lot of gambling, illegal card games, all kinds of crooks hang out there. Look at those convicts who escaped. That's where the cops caught them. Who knows who Mike is getting mixed up with."

"He's your brother," Lukia said. "We have to look out for him."

"Like he looks out for you? Like he looks out for me?" Egnat shook his head and took another puff of his cigarette. The ribbon of smoke wove upwards like a snake, searching for a branch to curl around.

"I'll talk to him."

Egnat stood in shadow. Behind him, the sun was disappearing in a darkening sky. He mumbled, "Like you did last time, and the time before that, and the time before that." When Lukia moaned, Egnat's eyes softened. "Mama, I can't go on like this. No matter what you say or I say, Mike doesn't listen. I have to think about what's best for my family."

Lukia felt the ground giving out from under her feet. "Please wait. Wait until after Dunya gets married. She'll be leaving soon, and if you leave too, what will I do?"

He took a long drag of his cigarette and studied his mother for a moment. "Only until she's married. But if nothing changes, I'm going to look for another farm."

Her throat constricted, as if it couldn't take any more of anything. She swallowed hard. Only three more months before Dunya married. That's all the time Lukia had to talk some sense into Mike. She couldn't imagine managing the farm without Egnat's help. Would he really abandon her and move? There was also Harry, but it would break his heart if he had to return home to help his mother. No, it was Egnat who would leave the biggest hole by his absence. Where had she gone wrong? Egnat had accused her of coddling Mike. Had she? Her mind wrestled with so many memories of Mike returning from the city drunk and making excuses as to why he'd been paid less than expected. Egnat was right; she knew it. He would wait, but she knew it was only a matter of time before he left with his wife and children. If he didn't, her sons could end up killing each other. That kind of disaster no mother could live with.

Not What She Expected

olly held a basket of mushrooms between her knees and cut off the tough ends of each fungus with a paring knife. On the kitchen table were three more baskets filled with mushrooms, freshly picked that morning in a forest near their home.

Her mother was at the stove, sterilizing the sealers in a tub of boiling water. When she returned to her seat at the table, she grabbed a paring knife and said, "We should go to Oretzki's and buy some fabric for a wedding gown."

Dolly deftly sliced the end off a mushroom. "We don't have to go. Michelina is going to make me a dress, and we've picked out the fabric."

"What?" Lukia glanced at her daughter. "You talked to her already?"

"Of course."

Lukia's forehead pleated. "My work isn't good enough?"

"Mama, your work is beautiful, but you have enough to do. Besides, Michelina will sew it for me at a discount. You know the beautiful work she does."

"I know," Lukia said, nodding. "I admired her stitching on the ivory suit she designed for you last year. She's an artist."

Dolly took a large knife from the table and began slicing the mushrooms and placing them in the empty bowl beside her.

"Nu, what kind of gown is she making you?"

"She showed me a photo in a magazine. It's beautiful. A white satin gown, with matching covered buttons from the neckline to the hem."

"That's the style?" Lukia said, slicing a mushroom into the bowl on the table.

"Yes. And on my head, I want a tiara of seed pearls and a long net veil, like a train, so that when I walk down the aisle in the church, it'll trail along the carpet."

"Oy, so fancy."

"Olga said I should send the invitations out now. Just in case there are other weddings happening after harvest time."

Lukia grunted. "I have to talk to Peter's parents. I hope they're not expecting me to pay for the whole wedding. Did they say anything to you about it?"

"No."

"You don't put the cart before the horse. I have to talk to them."

Dolly had low expectations of her fiancé's parents. Peter's father wasn't a generous man; he still hadn't given Peter the lot he had paid for. She and her mother continued to slice more mushrooms, but a silence fell over them like a heavy blanket.

Marrying the girl of your dreams wasn't as rosy as the movies made it out to be. That's what Peter was finding out. Not rosy at all, when your family disapproved of the girl you loved. He appreciated Dolly was no pushover, but that quality rubbed his family the wrong way.

The problem that disturbed his family started one late-August evening, when Peter visited Dolly at her farm. After they'd eaten, they sat down on the bench by the front door. As she stretched her bare legs, the skirt of her rayon dress fluttered in the light breeze over her shapely calves. His desire for her was hard to contain, and he had to adjust his trousers and force himself to pay attention to what she was saying.

"I'm going to ask Olga to be my maid of honour," she said.

"I like her." He'd met her at Dolly's

church. A pleasant young woman whose body had been affected by polio. Puppy ran over to them and jumped up to get petted. "Hey, Puppy," Peter said. "How're you doing, fella?" He stroked the collie's golden hair. Puppy nuzzled his head against Peter's thigh, then moved over to Dolly.

She petted the dog, running her hand along his back. "I'm not sure about the bridesmaids yet, but Mike suggested I ask some of his friends, nice girls. I'm going to have five altogether. What about you? Have you thought of who you want for best man and who you want as ushers?"

He hadn't. Her question unsettled him. He hadn't thought of who'd be in the bridal party, but now that she'd brought it up, he thought of his sister, Mary. Though Dolly had yet to meet her, he wondered why Dolly would ask Mike's girlfriends to be bridesmaids and not his sister. Mike's girlfriends were strangers, not as close as a prospective in-law would be.

"Who are you going to ask to be your best man?" Dolly asked again.

"Bill. I'll ask Bill."

"And what about the others?"

He turned to her. "Dolly, have you thought of asking Mary to be one of your bridesmaids?"

She twisted her lips. "I don't know. I don't want to embarrass her. Would she have money for a dress? The girls have to buy or make their own gowns."

His brows knitted. "I'll pay for her dress."

"How? You have hardly enough to buy a suit for the wedding. How are you going to afford a bridesmaid's gown, too?"

He tightened his mouth. "I'll figure it out."

She let out an exasperated sigh. "Peter, I know what happened to your sister. I heard from a neighbour that she has a child, that she got in the family way when she was seventeen. That's why she's living so far away."

"Who told you? Some busybody—"

"It's true, isn't it? And she's living in Cypress River with her daughter?"

Distressed, his cheek twitched and his legs felt restless. He hadn't told Dolly about Mary because he suspected she wouldn't understand. Society didn't understand.

When he didn't answer, she said, her face serious, "How would it look to have an unwed mother as a bridesmaid? Bridesmaids are girls who've never been married before or have children. They're single women."

"Who the hell cares what it looks like?" His voice sounded harsh to his ears. He wasn't accustomed to showing his anger, not like his father, who had no trouble yelling at his wife and children. "Mary was young. It wasn't her fault. A man took advantage of her."

"You don't know who it was?"

"No, she wouldn't say." He stared at the starless sky; it looked as bleak as he felt when talking about Mary. He lowered his head. "Mary knows her brothers. We would've beat the crap out of him for ruining her life."

"Poor Mary."

"She kept her baby. You can imagine how hard that was." It pained him to think of what his sister had gone through. When their father found out, he kicked her out of the house with no place to go. His mother learned of a home for unwed mothers, a Catholic one in Manitoba, near the Ontario border just west of Kenora. Mary had to scrub floors and do other menial jobs to earn her keep. What surprised Peter was her decision to keep the baby. She was supposed to give it away when she delivered, but the nuns couldn't find anyone to adopt the infant, so Mary kept her. She had wanted to all along, she said; she couldn't imagine anyone else raising her. Tears filled his eyes as he thought about how brave his sister had been. Feeling self-conscious, he blinked the tears away and hoped Dolly hadn't noticed.

He cleared his throat. "You were asking about the ushers. I think I'll ask George and my friend Leslie."

"The friend you got in trouble with at school?"

He nodded. "And I'll ask Mike and Harry, too."

"My brothers?"

"Yes." He hoped she'd get the hint it was proper to ask your kin, whether it was yours or your prospective spouse's, to stand by you on your wedding day.

"That's nice," she said. Seemingly satisfied, she swung her legs back and forth. "We have to get our invitations out. And Mama's going to talk to your parents about the reception, see what they'll pay for."

He muttered in agreement, then watched a hawk sail across the sky in the fading light.

A few weeks later, Dolly drove with Egnat in their truck to the store in Stony Mountain. She told her brother that while he bought staples and talked with some of the local farmers, she'd visit Peter. But when she got to his house, he wasn't there. Panye Klewchuk and a young woman greeted her.

"Come in, Dunya," Peter's mother said.

With a hint of a smile and serious eyes, the young woman said, "So, this is Peter's girl. I've been wanting to meet you. I'm Mary." She was polite, well-spoken, and well-mannered, and if Dolly hadn't known her roots, she might have thought she was English or Scottish.

Dolly had met all of Peter's brothers—Bill, George and Johnny—and expected Mary to be tall, like them. But she was the shortest of the five. Slimly built, like her brothers, she bore a strong resemblance to her mother, with her kind, round face and brown hair. Her bob haircut and clothing—a short-sleeved sweater over a knee-length black skirt and Mary Jane shoes on her feet—showed she was fashionable despite being poor.

"Please, sit down," said Panye Klewchuk.

They gathered around the small wooden kitchen table covered with a flowered oilcloth.

Dolly said, "I'm so glad to meet you, Mary. Peter has told me you're his favourite sister."

Mary laughed, her face relaxing as she said, "I'm his only sister. I better be his favourite."

While Peter's mother placed a plate of peanut butter cookies on the table and made some tea, Dolly said, "I'm the only girl in my family, too. I lost a sister in the old country. Hania died after she gave birth to a son."

"That's too bad," Mary said.

Panye Klewchuk put the teapot on the table and Mary took three cups out of the kitchen cupboard to the left of the wood stove. She got a glass bottle of milk out of the icebox at the end of the kitchen counter and poured some milk into a small pitcher, which she put on the table along with a matching sugar bowl.

"How are your wedding plans coming along?" Peter's mother asked.

"So far, so good."

Panye Klewchuk's eyes narrowed as she said, "Have you picked out your bridesmaids?"

"Yes."

"But you didn't pick Mary."

Dolly looked at Mary. "I thought it would be too hard for you. The cost of a dress and ... you know, bridesmaids are single." Dolly swallowed. "And they're not mothers." Since she knew Mary had a daughter, she glanced at the bedroom and thought that maybe the little girl was sleeping there.

"What are you saying?"

Dolly hesitated. "Mary, I know about your girl."

Mary's eyes widened. "Who told you?"

"A month ago, I hitchhiked to Stony Mountain, and the driver asked me where I was going. I told him I was going to see my fiancé in Stony Mountain. And he said 'What's his name?' and I said 'Peter Klewchuk.' And he said, 'Oh, I know him. His sister got pregnant and had to leave home.'"

"What?" Mary turned to her mother.

"You're lying," Panye Klewchuk said to Dolly.

"No, I—"

"That's a lie!" Mary said.

Dolly trembled. She hadn't expected Mary to take umbrage at the truth. Taken aback, she said, "I just told you what this man told me."

At that moment, Peter's father stepped into the house. "Who's yelling here?"

"Your soon-to-be daughter-in-law," his wife said.

"Get out!" Pan Klewchuk said. "Get out of the house. The only place for yelling is the barn. You can yell all you want with the cows."

"I'm sorry," Dolly said. "I was just saying—"

"Enough!" he roared. "Get out before I chase you out!"

Peter's mother folded her arms; his sister stood stone-faced beside her.

"Thank you for the tea," Dolly said as she left, her legs shaking. She hadn't expected such a disastrous meeting. She shook her head as she walked past the fading flowers of summer that lined the path alongside the house. She kept thinking of how Peter's family had yelled at her. They'd thrown her out of the house. They'd accused her of lying. She didn't lie. She'd told the truth. What would people think if she'd asked Mary to be a bridesmaid? Peter had said, 'Who the hell cares?' Well, she cared.

When she saw Peter next, he acted as if she had committed a horrible wrong. He had ridden to the farm on his bicycle and found her outside, throwing feed to the chickens. He wasted no time telling her what he'd heard from his mother and sister.

"It's the way you said it, Dolly. Out of the blue."

"What do you mean, out of the blue?"

"It's gossip. You were sharing gossip. You don't say things like that."

"But it's true. I only said what's true." She threw more seed down. The chickens ran to the spot where she'd thrown their food. "Your mother wanted to know why I didn't take Mary for a bridesmaid." She stopped throwing seed and faced him. "No one asks a woman who's shamed herself to be a bridesmaid. No one."

With his normally soft eyes fierce, he said, "I'm proud of Mary. She was brave to have a child out of wedlock and raise her. It wasn't her damn fault!"

"I know," she said, contrite. "I'm sorry, Peter. I'm proud of her, too. I was just trying to explain. You know my English isn't so good. I just say what I hear from this man who knows Mary." When Peter remained sullen, she said, "Did you think that was right that your father yelled at me, told me to get out?"

Peter thrust his hands in his pants pockets. "Of course not, but you have to understand—"

"People laugh at me because I'm just a farm girl. I don't want anyone to laugh at my wedding." With the seeds dispersed, she wiped her hands on her pants and marched towards the barn. Peter stayed back.

Let him sulk, she thought. *Let him sulk.* She had feelings, too. She didn't tell Peter that the driver who'd told her about Mary used the word *bastard* to describe her illegitimate birth. Dolly prided herself that at least she'd had the good sense not to repeat that awful word.

Not the Old Country

The aroma of freshly baked honey cakes filled the air in the kitchen, along with the excitement Dolly was feeling now that her wedding was only a day away. The women in the house had been cooking and baking tirelessly for days. Maria Karpinsky and Natasha Chimiuk had come over to help—bringing some baked goods and rolling up their sleeves to make varenyky and holupchi. With all the chattering and laughter, time passed quickly.

While her mother set the honey cakes to cool, Dolly began rolling out the dough to make hrystyki, a sweet treat that would be deep-fried and dusted with icing sugar.

Elena stood at the stove, stirring poppyseed filling for sweet rolls.

Dolly cut the pastry dough into small rectangles, then cut slits in each piece. After cutting the slits, she said, "I wish one of my bridesmaids would sing me a song at my wedding."

"What song?" Elena asked.

"The one about a girl getting married without her father there to give her away. But no one knows the song." Dolly sang, "Dunya, Dunya, look behind you to see if your father is standing there. I looked and looked, but he wasn't there. He died in the raw ground, newly dug."

"That's how it is," her mother said, as she heated a pot of oil on the stove.

Dolly muttered and inserted one end of a rectangular piece of dough through the slit, pulled and twisted it into shape. She picked up another rectangle of dough and repeated the action.

Her mother wiped her hands on her apron and began creating hrystyki as well.

"It's too bad this isn't the old country. The girls don't know this song." She shrugged her shoulders. "At least Nick Meronek's mother made you a nice shower. A dozen women came! I didn't know there were so many Ukrainians in Stony Mountain."

"Two were English," Dolly said.

"I know," her mother said, frowning.

Dolly understood immediately that she had offended her mother by suggesting she hadn't noticed the English women. She said, "I know you know."

Her mother grunted and gave her a sideways look.

"That's a pretty set of china dishes they gave you," Elena said, as she spread the poppyseed filling on a large square of dough. "And a fine roaster for holupchi."

Lukia tsked. "Good to have nice dishes, but you need food to put on them."

"Mama," Dolly said, "don't start."

An unease settled over the women. Dolly exchanged looks with Elena, who

quickly broke eye contact—a sign she was
not about to side with her if it meant
displeasing her mother-in-law.

Dolly resumed making hrystyki. She
wished her mother would stop
complaining about Peter. He was
wonderful. Everyone who met Peter loved
him. Nick Meronek called him a prince
among fellows. Bill said his brother
could've had any girl in the village. And he
was intelligent and kind. Though these
thoughts circled in her mind, she knew
her mother was right. The road ahead
wouldn't be easy. Dolly knew she'd have
to work, too, but she'd been working ever
since she left school, so she didn't expect
that to change. And with conditions
improving on the prairies, there was a
glimmer of hope on the horizon. As long
as there was hope, she'd find a way.

Dolly had been up since before the cock
crowed the day of her wedding. After she
milked the cows with her mother and

Elena, she ate some porridge hurriedly. She washed her hair in rainwater and, in front of the bureau mirror, she fashioned some waves in her dark brown hair that now had burnished red streaks from the sun. As she styled her hair with a few dabs of gel, she caught a glimpse of her white satin gown hanging in the open wardrobe closet she shared with her mother. Michelina had sewn matching satin-covered buttons from the neckline to the hem of the long-sleeved gown. It was a classic design that fit Dolly perfectly, showing off her ample curves. Alongside the gown hung a seeded pearl tiara and a cathedral veil that would form a long train behind her when she walked down the aisle. And on top of the bureau lay a sprig of myrtle, for purity—to be tucked into her headpiece when the time came.

She was fortunate Michelina had sewn the gown for only nine dollars, the cost of the fabric. She had charged nothing for her work—an unbelievable bargain. Dolly had purchased her veil and crown separately for two dollars and fifty cents each. And Peter's shirt cost one dollar and fifty cents and his tie another fifty cents. He was so sweet to pay for it all.

She was still fussing in the mirror when Peter showed up. He'd come to the house to ask for her mother's blessing, as was the custom.

In the living room, he and Dolly knelt on an embroidered rushnyk in front of her mother and Egnat—who stood in place of her father. Holding a loaf of bread and a framed icon of the Holy Supper, her mother said, "This bread is life itself. It stands for abundance, which I wish for you. Your tato would've wished the same." She handed the bread to Peter and then moved the framed icon through the air in the shape of a cross. Raising her face skyward, she added, "As these two children stand before their mother, we know there were times they did not listen, but I ask you to forgive them and bless them." Handing the icon to her daughter, she said to them both, "May God bless you with a prosperous life together."

"Thank you, Mama, for your blessing." Dolly wished Peter's parents could have taken part in this ceremony, but his mother had taken ill. She hoped to attend the service later that day.

Lukia took Peter's hands and said, "You have to be good to my daughter. She's the only one I have now."

"I will, Mama," he said, addressing her more intimately now that the wedding day was upon them.

Her mother got her handbag and opened it. She took out her wallet and pulled out five twenty-dollar bills. "For your home. Put it aside and use it towards a down payment on your own place."

"So much?" Dolly said.

Lukia pursed her lips. "I saved it for your wedding. You will need it. Go with God." She embraced her daughter and

Peter, looking at them intently, as if they were leaving her for the last time.

While Mike drove Peter home, Dolly bounced from room to room getting ready. The only niggling thought she held had to do with their wedding night. Neither had been intimate with anyone else. This would be their first time. She knew there would probably be some discomfort, but that wasn't what worried her. She worried she might not bleed to prove she was a virgin. She thought she had broken her hymen the time she'd fallen off a horse, but she wasn't sure. If she didn't bleed, as expected, would Peter think she'd had sex with someone before him?

In the bedroom, she noted her sour expression in the bureau mirror and did her best to push her troubling thoughts away. *Nothing is going to spoil my wedding day. Nothing.* She forced a smile and donned her gown.

Next was her headpiece. As she was fastening it, her mother, dressed in a navy crepe dress with a lace collar, came into the room and sat on the bed. "Docha," she said, "I can't believe you're getting married already. So fast."

"Not so fast, Mama. I'm twenty-three. Peter's twenty-eight. How much longer can we wait?"

"Oy, a tragedy."

"What do you mean, a tragedy? You should be happy for me."

"What's happy? You're marrying a poor man. How can I be happy?"

Dolly tucked the myrtle in her headpiece. "If you're going to sit there and complain—"

"I'm not complaining. I'm just saying how it is." Her mother paused, then said, "When you're in church and you and Peter have to kneel in front of the priest, remember to put your knee down on his pant leg. That way, he'll listen to you in your marriage."

"Yes, Mama." Dolly understood that Peter would have to listen if they were going to get ahead in life. She'd seen too many women disrespected by their men in their own homes. Peter's mother was one of them. Dolly was pleased Peter had noticed his mother's plight and sympathized with her. That gave Dolly hope he differed from the men who expected their wives to cook and clean and raise the children but have little voice in other matters. Since she worked as hard as any man, she wanted a marriage of equality, one in which she'd have a say in what mattered, like the household finances. She wanted her voice to be heard as much as his. Besides, she'd had enough of her mother telling her to be quiet when she was in a talking mood, and her brothers teasing her as if her ideas had no merit. In her marriage, she would make sure her opinions counted.

A Hole in the Party

riends and relatives of both the bride and groom had packed St. Mary the Protectress Church—still only a basement. Lukia had hoped her brother, Petro, would come to the wedding, but the cost of a train ticket from Toronto to Winnipeg was too much for him and his family. The rift between them remained, but at least he'd answered the letter Egnat had sent along with the wedding invitation. His sons, Alex and Ted, were here, as were all the Klewchuks. Except for Bill, the best man. He hadn't shown up yet. Lukia didn't know why. She hoped he hadn't had an accident.

Pan and Panye Klewchuk and their

children sat on the opposite side of the main aisle. Peter's mother, dressed in a lovely print dress with a beaded necklace, looked pale and frail in a wheelchair that Johnny and her husband had carried down the steps to the basement. Peter's father, though handsome with a handlebar moustache and silver hair, was reed thin, not at all like most of Lukia's countrymen, who tended to be stockier. Peter had obviously inherited his father's lankiness and good looks. Dunya had mentioned the family had no vehicles and that Peter's father walked everywhere, which could explain his slim body. Lukia wasn't sure what Panye Klewchuk was ailing from, but she'd heard some gossip that she had rak. Cancer was a disease you didn't recover from.

Luckless woman, Lukia thought. *At least she's seeing her eldest son get married*. Her poor Gregory had died so young, he had seen none of his children marry. He missed both Hania's and

Egnat's weddings, and now he was going to miss Dunya's. *Oy, Gregory, why didn't you listen to me? I told you I had a bad dream, and you laughed. And when you insisted on going to the forest to chop some wood, I asked you to cross yourself. Again, you made fun of me. You could've at least crossed yourself.* Her brow furrowed. *Maybe God would've protected you.* She stared at the iconostasis with paintings of the disciples, Christ, and Mary, and crossed herself three times.

A commotion behind her caused Lukia and many of the guests to turn. Father Mayewsky was receiving Peter and Dolly as they entered the basement with their bridal party. He tied an embroidered rushnyk around Peter's left hand and around Dunya's right and led them down the main aisle, followed by the bridesmaids and ushers. When they had settled at the front by the altar, the priest prayed. Lukia crossed herself again, along with the rest of the congregation. She saw

Peter look towards the entrance, straining to see over the crowd. Lukia assumed he was expecting Bill to appear at any moment.

Facing the iconostasis, her daughter looked like a princess in her white satin gown and pearl tiara, her long veil trailing behind her. Tiny twigs of cedar had been placed around its lace edge. In her hands, she held a bouquet of red roses with ferns tied with a white organza bow. What a difference between her daughter's Canadian wedding and the one Lukia had in the old country! Lukia had worn a beautifully embroidered shirt indicative of her oblast and a wreath of red poppies in her hair. She had carried a bouquet of sunflowers. Gregory had also worn an embroidered shirt. Little by little, their traditions were being eroded in this English-speaking land.

Lukia heaved a sigh and gazed at Peter's ushers. His brother George, his best friend Lesley Woods, Mike, and Harry stood to Peter's right, all dressed in their fine suits, white shirts and dark print ties, with a rose in their lapels. Peter distinguished himself from his ushers by wearing a vest and a white tie over his shirt. To the left of the couple stood Olga Chimiuk, the maid of honour, in a blue gown with a matching headpiece, and the bridesmaids—Leila Katchuk from Dauphin, Olga Pashen and Anne Lacoma from the church and another one Lukia didn't know. Holding bouquets of carnations and roses, the bridesmaids wore long, pastel-coloured taffeta gowns, each one a different colour—green, pink, yellow and beige—and adorning their hair, a matching band of small satin flowers with a veil.

Lukia regarded Olga, her hair nicely coiffed, her long face composed and yet hard to read. Perhaps she would be the one to catch the bouquet at the wedding, a Canadian custom that her daughter said she'd follow. Whoever caught it would be the next one to be wed.

As Father Mayewsky handed the couple lit beeswax candles to hold, signifying joy and warmth, Dunya handed her bouquet to Olga. The priest blessed the couple, then placed wedding rings on the bride's and groom's fingers. He positioned gold crowns on their heads, then bound their hands together again with the embroidered rushnyk. Holding the ends of the cloth, he led them around the altar three times, while George and Olga followed behind and made sure the gold crowns remained on the bridal couple's heads.

After communion, the priest instructed Peter and Dolly to kneel on an embroidered cloth. Lukia smiled when she noticed her daughter kneeling on a bit of Peter's trousers. It pleased her that her daughter had paid attention to her advice. She would start her marriage with a voice that mattered. Her husband would listen to her. Then Lukia thought of her own wedding. Kneeling on her husband's pants hadn't helped; Gregory hadn't listened. Lukia prayed her daughter would have better luck with her man.

The choir sang beautifully, but Lukia couldn't help crying. Tears streamed down her face as her daughter and Peter vowed to honour one another until eternity. Her daughter's future was now sealed. She must have groaned audibly without thinking, as Elena gave her a nudge. Egnat, who stood on the other side of Elena, handed his mother a handkerchief, the one thing she'd forgotten to put in her purse.

Wiping away her tears, she looked over at Peter's mother and father, who appeared to be observing the ceremony with grim faces. Their expression showed they weren't any happier than she about the union. From what Dunya had confided, they were unimpressed that their son was marrying a farm girl. As if their son was so much better. And as if they had so much! Dunya had told her mother that they lived in a two-room house in town and owned the double lot next door, the property Peter was to have. They'd been cordial enough when she met them, but they'd kept their distance. For Lukia, this was appalling. In the old country, when couples married, their two families came together to give their children a joint blessing. She understood sickness had prevented Peter's mother and father from travelling to her farm, but she'd expected a warmer reception when they greeted one another in church.

The Klewchuk children carried themselves well. George, the third eldest, had finished high school, as had Bill, the second. Though he was the best man, there was still no sign of him. Where was he? Lukia noticed Peter checking the crowd, probably wondering the same thing. What an insult to ignore your brother's wedding! Only a near-death illness should keep a close member of the family away.

At least Mary had come to the wedding. She sat beside her mother, dressed in a stylish dress, with a hip belt of the same rayon fabric. Since the children were so well-dressed and groomed, they couldn't be doing that badly, thought Lukia. Yes, it was good Mary came. Lukia learned from Dunya that she'd been disappointed not to be part of the bridal party. That was understandable. But it was also understandable that Dunya was following what was right. How could she have chosen Mary to be a bridesmaid when she was no longer a virgin?

As Father Mayewsky pronounced them man and wife, Lukia's heart sank. According to church law, they had become two people in one body and soul. She liked Peter, but she could not see how this union would make her daughter prosper. More tears fell as she prayed, "God, God, please take care of my children."

Dolly fumed, but refused to let Bill spoil her day. He hadn't had the courtesy to show up for the wedding ceremony, nor for the photographs at the portrait studio. She and Peter would have wedding photos with an uneven number in her bridal party: four men and five women. She was sure Bill was being spiteful. Peter had mentioned that Bill fancied himself as the brightest in the family, and also the one who couldn't pass a mirror without admiring his features.

Peter shared nothing of how he was feeling about Bill, but she could tell he was anxious by the way he fidgeted with his collar, and in the car, his socks, pulling them up more than necessary. Bill had snubbed him, the brother he'd been closest to. Peter kept looking at the photographer's studio door, as if Bill was about to burst in at any moment with some excuse for why he was late.

Her brother Mike had paid for the hall in Brooklands, a convenient location because it was a community on the north edge of Winnipeg with easy highway access to their farm and Stony Mountain. He had also paid for all the ingredients that Lukia, Elena, Dolly and their friends needed to make the food for the reception. He told their mother he was getting good money from hauling goods. Dolly, like her mother, appreciated his generosity, but, having seen this kind of help before, worried he'd soon return to his old ways.

Victor Karpinsky's trio—accordion player, tsymbaly player and violinist—who had played at Nick's wedding, agreed to play at theirs, too. Her family knew Victor from the days his family had lived with theirs on the Rosser farm. Dolly and Peter stood in the receiving line at the door with their parents to greet their guests, while the band played the Ukrainian wedding march. Her feet tapped as they shook hands and hugged people from their communities and her church. She couldn't wait to dance in her beautiful gown.

She hadn't been standing long when Peter suddenly left the receiving line with one of his friends for a drink of horilka that her brothers, Harry and Egnat, were pouring for the guests. Her mother saw him go as well and made a face. Dolly wondered what he'd been thinking to leave her alone to greet the guests. Frowning, she turned to see him kibbitzing with two of his friends. She tried to catch his attention, but he didn't turn around.

Mrs. Babiak, a church member, had noticed Peter's leave-taking and said to her mother, loud enough for Dolly to hear, "His leaving like that. Tsk, tsk, tsk. That's bad luck." Mrs. Babiak harrumphed before she moved further into the hall.

"Not good," Lukia said.

Dolly pretended not to hear and smiled at the next guest. Was Peter's behaviour something to be concerned about? Before she thought any more of it, Bill showed up with his face flushed. Dolly wasn't sure if it was from drinking beforehand or from embarrassment. He said, "I'm so sorry, Dolly. I had to hang around the barracks for one of the other soldiers to show up. It's my job to hold the keys, and I couldn't find them."

Dolly didn't know what to say. Was he telling the truth? She hesitated, then said, "Okay, Bill."

"Where's Peter?"

"Over there." She pointed to where Peter was standing with his friends.

Bill smirked and went to join his brother. Dolly followed him with her eyes. Peter patted Bill on the back, as if his brother had done nothing wrong and needed to be congratulated instead of reprimanded for not showing up for the service. Why did her husband let his brother get away with such nonsense? There was so much she didn't know about the man she married. He was a gentle sort, but there were limits, she thought. What Bill had done by not coming to the church or to the photo studio was rude. It was an insult. But what did she expect? Did she expect Peter to ream his brother out in public? No, that would be embarrassing. Again, she tried to calm her doubts. This was her wedding, and she was determined to have a good time.

Let Me Call You Sweetheart

A korovai, a braided round wedding loaf of bread decorated with flowers, graced the centre of each of the three long banquet tables. As the guests seated themselves, Egnat, Mike, and Harry went around the hall, ensuring everyone had another shot of horilka to toast the bride and groom. Their mother and Elena, along with their friends Maria and Natasha, carried plates and bowls of hot food—roasted chicken, pork and cabbage, kybassa, kishka, holupchi, fried mushrooms, varenyky with various fillings, nalysnyky, and cooked beets, peas and carrots, green and yellow beans—and set them down on the long tables. Dolly joked they were having everything from soup to nuts. So many serving dishes had to be borrowed. The Mazurecs didn't have enough china to accommodate all the guests. The feast showed that despite their years of hardship, they knew how to host a fine wedding.

A woman, prominent in the church, took Lukia's apron off and donned it herself. When Lukia protested, the parishioner waved her away, telling her to sit down with the wedding party.

Father Mayewsky said the Lord's Prayer and blessed the dinner. The toast "Daye Bozhe!" rang through the hall, along with the sound of glasses clinking against one another. Everyone began passing food around the tables. As guests sampled the various dishes, there were more than a few saying, "smachno," which had to be translated for the English-speaking guests.

"It means delicious," Mike said to Lesley, who sat beside him.

After coffee and dessert—cheesecake, honey cake, poppyseed rolls, and hrystyki—the ushers helped to clear the tables while the band took the stage. Guests placed the chairs along the walls to free the floor for dancing.

Victor grabbed the mike and said, "The first dance is between the bride and groom." Smiling, Dolly and Peter rose from their seats. She grabbed the loop of her gown's hem and took Peter's arm to dance to their song, "Let Me Call You Sweetheart." As they waltzed around the room, he sang along with the band, "Let me call you sweetheart; I'm in love with you. Let me hear you whisper that you love me, too ..." His vodka breath warmed her cheeks as their eyes met. There was no question; he loved her deeply.

The way he danced was one reason she had fallen in love with him. They were like butter and bread, good alone but better together. Feeling light as a feather in his arms, she glided with him across the floor, not missing a step. She thought, if only they could stay this much in step as the years went on, they would do well.

When the music came to a stop, Victor announced it was time for the bride and groom to dance with their parents. But since Dolly had no father there, she danced with Egnat. He beamed as if she was a child of his. He was the reliable man who had cared for her ever since her father died when she was five, and yet, when it came to advice, it was Mike she had gone to, to ask whether Peter was the right man for her. She knew in her heart that Egnat wanted more for her than what Peter offered, but he accepted her decision. His warm, calloused hands gripped hers tightly as they whirled past Peter, who had chosen Mary to dance with. His mother sat in her wheelchair, an unreadable expression on her face. Dolly had hoped for a mother-in-law who would embrace her, but it was not to be. She didn't know if Peter's mother had long to live, but Dolly suspected it wouldn't be long enough to forgive her for not taking Mary as a bridesmaid.

At the end of the dance, Egnat took her hands and stepped back to look at her. He said with a mischievous smile and a twinkle in his eyes, "For a squirt, you make a beautiful bride."

"Yeah, yeah, yeah," she said, beaming. In time, she would show Egnat that Peter was every bit the man her eldest brother was.

Another waltz began, and the bridesmaids and ushers rushed to the dance floor. Dolly encouraged her husband to ask her mother and watched him walk over to where she was seated. Dolly wondered why Pan Klewchuk didn't ask her to dance. He was standing with a couple of other men his age, each holding a glass of horilka. Not that she had any tender feelings towards Peter's father. He had yelled at her and told her to get out of his house. And he hadn't offered his son the property next door. She had been sure he was going to surprise them on their wedding day, but so far, all Peter's parents had done was pay for the horilka.

She loved having a Canadian wedding, but she missed some of the wedding traditions she'd observed growing up in her village. Like having one of her attendants sing a song about a girl getting married without a father. In the old country, a bride traded her wedding headpiece (a wreath of flowers) for a babushka. She didn't care for that tradition. A flowered scarf was for old women—babas—not for her. But she wouldn't have minded crying at her own wedding. Dolly wanted to cry, an old-country custom that meant the bride was saying goodbye to her youth and leaving a carefree life behind. But she couldn't muster the tears.

Another custom would involve Peter. She wanted him to take part in a dance where she would stand in the centre of a circle formed by the guests. The groom had to walk around the outside of the circle and try to break the hand-holding to get to his bride. When she'd proposed this to Peter, he said he'd find it too embarrassing.

"Embarrassing?" she said. She didn't understand that. There wasn't much that embarrassed her. It saddened her he didn't want to partake in this custom. She guessed it was because he'd immigrated when he was two, too young to have experienced the old ways. They held no meaning for him.

However, Peter liked one wedding tradition, even though he couldn't perform the Cossack kicks that everyone enjoyed watching. When the band played the koloymeyka, the dance floor quickly became crowded. The young and old alike formed a large circle. Mike and Egnat took turns in the centre, jumping in the air, showing off their Cossack kicks. Two of her bridesmaids followed her brothers into the centre and twirled with graceful arm movements and footwork.

Dolly and Peter cheered with the others. He said to her, "I saw my father do the Cossack kick when I was younger. But after years of working in the quarry, his back isn't what it once was." She noticed Pan Klewchuk on the other side of the circle. Though his eyes drooped, showing he'd had more than a few drinks, he clapped with the others

When it came time to throw her bouquet, Dolly tried to aim it Olga's way, but a young woman from Stony Mountain caught it. Olga didn't look disappointed. Maybe she never expected to catch the bouquet.

Afterwards, Dolly's brothers set up a long table for presentation, a Ukrainian wedding tradition. The band played the wedding march again and kept playing it over and over as the guests lined up to throw money gifts into the plate for the bride and groom, who stood behind the table with their attendants. Some money gifts were a few loose dollar bills; others presented their cash in envelopes. One young man was so drunk that after throwing his money on the plate, he kissed Dolly so passionately that two older men near the table hooted loudly. Peter also received some enthusiastic kisses from several young women. Dolly wasn't jealous. It wasn't her nature to be that way. The fact she'd married the man of her dreams gave her an unshakeable confidence.

Peter chortled as his brothers-in-law kissed him on the lips after throwing their money on the presentation plate. He'd never kissed men before he met the Mazurecs, let alone men with moustaches, even though kissing men as well as women in greeting was a common practice in their culture. The presentation line was winding down. His lips were sore from all the kissing, some from people he didn't even know. Soon, it would be his turn. He'd have to go around the table and present to his bride. He'd seen some grooms make a big joke of it and take off their shoes, jacket and tie, but he would never do that. Not with all eyes on him.

He loved Dolly, but now that he had tied the knot, he felt apprehensive. His inability to find full-time work did not bode well for their future. Sure, other men were in the same boat, but Dolly and her family considered men who weren't engaged in meaningful employment as slothful. He was far from lazy, but he had to admit he wasn't the aggressive sort, the kind that knocked on every door. When he'd tried to secure work in Winnipeg, employers rejected him again and again; it shouldn't have been surprising as white-collar jobs were closed to Ukrainians and Jews. Why would anyone keep trying when they knew all they'd get would be a door in their face?

The line had finished, and now it was his turn. He stood in front of Dolly, admiring her composure. Despite the long day, her appearance was as fresh as a daisy at dawn. He admired her full lips and teasing hazel eyes, a sparkle he couldn't get enough of. Tonight, he'd be taking her to bed for the first time. He was anxious about that as well. Though he'd had the odd offer in the past, it had been from a girl known to sleep with a few fellows. He wasn't interested in that kind of girl. Nor would he have wanted to get a girl pregnant. He'd had enough heartache watching his sister suffer.

He emptied his pockets of a couple of dollar bills and some coins and put them on the plate.

"More, more," Lesley and George hollered.

Peter laughed. He could feel his cheeks burn. Above him on the stage, Victor's fingers ran up and down the accordion keys, as the band played the wedding march with even greater enthusiasm. Bill clapped, along with Lesley and Dolly's brothers. Taking a deep breath, Peter took out the pocket watch he'd bought before he met Dolly and added it to the pile of money.

She laughed good-naturedly and said, "What else do you have?"

He took off his shoes and added them to the plate. He then leaned over the table and kissed her passionately to the cheers and shouts of encouragement from the crowd. He didn't care what they were saying. All he knew was that it felt good to have her lips on his.

No Honey on the Moon

Around eleven, a group of women brought more food out of the kitchen and set it on the long table below the stage. Despite having eaten a heavy meal, the guests quickly devoured plates of various cold cuts, garlic dill pickles, rye bread, and more sweets. Vigorous dancing had stimulated their appetites. It was also time to slice the korovai and the two-tiered dark fruit wedding cake with a plastic bride and groom on top from Gunn's Bakery on Selkirk Avenue. Her mother hadn't been in favour of buying such a fancy cake, but Dolly said it was the Canadian way and insisted on one for the end of the evening.

As the evening drew to a close, Dolly decided it had been a fine wedding. She had glowed in the admiration of many, especially the women who wanted to know where she'd bought her gown. Because her brothers kept stealing Peter away to have a drink with them—not that he needed much urging—she had been free to dance with others. She danced with Alex, Ted, Lesley, Nick Meronek, and George. All spoke fondly of Peter, which warmed her and quelled any concerns she had about their honeymoon night. She even danced with Bill, though he reminded her of how she'd rebuffed him the first time.

She said, "No hard feelings, Bill?"

He said, "No hard feelings," and held her tightly as he whirled her around the floor.

The dance was over by midnight. Seeing the band pack up, Dolly walked over to the stage and thanked Victor and the other musicians for their wonderful playing. It took over an hour before the hall emptied. Guests, wanting to wish the couple a successful life, held Peter and Dolly back from leaving.

As they thanked them for coming, she couldn't help but think of the night ahead. She was full of anticipation and wondered what Peter would be like as a lover. Would he be like the actors in those Hollywood films who kissed their wives and then, fuelled by desire, led them to bed? Throughout the evening, she had watched her husband turn redder as the evening progressed. Since she'd grown up with brothers who never left a gathering sober, she had put her concerns about his drinking aside. She glanced lovingly at him and put her arm through his. She was now Mrs. Peter Klewchuk, a wife, and no longer just a grown child in her family.

She and Peter were among the last ones to leave the hall. Her mother, tired from all the preparations, and Elena, anxious to put the girls to bed, had left at least an hour earlier with Egnat. Mike and the hired hand, his brother's drinking companion, also left around the same time as they were so drunk they could barely stand up. Dolly looked around the hall; only a few guests remained, among them, Bill, who was sitting in a corner talking to Nick Meronek and his wife.

"Well, you two," Lesley said, coming up to them and putting his arm around Peter's shoulders, "you ready to hit the road?"

Peter, his face flushed, turned to Dolly. "You ready?"

She nodded. "Yes."

On the ride back to her mother's farm in Lesley's parents' car, Dolly sat on the front seat between Peter and his friend. She listened to the men talk, mostly about Lesley's work as an RCMP officer. She gazed out the windshield, the car's headlights cutting through the dark with two parallel rows of yellow light on the gravel highway. She thought of what lay ahead. It had been a wonderful wedding, except for Bill arriving so late. An insult, and yet Peter had said nothing to his brother when he finally showed up. She didn't understand a man like that, so different from her brothers. If one had insulted the other, they'd be on the floor, fists flying over some egregious remark. She had to put away her misgivings. Soon, they'd be back on the farm and she would be lying in Peter's arms.

When they walked into the house, it was so quiet you could hear the wind blow outside. The old wood floor creaked under their footsteps as they made their way to the third bedroom, past her mother's and Egnat's. When they opened the door to the bedroom, Dolly's face fell at the sight of Mike and the hired hand passed out on one of the two beds in the room, the smell of booze permeating the air.

"Oy," she said. "Why are they sleeping here? Mike knew we were coming back here. He was supposed to stay with a friend in the city."

"Maybe he forgot."

"What are we going to do?"

"Maybe I could move them."

"Where? Mama's cousin and wife are in the other room."

Peter looked perplexed.

"They came in from Sault Ste. Marie for the wedding."

Peter grabbed the headboard to steady himself.

"And how are you going to move them?" she said crossly. "You can hardly stand yourself."

"I could wake them."

"They're drunk. You wake Mike, he might throw a punch and start yelling. You'll wake the whole house up. Then what?"

His glum face was the answer.

Dolly felt deflated. Her desire for an intimate night had vanished like a puff of smoke. They had left a place full of merriment, extravagance, and laughter, and now they were alone in a miserable room with two drunks sharing one three-quarter bed; she and Peter sharing the other.

Peter shyly undressed. After taking off her pearl seed crown and veil, she began to unbutton her dress. Each satin-covered button undone brought her closer to the inevitable lovemaking in bed. She felt her mouth and jaw tighten. Why hadn't Peter arranged a hotel room? She looked again at her brother; his raven hair had fallen over his eyes. She wanted to shake him and say, 'What the hell were you thinking?'

She slipped out of her gown and laid it and her veil over a wooden chair in the room. Then she took off the slip underneath. Trembling in the cold, she climbed under the covers and waited for Peter, who was taking a long time to get out of his clothes. She wasn't sure if it was because he was nervous, or scared, or just inebriated. Or all three.

Peter took her in bed, his movements awkward and quick, with her glancing periodically at her brother and the hired hand, fearful they'd wake up and humiliate them with some untoward remark. The act was painful and she wanted to cry out, but again, the unwelcome company in the room made any utterances impossible. Dolly couldn't imagine a worse beginning of a marriage.

When Peter opened his eyes in the morning, his head felt as though it was being hammered on all sides. Mike and the hired hand had mercifully left the room. Dolly was also gone. He struggled to find his footing and put on his shoes. He hoped to make it to the outhouse before he embarrassed himself. He succeeded in throwing up there, but not long after, he threw up again at the side of the house, retching so much he thought his insides would explode. When he finished, Dolly was waiting by the front door. Without mincing words, she told him how horrible their honeymoon night had been. Her pounding words of disappointment competed with the pounding in his head.

Then she said, "I want a divorce."

"What? You don't mean that.... Honey," he said and immediately apologized for a night he barely remembered. He tried to take her in his arms, but she pushed him away. She would have none of his attempts to soothe her.

He would've loved a hotel room, too, but where was he supposed to get the money? She knew he didn't have much, and the little he had had gone for their rings and his shirt and tie. And how was he to know that Mike and the hired hand would be there? No one had mentioned they'd have to share a room. He wasn't a mind reader. Sometimes he felt there was no pleasing her.

"Come," she said. "I'll give you

something for your hangover."

Relieved she was talking to him, he followed her back to the house, his head bent, his shoulders stooped. He was not looking forward to seeing the rest of the family. When Dolly was angry, there was no hiding it.

Why had he drunk so much? He could blame Bill or her brothers, who kept bringing him shots of vodka to drink, but he'd blamed her brothers before when he'd had too much, and Dolly had said sarcastically, "Yeah, yeah, yeah, one brother held you down, and the other poured it down your throat." There was no doubt the drinks had helped to quell his anxiety about Bill, Mary, and his parents.

Peter muttered to himself. He had an excuse for his drunkenness, but not one Dolly would understand.

Sheepishly entering the kitchen, he exchanged "Good morning" nods with Lukia and Elena, who were busy preparing a meal at the counter and stove. Egnat's and Mike's drawn faces and slow movements suggested they were also suffering from hangovers. They had brought in saw horses and sheets of plywood to extend the kitchen table for a large gathering. Peter had forgotten that in a matter of hours, Alex, Ted, the Slipchenkos, the Karpinskys, and the Chimiuks would join the family for popravyny, a continuation of the wedding celebration. His mother-in-law had invited his family, but they had declined even when Mike offered to drive over and pick them up. He thought it was because his mother wasn't feeling well, but maybe they were still sore at Dolly.

She poured him a glass of dill pickle juice. He gratefully took it from her and swallowed the liquid, strongly tasting of garlic and vinegar. He wiped his mouth with his hand and hoped the drink would remove the taste of vomit in his throat.

"That should help," she said.

She regarded him like he was a

naughty child. He accepted her motherly act because she was acting calmer now. Maybe her mother's presence had quieted her down. He looked over at his mother-in-law and Elena. Did they know what had transpired between him and his wife? What he dreaded more than anything was her talking about him to others.

As people arrived, he did his best to put on a brave face. Dolly was charming as usual, as if there'd been no quarrel. Her brothers poured drinks freely, as though they hadn't drunk enough the night before. This time, he pretended to take a sip and set his glass down when no one was looking.

He took a little of everything that was passed around the table, but he had no appetite. He would have liked nothing better than to get on a bicycle and let the wind carry him wherever it wanted to. How could he have let his honeymoon night turn into such a disaster? He tried to remember what was going on in his head that evening. Though upset over Bill's lateness, he couldn't blame his brother entirely. Bill also had a soft spot for Mary. His whole family was angry that Dolly had treated his sister like she'd committed a terrible sin. Even at the reception, they sat stone-faced, as if they were at a funeral and not a wedding. Strange how his dad was the one who'd kicked Mary out when he learned she was pregnant, and yet, when Dolly only reported what she'd heard, she became the pariah. Looking back, Peter recognized he had allowed himself to become drunk to mask the pain of seeing his family reject the woman he loved. It had been hard to see their sad faces at what should have been a joyful event all around. Well, there was nothing he could do about that now. One thing he knew for sure. He was wrong not to have borrowed the money for a hotel room on their honeymoon night, as Dolly had wanted. Why was he so stubborn? He hated owing anyone anything, especially when he was unsure of how he would pay it back. He'd have to make it up to her somehow. She deserved that much, at least.

"Peter, you're not eating," his mother-in-law said.

"Mama, I ate so much yesterday."

She raised her eyebrows. He wasn't fooling her. She'd seen how much he'd drunk.

Mike peered at him sideways. Maybe he had heard them in bed. He hoped that Mike and the hired hand had slept through the night, oblivious to the creaking bedsprings, but he wasn't about to ask if that was the case.

Avoiding his glance, Dolly said little for the rest of the meal. He'd learned she had a habit of pouting whenever she didn't get her way. This was one day he would be happy to see the end of.

The Martians

olly's brooding extended into the evening as she helped her mother and Elena clean up. There was no place for Peter to escape her sullen looks. He tried to shake off the tension between them by tuning into a radio broadcast, but it only heightened his emotional upheaval. The Mazurecs liked to listen to the nightly news and weather, but that night, they stumbled upon a program that announced the world was being attacked by Martians.

The announcer said, "We know now that in the early years of the twentieth century, this world was being watched closely by intelligences greater than man's, yet as mortal as his own ..."

Peter turned up the volume. The announcer was speaking from somewhere in America, at a crash site, describing a Martian exiting from a large metallic cylinder. "Good heavens," he declared, "something's wriggling out of the shadow like a grey snake. Now here's another, and another one, and another one. They look like tentacles to me ... I can see the thing's body now. It's large, large as a bear. It glistens like wet leather. But that face, it ... it ... ladies and gentlemen, it's indescribable. I can hardly force myself to keep looking at it, it's so awful. The eyes are black and gleam like a serpent. The mouth is kind of V-shaped, with saliva dripping from its rimless lips that seem to quiver and pulsate."

The program continued and ended with newsflashes about Martian spaceships crashing into a farm in New Jersey.

From the calm expressions on the Mazurec family's faces, Peter realized he was the only one alarmed and that their understanding of the broadcast was different from his.

"What is it?" Dolly asked Peter. "You're pale."

"America seems to be under attack by people from space."

"Space? What space?"

"What's he saying?" Lukia asked. "Someone is fighting America?"

"That's what the announcer said." Peter put his ear to the radio. Reporters talked in anxious tones. They described squid-like beings rampaging New York City, killing people with heat rays and poison gas. Why, even the President, Franklin D. Roosevelt, came on the air to comment on the terror in the largest city in the United States.

Peter wished he could ask Lesley or his brother Bill if they'd heard the remarkable broadcast and what they made of it. Was the Earth in danger? Peter didn't know what to believe. It was another global threat, as far as he could see.

During the wedding, he'd talked with Bill and Lesley about what was going on overseas. Bill said talk about a possible war in Europe was ramping up. He wasn't sure what that would mean for Canadian soldiers if Great Britain declared war against Germany. The Munich Agreement, signed a month ago, was supposed to ensure peace. Neville Chamberlain, the British prime minister, almost guaranteed it himself when he convinced France and Italy to sign it. He thought Hitler was a leader who would keep his word. But Peter had heard the Fuhrer speak over the shortwave radio broadcast that he was able to pick up on his crystal set. His fiery speeches in German were electrifying; Peter could only imagine what it was like to hear him in person.

Though the radio program about the Martian invasion was over, Peter could not dampen his fears. His body shook, and he scanned the room to see if any of the family noticed. The women were talking about what some young woman wore to the wedding. They thought she looked like a whore in a low-cut dress. He didn't know who they were talking about. Peter had been so caught up in his own worries that he hadn't paid attention. He watched Egnat pick up the Saturday edition of the *Winnipeg Free Press* that Mike had bought in the city. He liked to check the grain reports.

Peter asked if he could read the front section and took it to the kitchen table, where he tried to put aside the disturbing radio program he'd heard. By the light of the kerosene lamp, he read how Hitler was taking over some place called Sudetenland in Czechoslovakia, because it had three million Germans. Britain and France appeared to have accepted Hitler's claim that it should be unified with Germany. The Fuhrer had also taken Austria. Was the rest of the world going to stand by and let him have his way? The Nazis were also deporting thousands of

Jews to Poland. Foreign Jews were being arrested in Vienna. It didn't say for what, but it said they were Polish, Czechoslovakian, and Hungarian citizens.

Strange times we're living in, Peter thought. He'd screwed up his wedding night. The radio said Martians were attacking New Jersey. And rumblings about another world war were in the paper. To calm himself, Peter went outside to look at the sky. There was no sign that anything unusual had occurred, like a spaceship visiting Earth. The air was cool, the sky cloudy, but he assumed that behind the clouds, the stars continued to spray the sky with their usual brilliance. He took several deep breaths and listened to an owl hooting in the distance. He could do nothing about what was happening in New York or Europe. But he could do something about the guilt and shame he felt over his failed honeymoon night. At least, he hoped he could.

The only positive news the next day came from the radio. The broadcast he'd heard about aliens killing people in New York turned out to be a staged dramatic performance by the actor Orson Welles, meant to scare the public. Fake was what the announcer called the reported Martian invasion. Not real at all. Peter found some comfort knowing he hadn't been the only one scared; it had affected listeners coast to coast, in Canada and America.

He went to the barn to clean out the stalls. It was the job Egnat had given him. He picked up a shovel and immediately felt his stomach roil at the smell of dung. As he shovelled the manure into the concrete boat, he kept reviewing what he could remember of his first night making love to Dolly.

Lilyfield Blues

That year's harvest had given the Mazurec family much-needed hope. The *Winnipeg Free Press* reported that Canada had a bumper crop, the largest wheat crop in ten years. Farmers could pay off their debts and start saving. Whenever Lukia went with Egnat to Stony Mountain for staples, the locals talked of little else. Good times seemed to be in sight.

And yet, good times seemed out of reach for her daughter and Peter. They had moved in the night of the wedding, for practical purposes. They had deposited their presentation money in the bank and hoped to save more so they could build their own house in the village of Stony Mountain. But first, they'd have to find a lot. And Peter would need to find a job outside the family farm. Until they could get on their feet, Lukia gave them free room and board, and paid Peter five dollars a week for farm chores, the amount the government gave her to support labour.

But within weeks of Peter moving in, Lukia noticed his change of mood. He wasn't a man to complain, but neither was he a man who could hide his feelings. When Lukia went to throw slops to the pigs, she caught him grumbling to himself as he stepped out of the barn.

Bothered by Peter's gloomy face as he went about his farm duties, Lukia decided to have a private talk with her daughter. In the evening, after Lukia, Elena, and Dunya had emptied their pails into the tall metal cans in the milk house and were heading back to the house, Lukia said, "Go ahead, Elena. I want to talk to Dunya."

"What about?" her daughter asked, folding her arms across her chest.

"Nu, I haven't talked to you since the wedding, and that was weeks ago."

"We talk every day."

"Come," Lukia said, beckoning with her hand. "Let's sit. It's cold, but it's a beautiful evening. The stars are out. There's no rush to go inside." Lukia buttoned up her wool jacket. It wouldn't be long before winter raised her fierce head again.

"Mama, this is about Peter, isn't it?"

Lukia said nothing as she sat down on the bench by the fence. Puppy ran over from the house. The collie rubbed against Dunya's leg, begging to be petted. Dunya obliged and massaged his head, back, and ears.

"Mama, I know Peter isn't happy."

"What's happiness? Look at me. I'm getting old. Old age isn't happiness; death isn't a wedding."

"Babcha used to say that all the time."

"Nu, she said the truth."

Dunya leaned back and stared at the fields in the distance. "This kind of work is hard on Peter. He's a proud man. He doesn't like Egnat standing over him while he works, like he's some supervisor."

Lukia said, "Of course, Egnat has to supervise. Peter knows nothing about livestock or crops. He's no farmer. He never was and never will be." She turned to Dunya. "Are you expecting him to be one? Egnat would teach him if he wanted to learn."

"No. It's not what he wants. I don't know what he wants." They sat for a few moments in silence. Outside of a horse neighing and Puppy scampering away, the barnyard was quiet, as if the birds and other animals were asleep. Dunya sighed audibly. "He likes to sing. He'd like to be a singer."

Lukia laughed. "A singer. Where's he going to sing? Who's going to pay him?"

"I don't know. We keep waiting for his

father to give him the lot next to his house, but the longer we wait, the more I think Peter's father is going to keep it himself."

Lukia snorted. "That's how it is. What little Pan Klewchuk has, he won't part with."

"I know," Dunya said, rubbing her hands. "I forgot to mention, cigarette smoke bothers Peter, too. You know how much Egnat smokes."

"Peter's too sensitive," Lukia said. "Most hard-working farmers smoke. It relaxes Egnat, like a shot of horilka. Would you deny your brother that pleasure?"

Dunya's brow puckered. "Of course not, but you see how it is."

Lukia saw, but what could she do about it? She couldn't ask Egnat to change his ways. That was asking too much. She turned again to her daughter. "Talk to Peter. If he's so unhappy here, he should look for a job elsewhere."

Dunya laid her head on her mother's shoulder. "I'm not so happy here, either. I'm a married woman now, but my brothers still treat me like their baby sister. And you know, a marriage bed should be private."

"It's private, sometimes," Lukia said.

"Yes, when Mike doesn't come home. At least we don't have the hired hand anymore." He had gone once the harvesting was done.

"Nu," Lukia said, "what can you do?"

They sat there, each lost in their own thoughts, until the cold became too much to bear.

The next day, as she gathered eggs in the chicken coop, Dolly mulled over the talk she'd had with her mother. She had hoped to save more money before they made a move out on their own, but it was hell watching Peter suffer under her brother's watchful eye. Her husband acted like a beaten man. Cleaning the barn was tedious. He had to fork the manure out of the shallow groove at the end of each stall and into a stone boat. Then he had to slide the heavy boat out of the barn, where the manure could rot and transform into fertilizer for the fields.

When she came out of the coop holding a basket of eggs, Egnat was waiting for her. He took a long puff of his cigarette that had shrunk to a stub, then stamped it out on the ground. His eyes narrowed, suggesting he wanted to talk to her about something serious. "Mama said she talked to you."

"Oy."

"Never mind oy," he said. "I'm not blind. I can see for myself."

"It's been such a big help living here, but you know—"

"I know." His mouth curved downwards. "You should be out on your own."

"We're going to look for property in the *Stonewall Argus*. Peter wants us to get some land in Stony Mountain. Build something ourselves"

Egnat squinted in the sun and pulled the brim of his straw hat lower over his forehead. "What kind of work can he get there? He's got no training in anything. Right now, he's getting some money from Mama. Does he think he can get more somewhere else as a hired hand?"

"I'll find something, too. I can find work as a maidservant again." She touched the eggs in her basket. They were still warm.

"Dunya, Dunya." He scratched his forehead with his nicotine-stained fingers. "Why don't you and Peter buy a farm?"

"You're joking."

"I'm not. Farmers are doing well, and—"

"You know he's not a farmer," she said, interrupting.

He put his hand up. "Let me finish. You know enough about farming; you could manage a farm yourself. And the way grain prices are rising, land value will go up, too. If it doesn't work out, you can always sell it."

"Have you mentioned this to Peter?"

"No." He cocked his head. "I figure he'd listen to you more than he'd listen to me." When she hesitated, he said, "I can ask around for you."

She wrinkled her brow. "I don't know. Let me talk to him first." Carrying the eggs into the house, she thought about how she could approach Peter.

Dolly found Peter washing the stalls. Immersed in his work, he barely glanced up. Leaning against a post, she sang a Ukrainian folk song. "Someone else's home is like this, crooked and leaning." She repeated the refrain.

Looking perplexed, he raised his head.

She continued singing, "But you make it a house of villains. Don't take me to one that's not yours."

"What are you singing?"

Realizing his grasp of the Ukrainian language was limited, she said, "Peter, the song means it's not good to live together with family. A home that isn't yours becomes a troublesome one."

"You don't have to tell me," he said in a low voice. He pushed the bristle broom harder over the wet barn floor.

She came up behind him and put her arms around him. He turned. She reached up and kissed him ardently.

He fondled her breasts and said teasingly, "What are you starting here?"

"What am I starting?" She laughed, then said softly, "Nothing." Now that she had his attention, she told him about Egnat's suggestion.

His face fell. "A farm? You told me you hated the farm; the work was too hard."

"Honey, it would be different if it was our farm. You'd be the master. It's no good living in a house where you're not."

But no matter what she said and how much she cajoled him, he kept shaking his head. "No farm, but you're right. It's no good living in a house where I have no say."

"Okay. In the spring, we'll look for land in Stony Mountain."

"If you say so, boss," he said. She left him grinning.

A Bit of a Bang

1939 had started off with a bang; at least, that's what Peter thought. *Time Magazine*, a popular and respected journal, proclaimed Hitler as Man of the Year. The Fuhrer certainly had grabbed the world's attention with his bold moves in Europe the year before. He'd torn up the Treaty of Versailles, took over Austria, and got Sudetenland, exactly what he wanted in the Munich meeting with Churchill, Chamberlain, Mussolini, and the French minister. And then, most shocking of all, after he'd been systematically throwing Jews out of all the land Germany occupied, there was Kristallnacht, what reporters called the Night Bf Broken Glass.

Nazis had marched through cities and towns in Germany and Austria, threatening every Jew they encountered and breaking plate-glass windows of shops, homes, and synagogues. They desecrated cemeteries; they had no shame. They rounded up thousands of Jews, took them to concentration camps, and forced them into labour.

Peter questioned the Times cover. He thought it was like a reward given to Hitler for his outrageous assault on Jews and takeover of neighbouring countries. He had lied to the British prime minister and terrorized so many, and yet he was on the cover of a prominent American magazine. It was all confusing, especially when there were some who thought Hitler wouldn't have sanctioned such an attack on Jews. It had to be hoodlums, they said.

His brother Bill told Peter he was sure a world war was brewing. How long could leaders of other countries give in to this maniac before they said enough was enough? Dolly listened to her husband's concerns, but she had no interest in world politics. She was more worried about how they'd live without steady work.

Peter wished the bad feelings his family had about Dolly would pass. Especially now that his mother was so sick and spent her days huddled in a wheelchair. The doctor said she had cancer for sure. He might as well have said she had a death sentence. They knew no one who'd survived that disease. Dolly tried to thaw the freeze by bringing over sealers of borscht and nalysnyky. Her gifts of food pleased his folks, but their opinion of her remained frosty.

But there was another matter bugging Peter. Dolly had been his first love, the first one he'd gone to bed with, but was he her first? He'd been thinking about it ever since they'd tied the knot. It was the way she flirted at community dances and the way men looked at her, lust gleaming in their eyes. She laughed and giggled, and occasionally told off-colour jokes that charmed the guys. If any man squeezed her too hard in a hug, or danced with her too close, she dismissed it afterwards. She said it meant nothing, though she took great delight in his jealousy, which also irked him and got him thinking about her virginity before marriage.

His jealousy got the best of him at a friend's winter wedding. Again, he had drunk more than he should have. With all the dancing, he had quenched his thirst with the free booze. His friends didn't hold back, either, so he had lots of company. He and Dolly had spun around the floor dancing to waltzes, polkas, a foxtrot and a schottische, but whenever he went to relieve himself or get another drink, she danced with some other fellow. She was light on her feet and showed by her glowing face that she was enjoying herself. He knew he should be proud she was so popular, but he couldn't help feeling jealous. It was doubly troubling she never showed the same jealousy about him. Girls were always throwing themselves at him. They'd come up and put their arms around his waist, lean in too close, or share a dirty joke that included a not-so-veiled invitation to meet them later. And yet, Dolly would laugh when he told her, like it was all innocent and nothing to worry about.

But he did worry. About her. When they got home from the wedding and he was undressing for bed, he said, "I saw the way men were looking at you."

"Yeah, yeah, yeah," she said, her face lighting up. "I know a couple would like me to be their wife."

"Yeah?" He watched her unclip her rayon stockings from her garter belt and take them off. "Was I your first?"

"What do you mean?" She stopped undressing and turned to him.

"Was I the first one? I don't know if you were decent."

"What?" Her eyes flashed.

"Mike Slep told me you had slept with Jerry." Jerry was a local farmer who'd been interested in her when her family held the barn dances on their farm.

"No. My God, how could you think something like that?"

Peter shrugged. He hesitated, then said, "You didn't show any blood on our honeymoon night."

"How would you know? You were too drunk to see anything."

His shame returned. He had been too drunk, and yet, he'd wondered afterwards. "Dolly, I didn't mean …"

"If you must know, you're right," she said bitterly. "I had no blood because I broke my hymen horseback riding. I fell off a horse and hurt myself." When he said nothing, she added, "If you don't know I'm decent, then you're crazy."

"You're calling me crazy?" He could feel his temperature rise. "If I was crazy, they'd put me in Selkirk." Selkirk was the mental institution outside of Winnipeg where they housed the insane. His cheek twitched as he said, "Don't ever call me crazy again."

"Okay," she said softly and continued to undress.

Somewhat mollified, Peter said, "Sweetheart, it's hard when you dance with other guys. I see the way they look at you. I know how guys think."

"I can't help how they look. If you don't know me by now ..."

He came up to her and put his hands on her shoulders. "You're right."

She turned and met his eyes. "I know I'm right," she said.

He took her in his arms and gazed at her hazel eyes, soft but determined. He kissed her tenderly, and the anger between them fizzled like a wet firecracker.

In bed, Peter thought once more about the conflict that had erupted. What was curious was the fact that Dolly rarely conceded an argument. The best he could

get out of her was a 'maybe.' A 'maybe'
she was wrong. She had the confidence he
was lacking. Or maybe his problem wasn't
a lack of confidence, especially when it
had to do with their future. Maybe he just
expected less out of life, and in that, there
was contentment. Why shoot for the stars
when they were so high? He'd been used
to living with poverty for so long, he had
become comfortable with that reality. But
she always wanted more. He wasn't
driven like she was. And yet, he was only
too happy to go along for the ride.

Dear Granddaughter

Lukia looked forward to February on the prairies, the last month of the truly cold winter days. With milder temperatures, she noticed that Genya no longer cuddled in bed the way she had during the frigid nights of January. Everyone's spirits in the household had risen with the promise of spring around the corner. But then—even though they often had storms late into spring—a snowstorm took them by surprise. Wicked winds, coupled with a heavy snowfall, created drifts that covered their barnyard and blocked their road out to the highway.

Egnat turned on the radio for the weather report. The weatherman said the blizzard would continue to howl through the night and to avoid highway travel.

As the sky darkened, Egnat lit the kerosene lamp early and moved it closer to Lukia, Elena, and Dunya, who were making another batch of varenyky. Peter sat on a stool near the front door and sharpened some knives with a whetstone.

Lukia stared at the window, coated with ice. "It's late. Genya's not home yet."

"Don't worry," Egnat said, "she's come back late before."

Elena said, "Maybe she stopped at a friend's house."

"She probably did," Peter said.

Lukia glanced towards the window again. "It's two miles. In these conditions, it could take twice as long. And what if she can't see, because of the blowing snow? What if she gets lost?"

"It's never happened before," Egnat said.

Lukia rolled another circle of dough. "There's always the first time."

Egnat went to get his coat from the hook by the door. Donning his tall felt boots, he said, "I'll take the sleigh."

"Take a kazshook for her, too," Elena said.

Lukia nodded. Their sheepskin coats from the old country had saved them several times from freezing. She glanced at Elena, her face lined with strain. She had rubbed the small round of dough in her hands so long that Lukia thought she had rubbed all the elasticity out of it.

"Do you want me to go with you?" Peter asked Egnat.

"No," Egnat said, waving his hand. "Keep sharpening the knives. We don't want the women yelling their knives are dull."

"Ha. As if we yell," Lukia said, annoyed.

Egnat tugged the front door. The snow had piled up against the house, which made the door difficult to open. But with a couple of hard tugs, he managed to get outdoors. Lukia watched him hook up their horses to their sleigh and ride off down the road, rumpled with waves of snow too difficult to drive on with their truck. She assumed Mike would spend the night in the city. Another excuse for a night of drink.

The racket of the wind did little to ease Lukia's mind. It whistled around the house as if it was some demon working desperately to find a crack to come in. The women took turns going to the window and scraping away the frost so they could see outside.

An hour passed, and still no sign of either Egnat or Genya. They'd finished making the varenyky, and with nothing but fear on their minds, they sat down on the chesterfield and picked up their handwork—Lukia, her rag rug, and Dunya and Elena, their mending. Vera, who'd woken up from her nap, was making cookies for her doll with the dough her mother had given her.

Dunya searched the sewing basket by her feet and found a spool of thread and a needle. When she started to sew a tear in the slacks she was wearing, Lukia yelled, "Dunya, what are you doing? Either take them off to mend them or put a piece of paper in your mouth so you don't sew your brains up."

"Yes, Mama." Dunya got up and tore a strip of paper from an Eaton's Catalogue lying on a side table and put it between her teeth.

Peter said, "She won't sew her brains up."

"You don't know that," Lukia said, pressing her lips.

Peter exchanged looks with Dunya, who kept the paper in her mouth while she repaired her garment. The women worked quietly. The only sounds were of the wind beating the house and Vera's chatter with her dolly.

It was impossible to keep all the cold air out. When the light in the lamps flickered, Lukia rose from the chesterfield and put another log into the wood stove and added some kindling to keep the fire going. The clock ticked mercilessly, each tick a reminder that Genya wasn't home yet. She imagined Egnat bringing Genya back, white with cold, her lips blue, like Ivan's were when he contracted pneumonia in the old country. They had lost no one in Canada yet, but Lukia remembered how frightened she was several years back when Harry had gone into the woods to hunt a rabbit and hadn't come back for hours. Egnat and Mike had to find him. The weather had been bad then, but not as fiercely frigid as it was today. Lukia could sit no longer and rose to prepare the meal.

"They'll be home soon and nothing is ready," she said, more to convince herself than Elena and the others.

Elena didn't reply. Lukia assumed she had her own ominous thoughts.

And then they heard the sleigh bells

tinkling, competing with the wind's harsh sound. Lukia, Elena, and Dunya rushed to the window and scraped it again to get a clear view.

"Can you see her?" Elena asked anxiously.

They remained at the window until Dunya said, "I see her. Egnat's getting her down from the sleigh."

"Thank God," Lukia said. "Is she walking?"

Moments later, a gust of cold air rushed through the house as Egnat entered with his arm around Genya. "She got lost," he said. "I found her wandering on a neighbour's field. The visibility was so poor, she couldn't see the usual landmarks." Her father took off her snow-crusted hat and coat. She held on to him as he lifted each leg and unlaced her grey leather boots.

"Come here," Elena said, ushering her daughter to a chair by the wood stove. Peter shook the snow from Genya's coat and hat outside, then closed the door, while Dunya went to the stove to make her niece some tea with honey.

Taking her daughter's hands in hers, Elena said, "Child, you're like ice." Genya's body shook as she warmed her hands over the stove. Elena unwrapped the strips of wet cotton flannel from around Genya's feet, ankles, and calves.

"Did you dry them at school?" Elena asked.

"Yes, Mama. I dried them by the stove."

"Getting them wet can't be helped," Elena said. "When the snow is deep, it's hard to keep it out."

Genya kept her long underwear on, and Lukia wrapped her with a warm perina from their bed.

"Oy, oy, oy," Lukia said. "We were so worried about you."

"Baba, you shouldn't worry. I would've found my way."

"In this kind of boora, not so easy. It's

a good thing Tato went to get you." She kissed her granddaughter's forehead and stroked her fine brown hair.

That night, Lukia thanked God for returning Genya to her family. God knew she'd had more than her share of losses.

Shantytown

By early spring, Dolly was desperate to leave her mother's farm. It bothered her to see Peter continue to suffer under Egnat's watchful eye, but it wasn't easy finding suitable land for sale. With no affordable property to buy in Stony Mountain, they rented a shanty on the outskirts of the village. It had an outhouse that was shared with five other families.

Their move into the old ramshackle building was relatively simple, since they had few possessions. Mike helped them transport the furniture they gathered—a double bed (from a family who was moving to Winnipeg and no longer needed it), a sofa (a cast-off from a neighbour), a wooden table (bought at an auction), and four chairs (from her mother). After viewing the shanty, her mother gave them a feather-filled comforter and said, "You're going to need this on cold nights."

This new life wasn't the great escape from family interference Dolly had imagined, nor the carefree life she'd envisioned. She did her best to make the three-room shack a home. They painted the old chipped-wood floor, washed the filthy walls, and scrubbed two inches of fly shit off of the ceiling. She filled an empty tin can with ashes from the old stove and placed the can on the floor of the outhouse to act as a deodorizer. In a month or so, she would plant pink petunias and white alyssum flowers along the exterior wall facing the street. The early years of prejudice on the prairies had scarred her; she planned to show the locals that even though they had little, she knew how to make a place presentable.

While she fixed up the shanty, Peter

went job hunting. Not long after they'd moved in, he found work. It wasn't what he'd hoped for, but it made Dolly smile. "You were right," he said. "French was the man to ask. He offered me a job in the quarry." Mr. French was the father of their neighbour in Lilyfield and in charge of employment for their district.

"You see? All you had to do was ask." Then, remembering his accident in the quarry, her smile faded. "You don't mind, do you?"

He shrugged. "It's relief work. Two weeks for twelve dollars. Better than nothing."

She nodded and recalled what Mrs. Hill, the woman who'd hired her to be a domestic, had said to her when she'd left her employment in a huff. 'Beggars can't be choosers.' It was true. What choice did Peter have? They had to eat.

After they paid their rent, they were left with barely enough for food and incidentals. Not wanting to touch their savings—earmarked for a down payment on a home of their own—they ran out of money so quickly they had to buy their food on credit from Dan Balacko's General Store. Though accumulating debt was worrisome, they weren't the only ones who had to rely on this method of staying afloat. Hard times were all around them, and buying on credit was the way to manage until the next paycheck. Dan kept track of his customers' purchases in a log book and reminded them at the end of the month—if they forgot—that it was time to pay up. Dolly made sure their debt remained manageable. She was used to scrimping and doing without during many years of drought.

As for Peter, he came home every day from work at the quarry with his face and arms covered in limestone dust. Dolly had a bucket of water waiting, one she got from the pump by the outhouse. While he cleaned himself up in the washbasin outside, she fried potatoes and eggs. Keeping him fed was a challenge. A plate heaped with potatoes barely filled the belly of a tall man, who'd been chopping rock all day. And for that, she was sorry. Occasionally, she ate less, so he'd have more.

When Dolly told her mother and Egnat that Peter had landed a job at the quarry, her brother said, "He'd rather shovel stone than manure? At least shovelling manure won't break your back."

Her mother also questioned the job. When Peter was out of earshot, she said to Dolly, "What kind of future is there in lifting rock? His father has been doing it for decades and what does he have to show for it?"

"It's only for a few weeks. Then Peter will find something else." She was tired of explaining to her mother how challenging it was for hundreds of thousands of men, including her father-in-law. Considering the last eight years, he hadn't done badly.

He'd supported his wife and five children
and he owned his house—paltry as it
was—and the double lot next door, which
should've been Peter's. That fact gnawed
at her, and she tried not to bring it up all
the time because she knew it bothered
Peter as well. And though the Depression
was ending and farmers' lives were
improving, that didn't mean others
weren't still lagging behind. No one could
deny what the Depression had created.
Lost years, that were hard to recover
from.

At the end of his two-week stint at the
job, he came home, his feet barely in the
door when she said, "You know what Dan
said when I asked him if we could have a
pound of butter?"

"What?" he asked, while he took off
his dusty shirt.

"'Oh, they want butter yet!'" She
pursed her lips as she seasoned the
kapusnyak simmering in a pot on the old

stove. "Dan thinks he's so smart."

"What did you say?"

"I said to put it on credit. That we'd pay him at the end of the month. But he wouldn't give it to me. Said you don't have a steady job."

Peter hung his head. "He's right about that. They've got no more work for me."

She was quiet for a moment, then said, "We could dip into our savings, but I don't want to touch it. If we start taking from that, we might not stop, and then what will we have? Nothing." She took two bowls off the shelf above the stove.

"You're right," he said, his face full of misery.

She ladled the sauerkraut soup into the bowls and set them on the table while he went outside to wash the chalky substance off his face and hands.

They ate in silence. After they'd finished eating, she said, "Why don't we go to Winnipeg? It's not that far. There would be more jobs there."

He made a face.

"What?"

"I still owe $10 rent for my room on Higgins Avenue."

"What? How many years ago was that? The owner probably moved by now. Besides, you think they'll find you in that big city?"

"Maybe."

"Look, maybe the owner understands. These are hard times. When you make enough, you can pay him back."

"I still don't want to go," Peter said.

Frustrated, Dolly clicked her tongue. "You're a homing pigeon."

"So what if I am?"

"What are you going to do here?"

"I'll find something."

"Oy, like you always find something."

He got up from the table and took the kettle of hot water from the wood stove and poured it into the large basin to do dishes. Though upset the conversation was over, she appreciated he wasn't afraid to do women's work. As she washed and he dried, she considered his desire to be close to his parents and brothers. They only lived four blocks away, but none ever visited. She didn't see them as loving, and yet he couldn't bear being far from them. *It's good he's such a family man,* she thought, *but now I'm his family*. There was little value living close to his parents, if there wasn't any work in Stony Mountain.

Then Peter and Dolly began a series of rotating jobs, a few weeks here, a few days there working for others. The pay for two was better than what Peter was making alone at the quarry, but the pay, she said, was peanuts. It wasn't enough to get them out of the hole that grew with each passing day. If it wasn't for her mother's generosity with food—eggs, cottage cheese, potatoes, cabbage, carrots, corn, sauerkraut, and the odd chicken—Dolly was sure they would be starving.

Still, she was happy to be with the man she loved—so gentle and supportive, she wanted to pinch herself to make sure it wasn't a dream. He was loving like her brothers, but unlike them, he listened to what she had to say. He didn't interrupt and tell her to be quiet. When she'd been talking for a while, she'd say, "I can't help it. I have to talk. My family always said, be quiet. How can I be quiet when I have so much to say?" He'd smile and listen some more. She figured that was why she'd fallen in love with him. That, along with the fact he was kind, smart, a wonderful dancer, and looked like Gregory Peck, the movie star.

And every morning, they woke up in bed and kissed and cuddled. They were careful when they made love; they both knew they weren't ready to have a child to support, not when they could barely support themselves.

But her mother's words, *love won't put food on the table*, troubled her. There were many nights she lay awake thinking about what her mother had said.

Bill was the first one of Peter's family to visit them in their shanty. He showed up in his brown wool serge army uniform and his private's cap perched on the side of his head. Like a big shot, he pulled a bottle of whiskey out of a brown paper bag. Dolly took three short glasses out of the cupboard and put them on the small square wooden table. While he poured the drinks, she heated the borscht she'd made that morning and sliced some rye bread.

Stirring the soup on the stove, she listened to her brother-in-law brag about the girls in Tuxedo—rich family's daughters, he said—who flirted with the young men from the army barracks. Dolly caught Peter's eye and made a face. She thought Bill was trying to make his brother jealous and make him wish he was still single.

She served the soup and bread and

sat down at the table across from Bill.

"Looks delicious, Dolly," Bill said as he soaked a piece of bread in his soup and swallowed it.

Peter said, "Have they changed the sign-up rules yet?"

"Why? Are you thinking of joining?"

Dolly looked askance at Peter. He hadn't mentioned his interest in joining the armed forces.

"There's no work here," Peter said. "I could make decent money in the army if they'd have me." Peter blew on a spoonful of borscht to cool it.

"Sorry, Peter," Bill said. "Nothing's changed since you went down with me to enrol. You'd have no problem with the height requirements, but you know they want at least a Grade 10 education. Otherwise, you'd qualify easily." Bill took another dollop of sour cream for his borscht. "And it helps to have a letter from a minister or a prominent businessman. But with your personality, that'd be easy." He looked from one to the other. "But what can you do? You're married now, and with cooking like this, what else do you want?"

"Yeah, yeah, yeah," Dolly said, pleased that Bill had praised her cooking.

"When did you try to join the army?" Dolly asked Peter.

Peter turned to Bill. "It was 1935, wasn't it?"

"Yep. I enlisted in 1935. Four years ago. Princess Patricia's Canadian Light Infantry. Would you believe it? They have weapons hanging over from World War I. Lee Enfield rifles, but no Ross. The Lewis gun and the Vickers machine guns are the same. Some of the old-timers are still around. And we have some low-lifes in the troops, but we new recruits are slowly changing that." He chortled. "Not fast enough, I say."

"Do you ever see George? I hear he's training in Tuxedo, too."

"Naagh. He thinks he's high and

mighty, joining the Lord Strathcona's Horse Regiment. Don't know how riding horses is going to help if we go to war. Who fights on horses any more?"

Dolly could see by Peter's face that he felt he was missing out somehow. His curiosity about the armed forces revealed his regret. His eyes had brightened when Bill talked about his life in the barracks. Well, she thought, if that's the kind of life he wanted, he should've stayed in school. So stubborn. He could've had good wages, like Bill. They wouldn't be struggling. But no, his pride got in the way. If he didn't want to do something, he wouldn't do it. She'd learned that about him, but she had also learned how to get around some of that stubbornness. A lot of sweet-talking helped. Not that she wanted him to join the military. From the way Bill talked, there was a lot of hanky-panky going on with those maids in Tuxedo.

After supper, Bill took a newspaper out of his khaki knapsack and laid it on the table next to the kerosene lamp. With the evening light fading, Peter turned up the flame.

"Look at this," Bill said, pointing to a headline on page one of the *Winnipeg Free Press*.

"Nazi plot to Seize Ukraine Revealed."

Peter peered over Bill's shoulder as his brother read that General Denikine, a leader of the White Russians during the Bolshevik Revolution, charged that Chancellor Hitler had a plan to tear the provinces of Ukraine, Georgia, and Azerbaijan from Russia. He was agitating for autonomy in Ukraine.

Bill said, "Denikine says the Nazis are wooing oppressed Ukrainians, who'd had enough sorrow living under Polish and Russian rule."

"But who can trust Hitler?" Peter said.

Dunya wondered what it all meant. She knew that with any war came lives interrupted, soldiers maimed and killed, citizens raped and pillaged, and families fleeing, the way her family had during the Great War, when she was a baby.

Bill turned the page. "Get this. An American ambassador said that Canada's a Nazi stronghold. And so is Mexico."

"I can see that," Peter said. "Some thugs beat up some Jewish shopkeepers in Winnipeg and the police did little about it."

Bill raised his head from the paper. "One incident."

Peter's brow creased. "No, I think there was more than one."

Bill grunted and tapped the newspaper with his finger. "Now that Hitler has taken Austria and part of Czechoslovakia, and with Ukraine and Romania next, he'll have over eighty million people under his control, and what then? Some maps on German university walls show Holland and Switzerland as German territory, too. And Hitler's also thinking about Belgium. The former ambassador thinks the entire world should unite against the Nazis." Bill scratched his chin. "I might go over sooner than you think."

"Oh, boy," Peter said, his face falling. Dunya guessed he hadn't considered his brother might have to go to war. She hoped that didn't mean Peter would be called up to go, too.

Lukia's Muddle

Lukia took a jar of pickled beets off the shelf in the cold pantry. Beside them were sealers of green and yellow beans, dill pickles, mushrooms, and on the floor, a crock of sauerkraut. The other day, when Dunya and Peter had visited, Lukia had loaded them up with a few jars of canned vegetables and a big bag of potatoes, a dozen eggs, and some kishka and studenetz. Peter loved blood sausage and jellied pork squares and thanked her twice for her generosity and exceptional cooking. Dunya never complained to her mother about their hardship, and Lukia didn't remind her daughter of her foolishness. Since they'd been married in the eyes of God, it was Lukia's job as a mother to support their union as best she could.

Realizing that didn't stop Lukia's worries. She had sacrificed her own chance at love for her children and, one by one, they were leaving her. She often thought about Orest and how she'd let such a good man get away. But as she reviewed how their courtship went, she concluded that, even now, she wouldn't have done anything differently. Knowing what she knew about other women marrying late in life, she couldn't trust that her children would be secure. What she hadn't considered, though, was that offspring become adults with ideas of their own.

Lukia tried not to worry about Dunya and Peter. Instead, she worried about Mike. Since his last fight with Egnat, an uneasy peace had settled over the house. It appeared he had accepted his faults and was working hard to address them. If he was hanging on to his old ways, he was doing a good job hiding them. Those unexpected overnight stays in the city were probably his way of keeping his carousing secret. She assumed Mike had adopted a more responsible stance at home because he knew his brother had run out of patience. Another slip and Egnat would leave with his family for good.

At night, Lukia talked to Gregory about her woes, even though her husband had died twenty-three years ago. Staring into the darkness, she asked, "What's to become of Mike? He's such a handsome and charming young man. You should see the young women around him. He's like a rooster in a yard full of hens." She could almost hear her husband laughing. *Not so funny, Gregory*, she thought, and scolded him in the dark of her bedroom.

The next time Mike came home with lipstick on his collar, she said, "I hope you keep it in your pants. You don't want to bring a bastard into the world. Every child needs a father and a mother."

He cocked his head, "Mama ..."

"Don't *Mama* me. I want to know you understand."

"Yes, Mama." He put his arms around her and kissed her, his alcohol breath overwhelming.

Perhaps her problem was she couldn't stay mad at Mike for long. Egnat grumbled that she had spoiled his brother. Maybe she did. Maybe his dark looks and mannerisms reminded her of Gregory. When Mike was sober, you couldn't ask for a better son.

Mike tested her tolerance again the following Saturday night. Egnat, Elena, and the children were already asleep when a noise in the kitchen woke Lukia up. She threw a sweater over her nightgown and found a chair knocked over on the floor and Mike ladling water from the pail into a tin cup. He stood there, wobbling as she approached.

"Again?" she whispered for fear she'd wake the others up. "You promised Egnat you'd be back in time to help him. Where were you?"

Bleary-eyed, he slurped water from a cup.

"My God. What's become of you? I can't keep defending you when you act like this."

"Go to bed."

"I was sleeping. You woke me up."

"Leave me alone," he said, his eyes darkening. He weaved his way to the staircase and stumbled as he climbed the steps to the bedroom.

"Oy," she said, feeling a sharp pang in her chest. She went back to bed and lay there, seemingly for hours, reviewing every conversation she'd had with Mike. She didn't know what he believed in anymore. He'd given up going to church altogether. Like his father, he'd lost his faith in God. Perhaps that was Mike's problem; he'd lost his moral compass. Or maybe he was just too hungover to attend.

In the morning, Lukia said nothing to Egnat about her confrontation with Mike the night before. After breakfast, Mike drove her, Elena, and the children to church. His sullenness kept her from saying anything more. She didn't want an argument while he was driving the truck. He said he'd return at noon to pick them up. Where was he going? She didn't ask. He hadn't answered her yesterday about his whereabouts, so why would she expect an answer now? Resigned, she knew in her heart it was only a matter of time before Egnat left.

Since the acoustics in the church basement weren't the best and her hearing wasn't what it used to be, Lukia sat with Elena and her grandchildren near the front. She let the Holy Liturgy sung by the choir wash over her like a gentle rain. Attending church on Sundays revived her, even though she stood and knelt more than she sat, and the service took well over two hours, which included the priest's announcements at the end. She felt a peace of mind she couldn't get on the farm. She knew peace was missing there because of her sons' ongoing arguments. But here, the choir, the incense, and Father Mayewsky's warm voice soothed her and took her back in time, to when she was a girl in Volhynia. So much lay ahead of her then. Had she known there would be so much sorrow in her life, would she have married Gregory? She answered her own question without hesitation. Of course she would've. A decent man, but oh, so stubborn. The choir was now singing the refrain, "Lord, have mercy." Gazing at the beautifully painted iconostasis in front of her, she forced herself to concentrate on the prayers being sung and crossed herself three times.

At the end of the service, she stood in line to kiss the cross Father Mayewsky held by the altar and to get a piece of blessed leavened bread. While she was waiting her turn, Natasha came up beside her and whispered in her ear, "The court of appeal removed the injunction. The judge said the courts couldn't interfere in a spiritual matter. He also said he didn't think Father Mayewsky got a fair hearing by the church court commission. That means he can keep performing his duties as a priest in our church."

Lukia squeezed Natasha's hand. "That's wonderful! Thanks be to God." A church court had formally suspended Father over a year ago, but the congregation had rejected the ruling and voted to keep him on as their priest. But some folks, the ones who had complained about him in the first place, decided to challenge the parishioners' decision legally. And now it appeared they had lost their appeal.

"Don't thank God so quickly," Natasha said quietly. "A few want to take it further."

"What?" The line moved and Lukia did as well. "Further than an appeal?"

"Yes. Ridiculous."

Lukia looked ahead at Father Mayewsky, who was smiling at a young family of four who took turns kissing the cross. Why couldn't these men who wanted to pursue legal action see what a jewel they had in their priest? She leaned in closer to Natasha. "Oy, what is the matter with those men? They keep pushing and pushing the matter, like it's a dying horse and they expect it'll get up if they push hard enough. Do you think they'll have a chance of winning?"

"Who knows."

"All because he performed the Divine Liturgy on the radio." Lukia said, keeping her voice down. "You know how modern he is. What's wrong with sharing our church service with more people? I don't know what those men have against him. Maybe they want him to kiss their hand, like we kiss the bishop's?"

Natasha harrumphed. "It's true what you say. Father Mayewsky tried to get approval first. He wrote to the Metropolitan in the States asking permission to record the service for the radio. He waited, but when he didn't get an answer, he went ahead on his own."

"That's strange he never heard back."

Lukia had arrived at the front of the line. She kissed the cross.

Father Mayewsky said, "How is everything with you, Panye Mazurets?"

"Everything's good, Father, thank you," she said and went to pick up a piece of holy bread from the plate on the altar. Everything wasn't good, but she wasn't about to complain to her priest, who had enough of his own problems. Chewing the bread as she walked down the side aisle, she glanced at the two men standing at the back. They were watching the dwindling group of churchgoers while talking out of the corners of their mouths to one another. Lukia wondered if they were the trouble-makers. When one of them caught her eye, she pretended not to notice and proceeded down the aisle, then outside to join Elena and her grandchildren.

A Royal Visit

The electric streetcar from Winnipeg to Stony Mountain stopped running at the end of April. The villagers bemoaned the loss, as it had run two to three times a day. Now, if they wanted to go into the city to see a movie or to shop, they had to take the bus operated by the Beaver Bus Line. Dolly had loved taking the streetcar across the prairie to Winnipeg. She always felt as if she was going on some new adventure with the wheels clickety-clacking on the tracks, the rest of the world just outside the car window. She kept hoping that one day, she and Peter would make the move to the city. It held so many more opportunities to advance.

There, with any luck, she'd be able to keep up with the fashions and see all the movies she liked. Owning only one dress to her name during her early teen years gave her a desire to emulate women who dressed to the nines, and they lived and worked in the city.

Despite her disappointment over the streetcar service shutting down, a new excitement filled her head. Everyone in the village was buzzing about the upcoming royal visit to Winnipeg near the end of May. She knew little about this king and queen, but she was sure their visit would be a wonderful show.

When the time came around, Peter and Dolly had no steady jobs to hold them back. They donned their church clothes— her flowered dress and his pin-striped suit—and took an early bus into Winnipeg to see the royals. There was a grand parade that evening, and the royal procession of King George VI and Queen

Elizabeth would take place the following day. Peter figured the King and Queen had arranged to visit Canada in order to drum up support for the war effort.

Peter and Dolly arrived early and found a spot to stand near City Hall. Already, the crowd was enormous. It seemed as if every citizen of the city and its surroundings had taken time off work, either to watch or be in the parade marching down Main Street. Three soldiers, each carrying the Union Jack, led the parade, followed by a dozen men in kilts and white spats playing the bagpipes and drums. A float with a giant replica of a jewelled crown and *Let Peace Prevail* written in large purple letters on its side rolled behind them. Cheers from the spectators greeted all the marchers and vehicles—Cree men in full headdress, a cowboy on a horse, a covered wagon, a brass band, majorettes twirling batons, a large group of young women in Ukrainian costumes, representatives of several other ethnic groups, and a float with the slogan *Build Better Boys* emblazoned on its side. Peter read the slogan to Dolly and wondered out loud what those who'd designed the float meant by that. It was followed by one with the banner, *Chinese Canadians Welcome Canada's King and Queen,* and one with a tree with blossoms from Morden, the town with an experimental farm.

After the parade, they walked more than a mile to her cousin Ted's house on Selkirk Avenue—where they had arranged to stay overnight because they had to get up early to see the royals. As they walked north on Main Street, they talked incessantly about the spectacle they'd witnessed. They weren't alone in their enthusiasm; the excitement of the shared event radiated from others walking behind and in front of them.

Ted gave them his bed while he slept on the chesterfield in the living room. In the morning, they asked him to come with them, but he said he had a painting job he had to do first. He hoped to catch the King and Queen's procession later in the North End.

To save streetcar fare again, they walked downtown. It had started to rain, but hundreds of people packed the sidewalks on Main Street four rows deep, most waving the Union Jack. Young and old wore their finest; even young boys wore a suit and tie, if they had one. In front of City Hall, civic employees had erected a red canopy, where Peter assumed the royals might make a stop to meet the mayor. He thought of waiting there, but the crowd had grown and the police had set up a roped barrier to keep citizens on the sidewalk.

Moving further south to find a better view of the upcoming procession, they walked past the Exchange District, then turned onto Portage Avenue, where a sea of red, white, and blue flags and banners hung down the front of most buildings.

Police officers in their dark blue uniforms and bobby helmets patrolled the street on foot, making sure spectators stayed well back off the road. Peter and Dolly found an open spot in front of Eaton's department store, which had, besides its regal banners, a giant photo of the King and Queen in royal dress over its shiny brass entrance. Some newspaper reporter with a movie camera filmed the crowd. The youth laughed and giggled as they strode past his lens, trying to get his attention.

Shuffling their feet and craning their necks from time to time, Peter and Dolly waited well over an hour for the royal procession. Members of the Lord Strathcona's Horse Regiment, escorting the royal car, were resplendent in their scarlet wool serge belted tunics, black trousers with a gold stripe running the length of the leg, and gold helmets with long red and gold tassels at the back. Peter spotted George and waved, though he wasn't certain his brother saw him. Though proud of his brother, a pang of envy coursed through his veins. How he would have loved to have been part of these ceremonies. He teared up thinking how George, at twenty-one, eight years younger and from their immigrant family, was part of the royal escort.

When the royal car drove by, Dolly nudged Peter and stood up on her toes, trying to get a better view over the heads of those in front. King George VI and Queen Elizabeth sat in a burgundy-coloured luxury convertible. The queen, attired in a pale blue dress with matching hat, held an umbrella over the two of them, waved, and smiled despite the steadily falling rain. In return, the crowd clapped and yelled and hooted. The poor and old alike glimpsed a world that would never be theirs. One woman fainted, and there was a rush from a few nearby to assist her. And then it was over.

They stayed another night at Ted's,

and he told them he had watched the royals in front of Holy Trinity Ukrainian Greek Orthodox Cathedral on Main Street. The church had placed chairs on the lawn for the old folks, and aides made sure no one blocked their view. He said, "When the King and Queen drove by, several parishioners waved banners with holy icons and the church bells rang. The queen looked up at the belfry and the king followed her gaze. I felt so proud of my heritage in that moment."

Thrilled with the event, Dolly insisted on buying a newspaper to mark it. Somebody at the corner grocery store remarked that she resembled the queen, which made Dolly laugh. Later, she cut out a picture of the queen and placed it in the corner of her framed wedding photo. Thereafter, when anyone visited, she could point out the resemblance, as if to say, *I could've been a queen, too.* Peter chuckled every time. Her delight in finding a resemblance was infectious. It was what

he loved about Dolly. She found pleasure
in the smallest of things and kept that joy
going for months on end.

For Want of a Shanty

Peter and Dolly hadn't been living in the shanty long when the owner unexpectedly put it up for sale. Wanting to seize the opportunity, Dolly said to Peter, "We should buy it. We can't afford to wait for your father to transfer the title to the land that's coming to you."

Peter's grim expression told her he hated talking about that land. He didn't want to admit his father had let him down. He lived by the creed, "Honour thy father and thy mother that thy days may be long upon the land which the Lord thy God giveth thee." He'd learned the Ten Commandments at the Anglican Sunday School in Stony Mountain.

With dreams of finally owning a home of their own, Dolly asked Mike to take Peter to Winnipeg so he could buy the shanty from the owner. While they were gone, Dolly spent the day helping her mother on the farm. Along with Elena, they made plum-filled pampushky, a deep-fried, sweet yeast bun dusted with icing sugar.

After several hours had gone by and Peter hadn't returned, Dolly became restless. She kept glancing out the window, hoping to see the family's truck.

"You're jumping around like a chicken with its head cut off," Lukia said.

"They should've been back by now." She gazed out the open window again. "I wonder what's taking them so long."

"You know Mike," said Elena. "Maybe they met someone he knows, and they got talking."

Dolly nodded and picked up a round of dough to fill.

She gasped when she heard the

truck's tires on the gravel road. She ran to the door with a dumpling in her hands. Elena laughed. "Dunya, look at your hands." Dolly giggled and ran back to the table to put the dough down, then ran outside.

Peter was the first to get out of the truck. When Dolly saw his flushed face, she stopped in her tracks. She could tell he'd been drinking. He normally looked happy when he drank, but this time, his face showed anything but happiness. He didn't move towards her. Her body tightened and her throat constricted.

"Peter, did you buy the shanty?"

He looked down at the gravel. His silence unnerved her. Mike got out of the truck and weaved towards her, as if someone was pulling him from side to side.

"Don't tell me …," she said, biting her lip and choking back tears.

Mike said, "I'm sorry, Dunya. You can blame me."

"No! No!" She stared at Peter, who avoided her gaze. She turned to Mike. "What did you do?"

"I didn't think there'd be a problem," Mike said. "We were thirsty, so we stopped at the Stock Exchange beer parlour."

"Oy, oy, oy." Dolly knew where that was. It was at the corner of Arlington and Logan, a short walk from Salter and Dufferin, where the shanty's owner lived. "You stopped for a beer? How could you? You knew how important this was."

"Dan Balacko beat us to it," Peter said. "He bought it."

"What? Dan bought our shanty?"

Neither Peter nor Mike would look at her. She clenched her fists and glared at her husband and brother with tears in her eyes. What a fool she'd been to trust them!

Refusing to look at them, she walked away, heading towards the open fields. She walked up and down the rows of grain, the golden stems and budding wheat so promising, a sharp contrast to the bleakness she felt about her future. Her legs were tired, but she kept walking until she reached the end of her mother's farm. She had exhausted her body, but her fury remained. She faced the wind and yelled gibberish into the warm air.

Back at the farmhouse, she bid her mother goodbye and marched past the complaining hens and over the uneven ground towards Stony Mountain. She willed herself forward, not wishing to look at the man she called her husband. Peter followed in silence a few steps behind.

She pouted the entire night, and the next day, and the next. Peter tiptoed around her as if she was a cake in the oven and any sudden sound or loud thump would cause her to fall.

Then Dan paid them a visit and told them he'd sold the shanty for a profit. His announcement, she told Peter later, was like salt poured on a wound.

"That was quick," Dolly said, gritting her teeth.

Dan shrugged. "Business is business."

She made a face, which he appeared to ignore.

"I'm selling a barn and outhouse," he said, "if you're interested."

She turned to Peter, who shrugged. He looked as grim as he did when he'd failed to buy the shanty. This time, she was taking matters into her own hands. She accepted Dan's offer, and they bought the barn—a stable made of logs—and an outhouse, for fifty dollars. As they negotiated the sale, Dolly noticed Dan smirking. She suspected he was gloating about besting her husband. She wished she could tell Dan off, yell at him about how he'd cheated them out of a home, but he hadn't. He wasn't to blame for her husband getting drunk. Peter should have taken care of what was important first. She wished she'd gone herself.

Peter felt ashamed. He should have gone straight to Salter and Dufferin. He should have said no to Mike, but his brother-in-law had given him a ride in his truck and wanted a beer. After a couple of days, Dolly forgave him, but she brought up his mistake again. After the third time, his right cheek began to twitch. No man liked to be reminded of how he had failed. She was peeling beets at the time and must have realized she was pushing him too far, because she shut her mouth after that. The peels flew with each stroke of her paring knife, as if they, too, wanted to escape the blame she couldn't help hurling.

After the shanty debacle, Dolly asked Peter to approach his father one more time about the lot next door to his home.

Peter went, but he came back from his visit crestfallen. It wasn't only his father who'd said no; it was also his mother. She said, "You want to build a fence between our houses so we won't see you." Peter didn't understand why his mother no longer trusted him to do the right thing. Dolly thought differently. She thought his mother had said no because she hadn't forgiven her daughter-in-law for slighting Mary. Peter didn't deny it. He blamed himself for not insisting his sister be part of the wedding party.

Though disappointed they'd lost the shanty, Peter and Dolly set to work making the barn a home. They cleaned and whitewashed the walls. Mike brought in fine gravel for the floor to offset the stable's foul smell. And to add to their meagre furnishings, they bought a grey and white metal Buck stove with a large surface for cooking. Peter called its legs a French name, which she had trouble pronouncing.

Peter said, "It's cabriole. Ca-bri-ol-e."

"Cabolly," she said.

"No. It's cabriole."

"Cabolly, cabolly. What does it matter

I call the legs of a stove?" Frustrated, she covered her hair with a kerchief, tied the ends behind her neck, and went outside and grabbed a hoe. She pummelled the strip of earth on each side of the barn doors until she calmed down.

A short time later, Peter came outside. "Honey—"

"You don't like how I speak," she said, interrupting.

"You speak fine. I was just trying to help you."

"I don't need that help."

"Okay then." He bent down and kissed her.

Seeing his remorseful face, she softened. Her resolve to stay angry at him melted, and the restored harmony helped to reduce her pain over the lost shanty.

A Place of Their Own

When a For Sale sign went up on the lot across the street from their barn, it revived Dolly's hope for a place of their own. The owner wasn't asking much, because it was uneven land and demarcated on an angle. But it was land they could afford, and, with no other options around, Dolly convinced Peter they should buy it. To ensure success, she went with him to seal the deal.

With the sale concluded, she said, "Are you ready to dig?"

"You don't waste any time."

"We already wasted time by not buying that shanty."

He gave her a pained look, then said,

"You really think we can dig a basement?"

"Who else is going to dig it?"

He chortled.

"Yeah, yeah, yeah, laugh," she said, and smiled.

They started digging as soon as they received the title to the land. They got up at dawn and dug the unforgiving soil with shovels they'd borrowed from their neighbours. The heavy clay resisted every time they pushed the blade into the earth. They dug all day, under a hot sun and a cloudless sky, each shovelful harder and harder to lift.

The next day wasn't any better. The sun beat down on them mercilessly as they heaved the stubborn earth to the side. Every so often, they took a break to get a drink of water. One time, while Peter was in the barn quenching his thirst, his brother Johnny rode over on his bicycle.

"Hey, Dolly. How are you doing?"

She wiped the sweat off her forehead

and stared at him. She was aware she had dirt on her cheeks and hands. Strands of her hair stuck out of the old flowered babushka she had tied at the back of her neck. "You see how I'm doing." She waited for him to offer to help, but he put his foot on the pedal and said, "I have to run."

"Run, run," she muttered into the dirt as he pedalled away.

Moments later, Peter came out of the barn, wiping his mouth with his hand.

"Did you know Johnny came by? He asked me how I was doing." She waited for Peter to respond, but instead of answering her, he picked up his shovel. She said, "How old is he?"

"Fourteen," Peter said, his lips twisting.

"Old enough to lift a shovel," she said.

The lines on Peter's forehead deepened.

Dolly clicked her tongue and dug into the soil again, this time with a stronger thrust, as if with that force she could summon the young man back to help.

They worked every day from sunup to sundown. They used the wheelbarrow they'd borrowed from her mother's farm to move the dirt to a pile beside the expanding hole. And in the evening, after a supper of fried cabbage, tomatoes, potatoes and bread, they took turns rubbing liniment on their backs, hips, and legs. They went to bed aching all over.

In the morning, they groaned as they stretched out of bed, every muscle in their bodies complaining. After they pulled on their work clothes, Peter made the coffee and Dolly fried more potatoes with eggs. She thought she could never cook enough to feed him. Rather than gain weight on the starchy vegetable, he grew thinner every day.

They only stopped working when there was a heavy rain that made it impossible to dig. They welcomed the sunny days, but that also meant standing in the black dirt, exposed to the blazing sun, with no escape. After weeks of excavating, they found they had to take more breaks to stretch their backs and legs to keep their bodies from buckling under the strain of the heavy lifting.

Some nights, when she lay in bed and thought of how much more there was to excavate, Dolly bit her bottom lip to keep from crying. With her back to Peter, she let her tears wet a spot on her pillow before falling asleep.

Out of curiosity and perhaps to cheer them on, a few neighbours dropped by periodically to see their progress. One shook his head and said, "Don't know how you two keep going."

"Have to," Dolly said and kept digging.

In a little over a month, they'd finished hollowing out a rectangle, six feet deep, twenty feet wide by twenty-eight feet long. Though every muscle in their bodies ached from the heavy toil, they stood over the large hole, relieved and proud they had dug a basement. Dolly thanked God for the strength He'd given them to complete the work.

That night, they collapsed in bed and didn't get up until the sun was halfway up the sky. She compared what they'd accomplished to conquering a mountain. They'd reached the pinnacle, with no more steps to climb. They congratulated each other, but they knew there was little time to rest. Inevitably, winter would be on its way. They needed more than a hole to live in.

Dolly's mother, Egnat, and Mike visited to see what they'd dug and to bring them some eggs, borscht, and sour cream. After admiring their work from all angles, Lukia said, "Nu, you did what you had to do. May God help you with the rest."

"Thank you, Mama," Dolly said. While she was talking to her mother, Peter showed Egnat and Mike the area that had given them the most trouble. Stones the size of a baseball had to be hauled out. She lowered her voice. "See, Mama. Peter works hard if he has to."

"I see," she said, nodding her approval." Good he can work."

Her mother had softened, but Dolly knew she would continue to reserve judgment. She couldn't fault her mother for her feelings; a promising future was what Dolly wanted for herself, too.

Now that they had excavated a basement, they set about finishing it with concrete. Peter was about to go down to Dan Balacko's store to order gravel, cement, and sand supplies when his friend Lesley pulled up in a late-model Ford. Peter hadn't seen him since his wedding. He was tall and slim, his blond hair cut close to his head, and his blue eyes showed a seriousness that comes with age.

After they'd greeted each other and Peter had admired his friend's new car, he said, "You home for a bit? Your dad said you joined the Royal Mounted Police and are living up north."

"Yeah. Had some holidays, so I thought I'd visit the folks." He walked around the gaping hole in the ground. "Pretty amazing. You dug this yourself?"

"Me and my better half. My body's still complaining," said Peter with a chuckle.

"Dad told me you've been looking for work."

"Word gets around, huh?"

"Some things never change." Lesley put his hands in his pockets and said, "Listen, I heard the government is hiring workers to improve the No. 7 highway. They need help widening the road."

"I appreciate you telling me," Peter said, patting him on the back.

"Well, I know it isn't easy ..." His voice trailed off. "Well, I best be going. Mom has me running some errands for her."

"Say hello to your mom and dad, will you?"

"Sure. They always ask about you." Lesley got back in his car and waved as he drove off.

Peter stood there for a while, watching his friend drive away. They'd both been at the top of their class when Peter's life took a turn sideways. Every time he thought of how he'd rejected Mr. Blackwell's offer to tutor him after school, he lamented his decision to quit in the middle of Grade 9. He'd screwed up any chance he had for success. He couldn't even join the army. Like many, he would have enlisted to serve his nation. But some, he figured, only joined because they were down to their last quarter and it was a last-ditch effort to get work. He couldn't blame them. *A man has to eat.*

With dashed dreams on his mind, he went into the barn, where Dolly was chopping onions.

"Lesley came by. He said they need men to work on the No. 7 highway. Sounds like a well-paying job, but I can't leave you to work alone on the house."

She put her knife down. "Take it. We need the money. It's not a permanent job. A few weeks, maybe a month. It won't be long." When he hesitated, she said with a twinkle, "Don't worry. There'll be lots for you to do when you're finished."

Peter grinned. He had a woman who wasn't afraid to get her fingernails dirty. As bad as things got, Dolly had a way of lifting his spirits.

Dolly was right. The job widening the highway didn't last long—three weeks of ten-hour days, using horses to pull a scraper that picked up the mud from the ditch and moved it to where the work crew needed it. While Peter was working on the road, Dolly contacted old man Meronek to help her cement the basement. She paid him, but she also helped him mix the compound and spread it on the cellar floor. She only took breaks to serve him lunch, snacks, and drinks.

One evening, after they'd finished eating a bowl of green borscht—made with spinach and topped with a sliced hard-boiled egg—she leaned back and said to Peter, "Bill came by today. He watched me mix concrete for a while. You know what he said?"

"What?" Peter tore a piece of rye bread and dunked it in his soup.

"He said, you don't deserve this, Dolly." She shook her head again. "What was he trying to do, start trouble?"

"Maybe he's jealous. I bet he'd like to have a good wife like you."

"Yeah, yeah." Bill's remark had bothered her, but then she thought of her brother Mike. He competed with his older brother, too. "Imagine," she said, "two brothers came by and neither one raised a hand to help us. What kind of family is this?" She took another slice of rye bread. "I asked Bill if he could loan us five dollars for an electric meter from Manitoba Hydro." They had a damaged radio with a cord, but they had no way to plug it in.

"You did?"

"You know what he said?" She shook her head in disgust. "He said, 'I need my money for a good time.'"

Peter kept his head down and swallowed more soup.

"A good time!" she said again for emphasis.

Though he agreed with her about his brothers, it wasn't in his nature to confront anyone about their unwillingness to help. He believed they should know themselves. And then she reminded him again that his father had promised him the lot next door.

"If he gave you what was coming to you, we wouldn't be suffering like this."

"Dolly, I already asked him."

Sighing, she got up and cleared the soup bowls.

Peter's shoulders slumped.

When she returned to the table with plates of potatoes, tomatoes and cabbage, she said, "Why can't we have the phonograph you bought?"

"Tato likes it. So does the rest of the family. How can I take it from him? You saw how he played it when you first met him. He loves it almost as much as he loves his plants."

"But you paid for it." She paused. "I miss having a radio. At least with a radio, we'd have some music."

"I miss it, too."

"Bill needs his money 'for a good time'! Ha!"

"You repeat like your mother," he said with a touch of annoyance.

Her eyes widened. "When you say I'm like my mother; that's a compliment. Like you're rubbing butter on my back."

He said no more.

She knew he disliked her speaking negatively about his family, but she had difficulty containing her frustration. They ate the rest of their meal in silence.

In the end, they got their radio

working. Peter got a loan from Pan Popowich, his old neighbour. Though excited, she agonized about how they'd pay the neighbour back.

With plans to begin building the house frame in a few days, Peter contracted with Jack Johnson, a local man, to give him a hand. Jack said the best deal for wood might be in Arborg, an Icelandic and Ukrainian community sixty-four miles north of Winnipeg.

Mike arrived the following morning to take Peter to the Arborg lumberyard. As he was leaving the barn, Dolly said to him, "Be careful today. I had a bad dream."

Peter nodded grimly. Every so often, Dolly cautioned him after some dream she had. He'd heard the story of his mother-in-law's bad dream and how it had foretold her husband's untimely death in the old country. That business of bad dreams gave Peter the willies, but he'd grown up with superstitions in his family, too. His mother had taken him to a fortune teller shortly after his birth to see if he'd live, so as far as he was concerned, there were some spiritual elements at play, and he wasn't about to question them.

All went well at the lumberyard. Peter and Mike loaded the wood, but by the time they were ready to head back, it was close to suppertime. With the light fading, Mike pushed the accelerator down, hoping to get home before nightfall. They were only a few miles outside of Arborg when the truck's tires burst. It made a hell of a racket, with the lumber shifting in the back, falling every which way. Peter braced himself as Mike quickly put on the brakes. His knuckles turned white as he gripped the wheel to control the truck swerving on the road. Dolly's warning—*I had a bad dream*—played in Peter's mind like a broken record. His body tightened, and he clenched his teeth as the truck shuddered and squealed in protest before it came to a stop by the side of the road. Peter shook for a more than a few moments, then exhaled deeply.

Mike, pale after his fright, leaned forward, his forehead on the wheel. "That was hell," he said. "I was afraid we were going to tip over."

"Me, too."

By the time Mike fixed the damage, with Peter's help, it was too late to drive home on the poor highway. They had to stay overnight at the Arborg Hotel, which suited Mike just fine.

When Peter got home, tired and groggy from the ordeal and a night of drinking, he had taken only a few steps towards the barn when Dolly came rushing out. "Where were you?" she shouted. "I've been crying all night. I thought you were dead and weren't coming home." Her eyes flitted from Peter to Mike, who stood behind his brother-in-law.

"I'm sorry, honey," Peter said. "We didn't know how to reach you." After they explained what had happened, Dolly calmed down. They were both glad her bad dream had not resulted in a fate worse than the one they'd experienced. They had survived.

The next day, Peter was up at the crack of dawn. Jack showed up not long after Peter had wolfed down a hearty breakfast of eggs, potatoes, and toast.

Heading to the lot across the way, Jack suggested how they might work together. Following his advice, Peter held up the boards while Jack measured and banged the nails in. Dolly prepared the meals and refilled their water glasses throughout the long day. They made satisfying progress until Jack broke the wooden hand plane he used to smooth the boards. When he told them that new ones cost several days' pay, Peter said his dad had one and asked Dolly to go borrow it.

It didn't take long before she returned
from her father-in-law's, with her face
puffy and red from crying. Peter gave her
his polka-dot handkerchief to wipe her
eyes and led her to a private spot behind
an oak tree.

"What happened?" he asked.

"Your father said, 'I don't have a plane
I can lend you.' I stood there like a
dumbbell. What kind of father doesn't help
their children?" Tears streamed down her
face, and she dabbed them with Peter's
hankie. "You've helped him since you
were fifteen. All the money you made;
you gave him."

Peter didn't know what to say. "He's
probably envious. He always wanted a
bigger house."

"What are we going to do?"

Peter thought for a second. "I'll ask
Glowatsky. He has all kinds of tools.
Maybe he wouldn't mind lending us his
plane."

Luckily, old man Glowatsky didn't

mind, but Peter's father's refusal stuck with them, like a wound that refused to heal.

One afternoon, Dolly watched Peter and Jack slowly erect the walls of the house, their sweat glistening on their tanned arms and necks, their white undershirts grey with dirt from lifting and laying the lumber.

While she was standing there, Mr. Monodar, a bachelor who lived nearby, walked over and said, "Coming along, coming along. Good to be young."

"I don't know about that," Dunya said. Peter and Jack were definitely coming along, but they would have trouble finishing before the snows came. They'd be lucky to get the frame up. Mr. Monodar watched them work for a few more minutes, then walked back to his home.

She continued to watch, but feeling a mounting headache, she raised her hand to her forehead to block the sun. A back tooth had been aching since early morning. Soon, the men would be in for lunch. Groaning, she went inside to make them some baloney sandwiches and to heat water for a warm compress. She planned to hold it against her cheek to dull the pain.

She got through the day, but the next morning she woke up with the same toothache. She rolled over in bed, and when she saw Peter stirring, she said, "Honey, would you go see Mr. French and ask him for a relief slip? Maybe he'll give me one so I can get my tooth fixed." She hated to ask, but Mr. French had been so kind to them in the past, she thought he wouldn't mind.

She was right. He not only gave Peter the relief slip but also a bus pass she could use to get to Stonewall to see a dentist.

After preparing food for the men and telling Peter to make sure he took care of

Jack's food and drink in her absence, she
set off early the next day for Stonewall.
Though her mouth throbbed, she enjoyed
the ride to the town six miles north of
Stony Mountain. It was a break from the
day's routine. She stared out the bus
window at the prairie landscape stretching
for miles in every direction. Her eyes
found a farmhouse with a couple of dogs
in the yard and a farmer on his tractor in
the field. His wife was hanging wash on
the line while their child, a toddler, played
in the soil nearby. There was comfort in
farming, an occupation that had supported
her family for generations. But Dolly had
no desire to be that woman who toiled
alongside her man bringing in the crops.
She'd chosen a man who wasn't a farmer.
But what would he be? That was the
worrisome question.

Dolly arrived at the dentist's office close to
noon, but he was already out for lunch.
Waiting for his return, she remembered

that Doug's sister, Ashe, lived in Stonewall. She was two years older than Dolly's old boyfriend, but had always been friendly to her in the past. Dolly looked at the clock on the wall and figured she could squeeze in a visit before the dentist returned. Not knowing where Ashe lived, Dolly popped into a few shops to enquire where she might find her. That was one advantage, she thought, of living in a small community; everyone knew everyone else; they made it their business to know.

Ashe, who lived in a two-storey house with a veranda, was pleased to see her. She was married and had a child who was down for an early nap. After coffee and a lunch of cheese and lettuce sandwiches and peanut butter cookies, she tried to sell Dolly a pink crocheted flower she had made. "Twenty-five cents each," she said.

"It's beautiful," Dolly said, twirling the flower with waxed green paper leaves in her hand. "I'm so sorry. I didn't bring any money with me." She didn't want to say she had none to give, and that all their money had gone to pay for the lumber for the house.

"It's all right," Ashe said, taking the flower and putting it in a vase full of crocheted flowers on the kitchen table. "Don't worry about it. I have enough customers."

"Good for you," Dolly said. She wished she could've bought one, if only to study its construction.

Her time with Ashe had given her more than embarrassment; it had planted the seed of an idea. Perhaps she could make flowers of her own to sell.

The Last Straw

It had been another long day of harvesting, and Egnat was only now coming in from the fields. Lukia glanced at the sky behind him. The horizon displayed a red setting sun, a sign of good weather for the following day. She arched her back to ease the discomfort of bending for too long over the stump holding a basin of sudsy water. She'd been scrubbing socks and other soiled clothing with a washboard. Nearby, Elena was taking the wash down from the line.

Egnat held half a glowing cigarette in his hand as he approached his mother.

"Mike's late again," he said.

"I know."

"He better not have messed up this time."

She feared Mike had, but prayed he hadn't as she wrung the socks and threw them into the pail of clean water beside her feet. She picked another pair of dirty socks from a basket of dirty clothes and submerged them in the soapy water.

Egnat said, "I wish we had a silo to store our grain. If we had one, we could wait a month or two to sell our wheat." He puffed his cigarette and exhaled, the smoke blurring the air between them.

"Why would you want to wait?" she asked as she continued to scrub.

"You know the price is fifty-five cents a bushel now. I talked to a farmer a couple of days ago, and he thought the price was going to go higher in a few months."

She cocked her head. "There's nothing we can do. That's how it is. We don't have a way to store the grain." When she saw his disappointed face, she said, "At least the price has gone up. Seven years ago, it was twenty-nine cents a bushel."

"Yes, it's better now, but not good enough yet." He took another puff, but this time brushed the smoke away with his hand.

Lukia couldn't see how investing in a silo made any sense. Not for a rented farm. Maybe when they got their own, they could do it. With no place for grain storage, they had to take it to a privately owned facility. Egnat, Mike, and a hired hand had loaded up the truck's five-foot-high box with the harvested grain and Mike had driven the truck to the Grosse Pointe elevator on Highway 6, ten miles northwest of Lilyfield. That was hours ago.

As Lukia was discussing grain storage with Egnat, Mike arrived back, the truck rumbling and kicking gravel on their road. When he emerged, he wandered slowly towards them. Thrusting his hand into his pants pocket, he took out a handful of bills and gave them to Egnat.

Egnat took one look and flew into a

rage. "What's this?" he asked, waving the bills at Mike. "I don't have to count it to know you've already spent some of it."

"No," Mike said, vehemently. "That's all they gave me."

"Don't lie to me. You went to the Exchange Hotel in Winnipeg again, didn't you?"

Elena shook her head as she walked by with a basket of clean laundry and headed for the house.

Lukia wiped her soapy hands on her apron and said to Mike, "Where's your head? Have you lost your brains?" She clicked her tongue. "You would test a saint." Bobbing on his feet, Mike averted his face from his mother.

Egnat said, "He's a piyak, and piyaks lose everything."

Putting up his fists, Mike said, "Who are you calling a piyak?"

"You can put your fists down," Egnat said. "I'm through fighting you. It doesn't help."

Mike's eyes welled with tears. "I won't do it again."

"Mama," Egnat said, "I can't do this anymore. I tried. I'm not working here just so Mike can piss it away."

"Egnat, son—"

"I'm sorry," Egnat said, interrupting, "but I've already been looking. There's a farm near Stonewall for sale. "

"Oy, don't say." Lukia's face crumpled.

"I've waited long enough. Other farmers are making their harvests pay off. They're getting ahead, and we're standing still. As long as I have to rely on Mike, it'll always be the same. I have a wife and a child. I have to think of them." Egnat gave his brother a fierce look and left Lukia standing with Mike.

With his head bent, Mike swayed before her. His shirt had a spot on it, either from a beer spill or food.

"See," Lukia said. "See what you've done now. Oy, oy, oy. Our family is breaking apart. This is what it's come to?"

"Mama ..." he said beseechingly.

"Don't talk to me. My God, my God. Children, children, what can I do with you?" Mike gave her a sorrowful look, then rambled off to the barn, where she suspected he'd have a good cry. When he drank, his tears flowed easily. If only his remorse could change his life for the better. She scrubbed the socks in the basin, wishing it was as easy to knock sense into Mike as it was to get out the dirt.

Turmoil on All Fronts

And then the unthinkable happened—what everyone was dreading. Hitler invaded Poland on September 1, 1939, a date that would go down in history. When Peter heard the news, he bought a *Winnipeg Free Press*. The headlines read: "Chamberlain and Hitler Agree on One Ominous Point—that if war should come, it would be long and bloodier than the Great War."

After reading one article after another about the tension building in Europe, Peter tossed all night. In the morning, Dolly complained, "You kicked me last night."

"You should've pushed me," Peter

said. "I must've had a bad dream."

Whenever he had a moment, he turned on the radio to catch the news. And, just as he'd feared, Britain and France had declared war on Germany.

The next day, The *Winnipeg Free Press* underlined what he'd heard on the broadcast: "It's War and We're In It" was the headline in large bold letters on the front page. What would become World War II had begun. Peter's thoughts turned to his brothers. There was no escaping conflict now.

The prospect of Canada going to war was in the back of everyone's mind. For those in Stony Mountain, so was the movie theatre being built on Main Street. It was where the locals gathered to share the news. Perhaps they thought the glamour the movies promised would make what was happening overseas disappear from their minds.

Eager to hear what others were saying

about the war, Peter stopped by the cinema's construction site on his way back from the post office, where he'd gone to pick up the mail. There were men who had taken a break from the construction and others who had just wandered over to have a look and give their opinion on the sturdiness of what they saw. The crowd grew after the penitentiary bell tolled quitting time. As usual, staff from the federal jail were walking home for the weekend, with white bags filled with leftover bread from the prison kitchen. They stopped to put in their two cents about the new movie house.

One fellow asked how long it would take to build it. Another thought the Oak Theatre, as it was to be called, was so badly built it wouldn't take long for it to fall down. Another asked if the roof tiles were going to be red or blue, or red, white and blue, like the flag.

Others wondered what the first picture would be. Peter knew Dolly couldn't wait to see a movie in their village. Ever since the walls had gone up, she had been giddy with the excitement of being able to see a show locally without taking the long ride into Winnipeg.

Peter's younger brother, Johnny, was just as excited as Dolly. He could talk of little else. With any money he made through odd jobs in town, he bought movie star magazines—*Photoplay, Modern Screen*, and *Motion Picture*—and cut out the pictures, which he used to cover the walls from floor to ceiling in the shack he lived in alongside the family house. There were black and white photos of popular stars: Jean Harlow, James Cagney, Clark Gable, Marlene Dietrich, Greta Garbo, Errol Flynn, Gary Cooper, and more. Johnny had moved into the shack after Peter got married. He told his brother he didn't want to listen to his mother and father fight anymore. Unlike Peter, who was the family referee, Johnny preferred simply to keep his distance.

Then the City Quarry's whistle pierced the air, and not long after, Peter's father ambled to the crowd in front of the movie-house building site. He put his tin lunch box down on the ground and offered his advice to Jim Snell, who was in charge of the cement mixer, on how to mix the compound. His father liked to throw in his ideas whenever he had the opportunity.

With war declared, the young men in the village talked about enlisting. Peter's brothers, Bill and George, were suddenly thrown into the spotlight. They'd done the right thing by enlisting, people told his father. The villagers said Bill and George were already learning what they needed to learn if they were called upon to fight the Nazis.

There wasn't any doubt about what Canada should do in the minds of most villagers, who were largely of Anglo-Saxon ancestry. They said that of course Canada should declare war on Germany and join the fight immediately, as it had done in the Great War. It was part of the British Commonwealth, and its citizens had sworn allegiance to the king.

But it wasn't a done deal. Not right away. It took a heated debate in the House of Commons for Canada to officially declare war on Germany on September 10th.

The other topic that got tongues wagging was the news south of the border. A neighbour who claimed to have inside knowledge said, "The Americans are worried Canada is going to pull them into war. Roosevelt wants none of it."

As gossip about the war grew, people discussed whose son had signed up and whose son wanted to but couldn't because of the requirements. A few were too short, some said. And then there was the schooling. Peter had to explain again why he hadn't enlisted. "I tried," he said, "but I don't have Grade 10." Embarrassed, he said it quietly more than once. He'd been the smartest boy in his class, but what was smart about dropping out? Now, when he walked the streets, he avoided some people, the ones he suspected would ask him why he wasn't joining the army or the air force or the navy.

"Your country needs you, boy," one said. "The forces need a strong boy like you," said another. When Peter mumbled his reasons, they said words like, "Too bad you can't go," and "What a shame." Peter's face flushed, and he looked down at his shoes as he quickly walked away.

Dolly's brothers were in the same pickle. They didn't have the education, nor were they tall enough. The three of them—Egnat, Mike, and Harry—were around five foot six inches tall, four inches shorter than the requirement. But they expressed relief when they were told farmers were vital to the nation. Soldiers needed to eat, and where would anyone be without farmers tilling the soil?

Those who couldn't go overseas to serve found other ways to show their patriotism. All kinds of organizations sprang up to support those fighting overseas. A group of women, calling themselves the Stony Mountain War Unit, planned to raise money to send the enlisted some comforts from home. When Peter mentioned the group to Dolly, she looked at him quizzically.

"You want me to join them?"

"Well," he said, "the women are planning all kinds of events. Whist-drives, dances, raffles, teas, garden parties, and toboggan parties. With the money raised, they plan to send goods their sons can't get overseas. Knitted socks, hats, cigarettes—anything that will raise the men's spirits."

"Do you know of any Ukrainian women in the village who belong?" she asked.

He didn't, and that ended the conversation. They hadn't invited Dolly to join, and with the ongoing prejudice, they'd probably be as uncomfortable with her in the group as she'd be with them.

An outsider she was, and an outsider she'd remain.

Lukia had her own woes and was quick to let Dunya know what they were when she and Peter came over for supper. She'd been quiet during the meal, but when they were having tea and honey cake, she said, "We have news, too." She nodded to Egnat, indicating he should be the one to tell his sister.

He put his cup down. "I bought a farm near Stonewall. With the higher grain prices, I managed to scrape enough to make a down payment. I got a mortgage through my bank in Stonewall. It's a quarter-section, 160 acres. There's a barn, but no house, so I've arranged for a boxcar to be delivered to the property."

"They're going to live in a *boxcar*," Lukia said, clicking her tongue. "Like we did in the Caucasus. Everyone's abandoning me. First Harry, then you, and now Egnat."

Egnat gave his mother a tender look. "No one's abandoning you, Mama. You know I can't live here with Mike. See, he's not even here now. He's in the city, running around more than he's on the farm."

Lukia said to Dunya, "You see how it is?"

Egnat grunted. "At least on my own, I can reap the rewards of my work. I won't have to pay for his drinking anymore."

"What are you going to do without a truck? What will you use to come see me?"

"I'll buy a car. And I have a bicycle." He cleared his throat. "I'm sorry I'll be taking my horses with me. You know Dan is special to me because I broke him."

"I know," she said, her throat closing with sorrow.

"Shoulder is old, but he can do small jobs. He can pull the stone boat when I clean the barn."

She rubbed her forefinger against her

thumb. "Nu, you have to do what you have to do. I don't know how I'll cope without you."

Lukia glanced at Genya, who was eating her stewed fruit. Ever since Vera was born, Genya had slept with her. Lukia would miss getting down on her knees with her granddaughter before bed, saying their prayers together, hearing her sweet voice mumble a prayer to her guardian angel. She'd miss her warm, slender body cozying up to hers in the middle of a cold winter night. The thought of the four of them leaving made her stomach fall.

How many nights had there been when Mike didn't come home? At least now she had Egnat and his family's voices for comfort. But soon they'd be gone. She would be alone, with only the animals and wind for company. Would she end up milking the cows by herself? How many other chores would be left undone?

To make matters worse, she had some

worrisome news from her grandson, Kolya, who was now seventeen. Though living in Argentina, he and his family had kept their Polish citizenship, and now that Poland was entering the war, Kolya had joined its navy, which had always been his dream. He told her he would be a crew member on a submarine and hoped to see her when he landed in Halifax the next month. With her life in turmoil over Egnat's decision to move, she asked Egnat to write Kolya and tell him she was sorry she couldn't make it to the east coast for a visit, but hoped to see him the next time he came to Canada. She wanted to add in the letter that her heart was aching to see him, but didn't because she wasn't sure he'd understand how much he meant to her. He was her connection to the daughter she'd lost.

How had it come to this? She'd arrived in Canada with four children, all bright-eyed and excited about the new land, the new language, and the new customs. They'd stuck together through the dismal years that had brought drought, grasshoppers, poor crops, and too many tears. Stiffening their backs, they had done the work. They even stood up against others' ignorance and prejudice. Rather than retaliate for the ridicule they received for their ways—the way they talked, dressed and smelled of garlic—they had stood even straighter and kept their focus on the land and the love they had for one another. Yes, they'd hung in together, even when Harry stayed in the city and Dunya got married and left the farm. But four leaving at once? That was too much to bear.

Lukia had always hoped she'd have a farm that would provide security for her children and their spouses and families. But this land had torn farming families apart. Egnat was the only one who had embraced the land, and he was leaving. That dream of hers, of family unity in one household, had collapsed like a fine spider web swept carelessly aside.

Paper Roses

Despite the fall rain, Peter and Jack continued to work on the house frame. Dolly appreciated her husband's hard work, but it wasn't putting food on the table. She thanked God she'd visited Ashe and figured out a way to make some money. Ashe had crocheted roses, but Dolly wanted to make ones that looked more realistic. She remembered seeing flowers made of crepe paper on a grave at a local cemetery. She went back to the graveyard, crouched down by the headstone, and examined their design. Over time, the sun and wind had faded their colour, but placed indoors, this crafted flower would stay lovely for a long time. She noted a petal's shape and counted how many she'd need to make a flower, as well as the number of leaves on each stem.

Excited by her idea, she stopped at Dan Balacko's General Store on the way home to buy red and green crepe paper, green paper leaves, and florist wire.

"What're you doing with that, Dolly?" Dan asked as he added the items to her bill.

"You'll see," she said, grinning.

Over the next few weeks—when she wasn't waiting on Peter and Jack—she fashioned dozens of paper roses under the sunlight streaming through their small barn window, and fashioned more under the dim light of the kerosene lamp in the evenings. She placed the completed ones in an empty wood crate in the corner. She stopped her work occasionally to admire the mass of paper roses she'd made or stretch her back from sitting too long.

On one of these occasions, she walked

down the petunia-lined path from the barn to the lot to check the men's progress. When she stopped to admire a bee landing on a petunia, she got another idea. Forgoing a visit to the lot, she hurried to the store to buy beeswax.

Dan raised his eyebrows. "You're up to something. I see it in your eyes."

"Yeah, yeah, yeah," she said, as she tucked the package of beeswax in her purse.

Back home, she melted the wax in an old pot, then dipped and twirled the crepe paper blossoms gently to cover every petal of the flower in hot wax. She lifted each rose, let it drip until it dripped no longer, and hung them on a line inside the barn to dry.

While she was coating her paper roses, Peter came into the barn to refill a jug of water. Noting the pot on the stove and the flowers on the line, he said, "You dipped them in wax."

"Yes," she said, beaming. "They'll last

longer now, and I can charge more for them."

"Brilliant," he said.

"Brilliant?"

"It means smart. Very smart."

"Oh yes, I'm brilliant." She laughed.

On the days when Peter wasn't able to work because of the heavy rain, she sent him to knock on the doors of the guards' houses and sell the paper roses to the guards' wives. She figured, of the two of them, he would be the better salesperson, because the locals knew him from when he was a child. His good manners and way with words would help with sales.

She was right. For their efforts, they earned enough to pay for a bicycle and shingles for a roof. That should have set their minds at ease, but unfortunately, the weather turned.

With construction stalled, Dolly bundled up in her fur coat and paced in front of the unfinished structure. There was still so much to do. Peter and Jack had put on a second storey, cut out the windows, and put on the roof, but because of the ice-cold strong winds, it had become too cold and perilous to work. Laying the shingles would have to wait until spring, as would adding the windows and the doors. They would not be able to finish their home before the snow arrived. They were at the mercy of Nature— sometimes a friend, sometimes a foe. She mumbled a prayer and went back into the barn to prepare some borscht. It was going to be another bitter day.

Father Mayewsky

Egnat and his family moved in the late fall to the farm he'd bought in Stonewall. Lukia shed more tears and prayed for the strength to continue without him by her side. With Egnat gone, Mike was forced to step into his older brother's shoes and take responsibility for the farm and his mother's well-being. As if suddenly splashed with cold water, Mike stayed sober causing Lukia to thank God for His mercy. She went to church with renewed hope. Maybe she and Mike could manage on their own.

As usual, she enjoyed the choir singing the Divine Liturgy. Nothing seemed amiss until Natasha grabbed her arm after the service, and ushered her outside, where they stood away from the others in the churchyard. "Have you heard? We're going to lose Father Mayewsky."

"What are you saying?"

"The Men's Brotherhood voted to throw him out of the parish."

"I thought the courts had settled the matter. They lost the appeal."

"The Men's Brotherhood keeps insisting he went against church rules. He might be defrocked because of his disobedience. They're taking him to Supreme Court."

"The Supreme Court? The church court and the court of appeals already tried him. Oy. How much is this going to cost?" Lukia tsked. "We have a church to build. We can't afford to pursue frivolous charges."

"I know," said Natasha.

A vehicle honking caused Lukia to turn towards the street. It was Mike, waiting for her in their truck.

"Nu, Natasha, we must pray for Father

Mayewsky." Lukia hugged her friend and left, feeling distraught. She didn't understand why some in her parish wanted to undermine a good priest. Was it jealousy or a fight for power? Either way, it would be a tremendous loss. Good priests were hard to find.

Back on the farm, Lukia gave Dunya and Peter, who'd dropped in to help pick potatoes, an empty burlap sack to fill for the winter. After they'd filled it, Mike lit a fire to roast some potatoes to eat.

Though the late afternoon air was brisk, there was little need for jackets or coats around the fire. The four of them sat around it on stumps, eating the charred potatoes they held in old newspapers. After they'd finished, Mike brought up the latest turmoil in Sobor. "If Father Mayewsky gets defrocked, that will mean Dunya and Peter are living under a bushel."

"No," Dunya said. "Everyone was at

our wedding. They saw us getting married in church. It won't mean we're living common-law."

"Maybe," Mike said, "but the law is the law. If he's no longer a priest, your license won't count. And if you have children, they would be considered bastards."

Lukia rubbed her thumb with her forefinger. "It's a shame Father Sawchuk and the Brotherhood are not letting this matter go. If what Mike says is true, you'll have to get married again."

Dunya and Peter exchanged looks of concern. "Mama's right," Dunya said. "If we buy property together, or sign anything as husband and wife, that could be a problem."

Lukia shook her head. "A few disgruntled people in the parish make trouble for everyone."

While Dunya and Peter discussed who would marry them a second time, Lukia packed some food for her daughter to take home. As she stuffed a shopping bag with dairy products, eggs, and root vegetables, she glanced back at her daughter and son-in-law. It warmed her heart to see such a loving couple, but she still agonized about their future, especially after she heard their house wouldn't be finished before winter.

The following Sunday, after the service, Natasha pulled Lukia aside again. "It's worse than I thought. I found out Pan Sawchuk never sent Father Mayewsky's letter to the Metropolitan like he was supposed to. He put it in his letter basket. I don't know if he forgot it or didn't want to send it. The church is going to suspend Father Mayewsky."

"That's how it is," Lukia said. "He's being punished, even though it wasn't his fault. My God, my God."

Lukia wondered why Father Sawchuk would do such a thing. He was now working for the Ukrainian Greek Orthodox consistory off of Main Street, but before that, he had been the priest at Sobor when she first started going to church in Winnipeg. And he was the one who had approved Father Mayewsky's appointment to their parish.

"Pan Bohonos and Pan Bugera are behind this," Natasha said.

Lukia did not know them, though she had heard their names mentioned in Father Mayewsky's announcements at the end of a few church services. They were Members of the Brotherhood in the court case. "It's odd," she said. "Most of the congregation is behind Father Mayewsky. I wonder what's really behind these court battles."

"We may never know."

Lukia and Natasha groaned about the unfairness of this attempt to oust their priest, but agreed there was little they could do to change the Brotherhood's decision.

Concerned about the validity of their marriage, Peter and Dunya heeded Mike's advice and got married again at the end of November, this time by a minister in an Anglican church near the Odeon Theatre on Notre Dame Avenue. She wore a simple dress and Peter wore the suit he got married in. Mike, along with a lawyer, served as witnesses. No photographer took photos, nor were any guests invited. Dunya hated paying for another service, but agreed with her mother. It was better to be sure than sorry later.

Good Neighbours

When Dolly awoke shivering in bed one December morning, Peter was already up, pulling on his long underwear. He came over and gave her a kiss. "I'll put the fire on," he said.

"Why didn't your mother and father take us in?" she asked as he headed for the pile of wood by the stove. "They have a warm house."

"Where would they put us?"

"The only one left is Johnny, and he sleeps in the lean-to."

"You're forgetting Mary slept on four chairs put together, and us four boys slept crosswise on one bed." He put some kindling in with the firewood and lit it.

"They bought a sleeper sofa for the living room. We could sleep there."

"Mama's sick. She probably wants quiet. Don't know how much time she has left."

Reminded of his mother's condition, Dolly felt a pang of remorse and stopped complaining. Peter said they were lucky that, so far, the winter had been mild. Dunya dismissed the notion they were lucky. Though Winnipeggers worried Christmas this year would be green, the snow was up to their knees in Stony Mountain. Living in a barn made of logs with no insulation was no picnic. Every walk to the outhouse meant bundling up and braving the winter winds. She didn't have good circulation—her feet were always cold—and she believed that if not for the feather-filled perina her mother had given them, she and Peter might have frozen in their sleep. But cold as she was, her pride kept her from running back to the farm for comfort.

Unexpectedly, their neighbour, Mr. Monodar, agreed with Dunya that the barn was no place to live with the threat of even colder days ahead. He came to their house one morning, and when she opened the door, with Peter right behind her, he said, "Children, you'll freeze to death here. Come to my place—you can feed the cattle and pigs for me. There's milk, and if you cook for me, I'll give you ten dollars a month for board."

Dolly didn't hesitate. She could've kissed him right then. However, Peter was more reluctant, and it took some coaxing to convince him that moving in with Mr. Monodar was better than staying in the barn and facing the bitter cold of January.

She appreciated the bachelor's generosity, but was shocked by how he lived. His place—two bedrooms, a living room, and a kitchen—was so filthy they had to shovel out the dirt. The ceiling was full of fly shit, and after cleaning it off, Peter and Dolly had to whitewash the walls and ceiling. They brought their bed, along with their paltry belongings, and hoped to live there until the spring.

Since Mr. Monodar had been so kind, Dolly tolerated him walking into the living room with his dirty shoes. His compassion helped them through the winter, as did the odd jobs Dolly and Peter secured in the village. While waiting for the snow to melt so they could resume building their house, Dolly nurtured her dream of moving to Winnipeg. No matter how much she tried, she saw no future for them in Stony Mountain. Living meagrely in a village was not the life she'd dreamt of.

Panye Adamovich, her mother-in-law's friend and neighbour, was also thinking about her life when she asked Dolly to come over for a visit one Saturday afternoon. Dolly thought she wanted to talk about Peter's mother, who was becoming more frail with each passing day.

But when Panye Adamovich ushered Dolly into her modest home, she said, "I want to show you something." There was no 'hello' or 'nice to see you' or 'welcome,' which Dolly found odd, but she followed the short, stocky woman with the curly, salt-and-pepper hair to the back room, where she kept her preserves. She wore a navy-blue sweater over her faded print housedress, brown lisle stockings scrunched around her ankles, and felt boots. She shuffled as she walked through the spotless kitchen with its worn linoleum floor and chipped, green-painted wood table. A plant in a small clay pot sat on a pink and white crocheted doily in the middle of the table. Like Dolly's father-in-law, the woman's husband had served in the Austro-Hungarian Army during the Great War and settled in Stony Mountain, where there were several other families from Bukovina. The house was quiet, so Dolly assumed the woman's husband and grown children were away working, visiting friends, or out on errands.

When Dolly reached the back room, she was surprised to see a plain wooden coffin up against one wall. Before Dolly could utter a word about the oddity of having a burial box in a house, the woman pushed up the hinged cover and, using a step stool beside it, climbed in. She stretched out on the satin lining, rested her head on the small pillow, and closed her eyes. ""I wouldn't wear this dress. I'd wear my good dress," she said, with her eyes shut. "Do I look good in it? Yes or no?"

Dolly stared at Panye Adamovich. "Yes. You look good. But you're not sick. Why did you buy a coffin?"

"Aagh," Panye Adamovich said, climbing out the box with Dolly's help. "I don't know what my children will do. I've been to enough funerals to see how poorly some people bury their family members. I don't want to leave the world worse off than how I came in."

Dolly knew little about her life, but she nodded solemnly. What her mother-in-law's friend said made sense. You couldn't always rely on those around you to take care of the important details. If you wanted things done right, you had to do it yourself.

When Panye Adamovich died, not long afterwards, Dolly wondered if her buying the coffin had hastened her death. Or was she already gravely ill but didn't show it?

When Dolly told Peter about her strange visit, he cringed. He found the whole coffin business disturbing, whereas Dolly understood the woman's fear. Since death for everyone was inevitable, Panye Adamovich wanted assurance that at least one part of her funeral would go well. Why wouldn't someone want to plan how they'd look after they were dead? Dolly hoped she'd live a long life—she planned on a long one—but when the time came, maybe she would do just what Panye Adamovich had done. Try out a coffin ahead of time.

And They Go

The prospect of an ever-expanding world war occupied Peter's mind. He continued to agonize over his inability to serve. Egnat must have sensed the same pull, because he told Peter he had joined the Ukrainian Society at Stony Mountain, an association organized to help Canadians fighting abroad. Their mission was to assist the Red Cross in their objectives, improve understanding between Ukrainian Canadians and other Canadians, and support the government and its war effort. The association elected Egnat to the executive council.

It seemed everyone was doing their part for the war effort. During a family supper at his mother-in-law's farm, Harry said to Peter, "John Slipchenko enlisted with the Winnipeg Grenadiers. He's asked me to run the service station in his absence."

"Has he already left?" Peter asked.

"Not yet."

Peter had met John at Sobor, when he'd gone to a church service with Dolly. A soft-spoken man, John was born in Ukraine, had travelled through Siberia, and lived in China for a couple of years before immigrating to Canada. Now, he was married and had a son. How would his wife manage in his absence? It seemed no sacrifice was too big for your country.

That Christmas, cheer was in short supply. Canadian soldiers shipped out for England in December. Bill was one of them, but George's regiment was to remain in Winnipeg. Peter, his eyes moist, hugged Bill when he stopped by to say goodbye. There were quite a few tear-stained faces in the village, as mothers, wives, and girlfriends worried if they'd ever see their loved ones again. The men, for the most part, kept their feelings hidden. There were a lot of pats on the back and messages: "Make us proud, boy!" "Don't let the Krauts win!" "Come home in one piece." But the unspoken fears that accompanied their wishes for a safe return hung in the air long after they'd said their farewells.

With so many young people gone, the town's population shrank significantly. Streets, normally full of bustling young people, were suddenly empty. There were no shouts or gales of laughter from those heading to the newly built ice rink or to the hills to ski on barrel staves or on store-bought skis. The newly built Oak Theatre rarely filled its seats on the weekends and during the week, the owner was lucky if he had enough customers to cover the cost of the projectionist. Villagers gathered in their homes to pray or cry or reflect on the madness that had sent their young overseas.

The long Manitoba winter—with its fierce wind whistling as it rattled the windows and tried to sneak in through the cracks in the sills or under the doors—added to Dolly's loneliness. She rubbed a circle of ice from the small barn window and looked out at the frozen landscape. No one was stirring in the village, not even animals. Few villagers had livestock in back of their homes, so there was no need here to get up early to milk the cows or tend to the chickens. Much as she loved Peter, she missed the liveliness of her former home—her brothers and mother singing folk songs after a hearty meal, the gramophone record playing a polka complete with scratches, her nieces and Mike jumping around in time to its beat, Puppy's barking, and the barnyard sounds. She also missed Elena. They'd grown close over the years, and now that she'd moved to Stonewall, they only got together when the family gathered for holidays or made it to the same church service.

Peter played his violin or banjo, which brought some cheer to the dark days of winter. Nick Meronek came over with his violin, and with Peter on his banjo, the two would play for hours, taking a break only when their fingers got tired. Dolly would get caught up in the music, too, and take a few twirls over the old boards, prompting Peter to look up, and wink at her.

Even Mr. Monodar clapped along, though he kept to himself as best he could. He ate the meals she cooked but said little at the table. The sounds of him slurping borscht, or smacking his lips after dipping a piece of bread in mushroom gravy, were the most they got out of him.

She looked forward to Peter's brothers' letters. George sent a photo of his wife, Anne Warren, a lovely brunette. With the war on, it had been a hasty marriage, and no one in the family had attended. And now she was pregnant. George was living in barracks somewhere in Ontario, waiting to be shipped overseas. She wondered how, when the time came, he was going to feel about leaving a wife and child behind. And how was poor Anne going to fare? It wasn't surprising that George had picked an English wife. She got the impression from her encounters with both Bill and George that their Ukrainian roots embarrassed them and they hoped to escape the prejudice that had plagued them in the village. Though, she thought, they must've known some Ukrainian, as it was their mother's only language, and yet Dolly had never heard either of them utter one Ukrainian word. It was as if by pretending they only knew English, they could pretend away their heritage as well.

Bill's letters were longer. She relished his stories. He was the brother who had the knack of imparting what he was going through with flair. When the first letter came, Peter tore open the envelope immediately.

Holding the letter up to the light of the kerosene lamp, Peter said, "He must've written this while he was crossing the Atlantic."

He read Bill's words: *We had boarded the ship in the evening and I slept solidly, perhaps aided by the screech.*

"Screech?" Dolly said. "What's screech?"

"I think it's an alcoholic drink that people in the eastern provinces drink." Peter turned his attention to the letter agai:. *Anyway, it seemed that a few minutes later someone shook my shoulder, said, 'Bob's your uncle. Here is our morning tea.' He pulled out a tray by my head and placed a cup of hot tea on it. You remember, Peter, tea was not anything I would drink on getting up. Still, it was hot and sweet and good for a dry throat. This type of treatment was not only new to me, but welcome. Later on, I found out that we were on a Pacific and Orient luxury liner, the SS Orama. It was called into action as a troop ship so suddenly that all the original crew for the luxury trade was still aboard and that was the kind of treatment we had all the way across the Atlantic. During meals, we had a waiter in a red jacket for every table and after dinner we went to the lounge for coffee, chesterfields and all, just like you see in the wealthy clubs. Or in the movies. The canteen sold everything and liquor was almost a giveaway.*

"That's something, huh?" Peter said to Dolly. Not waiting for a reply, he cleared his throat, then continued reading: *But to get back to the first morning, after the astonishment of the wake-up service, I was just burning to see what it was all about and impatient to see what a big ship was like. On leaving my bunk, it seemed that I was going through a hotel to get to the upper deck and once on top:*

Boy, what a sight. I guess the waves were small, but to a prairie boy, they seemed huge. And there was our ship, in the middle of this convoy. Three troop ships in the middle; next were three battle cruisers and two major battleships, surrounded by 19 destroyers. One battleship was the British Repulse, dark grey, low in the water, and very reassuring. The other battleship was the flagship of the French Navy, the Dunquerque, graceful, fast and a light grey colour. It was an awesome sight. We stood on the top deck forty feet above the water and gloried in the smell of the sea, and the blinking of signals from the command vessel. It was still very cold on deck as we had not yet reached the gulf stream, but we felt safe and gave little thought to the U boats that could be lurking nearby. Anyway, that's all for now. I'll write again when I have a moment. Keep the home fires burning. Cheerio, Bill

Peter said, "Boy, must've been quite

the sight." He folded the letter carefully and put it in an old cigar box the Perrys had given him. The other item in there was his pocket watch, which he'd bought when he was still a youth.

Dolly didn't understand half of what Peter had read and, truthfully, she wasn't that interested. The only part of the letter that had appealed to her was Bill's description of the luxury ship. She recalled her voyage across the ocean and her excitement at being on a large ship in the middle of the ocean. She had eaten in the third-class dining room, not as fancy as the one Bill had experienced, but she had also revelled in being served by stewards in white coats. They had that in common, at least. Having both grown up poor, they appreciated the finer things in life.

Peter rose from the kitchen chair to add another log to the fire in the wood stove. She understood the turmoil in his mind, but she prayed he'd never leave her to fight in a war that was consuming the world. She was too young to remember much of her father's distress, but her mother had recounted the effect the endless battles of the Great War had had on his health. Dolly understood he'd come home from the war a broken man. Never the same. Why would any woman want that for her husband?

The other big news that winter had to do with Elena. She was pregnant again, expecting at the end of May. Egnat and Elena were living with their two young daughters in a boxcar with an interior dividing wall. The girls slept on a sleeper sofa in their parents' bedroom, which also doubled as their dining area. The kitchen had a woodstove, and around it, thirty to forty chicks—kept in a shallow cardboard box—peeped at all hours. And on the ceiling, long curls of sticky paper caught the flies that tried to find a home indoors. Dolly expected it would take years before Egnat could afford to build a house on their property. Her brother's first priority was to ensure he had enough farm equipment and livestock to run a successful farm.

And yet, Egnat appeared to be more content, now that he was master of his own domain.

Her mother clicked her tongue the first time she went to Egnat's farm, but when she saw how happy he was, she stopped showing her displeasure.

With her eldest brother gone from the Lilyfield farm, Dolly worried about her mother's future security. Much as she loved Mike, she agreed with Egnat. Her middle brother was unreliable. When Egnat and Dolly heard he'd left their mother coughing and feverish to go to a dance with a young woman, they bawled him out. But their scolding didn't make any difference. Mike continued his merry ways, even when the young woman, upon discovering how he'd treated his mother, refused to go out with him again.

Genya settled in at her new school, two miles away. It was a long walk, but not much longer than the one she had taken to get to school in Lilyfield. She told Dolly she was knitting socks for the soldiers and writing them letters, too. All the students in her class were participating in this project. Dolly wished she could write the troops, but she'd never learned how to write in English. Peter was the one who wrote to his brothers. George was still in Ontario and Bill was stationed somewhere in England, training to be ready to fight whenever he was called. For the moment, it was only the English and the French battling it out with the Germans. The Canadians were on standby.

With more and more boys heading overseas, there was lots of talk about jobs opening up in the city. The possibility of full-time work fuelled Dolly's imagination. She had to find some way to get Peter into the city.

About the Lot

When the purple crocuses peeked through the snow, Dolly knew it wouldn't be long before they could resume building their home. Every time she walked by their lot on her way to the store, she stopped to examine their forlorn wooden structure. The walls were up, but the shingles for the roof lay in a pile by the foundation.

What had she been thinking when she told Peter they should buy the property? This community would never accept them as equals. Even though Peter's father had gained some respect with the English through his sociability and work, Ukrainian immigrants were outsiders. She saw no prospect of that changing anytime soon.

She thought of how foolish she'd been to drop out of school. She had been embarrassed to be so old in Grade 1 and have only one dress to wear. The boys' teasing about her breasts had bothered her as well. She had developed early, and no matter how much she slumped and tried to hide her chest's size, she couldn't. Fitting in was a problem that continued to trouble her.

She asked Peter, "Why did we pick this lot? Why did we rush to buy it? It's a terrible lot. Such an odd shape. And it's exposed to the hoodlums who raid gardens."

He was quiet, then said, "How did we know we'd have so much trouble?"

It was frustrating talking to Peter about it. He took everything in stride. He was sympathetic, but she knew that whatever direction they were going to take in life, she'd have to be the one to arrange it.

When Dolly had mentioned their lot was vulnerable to hoodlums, Peter wanted to say he had been one himself. In his teens, he had acted as the lookout while his friends raided gardens in town. He'd never thought about it being such a bad thing—until he got caught. He had been standing at a fence, looking in all directions, while his friends took the vegetables they wanted. But the next thing he knew, he felt a big hand on his shoulder. He turned and faced a policeman. The cop rounded the boys up, took each one home, and reported their wrongdoing to their parents.

Peter's father was so angry, he told him to stay in the corner, then grabbed a stick of cordwood from a pile by the stove and hit him across the shins and across the hands. He yelled, "How dare you embarrass me like that? What have I taught you? Thou shalt not steal. Do you hear me?"

"Stop it, Tony!" Peter's mother had

hollered at his dad. "What are you trying to do, kill him?" That stopped his father. Peter held no hostility towards his father for the beating. He didn't blame his dad; he blamed himself. He'd seen how hard his father worked, cutting and heaving hard rock, more hours than any man should to support his wife, four sons, and a daughter. He also knew his father worked hard to keep a half-decent reputation in the village, and Peter had sullied his family's name.

He had been thinking about all of this while he repaired a leak around the barn window. Dolly interrupted his reverie when she returned from the store, carrying the materials to make more roses.

"Nice colours," he said, admiring the yellow and variegated pink crepe paper she took out of the bag.

"Yes, but you know what?" Dolly asked as she took off her jacket.

"What? What are you so excited about?"

"Dan told me the City of Winnipeg is fixing the track to Stony Mountain. You should ask if they need more help."

"If they're already fixing it, they probably have enough workers."

"You don't know that." When he hesitated, she added, "Honey, your crown won't fall off your head if you ask."

He grumbled while he finished puttying the window frame. He hated the way she framed her suggestions. Not that they were bad—they were usually good—but she always wanted him to act on them right away. A man needed time to think.

She continued to prod him until he succumbed, got on his bike, and went looking for the job site.

Near to Stony Mountain, on the train tracks to Winnipeg, Peter found a small group of men fastening the steel rails with nail spikes, the sound of their hammers scattering any birds in the vicinity. Peter approached a worker wearing a railroad cap and asked who he could talk to about getting a job laying the tracks. The worker pointed to a tall, gruff-looking man in overalls. "Ask Huxley. He's the foreman."

Huxley was bent over one section of the rails, examining the work that had been done. Peter walked over to him and said, "Excuse me. Are you hiring?"

Huxley straightened up and studied Peter for a moment, his narrow brown eyes narrowing further. He took in Peter's size from head to toe and said, "What pay are you expecting?"

Peter hesitated, then said, "Twenty-five cents an hour."

"I'll give you thirty cents."

Peter grinned. "Suits me fine." He shook hands with the foreman and started work immediately.

He worked steadily for three weeks until his fellow worker misjudged a spot and accidentally drove a nail into Peter's finger, right to the bone. When he came home, Dolly was in the back of Mr.

Monodar's home, chopping wood for the stove.

She stopped chopping when she saw him. Knitting her brow, she said, "Why are you home so early?"

He held up his bandaged hand. "I was holding a nail and the German guy swung the hammer down so hard, he hit the knuckles of my left hand. A little closer and he would've smashed it completely. The foreman sent me home. I'm finished for now."

"Let me look at it." She unwrapped the bandage. One finger was red and swollen; the cut was deep. "Was anything put on it before it was wrapped?"

"No."

"It's going to fester if we don't take care of it. Come with me."

She took a piece of cotton batting out of a bureau drawer in their bedroom and led him to the outhouse in back of Monodar's home; trees and bushes along the property lines hid it from their neighbours.

"What are you doing? Why are we going here?"

"Never mind. Come in with me." Puzzled, he followed her into the grey, weathered outhouse.

He stood to the side while Dolly crouched over the hole and peed on the cotton batting. While she was peeing, she said, "You know, my baba healed people with herbs and she used urine to sterilize cuts and bruises."

Peter watched as she wrapped the urine-soaked cotton batting around his throbbing finger. When he had suffered from a cold this past winter, she'd made him drink hot milk with butter and minced garlic, then wrapped his throat with two cloth layers—a cold, wet cloth first, and on top, a wool babushka from the old country. He marvelled at her remedies.

For his injuries, the city gave him eight dollars in compensation. But when he reported what he'd received to Dolly, she grumbled, "That's not enough. Go back and show them you can't bend your finger."

He sighed heavily. "I'm not going back."

"Go back. That's not nearly enough. What are you going to do? How can you work now that you're hurt? They owe you more money."

Though reluctant, Peter had learned that Dolly had a wisdom of her own. She had a barometer of fairness he had grown to appreciate. Sure enough, when he went back to the labour department for the City of Winnipeg and showed them his injury, they gave him another eight dollars in compensation. When he returned home, she nodded knowingly and said, "See? Sometimes all you have to do is ask." He couldn't argue with that.

On the following Sunday, they set out to visit her mother, hitchhiking part of the way. Two miles from the farmhouse, Puppy came running to greet them, his tail wagging as fast as a hummingbird's wings. Peter and Dolly took turns bending down to pat him and rub behind his ears.

"Good boy, good boy," Dolly said, as Puppy jumped and ran in and out of their legs all the way to the farmhouse.

Egnat, Elena, and the girls had come for supper, too. It was the first time since they'd moved to Stonewall, and Lukia had prepared a feast. Passing her dishes around the table took a while before everyone could eat. But here they were, all together again. Lukia waited on Egnat and his family as if they were royalty.

Egnat teased, "I should've moved sooner."

"Don't say," Lukia said, giving him a cross look. She turned to her daughter-in-law. "Elena, eat, eat. You have two to feed now." She took a spoonful of beet horseradish and dropped it on her plate.

Elena stroked her pregnant body. "Yes. It won't be long now."

Dolly looked across the table at her

sister-in-law. "How far along are you?"

"Eight months."

Lukia said, "Maybe Genya can help when the baby comes. She's ten now, old enough."

"I can help, Baba," said Genya.

"I know you can."

Elena patted Genya, who sat beside her. "Only if the baby comes when you're not in school."

Vera said, "Me, too. I help, too." Her assertion triggered a few smiles from the adults.

When they had finished eating and were having their tea, Lukia said to Elena, "I wish you were still living here. You wouldn't be alone having the baby."

"Don't worry, Mama," Elena said. "I won't be alone. I have a midwife. Egnat will call her when the time comes."

"How? You don't have a phone."

"Our neighbour lives only a half-mile away. He has one."

"When I think of how I brought my

children into the world," Lukia said. "I had nobody when Dunya was born. I gave birth to her in a komora. No one was home. Gregory was in Lutsk, signing up for the Tsar's army. Not that he would've been much help. Oy. I bit down on a rag soaked with homebrew, and the smell of sauerkraut and garlic pickles in the barrels soothed me. It wasn't long before Dunya squirted out."

Elena said, "Hopefully, mine won't take long, too."

Lukia got up from her chair. "Come. Let's see if you'll have a boy. Dunya, bring me a needle with a long thread."

While the men stayed at the table to have another drink, Elena lay down on the chesterfield. Lukia took the threaded needle and made a knot, tying the two ends together. Then, holding the knot, she swung the needle over Elena's pregnant belly. Genya, Vera, and Dolly stood at the foot of the sofa and watched Lukia swing the needle in a circular motion.

"What's Baba doing?" Vera asked.

"Shhh," Genya said. "Watch."

Frowning, Vera pushed in closer.

"Nu, Elena," Lukia said, "you're going to have another girl. If it had swung straight, it would be a boy."

"As long as she's healthy," Elena said, groaning as she raised herself from the chesterfield. Massaging her back, she walked back to the table.

Genya said to Vera, "We're going to have a baby sister." Vera clapped her hands.

"Did you hear?" Lukia said to Egnat, as she sat down at the table. "You're going to have a girl." He raised an eyebrow.

Mike said, "Brother, were you hoping for a boy to help on the farm?"

"No matter. Each child is a blessing." Egnat grinned and raised his glass to his wife. Elena smiled back, exchanging a loving look.

Peter, whose cheeks had reddened from downing several glasses of whiskey, said, "Egnat, girls are a finished job. They're not born with something hanging, like boys."

"Ho, ho, ho. You're right." Everyone laughed.

"Daye Bozhe," Peter said as he clinked his glass with Egnat's.

Stirring milk into her tea, Dolly said, "Mama, I have something to tell you."

Lukia turned to Dolly, a smile still on her face from watching her grandchildren tickle one another on the carpet by the sofa. "What?"

"You know Peter got injured, so he can't finish the house. And even if we could finish it, there's no work in Stony Mountain. So, Peter and I are thinking of moving to the city."

"Oy, oy, oy," Lukia said, her brow lining like pleats in a skirt. "What about all the money you spent building the frame? Poof! All gone!"

"Not all gone," Dolly said. "We'll advertise in the local gazette. Maybe somebody will want to buy it and finish it themselves."

Lukia groaned. "Winnipeg? You'll be so far away."

"Not so far. If we can find a rooming house to rent, we'll have a place to stay and make enough money to pay for our own rent. And we can save to buy a place of our own."

"A rooming house?"

"People can't afford a house, so they're renting rooms in houses. You can make a lot of money renting to single men and women."

Egnat grunted. "You said yourself you weren't happy with your lot. You think you can get someone to buy it?"

Dolly set her jaw. "If the price is right, they'll buy."

Lukia said, "You have the stubbornness of your father. I hope you're right."

"We'll see," Egnat said.

Having exhausted the topic, they sang

folk songs, joyful and sad. Dolly felt her mother's eyes glance at her from time to time with sorrowful eyes, a reminder that she was deeply disappointed in her daughter's decision. *Well*, thought Dolly, *maybe I am stubborn like my father, but what choice do I have? Peter needs steady work.*

During one of the folk songs, Dolly looked out the window and saw a truck drive up. It was their neighbour, Doug Lawson. *What was he doing here so late? Farmers didn't usually visit when the sun was setting.* He stepped out of the car with a grim face.

"Doug's here," Lukia said. She had noticed Doug drive up, too.

Dolly got up to answer the door, joined by her mother. She greeted him at the door. "Hello, Doug. Is everything all right?"

He took his cap off. Fingering the brim, he said, "I'm sorry, Dolly. I accidentally shot your dog. I thought he was a fox after our mink. It was dark. He doesn't usually come that far."

"Puppy? Oh, no! Is he okay?"

Alarmed, Lukia touched her daughter's shoulder. "What?"

"No, he's not," Doug said, barely looking up. "I'm afraid he's dead."

Rocking her head from side to side, Lukia moaned, "Such a good dog."

Dolly said, "Where is he?"

"He's in the back of my truck."

Puppy's body lay limp on an old blanket. Dolly stroked his head, already cold. Tears filled her eyes as she patted the poor animal. Egnat and Peter wrapped the blanket around the dog and buried him under an oak tree. It was where he had often gone to find shade after his work was done herding the cows. Dolly would find him panting there, his tongue hanging out of his mouth, happy to be in a cool spot at the end of a hot day. Her mother and Mike would have to find another dog to help with the cows, but some animals were impossible to replace. Puppy was one of them.

With the milder spring weather and the snow gone, Peter and Dolly left Mr. Monodar's home and went back to living in their barn. She posted a notice about their building and lot for sale on the community boards in both village stores. She had instructed Peter to write the sign clearly and in large letters.

While she was hanging up the ad in Dan Balacko's store. Dan teased from behind his counter, "Going to miss you, Dolly."

"We're not gone yet," she said, putting the last thumb tack into the corkboard to secure the paper. She stepped back to admire the notice. She wondered if it was pure folly to think they could sell an unfinished house on an odd-shaped lot. Not wanting to give Dan any sense she had doubts, she straightened her back and walked out of the store with her head held high.

End Matters

Though his mother's health had declined rapidly in the past year, Peter was still shocked when she was hospitalized in Winnipeg. Wanting to visit her, Dolly asked Dan Balacko to drive them to the city in his taxi. Peter didn't feel bad about adding the fee to their bill. He suspected half the town owed the grocer money. In dismal times, buying on credit had become a way of life. As long as you paid your debt in full by the end of the month, there were no problems with this kind of borrowing. And so far, he and Dolly had paid their bill in a timely manner.

In the cab, Dan said he was glad to

take them, as he had to run some errands in the city anyway.

Sitting in the front, Dolly said, "You've done well for yourself. You have a nice taxi. You own a store, some houses—you must be a millionaire."

He laughed. "Not a millionaire, Dolly. Not by a long shot."

She snorted. "You have lots, I know. Since you're so rich, why did you buy the shanty out from under us? You knew we were interested."

"Business is business, Dolly. I told you that."

Dolly turned around and gave Peter a look: *see what you did*.

Moping, Peter stared out the side window. Some fields still had some snow, but it would soon be gone. He thought of the last time he'd seen his mother. She'd been feeling poorly, and Johnny had rolled her wheelchair to the front gate. She had said to Peter as he was leaving, "You're going to remember me." Her mouth was tight and her eyes serious.

The image of his mother at the gate, her face drawn and grave, bothered Peter. He couldn't get it out of his mind. Why had she said, *You're going to remember me?*

They drove down Logan Avenue towards the Winnipeg General Hospital and passed a group of men working on the railway tracks. "There's Huxley," Peter said, and leaned towards the window to get a better look.

"The foreman?" Dolly asked.

"Yes."

"I wonder if they need any more men," she said. "Now that your finger's healed."

Peter grunted. The work on the tracks hadn't been bad until he got injured. Still, he had hoped to find something less gruelling.

When Dan dropped them off at the hospital, Dolly said, "After we see Mama, go see Huxley. Maybe he'll hire you once more. Tell him you're living in Winnipeg now."

"What do you mean?"

"You can stay at cousin Ted's place."

Peter realized that Dolly's suggestion was reasonable, but it was one he had trouble embracing. And yet, what choice did he have? He had taken a wrong turn in life; it was hard to find that road of promise again.

The Winnipeg General Hospital was a massive building, with doctors, nurses and other staff bustling down corridors running north, south, east, and west. Patients in wheelchairs, others hobbling with canes or walking unassisted, made their way towards their appointments for X-rays and checkups. Several were accompanied by family members, old and young. Visitors mingled among them as they headed towards the wards, holding their loved ones.

The woman at the information kiosk near the entrance told Peter and Dolly where they could find Mrs. Tony Klewchuk.

Peter's mother was in a ward with five other patients, three beds on each side of the room. Mary sat beside her and stood up to kiss Peter when he arrived at his mother's bed, with Dolly close behind. Dolly stepped forward to give Mary a hug. He noticed his sister stiffen.

"How is she doing?" Peter asked.

"Not so good." Mary dabbed her red-rimmed eyes with a lace-edged handkerchief.

Dressed in a hospital gown, his mother lay listless and asleep on the pillow—her thin grey hair matted around her frail face, her skin sallow; her eyes, though shut, resembled hollow sockets. She'd lost so much weight, her once-robust arms were half their former size. The delicate wristwatch she'd been so proud of lay loose around her wrist. They'd only been in the room a few minutes before a nurse entered.

"I'm sorry," the nurse said. "You have to leave. I need to change her. You can come back in an hour."

Disappointed, Peter stroked his mother's hand, then left with Dolly and Mary. They waited until they'd left the corridor, with its glaring white walls, to make any plans. In the elevator, Dolly stood silently while Peter and his sister chatted.

"How's Eleanor?" Peter asked.

Mary smiled. "She's fine."

"I'm so glad the Icelandic family is treating you well."

"Me, too."

"Where are you staying?"

"With Father. I've nowhere else to stay."

"Mary," Dolly said, "Why didn't you come see us?"

"I came straight to the hospital."

Dolly gave Peter a pained look. Mary's reply had been curt. Peter knew his wife was still feeling the stings from his family, but there was nothing he could do to mend those fences. He hoped in time they'd accept her.

When they stepped outside, Dolly said to Peter. "Why don't you go see your old foreman? He's only a couple of blocks away. You have time. Mary won't mind, will you?"

Mary shrugged. "No, not if it's about a job. Good luck."

"What about you?" he asked Dolly. "What are you going to do?"

"There's a nice park nearby." She took Mary's arm. "We can go for a walk and meet you back here in an hour."

Peter exchanged looks with Mary, who put her hands up as if to say, *don't look at me*. Dreading the task in front of him, he swallowed and walked towards Logan Avenue.

On the way to the park, Dolly talked non-stop to Mary about her experience in Stony Mountain, how they had dug the basement by hand, the problems they ran into when Peter hurt his finger taking that railway job, and how and why they'd ended up at Mr. Monodar's. "Do you know him?" Dolly asked.

"No."

"Do you like living in Cypress River?"

"It's fine. People there treat us like family."

"Wonderful."

Dolly asked a few more questions, but after getting only short answers, she gave up trying to engage her sister-in-law. They walked for a bit without talking. It was a glorious day, a sharp contrast to the sterile interior of the hospital. The oak trees were leafing out; the lilac bushes showed new buds, and daffodils and red tulips brightened the path. They passed a young couple quarreling on a bench, two elderly men in serious conversation, and on the lawn, a young boy and girl throwing a ball back and forth. A robin flew down to the lawn and found a worm to tug.

Periodically, Dolly glanced at Mary, who kept her eyes forward. "Mary," she finally said, putting her hand on her sister-in-law's arm, "let's be like sisters."

Mary pulled her arm away. "Never. I'm never gonna be your sister."

"Mary, Mama's dying … Let's be friends."

"Never, never can we be friends." Mary, her expression fierce, rushed ahead, her head held high, her back stiff, her low-heeled shoes clicking on the concrete walk like angry birds pecking at hard seeds. Dolly resisted running after her, because she knew it wouldn't help. She'd created a barrier between them when she didn't ask Mary to be in her wedding party. Would her sister-in-law ever forgive her?

Taking Stock

Lukia shielded her eyes as she surveyed the tender grain shoots in the field. The Depression appeared to be over at last. It had taken ten long years. It was now 1940, and she, like every other farmer, looked forward to higher yields and better prices. Mike had seeded the fields on his own, but unlike Egnat, his heart wasn't in the work. Even the horses and cows suffered under his watch. They did not get the same loving attention that Egnat had showered on them.

Lukia tried to help, but she was now sixty-five years old and her body was not as cooperative as it once was. Eight childbirths and five losses—her husband

and four children—had taken their toll. And to lose the company of Elena and Dunya, as well as the joyous chatter of her grandchildren, made her heart ache. How do you heal a wounded heart? There was no treatment for that kind of heartache.

At night, her mind swirled with thoughts about her children. Harry had become like a stranger. He used to come home with his dirty mechanic's shirt and pants, which Elena washed for him. Now, he took them to some Chinese laundry in the city and Lukia barely saw him. The family fights had driven Egnat and his family away. How had she allowed that to happen? She was thankful, however, that Egnat stopped by weekly on his way to the city to sell his produce. Like Lukia, he sold his eggs, cottage cheese, butter, and sour cream to parishioners, who lived on and near Logan Avenue. Perhaps she should have thrown Mike out and kept her eldest by her side. But she couldn't do that. Mike was her most vulnerable child, the one who'd always soaked up most of her attention. The family's, too. Perhaps if she hadn't been so bent on helping him, she'd have paid more attention to the others. Especially to Dunya. Lukia liked Peter, but then, everyone liked him. She had never met such a gentleman. But none of that mattered if her daughter was going to live a life of poverty.

The sun disappeared behind a cloud like her dream of keeping her family together. She gazed once more on the land. It was decent farmland, but it wasn't hers. They were renting, and with only Mike to help, she saw no way they'd ever get their own property. Back in Kivertsi, if she ran into difficulty, she could rely on her own people for help. There were a few Ukrainian farmers she'd befriended, but without being able to drive, she was isolated. She relied on Mike for transport, and that was a sore point, as he came and went like a bird at a feeder.

She considered her daughter's wish to live in Winnipeg. Lukia enjoyed her trips to the city as well, especially the public market on Main Street, with all its stalls on wooden slats. She enjoyed the market even in the winter, when the sellers stayed in tiny huts and only came out when a customer showed up to buy root vegetables, frozen fish, or—close to the holidays—Christmas trees. From what she could tell, even though there was the odd Ukrainian seller, you needed to speak English if you wanted to compete. One seller told Lukia she bought her produce wholesale from the Jewish merchants in back of the market, then marked it up. She made enough from her sales to pay the rent of her stall and make a tidy profit besides. Lukia thought that if she was younger, she'd have a stall, too.

She wished her relationship with Mike was easier. When he was young, he listened, but overnight he had become like a wild horse, refusing to be tamed. He went through the motions of farming, but she knew he'd rather be rehearsing with the church choir for a spring concert, chasing some girl, or sitting for hours in some beer parlour, drowning his grievances. How had it come to this? One by one, her children had left, and the son who was the least dependable was the one who had stayed. She sought solace in prayer. At night, she stayed long on her knees, and when Mike wasn't too hung over, he drove her to church on Sundays.

The sun was high in the sky. It was time to make lunch. Mike would come in from the fields soon.

You'll Remember Me

Again, Peter had to admit that Dolly was right. His old foreman, Huxley, hired him to help remove the railway tracks from Logan Avenue to Provencher Boulevard. The first morning, he rose at dawn and rode his bicycle fifteen miles to the city. Though he'd told the foreman he was staying with his wife's cousin on Burrows Avenue, he discovered Ted wasn't there, which meant he had to ride back to Stony Mountain after work. Exhausted, he went to bed early. After rising with the sun, he told Dolly he didn't think he could keep the pace up. Rather than suggest he quit, she advised him to find Boris Karpinsky's address in the phone book and go there after work. She told him Boris would be more than happy to put him up, seeing as how the Karpinskys had lived with her family in harmony on the Rosser farm.

Luckily, Boris had fond memories of the Mazurecs, too, and welcomed Peter to his home. Peter was grateful for the accommodations, even though he had to curl his six-foot two-inch frame in order to fit on the narrow chesterfield in the living room. With his mother's days numbered, he wished he had the comfort of his wife's presence. He missed snuggling up to Dolly, feeling her warm, soft body against his. Ordinarily, he would have found it difficult to sleep on a sofa, but with the long days lifting rails and the evenings visiting his mother in the hospital, he slept soundly—a welcome escape from daylight's grim reality.

A week later, when he came into his mother's hospital room, he found her bed empty. It had been stripped and remade. Panicked, he rushed to the nurses' station, where a nurse told him his mother had passed away in the night.

He shrivelled inside. "Did the priest see her?"

"Yes. The priest from her church came by not long after you left."

"Was she alone when she died?" he asked, tearing up.

She tried to console him. "You'd be surprised how many die without a loved one present. It's almost like they want to save their families the grief of seeing them pass before their eyes." When he said nothing, she put her hand on his arm and said, "She went peacefully."

Peacefully or not, he had wanted to be there, and he was sure his mother would have liked him there as well. Had he known she was leaving so soon, he would have stayed longer. "Does my father know?"

"We're trying to reach him."

Peter worked the next couple of days in a blur. His mother's words when he left home haunted him—*You'll remember me.* Of course, he would remember her, but it was the way she'd said it. As if he wouldn't.

St. Michael's church, on Disraeli Street, held vigil all night for his mother. She lay in an open coffin near the altar. Parishioners came and went, paying their respects, as did Peter and Dolly and their families. His mother looked at peace in her best dress—a print jersey with a lace collar—but Peter hardly recognized her. The undertaker had applied light rouge on her plumped-up cheeks and drawn faint lipstick on her lips. His mother had never worn makeup, and it seemed wrong somehow that the undertaker had altered her in death without consulting the family.

Peter stood in a front pew with Dolly, his father, Mary, and Johnny. Bill and George, stationed overseas, did not know their mother had died. Peter had written them right away, his tears dropping on the paper as he described her ill health and passing. With the mail taking weeks to reach them, they wouldn't hear about their mother's death until long after the funeral.

The next day, Peter, Dolly, and his family followed the hearse in his friend's car down Logan Avenue. As their car passed his work site, his fellow workers stopped working, took their hats off and lowered their heads. His face solemn, Peter nodded at Huxley through the open window.

Peter had never been in a funeral procession before. The cars with their headlights on moved slowly, letting other vehicles on the road know they were heading to a cemetery. It was his mother's last ride. His eyes welled as he thought about her dismal life. He assumed she'd loved his father, but years of hardship had taken its toll.

He gripped Dolly's hand when they reached the gates of Brookside Cemetery, one of the city's largest. They rode past old stones marking people who had died many years before, then past the rows of Commonwealth graves of those who had fought in the Great War, fronted by a tall monument bearing a large cross. At one time, he'd read there were three hundred buried here, a fraction of the thousands who'd died overseas. He gazed at the rows upon rows of white rectangular tombstones engraved with a simple cross, the deceased's name, date of birth, date of death, and the words: *Lest We Forget,* and thought of his brothers, in training for the theatre of war. He blinked and tried to blot out of his mind the possibility of them perishing on foreign soil. The lead car, the hearse, directed the priest and the mourners to another section on the far side of the graveyard. His mother's plot was at the very back, near the wire and wood fence that enclosed the cemetery. Beyond the fence, the emptiness of an open field of tall, dry grass and a rundown farm in the distance underscored his sorrow.

Once the mourners had gathered, the priest waved his censer over Zoica Klewchuk's grave and began the prayers ushering her to heaven. Peter sang, along with the deacon and a few elderly parishioners, the mournful lament "Vichnaya Pamyat." The notes of Forever Memory stuck in his throat as he fought to keep from sobbing. He pulled a handkerchief out of his pants pocket and dabbed his eyes. The refrain, repeated in drawn-out, sonorous tones, caused a few others to weep as well. At the end, the priest and the mourners said the Lord's Prayer, crossed themselves three times, and watched as men in black suits lowered his mother's coffin into the hole. Peter glanced at his father, who stood dry-eyed. His marriage had been tumultuous, with many fights over his wandering ways. And yet Peter knew his father would miss his wife. They had raised five children in a land that often treated them as second-class citizens.

As the mourners dispersed, Dolly took Peter's arm. "Why did your father bury her here?" she asked. "Look at the stones around her."

He followed her gaze. In every direction, the headstones showed Chinese inscriptions, graves of Chinese immigrants.

"But she's not Chinese. Why did he bury her here?" she asked again.

"I don't know," he said, looking around. "Maybe it was the cheapest part of the cemetery. Or maybe it's where the city assigned him a spot." When he thought about Dolly's question again, he found the matter unsettling. He wondered whether discrimination had played a part in where his mother ended up being buried. In life, the Chinese had been discriminated against as well. And who was there to ask and even if there was someone to approach for an answer to his question, would they even admit they had acted with prejudice?

After the funeral, there was a luncheon in the basement at St. Michael's church. The Ladies' Auxiliary had prepared sandwiches, various sweet treats, and tea. His father had brought enough wine for the mourners to toast his mother's passing. His family stood around, making small talk with neighbours and friends who'd attended the prayers—the Meroneks, the Debiuks, and Pan Adamovich and his children. Nick Meronek was the only friend of Peter's who attended; the others had enlisted and, because of that, were scattered over the country or somewhere overseas.

While Dolly talked to Nick and his wife, Helen, Peter took Mary's arm and guided her to a couple of chairs in a corner, where they could sit down and talk in private.

Mary said wistfully, "I don't know how she managed. It couldn't have been easy for her in that village. They called us kids dirty Galicians, remember?"

"Yes. She was pretty alone. Outside of this church and doing some housekeeping in Winnipeg, I don't think Mother went anywhere."

"Too busy looking after us. God, she worked hard. She always had twelve dishes for Ukrainian Christmas Eve. She'd bake a kolach and put hay under the tablecloth. Remember?"

He nodded and visualized his mother with her apron on, bending down to get various hot dishes out of the stove and onto the table.

Mary said, "She always got me material for the Christmas school concert so I could make myself a dress. She was a wonderful mother." Mary crossed her legs towards him. "And those lowly prunes and apples she stewed. Boy, they tasted good."

"Yeah, lip-smacking," he said. "At Easter, too, she followed the traditions. Remember how she'd go by streetcar to Winnipeg to bless the Easter basket, and we weren't allowed to eat until she returned?" He smiled. "She made sure there were enough coloured boiled eggs for all of us." A few people were starting to leave. He looked at one woman hugging another at the door. "Yet she never hugged us."

"I guess she wasn't the hugging type."

They sat in silence for a few moments. Peter thought of how different the Mazurecs were. Perhaps that was what had drawn him to Dolly and her family. The love they had for one another was palpable.

Interrupting his train of thought, Mary said, "You know, when I saw her just before she died, she asked me to part her hair the way she liked it." Mary's eyes teared up. She glanced over at their father. "I don't think I ever saw him give her a kind word."

He felt an ache in his heart. His dad had been rough with all of them. But his mother had made sure they were all fed and clothed. She even made his dad's homebrew on the stove. How she put up with him—that was something Peter didn't understand.

Mary said, "I hated being the girl in the family. Everyone grabbed. I was always the last one to get chicken. All you guys left me were the feet."

Peter grinned. "Were we that awful? I didn't notice. I guess I was too busy grabbing for myself." He grew pensive as he tried to recall that time.

After a few moments, Mary said, "She stuck up for us, though there was one time she was away and I got the strap."

"You?"

"I never told you about that?"

He shook his head.

"She went to Winnipeg for something, and you know how Dad kept the strap by the door. Well, there was a pail of water by the door when I walked in. George and Bill were roughhousing and knocked the pail over. Boy, was Dad mad. He strapped all of us."

"Even George?"

"Yep."

Peter said, "When George did anything bad, he would run around the trees in the yard to avoid Dad."

"Can't blame him." She clasped her hands in her lap and looked over at Johnny, who was talking to a pretty girl. "What that woman went through. When Johnny was born, Mama was screaming something awful. She kept hollering for someone to get the axe to cut the umbilical cord. Dad had sent for the doctor in Stonewall, but the baby was coming too fast."

"Yeah. You were nine or ten."

"Nine. Somehow, Mama got through it. Dad had the cord tied before the doctor showed up. He was so mad the doctor still charged him."

He pondered Johnny, who was still talking to the pretty girl. Peter had been too occupied with his own life to notice how quickly Johnny had grown. He was almost as tall as Peter. Resourceful, too. He got a job running the film projector at the Oak Theatre in the village. He told Peter that as soon as he was old enough to enlist, he'd be gone, too.

Mary said, "I can't recall her speaking much English. Funny how we didn't talk to her much, either. She talked to Mrs. Adamovich across the street, but then she died. Other than that, she must've been lonely. People made fun of us. It does something to your soul."

She was right, thought Peter. He wanted to reminisce more, but the Men's Association was taking down the tables and folding up the chairs, so they had to leave. There was so much more he wanted to say, especially his regrets for all the hard feelings that had surfaced when he was preparing to marry Dolly. They parted, promising to write.

Because Peter had to work the next day on the tracks, Peter and Dolly stayed overnight at Mrs. Ewanoski's boarding home. They couldn't stay at Boris Karpinsky's; the chesterfield barely held Peter. Mrs. Ewanoski was her mother's friend from the time they had worked on Selkirk Avenue as domestics for the well-to-do Jewish residents. She asked them to pay twenty-five cents each for the night, but they had no money. Up to that point, Peter had worked only three days and hadn't received his pay yet. Dolly apologized and promised that as soon as he got paid, they'd give her what was owing. Mrs. Ewanoski also let Dolly use her phone to arrange a ride home with Harry, who often visited his mother in Lilyfield after work on Saturdays.

On the way back to Stony Mountain, Peter chatted with Harry about his recent fishing trip to Lockport and how he was managing the gas station while his boss was away. As the men talked, Dolly looked out at the flat farmlands, thinking her escape from farm work hadn't led to any financial improvement in her life. So far, they'd had no offers on their lot. The grey penitentiary building loomed ahead, its limestone walls so solid and harsh-looking. Prisons weren't the only structures built to keep certain people out of society. There were others, like the walls of prejudice that Dolly and Peter were facing in their pursuit of work. Never mind, she thought, where there was a will, there was a way. And she was determined to find it.

When months had gone by with no response from their ad, some pessimism crept into her daily thoughts. What if their property never sold? She tried to suppress her misgivings by making paper roses. As she was fastening leaves on the stems, she came up with a plan she was eager to share with Peter. She waited until he came home from his job for the weekend.

She was making another paper rose when he walked in the door. Eyeing the wood crate full of crepe flowers at her feet, he said, "You make them so fast."

She beamed. "Money, money, money."

He laughed. "I forgot to tell you. Huxley says the job might take longer than three weeks."

"Wonderful! Such good news." She got up and kissed him. He responded passionately. "Wait, wait, wait," she said, giggling.

"For what?" He kissed her again.

"Peter, I was thinking, we shouldn't wait to sell the lot. We should move to the city now."

"Why?"

"You can't keep sleeping on Boris's couch. You'll get a cramped neck and a bad back. And Mrs. Ewanoski's place is too expensive. If we move, I can get some work in Winnipeg, too."

"What about our property?"

"Whether we're here or not, it'll make no difference. You can let Dan know how to reach us if anyone's interested in buying it."

"But we'll be so far from family."

"I thought you agreed to the move."

"I did, but I didn't think it would be so fast."

"You can still see your father. He goes into the city once a week to the markets; he stops in at the beer parlour. He can stop in to see us, too."

"I know, but where are we going to live?"

"Mike said Ted's back from Toronto. We can see if he has a room to rent in his rooming house."

Peter flopped down on a chair, looking more exhausted than when he had walked in the door. She let him mull over her idea while she made more flowers. Later, to ease his mind, she suggested they walk to

the Oak Theatre the next evening, to see
Gone with the Wind, with Clark Gable and
Vivien Leigh. The Stonewall Argus had
advertised it as the picture of a lifetime.
All seats were reserved and cost seventy-
five cents for the matinée and a dollar and
ten cents for the evening show, but
Johnny had told them that since he ran
the projector, they could get in for free.

The film was over three hours long,
with an intermission. Afterwards, they
said goodnight to some people Peter
knew, then walked home in the dark,
holding hands. The air was crisp and the
streets so quiet, it reminded her of the
welcoming stillness on the farm when the
livestock settled for the night. A black and
white cat ran out from the trees' long
shadows in the moonlight and dashed
across the road. They watched it
disappear into some low-lying bushes.

As they turned the corner to their
street, Dolly said, "What did you think of
the movie? Did you like it?"

"It was a wonderful film, but seeing the scene with all the injured soldiers made me think of Bill and George."

"Yes, that was sad. That's why I'm glad you don't have to go."

"Hmm," he said, and they walked several yards in silence.

"How about the love story?" she asked. "I can't believe how Scarlett played with Rhett's feelings. And the way she went after Ashley! He was married to her sister. What a hussy. But I admired her spirit."

Peter chuckled and squeezed her hand.

Dolly sighed, "At the end of the movie, Scarlett was all alone, crying for Tara, her land, just like Mama cried about hers."

"What do you mean?"

"Mama has always believed in land as security. She thought we'd all live on the farm together."

A dog barked as they passed a yard. Otherwise, the quiet of the night took over, leaving Dolly to her thoughts. She hoped they could move soon.

They left the bed and the buck stove for now and only took what they needed—clothes, sheets, towels, pots and pans, dishes, cutlery, and the perina her mother had made them. If their move was successful—that is, if they found steady employment—they would sell the barn, too.

Packed and ready to go, Dolly moved the wood crate of paper roses to the side. She said to Peter, "Mike won't be here for another two hours. Why don't you knock on one of the guard's houses and see if you can sell some paper roses?"

"Now?" Peter frowned. "Why not wait until we get to Winnipeg?"

"Honey, they know you here. We're more apt to sell them here than in the city. You can buy all kinds of artificial flowers in Winnipeg."

"Oh, brother."

"Never mind, *oh brother*." While he paced, she wrapped a dozen roses in the tissue paper she'd saved.

After Peter left Dolly with the roses in his hand, he turned back twice, only to turn forward again. He thought of telling her he had tried a guard's house, but his wife wasn't home. But knowing Dolly was no fool, he steeled himself and kept walking. When Mrs. Newman opened the door, he could feel his face turn red. He felt like a beggar holding out his hat for a handout.

"Peter," said Mrs. Newman, acting surprised to see him on her doorstep. Behind her were a couple of policemen he recognized. They stood in the doorway of her kitchen with a bottle of beer in their hands. "What do you have there?" she asked.

"Paper roses my wife made. Would you be interested in buying some? They're sixty cents a dozen." He handed her one.

"They're lovely."

Laughter rang from the kitchen. "I'm having a party. Could you come back tomorrow?"

Peter pressed his lips. "I'm sorry, Mrs. Newman, but we're moving to Winnipeg this afternoon."

She studied him for a moment, then said, "Well, all right then. Come to the kitchen and I'll buy these beautiful roses from you."

He followed her. The policemen who'd been standing in the doorway moved over to let Peter and Mrs. Newman into the kitchen, where five other men were chatting around the table. Some in uniform, some not.

"I'll be right back," she said and went through the other open doorway that led to the living room, where the policemen's wives sat dressed in fashionable dresses like the ones Dolly had described to him. She'd mentioned how much she admired the frocks in the shop windows of Clifford's on Selkirk Avenue. It was a shame he wasn't making enough money to buy her one. She got one on credit—not as nice—a few months back at Dan Balacko's store. She wanted a new dress so she would look presentable when she applied for work in the city.

One wife caught his eye, but out of embarrassment, he quickly turned away and pretended to look at the plaque, *Bless This House*, on the kitchen wall, and at the food spread out on the table: platters of cut-up roasted chicken and sliced salami, bowls of mashed potatoes, canned corn and canned peas, and various pickles. It made him hungry. When he thought of how little he and Dolly had in comparison, it made his stomach turn.

He waited awkwardly for Mrs. Newman to return while the men continued talking amongst themselves. She reappeared and gave him sixty cents for the roses.

"Good luck in the city," she said.

"Thank you again." He left, thinking

that was one thing he wouldn't miss about
Stony Mountain; he hated feeling second-
class.

Something Wrong

There was something wrong, thought Lukia. The last time she had seen Egnat was a month ago, when he and his family were over for supper. With Elena so close to delivering, Lukia felt uneasy. She'd had another bad dream and, with looming calamity on her mind, she skipped church on Sunday and asked Mike to drive her to Egnat's farm instead.

Lukia sat beside Mike in the front seat of the truck as he drove ten miles on the gravel country road from their home in Lilyfield. Dust flew in every direction, clouding their view of the farms they passed. Fields of flourishing grain should have lifted her spirits, but with Elena on her mind, she couldn't fully appreciate the change in fortune for local farmers, brought about not only by the weather but also by the war. The demand for grain had risen and, along with that, the prices.

They turned down the quarter-mile dirt road that led to Egnat's farm. Lukia gazed at the wheat growing in his fields. Her heart swelled with pride. His grain looked healthy, and he had created a fine-looking entranceway to his home. He had edged both sides of the road with the large stones he'd removed from his land. But again, she worried about his health. That kind of lifting wasn't good for any man.

At the end of the road, Mike turned again. The remaining lane took them a few hundred yards through a small forest of poplar, birch, and maple trees. They stopped just outside the outhouse. Upon exiting the truck, Lukia found a turkey gobbling at her heels. She shooed it away, then walked past chickens pecking at seeds on the ground and the henhouse, where a hen squawked at them through the open doorway.

As Lukia and Mike approached the boxcar, two mutts came bounding down the yard, tails wagging. Patting the dogs, Lukia said, "Have you been good boys?"

The screen door of the boxcar opened, and Genya and Vera rushed out. "Baba," Genya shouted, "have you come to see the baby?"

Lukia clasped her hands. "Is everything all right?"

"Yes. Mama's feeding Nina now."

"Nina, lovely name. Thanks be to God." Lukia embraced both girls. She said to Vera, "And look how big you're getting." Delighted by her baba's comment, Vera danced alongside to the boxcar.

While Mike stayed outdoors and took turns swinging both girls in the yard, Lukia opened the boxcar door and went inside. Set with the woods at its back, the dimly lit home had tiny windows, making it difficult for the morning light to brighten its interior. Strips of flypaper, covered with dead flies, hung from the ceiling. Lukia set the sealers of borscht and the bowl of sauerkraut-stuffed piroshki she had brought from home on the table.

"Elena," Lukia called through the open door to the bedroom.

"I'm in here, Mama."

Propped up in bed by a few pillows, Elena smiled, as her baby sucked hungrily on her breast. Lukia wiped her glasses on her sleeve, then put them on to get a good look at her new grandchild.

"My God, so sweet. I was so worried. When I didn't hear from Egnat, I thought maybe something had happened."

"No, Mama, everything's fine."

"Where's my son?"

"You know Egnat. Every Sunday, he walks up and down the fields to make sure his crops are doing well."

Yes, Lukia knew her son. He had started young with adult responsibilities;

those early farm duties had served him well.

Lukia sat down on the sleeper sofa next to Elena and watched Nina nurse. "You're careful you don't sit on the stove?"

"Mama, you tell me that every time. When Hania did that, it was winter. She was cold. I'm fine. Don't worry so much."

"I know. Worry doesn't help. But what can you do? It's a mother's curse." Her beautiful daughter Hania's death, like that of her other three children's, would never leave her.

The screen door opened and shut again. Mike appeared in the bedroom doorway. "Good day, Elena. How's the little one?"

"You can see for yourself."

He stood there, looking tenderly at his niece, then at Elena. "And how are you?"

"Fine." She adjusted the pillow under her arm.

Lukia said, "I brought you some borscht and piroshky."

"Thank you. We can have your food for lunch as soon as I'm finished here." She said to Mike, "Egnat's in the field. If you don't mind, tell him Mama's here and to come get a bite to eat."

While Elena swaddled Nina and placed her in a hammock outside, Lukia heated the borscht on the wood stove and Genya set the table. Not long after, Egnat entered the boxcar and embraced his mother.

She held his face and breathed in his tobacco smell. "You've done well, son. Another sweet child."

"Thank you, Mama." He poured the adults a shot of homebrew, which they cut with 7-Up.

"I guess you'll have a christening soon," Lukia said. "We can have lunch at my farm afterwards."

Egnat said, "That would be nice."

Elena put her arm around Lukia's waist. "We'd like Dunya to be godmother for Nina."

"Wonderful," Lukia said. "She would be proud to be Nina's godmother."

Once they were all seated at the table, Egnat raised his glass. "Daye Bozhe." He clinked his mother's glass, and Mike and Elena followed suit with the toast.

Lukia slurped her soup, content that her dream hadn't been a bad omen after all.

Winnipeg Bound

Mike moved Peter and Dolly to Ted's place, a two-storey wood rooming house with a veranda on Selkirk Avenue, east of Main Street, away from the business district. Ted rented them a room on the second floor with a hot plate, double bed, davenport, and bureau. The bathroom was down the hall, shared with three other tenants. They hoped to get a better place once they secured permanent jobs. Peter's job on the tracks would be over by the end of the summer, and Dolly would continue to do casual domestic work while dreaming of something better.

But their excitement about their future dimmed when Peter doubled over with stomach pain one evening after work. At first, they viewed his agony as serious, but then—because he had been such a healthy man—they figured it was probably something he ate and with time, it would go away. While he lay moaning on the davenport, Dolly took the little money they had from Peter selling her paper roses and left to repay Mrs. Ewanoski for the night's lodging after her mother-in-law's funeral.

When Mrs. Ewanoski opened the door, she immediately welcomed Dolly into her home. "Would you like some tea?"

"No, I can't stay. Peter's sick." She opened her purse and handed her mother's friend the money they owed. "Thank you again for putting us up for the night."

"Is it serious?"

"Stomach troubles. They should pass."

"My dear girl." Mrs. Ewanoski pressed the money into Dolly's hands. "Keep it. Forget about what you owe me. Keep it for good luck. You can buy Peter some whiskey to soothe his stomach."

"Oy, Panye Ewanoski, you're so kind."

"Go take care of your husband."

Dolly left her mother's friend, feeling richer than she had in a while. When she arrived home with a bottle of whiskey, Peter grinned despite his pain. The liquor dulled his agony and his stomach problems abated. He felt better in the morning and went to work.

Peter had never known a woman like Dolly. He had fallen in love with her spunk and beauty, but it was her resourcefulness that pleased him. Even with her waxed crepe paper roses, she wasn't content to make only red ones. She made yellow roses and various shades of pink ones, too. Parishioners at Sobor bought them, as did the dressmaker, Michelina, and Ted's friends.

Not knowing what lay ahead, Dolly said they had to keep scrimping. They had to save what they could, especially when they didn't know if or when their lot would sell. And since they had established a home in the city and wouldn't be returning to live in Stony Mountain, they also decided to sell their barn. To ease their money situation, Dolly invited Harry—who was looking for a place to rent—to share their quarters until a room became available on their floor. He used the davenport in their room, which made it awkward for both Peter and Dolly, but Harry helped with the rent, and for Dolly, the added income offset the loss of privacy for the time being.

Peter helped Harry carry his belongings into their room. As he watched Harry place his undershirts and socks in the bottom drawer of the bureau, he said, "Have you seen John Slipchenko lately?"

"No," Harry said. "He shipped out in May with the Winnipeg Grenadiers. They went to Jamaica."

"Jamaica? What the hell are they doing

there? Is Hitler threatening that island, too?"

Harry closed the drawer and sat down on the davenport. "The British government's worried France is going to fall. Jamaica's far away, but they want some military to man a garrison there. John said, they're going to send some troops to Bermuda, too."

Peter shook his head. He didn't know how a base in the Caribbean would assist the French, but the war was expanding all over the globe. In elementary school, he had meticulously drawn a map of the world. He thought of all the countries whose borders he'd drawn when he was in school. More than a few were quaking once again with enemy fire. You'd think humanity would have learned its lesson after the Great War. Its tragic consequences had affected everyone. Dolly had told him of how her father had suffered as a soldier in the Tsar's army. No one believed they'd face another world war in their lifetime, and yet, the world was once again engaged in a battle that was escalating rather than stopping.

He was proud of the map he'd drawn. It had been so accurate that his teacher had accused him of tracing it. She'd thrown his work in the garbage. She was also the one who had struck his knuckles when he wrote with his left hand.

Harry said, "You're deep in thought."

"It's this damn war," Peter said. Harry nodded. Pretty well anyone you met felt the same way.

Peter and Dolly adjusted to sharing their space with Harry, but then her cousin Alex arrived, asking if he could stay a few nights. His wife, Nancy, had kicked him out. Dolly thought he had a lot of nerve asking, especially when they hadn't been invited to his wedding. Alex was one of Petro's sons who had largely kept to himself. He had teased her mercilessly when they were children and their families lived together on the farm in Rosser. But she couldn't say no to a relative, so she let him sleep with Harry on the sleeper sofa. When Harry grumbled, Dolly said, "We're family. We don't turn family away."

They were all happy, though, when Nancy showed up a couple of days later, saying she was willing to try again. At first, Alex said, "No. I can't stand your mother. She's always bugging me."

"I'll talk to her," Nancy said, taking his arm and cozying up to him. In a sultry voice, she added, "I miss my big boy." She purred like a cat.

He laughed. He couldn't resist her Lana Turner looks—her flaming red lipstick and wavy blond hair.

Witnessing how they behaved—Alex and Nancy kibbitzed like kids—Dolly doubted they'd ever have children of their own. They were too intent on having fun, and having kids would only tie them down. At least, that's what Alex had told Peter privately.

Peter thought Lady Luck was looking out for them, because a day after Alex moved out, the tenant a few doors down gave his notice, prompting Harry to ask Ted if he could rent the room. Harry hadn't given them any trouble, but theirs was a small room and any intimate acts had to be placed on hold while he was there. Peter and Dolly were relieved when he moved down the hall.

One morning, when Dolly came out of the house carrying a basket of wet laundry to hang on the line in the backyard, she found Maureen, a tenant on the same floor, hanging her wash.

Maureen said, "Glad you took the room next to mine. The guy who was in there before you must've been a night owl."

"Night owl?"

"He stayed up all night playing his radio. Most folks have to get up in the morning. I complained to Ted about him.

Told him I was moving out if he didn't do something." She picked up her basket. "I have to get going."

"You have a job?" Dolly asked as she hung up some towels.

"I'm going downtown to wash store windows on Portage Avenue."

"You can do that?"

"Sure. Anyone can. All you need is a bucket, cloth, and hot water. The store owners supply the hot water. I supply the muscle."

"That is smart of you to find work like that. I have to find a job, too."

Maureen regarded her for a moment, then said, "Tell you what. Why don't you come along? We can work together. Get more windows done that way. Plus, I wouldn't mind the company."

Dolly hesitated. Though she was dressed respectably, she hated to get her good blouse and pants dirty. "Can you wait for me? I'll change fast."

Dressed in an old pair of pants and

one of Peter's old shirts, Dolly went with Maureen to board a streetcar going downtown. They walked up and down Portage Avenue, stopping at stores where the windows looked dirty. While Dolly waited outside with the bucket and clean cloths, Maureen went into a dress shop to ask the manager if he wanted the windows washed. It wasn't the type of activity Dolly had envisioned when she rode through this shopping area with Peter on the day of her engagement. That day, she had dreamt of being one of the fashionably dressed women flitting from shop to shop, admiring the dressed mannequins in the windows and deciding which outfit to purchase. While she waited for Maureen to come out, she stood to the side so she wouldn't block the window display. She watched shoppers stride by, holding their purses with white gloves, as if they had not a care in the world.

She recalled one of her mother's stories about how she'd seen an ex-suitor

and his wife driving by in a fancy carriage
while she was walking on the road to
Lutsk in the old country. An embarrassing
incident because she was dressed so
poorly. Dolly then thought about her
former fiancé, the Russian stock broker.
What if he drove by and saw her in a worn
man's shirt and ill-fitting pants washing
windows? That would be embarrassing,
too. He'd ask her what she was doing, and
she'd say, "What you see." And he'd say,
"Whose store is this?" And she'd say, "It's
mine. What does it look like?" She
imagined she would brush off her
discomfort with a toss of her head.

Maureen came out of the store and
winked. She grabbed the bucket from
Dolly and went back into the shop to fill it
with hot water.

By the end of the day, they had both
earned more than farmers paid hired
hands for a day's labour. Dolly was
grateful to Maureen for letting her tag
along, but she needed to find a better job,

one that didn't expose her to the public in that way. Life was tough enough without adding humiliation to the mix.

Bad June

Working on the tracks, Peter learned about all the political wrangling in the city and in the country. Outside of sharing the odd joke, his fellow workers talked of little else while they pulled up old rails.

That June, the Canadian government had proclaimed the Defence of Canada Regulations under the War Measures Act. Now that Benito Mussolini, the dictator of Italy, had declared war against France and the United Kingdom, all fascist organizations in Canada would be illegal. Though the idea of communism threatened many citizens—especially those who'd escaped the terrors of bolshevism in Russia—the police showing up unannounced at Jacob Penner's home shocked Peter and the men he worked with. Jacob Penner was a Winnipeg city councillor and a member of the Communist Party of Canada. Even Peter's foreman, Huxley, joined in to talk about the Commies.

"They arrested him because he's an avowed Communist," Huxley said.

The men alongside Peter grumbled about the arrest. Penner was starting his third term as city councillor, and was popular with the city workers because he listened to their complaints and tried to do something about them. Sympathetic, he was fighting the bigwigs on their behalf.

Huxley said, "They sent him to a camp for political prisoners outside of Calgary."

Joe, another worker, said, "That's where they're holding a few hundred Germans, who they suspect are Nazi sympathizers."

"Maybe so," Huxley said. "Maybe so."

Peter shared their concern but feared any alliance with those who supported communism. He remembered the Winnipeg General Strike, when thousands of workers walked out on their jobs. They marched down Main Street, demanding decent pay and better working conditions. He was nine years old at the time and, along with his friends, watched a crowd overturn a streetcar in front of City Hall. One man died; others survived beatings. Men, hired by the bosses, wielded billy clubs as they rode their horses through the mob of workers, striking anyone in their path.

His father had been one of those workers who complained about prices rising, unfair wages, job discrimination, and poor housing. He was a member of the Labour Temple on McGregor Avenue, a workers' organization that was considered communist because its building had been erected by volunteer Communist labour. That was also the time when thousands of soldiers were returning from fighting in the Great War. They were looking forward to civilian employment, only to find jobs scarce. They blamed the immigrants, like his dad—considered a "Bolshie" because of his Slavic name and ways. With the workers' march down Main Street broken up, his father was returning to his home on Dufferin Avenue when three veterans of that war began chasing him and calling him names. They chased him several blocks to his house, demanding he kiss the Union Jack. When Peter and his mother showed up at the door wondering what the ruckus was all about, one soldier grabbed her breasts. Peter looked for a stick to hit him with, but by the time he could find one, the soldiers had done their damage, leaving his father bruised and bleeding in the front yard.

Because of the unexpected beating, his father decided he'd had enough of the city and moved with his family to Stony

Mountain. The Winnipeg General Strike had left its scars on Peter, too. He developed a fear of being labelled a Commie. Lodged in his stomach, that fear gnawed at him, and he considered mentioning it to Dolly, but he did what his mother had always recommended when his stomach was upset: he chewed raw garlic. His mouth curled when he thought of how Ukrainians were called *garlic stinkers*. Well, stinkers or not, he thought, if something works to minimize your stomach cramps, then it had to be good, and who the hell cared what non-Ukrainians thought. As long as they didn't think he was a Communist.

June, typically a glorious month with lilacs in bloom and fields sprouting with vegetables and grain, turned out to be difficult one for Lukia. With only one son to help her, she was working much harder than when Egnat and Dunya were at home. Rheumatism had set in, and she had to wear heavy cotton stockings to relieve the aches in her legs. At night, she slept with a hot-water bag between them. Occasionally, she felt a twinge in her chest and knew she'd have to go into the city soon to get her blood pressure checked by Dr. Ryback.

Exhausted at the end of one day in June, she fell asleep instantly, her dreams churning with images of rotting fields and uncut grain and Mike's contorted face and mouth agape wandering aimlessly down a road. She woke up at dawn to a quiet house. At first, she thought Mike had risen earlier and was already out in the barn, but when she passed his room, she saw that his bed hadn't been slept in. His truck wasn't parked out front, either. Where was he? He'd stayed in the city overnight before, but now, thanks to her tortured dreams, she worried he'd had an accident. She threw on a sweater and rushed to the barn, thinking that maybe his truck had broken down and he got a lift home and was already milking the cows. But the only sounds that greeted her in the barn were the gentle mooing of Bossie and the shuffling of the other cows' feet. Bossie nodded when Lukia approached, setting the milking stool beside her.

"Yes, just you and me," Lukia said. Pulling the teats, she thought of what she might do if Mike didn't show up by nightfall. One of her neighbours had a phone. Perhaps she could walk there and ask them to call someone, but who? Neither Egnat nor Dunya had a phone. In her ruminations, Lukia must've yanked Bossie too hard, as she stomped her feet and moved back. Lukia patted her rump and said, "Sorry."

Later, after Lukia had milked the cows and fed the animals, she went back to the house and began mincing garlic, its fragrance soothing her troubled mind. She was cutting slivers of raw beets when she heard a vehicle pull up on the gravel road, then car doors slamming. She looked out the window to see both Egnat's car and

Mike's truck. Her sons walked towards the house, Mike with his head bent.

She opened the door. "What happened?" she shouted, her voice cracking.

Egnat wore a pinched expression. Mike kept his dishevelled head down as he brushed past her into the house. Egnat took off his soiled cap and held it in his lap as he sat down at the kitchen table. Mike stood, looking as if he had come home in duress, wanting to be anywhere but here.

She sat down, too. "Nu, tell me what happened."

Egnat stared at Mike. "Are you going to tell Mama?"

Lukia waited a moment, then said to Mike, "You don't have a tongue?"

When Mike kept his eyes down and stayed silent, Egnat said, "He told the police he had a brother in Stonewall. They came to my farm early this morning. It was still dark out. They told me Mike was in the city jail."

"What? Jail?" She turned to Mike. "You were in jail?"

"He and another man got picked up for speeding down Main Street and Logan Avenue at three o'clock in the morning. The police found two gallons of homebrew in the car. They said he had to pay two hundred dollars in costs or face three months in jail."

"Oy, oy, oy. What a durak!"

At being called a fool, Mike quickly turned away.

"What am I going to do with you? You're not a little boy anymore. Did Egnat bail you out? Is that why they let you out?"

Mike didn't answer and kept his head bowed.

Lukia glared at Mike. "I don't know what to say. Two *gallons*? Have you nothing to say for yourself?"

"I'm sorry, Mama."

"You're always sorry."

"What were you doing with all that horilka?"

Mike avoided her eyes. Egnat said,

"He's been selling it. Bootlegging."

Lukia groaned. "What were you thinking? Do you want them to send you back to the old country?"

Egnat said to Mike, "I should've left you in jail. Maybe you'd learn, then."

Mike mumbled something and headed for his room.

Lukia shook her head. "Now he's going to sleep half the day. Why has God punished me like this? Two hundred dollars! My God. I'll pay you back."

"Mama," said Egnat, "how can you pay me?"

"Nu, I'll pay you."

"No." He stuck a cigarette in his mouth and dug into his pockets for a match. "Elena was very upset."

"Of course. You're living in a boxcar, and he's running around like a big shot. Hanging around with the wrong people." She murmured, "It's a tragedy. He's lucky he has you, but how long is this going to go on?"

Egnat had no answers. Having slept little, he looked haggard. "I have to go. My work is waiting."

"I know. Thank you, son." She followed him out the door and didn't wait for him to drive off. Moaning, she walked to the barn; their new dog, a black-and-white mutt, ran ahead. It was time to take the cows to pasture. There was no point talking to Mike. He didn't listen. What else had to happen before he came to his senses? What would Gregory say? There was only so much a mother could do. You raise your children, teach them the Ten Commandments, ask them to be respectful to their elders, and to work hard to get ahead in life. You tell them to treat others as they would like to be treated, and not to be foolish. What a fool her son was! *Dear God*, she asked, *what shall I do? What else can I tell my son that will change his course in life? If he hasn't seen by my example and his brothers' how to live, what else can I do to open his eyes?* She muttered under her breath, opened the barn door, and let the cows out.

Weeks later, Lukia received more bad news. Sitting in a front pew at Sobor, she listened attentively to Father Mayewsky, who, after reading from his list of church announcements, gazed at the congregation and said, "Hitler has invaded Ukraine." Lukia gasped. She turned to see several parishioners buzzing; a few nodded as if they'd already heard this tragic news. So many had relatives in their native land. The priest added that there were German troops assaulting the Soviet Union on several fronts. He then said, "Let us pray for Ukraine."

They prayed and sang Ukraine's national anthem, "Ukraine has not yet perished." The voices of the choir and congregants resounded through the basement with more than the usual fervour. Lukia shivered when they sang

the lyrics: "Our enemies will die, as the
dew does in the sunshine, and we,
brothers, will live happily in our land."
Yes, enemies might die, Lukia thought,
*but also her countrymen. War wasn't kind
to either side.*

The choir followed the anthem with a
prayer for Ukraine, written in the last
century by the composer Mykola Lysenko.
"Lord, of the Great and Almighty, protect
our beloved Ukraine. Bless her with
freedom and light of your holy rays." As
the choir continued to sing the hymn,
Lukia searched in her purse for her
handkerchief to dry her tears. She joined
in the last chorus, her voice rising with the
others as she came to the end. "Bless us
with freedom, bless us with wisdom; guide
us into the kind world; bless us, oh Lord,
with good fortune, for ever and
evermore." The passion with which the
congregation sang made their sorrow
even more palpable.

After the service, Lukia sought Maria

Karpinsky in the churchyard. They discussed their children first, then brought up their fears about Volhynia. Maria said, "You know how it is. Some Ukrainians will think the enemy of their enemy is their friend. They'll think the Germans are going to help them gain independence from the Russians."

"Aagh," Lukia said. "Who would believe them? Look what they've done to Poland. Father Mayewsky never mentioned if Hitler's army is in Volhynia."

"Who knows."

"I'll have to ask Egnat to write my brother. Give my best to your sons and daughter."

"You, too, Lukia. Stay strong."

Lukia looked at her watch. Mike should've been back by now. Thinking he might've parked around the corner, she walked towards the street. Natasha, who had been chatting with a few other women on the other side of the lawn, broke company with them and came up to

Lukia on the sidewalk in front of the church.

They greeted one another with hugs. "Nu, Natasha, how is everything with you, your husband, your children?"

"Good, And with you?"

"You know how it is since Egnat left."

"That's how it is. But what can you do?" Panye Hyworon waved as she walked by and both women waved back. "Listen, I have some news about Father Mayewsky."

"What news? Are we going to lose him?"

Natasha laughed. "No. The Supreme Court decided once and for all he can stay on as a priest, but he has to return the antimins to the Consistory."

"What is that? Antimins?"

"It's the consecrated cloth square he uses to celebrate mass."

Lukia recalled the delicate lace-edged square Father Mayewsky used to hold the chalice of wine for communion. "Are they going to take it away from him? What will he use then?"

Natasha sighed. "He'll need something. If they take it away, they'll have to get him another one. At least our priest can attend to church business now instead of fighting for his rights in court."

"Thanks be to God." Lukia watched Mike drive up in their truck. "Nu, Natasha, take care of yourself. Until we see each other again."

On the way home, Lukia told Mike what she'd heard in church about the war reaching Volhynia. "Good thing God gave us the courage to leave when we did," she said. She could not fathom living through another world war and having to run for her life again.

Chrysler Imperial

Sundays were a day of rest. After church, Harry offered to take Dolly and Peter for a ride in John Slipchenko's car to a community picnic in the country. John's wife, Anna, didn't drive, and she had asked Harry to take the car for a run. It had been sitting idle in their garage ever since her husband had joined the Winnipeg Grenadiers.

Eager to get going, Dolly kept glancing at her watch and running to the window of their room on the second floor to see if her brother had arrived. He'd taken the bus to Slipchenko's home to pick up the car. Looking down to the street, all she saw was a parked car—banged up and black; it wasn't John Slipchenko's late-model navy blue Chrysler. She knew his car, because he had driven it to church a few months before he'd enlisted. It had caused quite a stir. Though quite a few parishioners owned cars and trucks, there was only one other that compared in luxury to the one John drove.

"You're jumping like a rabbit," Peter said, putting his suit jacket on.

"So what if I am?" she retorted. It was a beautiful day and a drive in an automobile would be a treat. It would take her mind off their property in Stony Mountain, which still hadn't sold. When they last visited the village, Dan Balacko said he'd seen a few people sniffing around their notice pinned to the community board, but didn't know if they had taken the information down. Dolly asked him if he was interested, and all he did was laugh.

She returned to the bedroom bureau mirror to adjust the combs in her hair and

the suspenders on her trousers. After
she'd seen films with Katharine Hepburn
and Marlene Dietrich wearing trousers,
she saved to buy a pair and wore them
more often than a dress. Olga told her
that Miss Hepburn had been wearing
slacks for almost ten years and had had
half-a-dozen custom ones made. And just
last year, *Vogue*, a rich woman's
magazine, had its models photographed in
trousers. The photos showed that women
in pants were daring, sure of themselves,
and liberated.

Growing up with three brothers, Dolly
had learned early on to hold her own with
them. She regarded men's work as work a
woman could easily do. She'd done her
share of manly labour on the farm: driving
the tractor, helping with threshing, and
shovelling what needed to be shovelled.
And she liked to show her strength by
squeezing men's hands when the
opportunity came to shake them. It didn't
matter if they wore rings. She delighted at

seeing them spread their fingers in pain afterwards. She chuckled every time she thought of the hands she had pressed. She wanted men to know she was not a woman to be dismissed easily.

When she heard a car honk, she quickly tucked her white shirt into the waistband of her slacks and ran to the window. "He's here."

She took the picnic basket, packed with a potato salad, a jar of dill pickles, a dozen oatmeal cookies she'd baked in Ted's oven, four plates and forks, and rushed downstairs. Peter carried a blanket and a brown paper shopping bag containing a mickey of homebrew and four glasses.

Harry was standing on the curb, waiting for them. He had arrived with his new girlfriend, Betty, who showed up dressed in a modern pantsuit, with her curly dark-brown hair pinned back, like the style Ginger Rogers wore in all the musicals.

"Did you bring the kybassa?" Dolly asked.

Harry grinned. "Yes, and a loaf of rye bread."

After introducing his girlfriend to Peter and Dolly, Harry showed them the car.

Peter whistled. "It's a beauty."

"It's a 1935 Chrysler Airflow Imperial. All-steel body. Whitewall tires. Safety-glass windows."

"I love your suit," Dolly said to Betty. "Where did you buy it?"

"Dayton's, on Portage Avenue." It was a shop known to have the latest styles of dresses and suits for ladies. Just the other day, Peter had read their advertisement in the newspaper, illustrating a man-tailored suit for ladies. The ad said it was a friendly credit store. All you needed was a small down payment and you could pay the balance at your convenience. Admiring Betty's suit, Dolly figured that as soon as she had a little more saved up, she would buy herself one, too.

Harry opened the hood of the car for Peter. "It's a V8 engine, eight cylinders, lots of horsepower. Double-acting shock absorbers, automatic choke. And it's not too bad on gas." He closed the hood.

"How many miles to a gallon?" Dolly asked.

"About twelve. If I keep the speed at twenty miles an hour, I can get fourteen."

"That's impressive," Peter said.

Dolly said, "Let's go." Not waiting for Peter to open the car door, she opened it herself and climbed into the back seat. Peter followed. The car was as beautiful inside as it was out, with cream leather upholstery on the bench-style seats and a woodgrain dashboard.

"Make sure your hands are clean," Harry said, getting into the driver's seat. He turned to Peter. "It has a three-speed transmission."

"Can we go already?" Dolly said.

Harry chuckled. "Hold your horses," he said, and started the car.

Dolly relaxed and sat back as they pulled into the street.

Though she couldn't wait to get out into the country and see how the car performed on the highway, she delighted in the looks they got from the pedestrians they passed and from other drivers that pulled up next to their car at stoplights. She sat up straighter and smiled as if she was royalty.

When they got to an open stretch of highway, she said, "Okay, Harry. Show us what the car can do."

Harry pressed the accelerator down. Dolly opened her side window and stuck her head out to feel the wind on her face. "Can you go faster?" she asked.

He pushed the pedal down and she watched the needle on the speedometer move to forty-five miles per hour. At that speed, the motor purred.

Harry said, raising his voice over the sound of the engine, "At forty-five miles per hour, it goes into overdrive and the hum of the motor fades."

Peter leaned forward to inspect the instrument panel. "You've even got an ashtray, front and back. That's really something."

When they arrived at the picnic, put on by the church Betty attended, their arrival caused quite a stir. Most people had come by wagon or truck or bicycle. Theirs was one of only a few vehicles there, and the others were no match for the luxury car Harry had driven. She saw her brother's chest puff out as he showed a few locals the engine and the interior. Some of Harry's pride rubbed off on her, though she knew it would be a long time before she and Peter could afford any kind of car.

Afterwards, Betty took photos of Dolly and Peter sitting on the hood of the car, and Peter took one of Betty, Harry, and Dolly perched on the hood as well.

When the men began to talk about the war overseas, Dolly suggested to Betty they take a walk around the grounds. She didn't want any bad news to spoil an otherwise lovely day. On the way home, they planned to stop in to see her mother. How she was getting along was another worry. Dolly had talked to her mother about giving up the farm, how it was too much work with only one son left to help her, but her mother didn't want to hear any of it. She said she wanted to help Mike improve his lot in life. But how could her mother do that when her brother showed no interest in following her guidance?

Canada Packers

Hoping to get a better job than house cleaning, Dolly thought again about the pant suit Betty had worn to the church picnic. With so many men overseas, women had taken over their jobs in the factories and had also adopted wearing pants to work.

One afternoon, she took the streetcar to Dayton's Dress Shop, across from Eaton's on Portage Avenue. She tried on several pantsuits, but the one that caught her eye was a dark green wool and rayon one with thin orange stripes, on sale for $15.95, regular thirty dollars. She turned in the three-sided mirror to view it from all sides, while the store clerk issued flattering statements. "It fits you perfectly, dear. The colour brings out your hazel eyes."

The clerk was right. It fit her beautifully, nipping in at the waist to show off her curves, but it was expensive, even with its marked-down price. She hoped to put down a deposit, but when she got to the till, the clerk said, "I'm sorry, but you'll have to get your husband to come in and sign for you."

Taken aback, Dolly stood there with her mouth agape. Peter didn't have a steady job. He wouldn't qualify, either.

"Ma'am," the clerk said, "do you want me to hold it for you?"

"What do you mean?"

"I'll put your name on it and hang it on a rack at the back until your husband comes in. We can hold it for three days."

"Yes, please," Dolly said.

"Three days, no longer."

Dolly left the store upset. How was she possibly going to buy it?

Back home, Dolly complained to Peter over supper. "How am I going to be taken seriously in a dress? I need a pants outfit. Peter, it fits me like a glove." Poking at her food, she ate her fried liver and onions with a fallen face. She kept thinking of how she could get the trouser suit she needed.

"What about your brothers?" Peter asked. "Could one of them help?"

She pursed her lips. "Egnat and Mike are farmers. I don't know if their income would count. It's so unreliable. I'd hate to drag them to the store and get rejected again." As for her brother Harry, he'd recently bought a car on credit and was making payments. She didn't think he could afford to sign on to another debt.

They ate in silence for a bit, then he said, "I think I know who to ask."

"Who?"

"You'll see," he said, smiling.

Since she had criticized Peter's family so much, it surprised her when her father-in-law agreed to co-sign the credit application. He accompanied her to Dayton's so she could buy her much-desired suit. Thrilled, Dolly wore it home on the streetcar. Sure that all the glances in her direction were admiring ones, she couldn't wait to apply for jobs.

On Saturday, she bought a *Winnipeg Free Press* newspaper at the grocery store and, with Peter's help, combed the Help Wanted ads. Outside of domestic help ads, there weren't many she was qualified for. Her broken English made it impossible to get a job in a department store or any other place where you had to meet the public. Her accent was a dead giveaway, and even though Ukrainian Canadians had signed up to fight in large numbers, prejudice hadn't abated.

Discouraged by the ads she'd seen in the paper, she wondered how she'd be able to find a well-paying job. These thoughts consumed her as she left the house Monday morning to buy fixings for that evening's meal. As usual, the public market filling one square block on Main Street was busy with shoppers checking one stall after the other to buy vegetables, fruit, fish, meat, and poultry.

While she was standing in line to buy a chicken—freshly killed, with its feathers still on—she saw Michelina, her previous employer, standing at another stall nearby. Dolly had stopped working for her when the seamstress's uncle wouldn't leave her alone. His remarks and attempts to fondle Dolly had become too much, so she quit. Michelina understood, but she couldn't throw her uncle out on the street. He was her mother's brother, and Michelina had made a promise to her family to care for him.

Dolly paid for the chicken—which the seller wrapped in brown waxed paper and placed in her shopping bag—then waited at the other stall for Michelina to complete her purchase. After exchanging a few pleasantries and asking whether her uncle still lived with her—he did—Dolly told the dressmaker she was looking for employment in the city and wanted to make more per hour than what domestic help was getting.

"Canada Packers are hiring women," Michelina said. "My cousin got a job there."

"What's Canada Packers?"

"A big meat-packing plant. They process beef and pork. They make wieners, bacon, baloney, sausages ..."

"Do they ask about schooling?"

Michelina shook her head. "No. They don't care if you went to school or not, as long as you can do the job."

"Where's Canada Packers?"

"In St. Boniface. Next to the Union Stockyards."

Dolly scrunched her forehead. "Not in Winnipeg?"

"It's the French city, right next to Winnipeg."

Michelina dug in her purse for a pen and wrote the information on Dolly's paper shopping bag. "You can take a streetcar there. Good luck."

Excited about the possibility, Dolly barely slept a wink that night. In the morning, she got up with Peter to make him breakfast. She put on her new pant suit, fastened her hair back with combs, and made sure she had enough money for the transit fares to the factory and back. Peter told her she'd have to transfer from a streetcar to a trolleybus to get to her destination.

Anxious, she sat near the driver in both vehicles, and kept asking how much further she had to go. When she saw a series of train tracks, a water tower, and hundreds of sheep and cattle herded into pens, she stood and asked to be let off. Stepping off the trolleybus, she inhaled the most awful stench. She assumed it came from the droppings of the penned-up livestock, but maybe, she thought, the overwhelming smell had come from the actual slaughter of the livestock. She curled her nose and strode to the factory.

When she reached the front door, she took a few deep breaths before grabbing the door handle. She needed to calm herself before entering the meat-packing plant.

Inside the entranceway, the smell of freshly cut meat assaulted her, and she wrinkled her nose. Though the odour was unpleasant, the corridor was spotless. The first person she met was a man dressed in a tweed cap and white coveralls stained with blood and unknown brown marks. He inspected her as if he was appraising cattle.

Ignoring his rude behaviour, she said, "Please, sir, where is the office?"

He cocked his head. "You're looking for a job?"

"Yes."

He asked her to follow him to the office, and when he opened the door, he said to the clerk at the desk, "Here's another one for you," then left.

The clerk, a young woman with a pleasing, round face and red hair, looked up from her papers and smiled. After Dolly asked about a job, the clerk gave her a pen and a form to fill out.

For a few moments, Dolly stood there, unsure of what to do. She didn't want to admit she couldn't read, so she said, "I'm sorry, but I forgot my glasses. Please write it for me?"

"Sure thing, honey."

Dolly gave the clerk her name, address, and previous work history. After filling the form out for Dolly, the young woman picked up her phone and called someone. "The foreman will be right out." She smiled again. "Nice suit."

"Thank you," said Dolly, beaming. "I got it at Dayton's."

While Dolly waited, the clerk busied herself with some papers on her desk. Soon, a short, bald man in stained overalls walked into the office. "Here you go, Elmer," she said, handing him Dolly's application.

Elmer studied the form and appraised Dolly as well. "Okay then, Mrs. Klewchuk. You can start tomorrow. Be here at 7 a.m."

"I got the job?"

"Yes, madam. You got the job."

"What will I do?"

Elmer said, "You'll get trained in cutting bacon or wrapping hams or lard. All depends on what we need. Don't wear anything good here if you want to keep it that way. We'll give you coveralls. Cover your hair with a hairnet and scarf. Stuff flies around here. You wouldn't want any of that to get in your hair."

"And how much pay, please?"

"Thirty cents an hour to start."

"Okay," Dolly said, and shook his hand. She felt like jumping up and down with joy. Though she contained her enthusiasm, she couldn't help but beam.

Thirty cents an hour was more than she'd made anywhere else.

The foreman left first. As Dolly turned to exit the office, the clerk said, "The pay's good, and sometimes you get overtime. Then they pay time-and-a-half. And you can buy bacon ends at the end of your shift for a fraction of the cost of store-bought bacon. See you tomorrow."

"Yes. See you tomorrow." Dolly skipped out of Canada Packers and down the sidewalk to the trolleybus stop. She left feeling she could accomplish anything.

Letters Home

After his job dismantling tracks ended, Peter—encouraged by Dolly's success at Canada Packers—secured a position at Western Packing, pumping salt into hams. The meat-packing industry was one workplace that hired Ukrainian immigrants. Factories were full of them. The bosses knew Ukrainians worked hard and were willing to put up with lousy work conditions. Every morning, unemployed men and women lined up at the gates looking for work. Peter was hired because he was young and strong. Men made more per hour than women, so his take-home pay was better than Dolly's. Though irked by the inequality, she appreciated the steady work and paycheck.

Peter, however, found his job tedious. He stood on his feet all day in a cold, windowless room with the floors and walls wet from the carcasses being hosed down. It was also challenging work because of safety concerns. He had to be careful because of the slippery floors and crowded workplace. After work, he and Dolly would soak their hands in hot water to soothe their aching muscles and the occasional cut. Slicing bacon, Dolly found it hard to avoid cuts, but she never complained. He thought her stamina and tolerance came from being raised on a farm, where it was common to get scraped and bruised doing chores. Though she agreed they had tough jobs, she teased him when he groaned or muttered about the work, and reminded him they were lucky to get employment. In his wildest dreams, he had never imagined this was where he'd end up. He had once dreamed of becoming a singer or a musician, but that kind of work wouldn't support a wife—or the family they both desired.

His brothers continued to write. Their letters took Peter's mind off the dreariness of his job. They were still waiting for deployment to the front lines. Bill continued to train in England and George hadn't left Canada yet. He had moved east to Ontario, where he was training at Camp Borden. His wife Anne had given birth to a baby girl, Barbara Anne. George wrote: *Poor Anne almost died giving birth. I visited her in the hospital, and as I was leaving her room, a nurse said to me, 'That lady isn't going to make it.' She didn't know I was that lady's husband.*

Peter wished he could reach across the pages and see his niece. It was going to be tough for Anne, with her husband across the ocean. George also wrote: *We had to give up our horses. Lord Strathcona's Horse (Royal Canadian) is now an armoured regiment. The higher ups now say we're the 1ˢᵗ Canadian*

Armoured Brigade. It appears we're going to get training commanding the tanks when we head overseas.

Peter couldn't believe that his younger brother would be in command of such heavy artillery. In their teens, they had shot .22 rifles, hitting tin cans off posts and trying to get the odd rabbit for Mother, but this was something else. But the part that really hit him in the gut was George's next lines: *I don't know how you'll feel about this, Peter, but both Bill and I changed our names from Klewchuk to Kendall. We don't want to just be the grunts in the armed forces. You can't advance or get decent treatment if you're a Hunky. I hope you understand. I haven't told Father and you can do as you like, but I'm pretty sure he won't be happy.*

There was no way Peter would be the bearer of that news. His father was proud of his roots, even though he hadn't had an easy go of life in the village. Peter stared at George's beautiful penmanship. He didn't like the fact his brothers had changed their name, but he understood their dilemma. Men of Anglo-Saxon stock held the top leadership positions in the forces and would be the ones recommending advancement. They could make or break your career, and like anywhere else in Canada, many of them looked down on people of his ancestry. Nothing you could do about that.

Peter thought it was funny that Bill hadn't mentioned the name change in his letter. Perhaps it was because they'd been close and he knew Peter would frown on his giving in to the British in that way.

Bill had described life in Britain as exciting but grim, given the daily fears of its citizens. With the way Hitler was behaving, the British feared they'd be next.

And sure enough, in September, the Nazis began bombing Britain. Newsreels at the movie theatres showed German planes raining bombs over London and

Londoners clutching their children's hands and running scared into the bomb shelters. Many families in England, afraid their children would die in one of these raids, sent them away, many to Canada.

What surprised loyalists everywhere was the fact that King George VI and Queen Elizabeth didn't escape the city but stayed in London and toured the shelled areas to give the locals support. But when a bomb hit the grounds of Buckingham Palace, people wondered about the wisdom of their decision. People sang "God Save the King" with more emotion than ever before.

On their next trip to Stony Mountain to see Peter's father and see how the structure on their lot was holding up, they met locals who admired the royals' bravery and were busy providing bundles for Britain. Patriotism was in plain view everywhere they walked. Though the village was small—only three hundred and eighty inhabitants—the residents bragged they had the highest per capita number enlisting in the entire British Commonwealth. To pray for those in England who were in harm's way, the village held a joint dedication service one Sunday evening in the Stony Mountain school auditorium, conducted by the rector of the Anglican church and the minister of the United Church. People brought their bundles and piled them in front of the platform. Choirs from both congregations, along with school children, sang, "O God Our Help in Ages Past," and "Fight the Good Fight." Peter wished he could have attended.

Knowing how the war had escalated overseas and how powerless he was to serve added to his frustration. He choked up when he received a letter from the Canadian government saying, *What will your kids say if you don't go to war?* He had no kids, but someday he might, and he expected they'd ask him what he had done during the war years. All around him, people talked about their sons and daughters in the forces. He tried to avoid these conversations, but it was impossible. There were signs everywhere dedicated to the war effort: signs to enlist, signs to buy war bonds, signs to write letters to soldiers.

There was some talk the government might loosen the requirements to join. He tried to talk to Dolly about his feelings, but she didn't understand. Instead of offering words of sympathy, she said, "They didn't want you when you were single; there's no point in you going now under the bullet."

For now, he couldn't join if he wanted to. He didn't tell her he had high hopes the recruiting offices would soon open up enlistment to those less educated.

Then in early fall, Peter had an accident. Perhaps it wouldn't have happened if all the problems on his mind hadn't affected his concentration. He had woken up tired that morning, which wasn't surprising given that he cycled miles to work there and back to save on streetcar fare and stood on his feet for eight hours every day. But he was more tired than usual because they'd gone to the theatre the night before, watched two films, and didn't get home until after midnight. Usually, he was cautious as he cycled through intersections and passed parked vehicles, but today, his mind kept reviewing what George had written. His brothers' name change troubled him. He expected now that George had an English wife and an English name, he was passing as such. It seemed obvious his brothers were ashamed of their Ukrainian roots. Absorbed in these thoughts, Peter didn't see the truck coming. The next thing he knew, he had tumbled to the ground. As he lay there, sprawled in the middle of the street, the first thing he thought of was the condition of his bike.

"Are you alright?" a gruff voice asked.

Stunned, Peter looked up at a robust man in a plaid shirt standing over him. He put out his hand and Peter grabbed it, groaning as he stood up on shaky legs. His back and side ached from the fall and his head was a cloud of confusion.

"You came out of nowhere," the man said as he picked up Peter's bicycle. The fender was bent, but the man straightened it enough for Peter to ride.

"I'll be okay," Peter said, though he wasn't sure if that was true. He stretched his shoulders one way, then the other, hoping to loosen the kinks and minimize the pain.

"You sure now? I can take you to the hospital to get checked out."

"No, no, I'm fine." The thought of going to a hospital scared him more than the thought that he might have injured himself for life. He couldn't afford to pay for an X-ray or any other medical procedure. The political parties had talked about setting up a public health care system, but so far, it wasn't happening.

Though shaken up, he took the bike from the man and said, "Thanks for your help. I'll be on my way." His tweed cap had flown off in the crash. He found it across the street, where it had landed next to the tire of a parked car. He dusted it off and put it back on. He could feel the pain streaking down his back, from his neck to the base of his spine, but he climbed on the seat and pedalled north. Every turn of the pedals irritated his limbs, the pangs reminding him of his almost fatal encounter. What if the truck had run over him, rather than clipped him at an angle? He would have been a goner. Life could be taken away in an instant if you weren't paying attention.

When he told Dolly about his mishap, she said, "Oy, Peter. God was looking out for you." She helped him take off his shirt and trousers and had him lie down on the bed while she rubbed his sore spots with liniment.

In the morning, he awoke early as usual, but he had trouble getting out of bed. His back and side ached from the fall. His body told him it would take a long time to recover from what he'd lost in the accident.

A Welcome Proposition

It had been almost a year since Dolly and Peter had moved to the city. Their lot still hadn't sold, but their barn had. They got fifty dollars—what they had paid for it—and Dolly immediately put the money into their savings account at the bank. They figured their lot hadn't sold because, rather than growing, the village seemed to be dying, or maybe it only felt that way because of all the missing youth. The only ones remaining were those who worked in the penitentiary, the quarry, or the few stores in town. The mayor had hoped that the new movie theatre would spark some interest, but so far, the number of residents had remained the same.

Their unpaid taxes on the lot now included additional penalties for failure to pay on time. With money owing to the municipality, Peter received regular warning letters stating they were in arrears and would lose their property if they couldn't pay. Not wanting to lose their investment, Dolly rode their bicycle several miles to the home of Walter Swystun, the lawyer and choir director at her church, to ask for his help, but he said there was nothing he could do if they didn't pay their taxes.

The problem gnawed at Dolly, causing many sleepless nights. It continued to gnaw at her during the Easter Sunday service at St. Mary the Protectress Church. The lively hymn, "Christ is Risen," sung repeatedly by the choir, did little to quell her anxiety. She gazed at the two vases of white Easter lilies on the altar, the fresh flowers pinned by the Ladies' Auxiliary on the lapels of parishioners, and the new straw hats the women wore. The most joyous day of the year, her mother's favourite holiday, should have raised Dolly's spirits, but all she could think of throughout the Divine Liturgy was the impending loss of their investment—all their money, time, sweat and tears.

During the priest's sermon, Dolly glanced at her mother listening, her hands folded in her lap, while he droned on about the need to repent and how you couldn't be saved if you didn't ask God to forgive your sins. How her mother could continue to rely on God after what she'd been through was a mystery. Dolly prayed, but she knew God wouldn't save her from her current woes. And He wouldn't save her from her mother's scolding. She'd warned Dolly about marrying Peter. How was Dolly going to tell her mother they were about to lose the property they'd bought with the money they'd been given? Dolly swallowed hard. Perhaps she'd raise the problem after they'd had a few drinks at the farm. Her mother would find out soon enough, and Dolly would rather be the one to tell her.

After the service, the congregants gathered in a large circle in the churchyard and placed their Easter baskets at their feet for the priest to bless. Her mother unfolded the embroidered cloth that covered her basket to reveal two tall paskas, a ring of kybassa, a thick square of butter with a cross made of whole cloves on top, two peeled hard-boiled eggs, five eggs coloured with beet and onion dyes, and a small dish of red horseradish. Now that she was a married woman, Dolly felt badly she hadn't prepared a basket of her own, nor had she made anything for the Easter lunch afterwards, but with the long hours working in the city she'd had no time.

Elena positioned her basket next to Lukia's on the ground. Genya and Vera hovered nearby, admiring all the different baskets and watching the priest walk among the parishioners, waving his censer and making the sign of the cross while he and the deacon sang the hymn, "God is Risen."

Dolly said to Elena, "How's Genya feeling?"

"Better." Genya had left the service earlier. Her mother had taken her outside when the smell of the incense had made her nauseous and dizzy.

Dolly looked back at a group of men standing outside the circle of women. Peter stood talking with Egnat and Mike, who'd both lit up a cigarette. She saw her husband take a quick step back; he hated being too close to smoke. He said it bothered his lungs. Arkady Karpinsky and his two sons, Boris and Victor, joined them, and she guessed they were catching up with one another about the farm and how Peter was managing in the city. She glanced again at her mother, who was following the priest with her eyes as he blessed the baskets of the worshippers. She would not be happy when she learned about the lot.

Back on the farm, Dolly's stomach churned as she helped her mother and Elena get the dishes to the table. Though she planned to tell her mother about the lot after the meal, it was hard to wait. She fidgeted, but her mother and the others didn't seem to notice. There was too much excitement. Easter was always the time for a feast, and Lukia and Elena didn't disappoint. They had prepared a roast chicken, kybassa, kishka, holupchi, nalysnyky, studenetz, varenyky with three different fillings—potato, bacon and onion; cottage cheese and potato; and sauerkraut—plus mushrooms fried in butter with onions, pickled beets, garlic dill pickles, cooked carrots and yellow wax beans. And three different offerings of dessert—honey cake, cheesecake, and hrystyki.

But the other excitement in the

household involved Harry and his new girlfriend, Marike Bartosh. She had curly brown hair, a round face and sparkling brown eyes, and she stood a shade shorter than Harry. Quiet like him, she offered to help in the kitchen, which pleased Lukia. He'd met her at a café on Main Street, where she worked as a short-order cook. Dolly told her brother privately that she thought he and Marike went together like bread and butter. His face reddened, but he looked delighted his sister had given her approval.

With the dishes on the table and horilka poured into all the short glasses, Lukia stood at the head of the table, crossed herself three times and, along with the others, said the Lord's Prayer. She then passed the plate with the blessed hard-boiled egg cut into ten pieces, one for every member of the family and Marike. Each piece represented family unity and hope for a happy and prosperous year until next Easter.

The entertaining part of the meal was at the end with the cracking of coloured eggs. Dolly laughed as Egnat made a big production out of checking the hardness of his egg. He clicked his teeth on the shell twice and, dissatisfied, traded it for another coloured egg in the bowl. Harry looked on with interest, but waited to pick one to crack. Mike had an ongoing rivalry with his older brother and took a little time selecting his, picking up one egg, then putting it down before testing another.

Approaching Peter on the other side of the table, Egnat led the egg cracking ritual. "Hrystos Voskres!" he said.

Peter replied, as was the custom, "Indeed He is risen."

Egnat successfully cracked one end of Peter's egg and chortled. Then Peter turned his egg over and Egnat cracked the other end as well. Leaving his brother-in-law to peel his boiled egg, Egnat went on to find another family member with an unbroken egg.

Once everyone had had a turn with this ritual, Egnat poured more horilka. Dolly tried to catch Peter's eye, but he was looking at his glass as Egnat refilled it to the brim. She knew she'd have to say something soon, before her family started singing and drinking too much to listen.

Dolly cleared her throat. "Mama," she said sharply, which caused her mother to turn towards her. "Mama, I'm afraid we're going to lose our lot. We can't pay the taxes."

Egnat straightened up in his seat and leaned towards her. "So, you're going to walk away and leave everything there for people to take?"

"We're trying to sell the lot and the house frame, but with the men gone to war, there isn't anyone interested in buying an unfinished home." She threw her hands up in despair.

There was silence around the table, except for her mother. "Oy, oy, oy. Tragedy."

Her mother's words echoed in her ears. Unable to tolerate her mother's disappointment, Dolly stood up to clear the dishes.

"Wait," said Egnat. "Sit down."

"Why?" Dolly remained standing.

"How much were all your materials, including the roofing tiles?"

"Two hundred and fifty dollars."

Egnat said, "We're living in a boxcar now, but I want to build a house. How about I give you the money for your structure and I'll move it to my farm in Stonewall?"

Dolly and Peter exchanged wide-eyed looks. She said to Egnat, "You'd do that?"

He nodded.

Lukia raised her eyebrows. "You have a good brother."

"Yes," Dolly said, her eyes welling. "A wonderful brother."

"But first," he said, "I would have to dig a basement."

"Of course."

"Now you can clean up," Egnat said, grinning, and raised his glass.

"Daye Bozhe," Peter said, raising his glass to Egnat. "Thank you."

As Dolly removed the plates from the table, she couldn't believe her good fortune. The money would help them get started in Winnipeg. They couldn't recover the time and effort they'd put into building the house, but at least not all was lost.

Behind the Scenes

Peter continued to stew about the war. The news on the radio reported the number of casualties mounting up—a daily reminder of the sacrifice his generation was making. What surprised him was the fact that neither Bill's nor George's division had been called up to fight. With battles raging on more than a few fronts in Europe, Peter didn't understand what the holdup was. His brothers both wrote that their units were eager to see action.

Bill had mentioned in his last letter they were moving around a lot, doing field training in various parts of Britain: *We learned how to use the Bren gun, a fine shooting weapon with a cyclic firing rate of 500 rounds per minute. As strange as it seems, it's considered to be too accurate. It has a very small beaten zone at the target. In other words, why put five bullets in almost the same spot when one can do the job?*

But it wasn't all war games. Bill also wrote they had time to go to nightclubs and visit Westminster Abbey, the Tower of London, Petticoat Lane, and Soho. Peter recalled pictures he'd seen of those places in magazines, and a touch of envy crossed his mind.

Peter laughed out loud when Bill described some of the local folks and their sayings. He wrote how one local fellow at a pub asked: *What does a Canadian girl call a good screw?* Then Bill elaborated: *To the Limeys, screw means wages. Knock me up means wake me up, and keep your pecker up means keep cheerful.*

Peter didn't bother explaining these terms to Dolly, even though her command of the English language had improved since he'd met her. There was no point in confusing her. Some things were better left unsaid.

And then there was the letter in which Bill wrote about the girls: *Some of the English girls say, 'Marry a Conidean (Canadian), they get a larger pension than our boys if they get killed.'* That gave both Peter and Dolly pause.

Bill went on in the same letter: *At times there's a brutal mix up in emotions, and cheating on both sides of the Atlantic. One of our dumbbells wrote one letter to his wife and one to his girlfriend, put them in the wrong envelopes. Result, no girlfriend and a hostile wife. And then there's this corporal, he came to me later on telling me that he had been overseas two years yet his wife at home was going to have a baby. He was a decent sort, we called him the padre.*

Peter and Dolly shook their heads at that. It seemed morals flew out the window even more when you were at war.

Peter turned the page and read some more: *So far, I have not mentioned the bombing raids on England. As anything else, they seemed to start slowly and kept increasing in numbers and damage. I was in Croydon, a suburb of London on the first raid. It was 12 Heinkel bombers and I watched all get shot down by the R.A.F. We used to watch the fights almost daily, some times the fight started so high that all you could see was the contrails and as the fighting progressed the planes got lower and lower and we would have a good view. The biggest problem the Air Raid Precaution people had was to get anyone to go under cover. All sorts of air-raid shelters were made, but the most used shelters in London were the tube stations (underground railway). Most of us had been in the raids in London, in the open and along the coast. The British radar was getting quite good and could give at least a fifteen-minute warning of approaching bombers. A lot of the sights* were disturbing, especially in London, where a lot of the homes and buildings were old brick and old stone and flew apart easily. Sometimes on a raid, the bombs broke the water lines, leaving the fire fighters no water. It was hard moving ambulances through the rubble. Of course, the searchlights would be on and the anti-aircraft guns would be booming.

Peter went on to the next page: *It was sad to see the daily workers coming from the underground going back to work in the mornings, tired with black circles under their eyes. How could they rest with people walking around you, over you, plus rumbling trains? Still, they stood up remarkably well. One day, walking in the London streets, I saw a child's small arm lying on the sidewalk. I still feel sick and upset just thinking about it. That these little people, so helpless and so small, should have been made to suffer and get killed in this sheer madness called war.*

Peter stopped and his eyes teared up.

"Can't believe what he's going through." He read the rest of the letter through blurry eyes. Bill said he was now a sergeant with thirty men under him. He signed off, asking Peter to pass his love on to Dolly.

House on the Move

Moving a home to Stonewall turned out to be more complicated than her brother had thought. He told Dolly he had to contact both the district authorities and the Manitoba Power Commission to get permission and help to raise the power lines hung over the roads. There were more than a few of them on the route between the lot in Stony Mountain and his farm in Stonewall. And he hadn't counted on the cost of moving, either. He didn't complain to her, but Dolly's mother told her about his challenges. She said if Egnat had known beforehand, he wouldn't have offered to bail her and Peter out. But, being a man of his word, he said nothing to either.

Her mother also said, "He's having the cement for the basement poured on a spot close to the farm road."

"Not where his boxcar sits?" Dolly asked.

"No. That'll stay. Egnat said it could be years before they can save enough money to finish building the house."

Dolly couldn't thank her brother enough. She marvelled at how seriously he had taken on his father's role. He was still looking after his sister, decades after their father had passed.

Several weeks later, Egnat showed up in his car at the Stony Mountain lot to meet Dolly, Peter, and the professional house movers, who'd arrived with a large flatbed hitched to a truck. Using a hydraulic lift, cribbing, and beams the length of the unfinished house—which Egnat had measured in advance—the three movers lifted the wood-framed construction off the foundation. Dolly and Peter stood to the side, watching what they'd built rise above the basement and move to the truck's flatbed. She watched with mixed emotions, sad to see what they'd sweated over being moved, their dream of having their own home shattered, and yet there was some lightness in her heart, as if the weight of all that worry over money and completing their home before winter was being lifted along with the house. Then the movers fastened the house frame down with multiple wires to keep it from bouncing off the flatbed during the drive to the farm.

Dolly and Peter climbed into Egnat's old Ford and followed the movers out of town and down the highway. It was both exciting and scary. People came out of their houses to gawk, make comments on the stability of the move, and gasp when the frame unexpectedly shifted and the movers had to stop their vehicle to fasten it once more. The fear it could slide off the flatbed because of an unexpected bump or a turn that was too quick was a fear Peter and Dolly shared, especially when the house frame trembled with every turn in the road. The locals waved and wished them well as they drove past.

Leading the movers were workers from the Manitoba Power Commission, who halted their progress whenever they had to raise or cut a line in order for the house to pass. There were also periods when the traffic on Highway 7 had to be stopped to let them through. The whole move—close to eight miles—took most of the day.

With every mile, Dolly reasoned that at least her brother would benefit from their hard work, but that thought did nothing to reduce the lump in her throat. Peter sat stonily beside her. She knew he was probably feeling the same way. They'd never worked so hard in their life as they had, digging that basement. All the agony and pain of that endeavour remained with them. The hole in the ground—evidence of their back-breaking labour—would now benefit whoever bought the lot from the municipality. Because they couldn't pay their taxes, they would get no compensation for all those hours of toil.

Thanks to her brother, they had recouped some of their costs. However, this didn't stop Dolly's mother from shaking her head about their foolishness. She'd never wanted her daughter to move to Stony Mountain, and to her, the fact it hadn't worked out proved her point. Dolly could see no sense in arguing with her mother. When she adopted a viewpoint, it was hard to change her mind.

Rooming House

In the fall, Ted announced he was moving to Toronto to live near his family. His father had bought an apartment block on King Street and wanted his help to spruce the place up. Ted didn't say so, but Dolly figured her uncle must have got the money from selling his place in the old country.

Realizing the opportunity Ted's decision gave them, Dolly didn't wait for Peter to take his shoes off when he walked in the door from work. "Ted's moving," she blurted. "Let's take over the rooming house. We can rent the whole house. The landlady wants $25 a month. We can move into Ted's suite and rent our room and the other large room upstairs for seven dollars a month, and the small one for five dollars." She mentally calculated what the suite downstairs would cost them—she was always good with numbers. "After we collect the rent, we'll only have to pay six dollars for our rooms downstairs. That's a dollar less than what we're paying now. We can't find anything that large for that price."

"I don't know," Peter said, sitting down heavily on a chair.

"What don't you know?" Though she was used to Peter's reluctance whenever she proposed something new, she couldn't help but feel frustrated.

"Do we want to be worried about roomers?" he asked. "What if they don't pay? They'll move out and we'll have to find strangers to rent the rooms."

"Strangers!" she said, almost spitting the word out. "Of course, strangers. Who else? Peter, how are we going to get ahead? This way, the roomers will help pay for our expenses and we can save for a place of our own."

"What about all the extra work? You have to provide clean bedding and towels. Don't you have enough work with your job at Canada Packers?"

"Yes, but I don't want to work there for the rest of my life. Together, we can make something of ourselves." She kept talking about how they'd benefit from running a rooming house.

It took him several days to come around to her way of thinking. He finally agreed when she said she'd be the one to interview and deal with the roomers. He'd be there for support, he said, but he hated telling people to pipe down when they were making too much noise or to stop having guests at all hours.

They used some of the money they got from Egnat to pay Ted for all his furniture, including a Zenith floor-model radio and an icebox. Dolly could barely contain her excitement over the radio. Now she could listen to Lux Radio Theatre in the evening while she ironed and mended clothes, or crocheted doilies for the furniture. And Dolly loved the fact that Arctic Ice's red truck delivered a block of ice for their icebox on a regular schedule, which kept vegetables, fruit, fish, baloney, kybassa and eggs fresh longer. The driver cut a cube of ice out of a gigantic block in the back, then slung it onto a rubber mat on his shoulder and carried it into the house. Dolly marvelled at these modern conveniences, which proved to her she had done the right thing by encouraging Peter to move to the city.

Harry took over Dolly's and Peter's room, and they rented the smallest one to a middle-aged couple. The wife, Jean Pshybylski, worked in the shmata district, sewing coats and suits at the Jacob Crawley garment factory. And Dolly rented the third room on the second floor to a young woman—who said she was a secretary—but she gave her notice after staying less than a month.

With one room vacant, Dolly put a sign—Room to Let—in the front window of the house. Two men in their thirties—a shoemaker, nice-looking and lanky, the other a taxi driver, stocky and balding—showed up the next day. The lanky one said, "Is your mother home? We've come about the room."

"I'm the landlady."

"You look too pretty and young to be one," the lanky one said in Ukrainian.

Dolly laughed. "Ho, ho, our people. But don't think because you flatter me, I'll rent you a room."

Smiling, he said, "I thought it would help."

"Come in. It's upstairs." They followed her to the room, which Dolly and Peter had freshly wallpapered in a design with pink roses. It had a double bed, a hot plate, a bureau, and a small closet. She showed them the bathroom. "All the tenants share it. We've had no trouble. I supply the sheets and wash them once a week. No guests in after ten o'clock or staying overnight."

The taxi driver said, "Sounds good to me. What do you think, Eugene?"

The lanky one nodded. "Yeah. It'll do."

She invited them into her living room and asked them some personal questions, like why they were moving, what was wrong with where they were staying, where they worked and how long they'd been at their jobs. Satisfied with their answers, she said, "You can have the room."

The shoemaker said, "How would you like us to pay you?"

"On time. You have to pay me on time. And a deposit, please, to hold the room for you."

When Peter got home from work, she waved five dollars at him. "I rented the room."

His mouth fell open. "That's great, honey."

Much later, Dolly thought she should have known there might be trouble renting rooms to men, especially a fine-looking one like Eugene, but all she saw then was a fattening bank book. Peter was happy with the money coming in from the roomers, but only until he met the shoemaker.

Eugene was a little taller than Dolly and had come to Canada from Ukraine around the same time she had. He spoke Ukrainian well, but she made the mistake of telling Peter how much she admired Eugene's command of the language. Perhaps she was needling her husband unnecessarily. But he had the habit or correcting her English, and she wanted him to know that English wasn't the only language worthy of correction. On Sunday evenings, Eugene would join them on the porch to watch neighbours walk by. They'd stop to talk and share some of the local gossip. It seemed the whole neighbourhood was out then, savouring the warm air, a pleasant change from their houses, still hot from the day's heat. Though people walked about, the streets were quiet, except for a group of children running amongst the trees on the boulevard, trying to get the last bit of playtime in before the streetlights came on and their mothers called them in for the night.

During one lovely evening in August, when she and Peter were sitting on the front steps with Eugene, she said to him, "When are you going to find a nice girl and settle down?"

"I'm looking, Dolly. I'm looking."

"It's about time you found someone. You're not getting any younger."

Eugene guffawed.

"Laugh, laugh," she said, somewhat annoyed. Dolly wasn't sure he was laughing at her or with her. She folded her arms. The street lights came on, illuminating the kids, now accompanied by shadows as they ran to find hiding spots after their friend shut his eyes, leaned against a tree trunk and yelled, "Hide and Seek!" The friend finished counting to ten and shouted, "Ready or not, you must be caught."

Eugene said to Peter, "When are you going to let Dolly stay home?"

It was twilight, but Dolly could see Peter's cheeks twitch, a sure sign he was upset.

Before Peter could reply, Dolly said, "I like working. It's how we're getting ahead."

Peter's cheek relaxed. He shrugged and said, "What can a man do? She's the boss."

Dolly laughed. "Yeah, yeah, yeah."

"You're a lucky man, Peter. A lucky man."

"I know," Peter said, looking fondly at Dolly.

Though their exchange had been agreeable, Peter complained later, as he was getting ready for bed. "He's interested in you, alright."

"Naagh," Dolly said, dismissing the comment with her hand. "What's he want with a married woman like me? He's looking for some young girl."

"If you were available, he'd come after you." Peter pulled on his pyjama bottoms.

"Why are you pouting? I love you, nobody else."

"Yeah?" He got that sheepish look, as if he was hearing it for the first time. He climbed into bed beside her and kissed her tenderly. She fell asleep in his arms, satisfied her husband cared for her that much.

They didn't see Eugene again until the following Sunday afternoon. They had walked two blocks from their home to Banana Park, a public park that sloped down to the Red River. Families, couples, and the odd lone person sat on benches or lay on blankets, soaking up the sun's rays and chatting amongst themselves. Over on one side, a father and young son threw a rubber ball back and forth, while their dog ran along, hoping to join the fun.

Seated on a blanket, Peter and Dolly were watching the boats go by when Eugene appeared out of nowhere and plunked himself down on the grass beside her.

"What a wonderful day!" he said. He looked carefree with his shirt sleeves rolled up and his collar unbuttoned at the neck. He had slicked his hair back with pomade, and the scent he'd splashed on reminded her of freshly washed sheets. It was such a pleasant fragrance that Dolly thought of buying Peter a bottle of cologne for Christmas—that is, if she could squirrel away any extra money by then.

Peter leaned around Dolly and said, "It is a beautiful day. Don't you have any family, Eugene?"

"My folks live in Dauphin. I should get

up to see them, but I have to get a car first. One of these days."

"I keep telling you, you need a wife," Dolly said.

"Guess so." Eugene looked at Peter. "But where am I going to find a woman like yours, eh?" He then winked at Dolly.

"Yeah, yeah, yeah," she said.

Peter half-smiled. "I know. You don't have to tell me."

Eugene took off his socks and shoes and wiggled his feet in the grass. "Boy, this feels good."

In front of them, several children ran up the hill, then lay down and rolled all the way down, laughing as they went.

"Looks like fun," Eugene said. He turned to Dolly. "Want to try it?"

"No," she said, giggling.

Standing up, Eugene extended his hand.

She said to Peter, "He's like a little boy."

Eugene smirked. "Who said you're only

young once?" Though she didn't take his hand, he wasn't deterred and cocked his head. "Are you coming or not?"

Dolly hesitated, then got up from the blanket. She said to Peter, "Are you coming?"

"I have my suit on." Every Sunday, he wore his suit. It gave him a lift after wearing smelly overalls all week.

"Okay," she said, and followed Eugene to the top of the hill. She lay down near him, parallel to the river bank. He said, "Ready, set, go!" She rolled down the hill, with Eugene a little ahead of her. At the bottom, she rolled right into him, their legs tangling. They howled with laughter as they helped one another up.

By the time they got back up the hill, Peter had their blanket folded and draped over his arm.

Bewildered, Dolly said, "We just got here."

"We have so much work to do."

"But Peter, it's Sunday."

"I know, but you've said yourself, you've been worried about all the stuff in the house that needs fixing. We've been to church. We've paid our respects to God. I'm sure He won't mind if we tackle a few jobs around the house."

Walking away from the park, Dolly realized her flirting had gone too far. Peter was not that religious. His bringing the Lord into the conversation was his way of putting his foot down. From then on, the only time she and Peter sat on the porch steps was when Eugene wasn't home.

Mrs. Pritchard

Dolly stopped scrubbing the old linoleum floor in the kitchen to look at her watch. It was ten at night and Peter wasn't home. His work ended at five. Even if he had missed the bus and walked, he should have been home hours ago. She wondered if the threat of layoffs at Western Packing had kept her husband out late again. He had mentioned he liked to talk after work to his co-workers about what was going on in the plant.

She recalled the first time he'd come home late; that was a month ago. He said he'd gone to a meeting with some employees who wanted to organize a union. Peter told her Western Packing had a union before, but it had been crushed after a violent strike in 1934. Wages improved after that, but the workers still got paid far less than those at Swift and Burns meat-packing plants. And they complained about more than pay; they griped about long hours, threats of layoffs, foremen who played favourites, overtime without extra pay, and hazardous working conditions.

She snorted as she wrung out the cloth in the pail of hot, sudsy water. She was in favour of unions—workers at Canada Packers were also motivated to organize a good one—but her husband coming home drunk after a meeting didn't suggest much had been accomplished. It was a good thing she knew Mabel, who lived nearby and also worked at Western Packing. When Dolly had bumped into her the previous Saturday afternoon in the ladies' blouses section of Wolch's Department Store on Euclid Avenue, she started talking about the coming layoff and what the workers were going to do about it. Mabel said that so far, the workers hadn't figured out how to respond to the bosses. As far as Dolly was concerned, if they spent less time drinking, and more time problem solving, they'd get somewhere.

Dolly stood up and massaged her lower back. Groaning, she got a knife out of the cutlery drawer to scrape the bit of guck she couldn't get off the floor with a rag. She had to do something about her husband's late nights. A man running to the beer parlour three times a week was a man with a drinking problem. She'd seen at close hand what too much alcohol did to a man. Mike had had a couple of run-ins with the police. Her brother also got black eyes from fights he got into after drinking too much at the Yale Hotel on Main Street. Fortunately, Peter wasn't a violent man when he drank, but drinking till the beer parlour closed meant money and time wasted.

She paused her scrubbing and thought again of what had changed Peter from a man who was home every night for supper to one who staggered in hours later. Dipping her cloth back into the pail of sudsy water, she resumed her washing and recalled the night he started his brooding. They'd gone to the movies to see a doubleheader at the Starland Theatre. Perhaps they shouldn't have gone. There was no escaping the war, because both the theatres they preferred, the Starland and Fox, showed a newsreel beforehand—Canadian soldiers marching to the ships that would take them across the ocean and British troops yukking it up in camps near the front. There was even some film footage of British soldiers fighting on an open battlefield, bullets whizzing by, with no protective shelters in sight. That should have scared Peter, but it didn't. He felt he wasn't doing his duty, no matter what Dolly said. It wasn't his fault he couldn't go, but that knowledge didn't keep him from feeling ashamed.

Dolly rinsed the cloth in the pail and watched the dirt colour the water a dark grey. Every time he was late, she stayed up, waiting for him to come home. She didn't know why she bothered, as she couldn't talk any sense into him. Whatever she said fell on deaf ears.

After Dolly had cleaned the floor, she went out on the veranda to wait for Peter. It had been a hot summer day, and she was sweating from washing the floor. The day had cooled some, and luckily for her, the mosquitoes had taken the night off. It was a calm, still night, with the stars dotting the inky blue sky, like a polka-dotted blanket over the quiet street. Earlier in the evening, she'd exchanged a few pleasantries with their neighbour, Mrs. Pritchard, a woman Peter knew from Stony Mountain. She'd been out for a walk, but now, the streets were empty. She sat down on the porch steps and stared at the streetlights, thinking of what she could do to stop Peter from drowning his cares in a beer parlour.

Tired of waiting, Dolly went to bed around eleven. Not long after, she heard the front door creak open. A short time later, Peter stumbled into bed, his breath reeking of beer. Knowing there was no point in talking to him when he was drunk, she went to sleep. She didn't know how long she'd slept when Peter's retching in the toilet down the hall woke her up. She threw on a robe and went to the bathroom. He hadn't even bothered to close the door.

"Peter," she said, "you're going to wake the whole house up." Sound travelled easily from one floor to the other. She believed if she could hear the roomers upstairs, they could hear her and Peter below.

The toilet bowl showed pieces of corn and some unrecognizable food.

Dolly grumbled and went into the kitchen, where she took a jar of dill pickles out of the icebox. She poured some dill pickle juice into a glass and took it to Peter.

"Here," she said, "drink this." Peter drained the glass as soon as he had it in his hand.

Unfortunately, thought Dolly, giving him a hangover remedy was becoming routine. She needed to find a better way to get him to stop his nasty habit. While he was retching one more time, she came up with an idea she hoped would work.

In the morning, Peter sat down at the table gingerly, as if he was carrying a heavy load. His brow creased, and he held his head with one hand while he ate his porridge with the other.

Dolly watched him eat one spoonful after another without looking up. When he got near the bottom of the bowl, she said, "It was lovely sitting on the veranda last night. I saw Mrs. Pritchard; she stopped to say a few words. She asked about you."

Peter, bleary-eyed, looked up from his cereal. "Did she?"

"She remembers you always had a smile and a kind word for her."

Peter took a sip of coffee. "She was always very nice to me."

"Yes, she asked me where you were. 'He isn't sick, is he?' she said. When I said no, she said, 'I haven't seen him sitting on the porch with you for quite a while.'"

Peter said nothing. He avoided looking into Dolly's eyes.

"I told her you were working overtime."

"Huh," Peter said. She noticed he had blinked when she said he'd been working overtime.

Dolly said nothing more. She got up from the table, removed Peter's bowl, and carried it to the sink. She could feel Peter's eyes on her. She didn't turn. She wanted what she'd said about Mrs. Pritchard to sink in. She hoped he'd be embarrassed and would think twice about going to the beer parlour again.

But it was not to be. He did it again, this time blaming a new worker, saying he just wanted to be friendly and saw no harm in inviting him for a quick drink at the Yale Hotel.

Dolly waited until Saturday morning to try another approach. When Peter came down for breakfast, she made him his toast and coffee and then opened the front windows wide before going outside to sit on the veranda. She glanced back through the open lace curtains in the living room and saw him sitting at the kitchen table. She knew she had a loud voice that could travel through the open window. Peter had overheard a street conversation before and had complained about her telling people too much about their business. He was a private man, so what she was about to do would have its effect. At least she hoped it would.

"Good morning, Mrs. Pritchard," she said to an empty street. "How are you today?" Dolly paused, then said, "Yes, it's a lovely morning for a walk."

Dolly looked back through the open window to the kitchen, where she saw Peter straighten up. His body leaned in the direction of the living room. He appeared to be listening.

"No, I'm sorry you haven't seen Peter lately. He's been coming home drunk every night." She paused again. "Yes, it's awful. Other women's husbands work and come home to their wives. My husband goes and gets drunk. We've been talking about having a family, but what would be the point if there's no father at home?" Dolly sat silently for a bit, watching a sparrow land in an oak tree. The bird pecked at the bark; she'd probably found an insect. Then Dolly said, "I'd better get going. With Peter away so much, I have lots to do." Another pause, then she said, "Yes, please say hello to Mr. Pritchard. Tell him I was asking about him."

When Dolly came back into the house,

she noticed Peter had risen from his chair and was rinsing the dishes in the sink, something he hadn't done in a while. She walked into the kitchen and picked up a cloth to wipe down the table. He looked over and said, "I heard you talking. Who were you talking to?"

She looked blankly at him. "No one."

He regarded her for a moment, then said, "I think I'm going to fix that door to the basement. I figure it's about time I fixed it. You know how it's been sticking."

About That Roomer

Life seemed rosier with rents coming in, and both of them employed at the meat-packing plants. She'd convinced Peter to leave Western Packing and get a job at Canada Packers, where she worked and where they paid their workers more per hour. She was sure he'd land a position in the fancy meat department, where the workers sliced and packaged the cold cuts, but she was mistaken. Because Peter was tall, the foreman gave him the job of taking sides of beef down from the ceiling hooks in the killing room. It was heavy work. Dolly worried Peter would die if a side of beef ever fell on him.

Yet she was thankful they had jobs, but

for how long? With the country deep at war, men weren't coming home anytime soon, but she expected that once they did, she might have to look elsewhere for work. In the meantime, she kept close watch on their dollars, making sure there was something to save from every paycheck.

But one Saturday in late summer, the owner of their rented rooming house showed up at their front door. After asking how they were managing, she said, "I'm sorry. I don't have good news. I'm selling the house. My daughter lives in Fort William and I want to move close to her. I'm not getting any younger. If I don't move now, I'll never move."

Dolly reeled from the news. "Oh, no," she said. Then, quickly recovering from the shock, she asked her landlady how much she wanted for the house. The amount was in line with what other houses were selling in the district, so she asked, "How much do you want for a down payment?"

It was an extraordinary amount, but Dolly said, "Let me talk to my husband. We might be interested."

The landlady arched her eyebrows. "Don't wait too long."

Dolly waited anxiously for Peter to return from Wolch's Department Store, where he'd gone to buy a new undershirt. She kept running outside to look up the street for any sign of him. The next time she came out, she greeted him coming up their front walk, carrying a newspaper and whistling "You Are My Sunshine." She quickly poured out the owner's plans, as if a dam on her thoughts had broken.

"We'll have to move," he said in a matter-of-fact tone. He opened the screen door and went inside. Annoyed by his abrupt response, she followed him in, but let the screen door snap shut behind her with a loud bang.

"Weren't you listening?" she said to him in the kitchen. "We could buy it. We have some money left from the sale of our building, and with our savings, we could afford it. It will be tight, but we'll have our own house."

He made a face, then poured himself a glass of water from the tap. "The house is too cold in the winter. It costs too much to heat." They'd been heating with coal, but he was right. The house was drafty. It had poor insulation. They had to lay old cloths at the bottom of the doorframes to keep out the cold, but it still got in. She'd even found a thin coating of ice in the corner of a bedroom wall.

"And we have too many mice," he said. Peter had placed mice traps everywhere, outside the cupboards and in.

Her face crumpled. "Every house has mice." She couldn't buy it without his agreement. No bank would sign a mortgage on her say-so alone. She gazed out the window at the backyard. The leaves on the lilac bush fluttered in the breeze. The flowers were no longer in bloom; the remaining brown petals were the only reminder of their former glory. It wouldn't be long before fall arrived. "We could get a cat," she said.

"Let's look for another suite," Peter said.

"What am I going to do with all the furniture? Suites for rent come furnished."

"I don't care. I don't want another rooming house."

"What's got into you? Do you know how much we'd lose in revenue?"

He opened up the newspaper and began to read. Dolly had learned that when Peter adopted that attitude, he wouldn't budge. He was one stubborn man.

All that evening, Dolly considered their options. If they waited too long to see if the property sold and to whom, they could be out of luck finding another suitable place to live in. She knew his refusal to consider a rooming house was about their male roomers. It wasn't about the heating or the rodent problem. Why had she teased Peter so? Women flocked to her husband like bees to honey, but she didn't see them as a threat to her marriage. But Peter was the jealous type. She blamed herself. She liked to see him get worked up when she flirted and when the men responded in kind. It was her way of keeping his interest. Couldn't he see that?

Though Dolly patted herself on the back for curtailing Peter's late-night drinking at beer parlours and their landlady had decided to wait until spring to sell, her problems weren't over. Peter had made a new friend, Metro, a Ukrainian fellow at Canada Packers, who had the same desire to play chess as Peter did. Metro was single, with no responsibilities except to himself.

They played at the kitchen table on the weekends, starting from one o'clock in the afternoon until ten at night. They set pieces on the cheap plastic chess board Peter had bought before he met her.

Before playing, they pulled out their chess pamphlets, showing strategic moves by various masters, and tried to replicate them, exchanging thoughts on every move on the board.

On one occasion, while she was preparing them a bite to eat, Dolly overheard them talking excitedly about a recent match that Peter had in the back of a grocery store. He had gone to buy some milk and bread and didn't come home until hours later.

"So that's where you were so long," she said, bringing them a plate of kybassa sandwiches.

Metro said, "You should've seen Peter's moves. He beat this young champion."

"What champion?"

"Abe Yanofsky. He's beating everyone. He's only sixteen, but I predict he's going places. Peter won a game with a pawn and a queen."

Peter glowed with the compliment.

Dolly scowled. Their playing irritated her, because she felt obligated to serve Metro a meal and snacks while they played until late in the evening. She wouldn't have minded if they played once in a while, but this was a regular occurrence on the weekends, when she had so much work to do—laundry, ironing, mending, and baking for the week ahead.

At first, she said nothing, thinking this activity was better than his forgetting to come home from the beer parlour. But after too many chess-filled weekends, she complained. "Honey, I know you like playing, but waiting on you boys takes time I don't have."

"It can't be all work," he said. "A man has to have time to relax. Your brother Harry spends hours fishing on the weekends."

"Yes, but he brings food home to eat. What kind of food does chess bring?" When she saw his sullen face, she said, "Oy. play, play, but not all day and into the night. I can't do it all by myself."

"You're right." He agreed, but he left the argument muttering under his breath as he walked about their living quarters.

To soothe him, she said, "Why don't we play whist Saturday night? I'll ask the Pshybylskis. That way, we can both relax." She'd talked to their roomer, Jean, recently, and discovered she and her husband liked to play cards.

Peter shrugged. From his reaction, she understood whist was a poor substitute for chess, but she'd learned long ago that you can't always do what you want.

One of Theirs

Lukia and her family hadn't eaten all day. It was January 6th, Ukrainian Christmas Eve, and they were fasting, waiting for the first star to come out, which would signal that Christ had been born. Mike brought in hay to put under the tablecloth and Harry put a clove of garlic under each corner to keep the evil spirits away. Dunya lit a candle and placed it in the window. It was an old-country tradition that let any passerby know they'd be welcome to enter their home and join the family for their holy evening meal.

When Genya, who'd stayed at the front window to observe the night sky, said, "I see it! I see the first star!" the others rushed to have a look, too.

"Nu," Lukia said. "Time to eat."

After they had set twelve meatless dishes on the table, along with a kolach, a round braided loaf with a lit beeswax candle in the middle of it, Lukia stood to say the Lord's Prayer. Shuffling their chairs, her family rose to join her.

Lukia thought this year's Christmas celebration should be the most joyous time. They'd weathered the Great Depression, and the life of a farmer had taken on a rosy hue. But with the world in turmoil and her family split, she had difficulty shaking her sadness at the table. While Egnat served the kutya—the dish of grains representing family deceased and living—she thought again of what she'd left behind and how she'd failed to keep her family together. In a few months, she would be sixty-seven. In Canada, people retired at sixty-five. But a farmer, she thought, never retires. You kept going until the Lord thought it was time for you to come to His home. How many more years did she have left? Dunya had found her love, and Peter was proving to be a good worker. As for Harry and Marike, who flittered around him, hanging on his every word, their relationship appeared to be serious. But she was from Czechoslovakia and Catholic. That was a concern. But then she reminded herself that Elena came from a Polish Catholic family, and Lukia couldn't ask for a better daughter-in-law. Egnat and Harry were both earning a decent living. They avoided the trouble Mike seemed to find every time he went out. That was the son Lukia hoped would settle down. Then she could die in peace.

Harry broke into her thoughts with news of his employer. "I have some sad news about John Slipchenko. The Japanese captured him in Hong Kong."

"No!" Lukia said. "How do you know?"

"Anna came to the garage a few days

ago to tell me. She said the Japanese killed hundreds and put about ten thousand more in prisoner-of-war camps."

Peter said, "Three boys from Stony Mountain are in the same company. I wonder if they're alive."

"My God, my God," Lukia said.

"Poor Anna," Dunya said. "Walter's only eight years old. Will he ever see his father again?"

Lukia knew full well what was going on in Anna's mind. To have your husband away, fighting a foreign enemy, was sure to fill her nights with dread. As it was, Anna was an anxious woman who had relied on her husband's calmness to get through the Depression. If he survived, what shape would he be in when he came home? Did the leaders of nations ever stop to think of the price their citizens paid with their lives and the families they left behind? Or were those who enlisted just pawns on a chessboard to be pushed around by men who were hungry for power at any cost? She'd seen it all before. She understood a monster like Hitler had to be stopped, but why had the British and the others waited so long? Why weren't they paying attention? The signs were all there. No one knew the full tragedy of war except those who fought and those who waited for their loved ones to come home.

While Lukia ruminated about the madness of war, the conversation around the table continued. Peter mentioned that the Americans were also entering the war. A month ago, the Japanese had bombed their navy base in Pearl Harbour. She wondered if Germany and Japan had a plan to divide up the world's spoils? The universe had gone mad with fighting in so many places. How many young men and women would be killed or maimed? How many families would be displaced and torn apart? How many mothers would grieve the rest of their lives for children who would never come home again?

They stopped eating and prayed for those overseas and for peace in the world. After what seemed like an interminable silence, they passed more food and filled glasses with horilka.

Lukia quickly forgot her woes amid the comfort of tradition. Following dessert, the family remained at the table to sing. In the old country, carollers from the church would come by after the meal to sing "God Eternal" and "In Bethlehem." Sobor had a group of young carollers, but they didn't go to the farms. It was too far and often too treacherous at this time of year, when the roads were icy or impassable.

"Never mind," Lukia said, when Egnat mentioned he missed the carollers. "We can sing. We always sing."

With Egnat and Mike's beautiful tenor voices filling the room, the family sang all the familiar Christmas carols late into the evening. For several hours, they welcomed the relief they got through raising their voices and celebrating the hope that Jesus Christ brought with His arrival.

Twelve days after Christmas, Lukia and Egnat drove to Sobor for Epiphany—the Feast of Jordan—to each get a small bottle of holy water. They lived too far for the priest to make the trip to bless their home, but with their own vessel of blessed water, they could do it themselves.

The priest's blessing of the water took place by a large ice cross on the snowy grounds of the church. The gathering was smaller, as most parishioners were at work. Families often chose one member to get what they needed. Anna Slipchenko was there with her son, Walter. Lukia told her she could count on them if she needed anything. Anna nodded with tears in her eyes, and squeezed Lukia's hand.

Upon arriving back on their farm, Egnat took his mother's glass container of holy water to the barnyard, where he blessed all the outbuildings and the animals before returning to the house to bless it and all the family members within. It was a day of thanks for all that they had. Lukia looked on approvingly as her eldest son maintained the rituals of the past. She knew he would go home and do the same on his farm. He hadn't forgotten what bound them to their faith and the land of their birth.

Nazi Invasion

The unthinkable happened in Winnipeg on Thursday, February 19, 1942. The Nazis invaded. There had been a warning in the papers two nights before, but many either didn't get the paper or missed reading about it.

On the evening prior to the invasion, Peter noticed warplanes flying overhead but couldn't tell what insignia was on the side. He assumed they were Canadian planes. But the following morning, he and Dolly awoke at 6 a.m. to the sound of air raid sirens. Peter recognized the sound immediately. He'd seen newsreels of the bombing of Britain, where that eerie sound warned citizens to seek shelter. But

Canada had no such shelters. His stomach sunk at the thought an attack was underway.

Dolly sat up in bed. "Peter," she said, her voice expressing alarm, "what is that?"

"I don't know," he said and rushed outside in his pyjamas. Shivering in the frigid air, he looked up and down the snow-covered street, but it was deserted, as it usually was this early in the morning. He could see no evidence that anything was amiss.

Returning inside, he said, "The streets are clear. Nothing unusual."

He quickly dressed and put on the radio in the kitchen. The broadcast was in German. He double-checked the station; it was CKY, the one that gave them the morning news. Startled, he turned to Dolly, who was packing their metal lunch boxes with baloney sandwiches. "Did you hear that? The announcer was speaking German." He rotated the dial to another station and was momentarily relieved to hear the host talk in English about the weather.

"How odd," he said. Winnipeg had residents from across the globe but, up until now, he'd never heard a local radio broadcast in a language other than English.

Dolly was too busy filling their thermos bottles with hot cocoa to pay any attention to his grumblings. He put aside his misgivings and prepared to leave the house. They donned their winter garb, grabbed their lunches, and left for work as usual. The cold air blasted them in the face as they stepped off the porch. Their breath formed tiny white clouds as they walked towards the streetcar stop on Main Street. Peter stopped to raise the collar of Dolly's muskrat fur coat. She pulled her matching fur hat down over her ears.

At the stop, Peter strained his head upwards and saw more planes overhead. It seemed one was dive bombing, and he instinctively clutched Dolly closer—but then relaxed when no one near them or elsewhere on the street expressed any panic. If there had been a threat, he was sure the city would have come to a full stop, but the streetcars were running and the one they needed was, at the moment, pulling up.

Boarding, Peter stopped to ask the driver what he thought was going on, but before the driver could reply, Dolly hurried him down the aisle to grab a seat before it filled with other passengers. As they rolled south down Main Street, Peter stared out the window, concerned he was missing something he should know, but all he saw were early risers going about their business. They passed a milk wagon pulled by a horse, two police officers dressed in buffalo fur coats walking their beat on the sidewalk, and the public market with its small huts, smoke coming out of their chimneys. They rode through the underpass, past the movie houses and a cafe where a customer was entering for breakfast. Again, nothing unusual. However, at city hall, a group of men in fine overcoats and fedoras huddled together outside the front entrance and talked with great animation. That was a scene Peter hadn't seen before. He glanced at his fellow passengers—an old woman with a *babushka* holding a shopping bag on her lap, an older gentleman sitting stiffly beside her, a middle-aged couple with two small children who were poking one another and laughing, a young man engrossed in a small detective novel, and several young women, fully made-up, chatting non-stop. As far as he could tell, they hadn't noticed the unfamiliar scene outside their windows, or they were taking this novelty in stride.

Anxious, Peter told Dolly he had to check what was going on and stood up, grabbing the strap overhead to keep his balance as the car swayed from side to side on its journey down the tracks. He moved to the front of the car to get a better look out the driver's window. Several police were setting up roadblocks at the intersection with Portage Avenue. When their streetcar got closer, he noticed a city worker on a tall ladder changing the name of the street sign. Peter strained to see what he was changing it to, but the man's position blocked his view. Later, he learned the worker had changed it to Adolf Hitler Strasse.

At the intersection, a policeman put his hand up for the streetcar conductor to stop. Streetcars only stopped here if the trolley pole separated from the electric wires overhead. Suspecting trouble, Peter's stomach lurched, and he returned to his seat.

"Why are we stopping?" Dolly said, peering down the front aisle.

"I don't know." Then Peter heard gunfire that seemed to come from downtown. His muscles tensed as he looked in that direction.

Dolly said, "Somebody's shooting." The other passengers began jabbering, fearful of what was going on. The middle-aged couple put their arms around their small children. A few stood or leaned towards the sudden sound.

"Were those gunshots?" one shouted.

"Stay calm, folks," the conductor said to the passengers.

"What does he mean?" Dolly asked, grabbing Peter's hand.

Peter didn't know whether they should try to get off the streetcar and rush back home, or hide somewhere in the vicinity.

The conductor stood up and said in a loud voice, "In case you missed it, the city is holding a mock Nazi invasion. It was in the papers last night."

"What?" The passengers buzzed amongst themselves.

The conductor said, "It's called the *If Day* exercise. The city officials thought it would be interesting to show us what it would be like *if* the Nazis occupied the city. If you're heading to work, I'm surprised your boss didn't give you the day off. The entire city is being attacked."

Peter heaved a sigh. This was insane. He said to the conductor, "What about the planes over the city this morning? Were they part of this?"

"Yes, sir. They were supposed to simulate German ones, with Luftwaffe markings." He scratched his nose. "It's where our tax dollars are going. I guess the military wanted to dress up like Nazis; they borrowed the uniforms from Hollywood. I don't see the point, do you?"

Seated near the driver, a woman in a long, fur-trimmed brown coat said, "The city is doing the exercise to raise money for Victory Bonds. They want people to know our soldiers need help if we're going to defeat Hitler."

The conductor jutted his chin towards Portage Avenue. "Here they come."

Dolly stood and said, "They have to

scare us? This is what they're doing to get money?"

Peter, along with several others, moved to the right side of the streetcar to see the tanks with men dressed like Wehrmacht soldiers ride towards them. In front and back of the tanks, hundreds more in Nazi uniforms and jackboots carried rifles and goose-stepped down Portage Avenue. When they reached the intersection, two soldiers marched over to the streetcar and boarded it.

"My God," Dolly said. "They're coming on board."

They shouted something in German to the passengers and motioned for them to get down from the streetcar. Then, with an affected German accent, the pretend Nazi officer asked each one to show their papers. His manner and speech were rough. He said to one man, "Don't even think of resisting. I will shoot you on the spot."

The Nazi imposter gave Peter and

Dolly a cursory glance as he examined their papers before moving on to the next passenger. But his manner was harsh enough for the old woman in the babushka to cry as she hunted in her purse for her identification. Perhaps she hadn't heard the conductor say the military exercise was all fake. The man behind her handed her a tissue to wipe her tears.

After enduring the scrutiny of the actors, the passengers returned to their seats in the streetcar and the other soldier, impersonating a German officer, gave the conductor a sign to proceed.

After that dramatic military encounter, the streetcar continued south down Main Street, as it always did, towards St. Boniface, where they'd have to transfer to a trolleybus to take them to Canada Packers on the outskirts.

A woman in front of them turned and said, "That was really somethin', wasn't it?"

Dolly proceeded to tell the stranger about her brothers-in-law being overseas and how Bill hadn't even given them five dollars when they needed it for a metre so they could have a radio.

Peter listened for a bit as the women shared their stories, then his mind wandered. He wondered if his brothers would ever experience an attack from the Nazis, or would the war end without them having fought at all? And if the war continued and Canada lost more men, would the government lower their enlisting requirements and call him up to serve?

When Peter and Dolly arrived at the meat-packing plant, they were late for work, but the foreman wasn't upset, nor were they penalized. The factory had been informed of *If Day* that morning. Peter wished he'd known, but he wasn't alone. Most of his fellow workers hadn't read the warning in the papers, either. It was all they talked about that day. He sat with his co-workers over lunch and told them of the tanks and Nazi uniforms he'd seen.

After work in the evening, Peter walked to Moishe's grocery store on Austin Street to buy a special edition of the *Winnipeg Tribune*. He wondered what the Jewish grocer thought of such a stunt, especially given the reports coming out of Europe. The Jews were under attack in several countries. Peter saw no sense in it at all. They were just like him; except they couldn't cross themselves. Not that they'd want to. Funny thing, though, since Christ was a Jew. The Fuhrer was supposedly Catholic. If Christ was alive, would Hitler be attacking him, too?

Peter couldn't believe how much trouble the city had gone to, simply to replicate a frightening event. The newspaper's headline on the front page was *Das Winnipegger Lugenblatt,* as if Hitler's men had really captured the city and taken over the press. "Can you believe it?" he asked Moishe, pointing to the headline. "The lengths the city went to, to stage an invasion."

"They went all-out," Moishe said, shaking his head as he peered at the paper. "The fake Gestapo even ordered soldiers to storm into the library on William Avenue, and they came out with armfuls of books, which they burned on the property."

"The city allowed them to do that?"

Moishe grunted. "They were books they were planning to destroy, anyway. It was all part of the show."

Peter read later that Manitoba had raised over three million dollars that day in sales of war bonds, an extraordinary amount. Extraordinary for sure, thought Peter, as he lay his head on the pillow that night. If it was going to help men like his brothers, who were far from home, then it was a worthwhile exercise indeed.

Fire in Her Belly

In the spring, their landlady's realtor put up a sign on the front lawn, advertising their rented house for sale. Though it could take months before the house sold, Dolly wasted no time looking for a new place to live. Unfortunately, there were no affordable houses for rent listed in the Saturday newspapers. Undeterred, she searched the ads for suites for rent. One landlord wanted fourteen dollars a month for two rooms, but it came with cockroaches. Another—a nicer place at eighteen dollars a month—had heating issues.

Knowing many landlords put signs in their front windows—cheaper than buying

ads—Dolly left Peter the following
Saturday to fix the toaster and walked up
and down the streets in the North End,
the part of Winnipeg catering to Eastern
European immigrants. She combed the
streets a mile in each direction. On
Manitoba Avenue, a half block off Main
Street, she found a sign in the window of
a three-storey home with a porch, painted
white with forest green trim, and attached
to two other homes identical in
architecture and colour. When she
knocked on the front door, a woman in
her fifties, with salt-and-pepper hair and
wire-rimmed glasses, answered. Mrs.
Wasiliuk said she was renting the attached
house next door. The lease was more than
what Peter and Dolly were already paying,
but with three rooms to rent out on the
second floor and one on the third, they'd
get enough rent to make up the
difference. Dolly didn't think twice. She
said she'd take it without even discussing
it with Peter. To reassure him, she

planned to tell him they would rent the rooms upstairs to girls only and maybe one to an old confirmed bachelor.

Peter knew he'd married a girl with fire in her belly, but sometimes he felt he could barely keep up with her desire to get them on their feet and keep them there. She'd found them a new home so fast it made his head spin. And to save on moving costs, Harry and Mike used their vehicles to move their furniture and other possessions. Hellbent on saving, she squirrelled away any change they had. His wallet had never been so bare. They'd opened a bank account, and if he had even a measly dollar in his possession, she trotted it down to the bank. And yet, she loved her fun, too. She made sure they had money for the movies once a week.

They could have gone to the Times Theatre, which was near their home, but they never cared for the movies playing there. Instead, if they weren't too tired after a long day at work, they'd trudge eight blocks down Main Street to the area between Higgins Avenue and City Hall, where the main movie houses were located. The cheapest was the Oak Theatre, where you could get in for half price if you brought your own apple crate. And kitty-corner across the street from the Oak were the Regent and the Colonial, but all three played B-movies, starring actors Dolly didn't recognize. They liked the Starland and the Fox theatres, with their grand lighted signs and elaborately decorated ceilings over the seats. They were the movie houses that showed the actors and actresses she cared about, the ones who appeared in the movie magazines on the shelves in the drug stores.

One evening, they went to see *The Maltese Falcon* with Humphrey Bogart and Peter Lorre. Peter normally liked film noir, its intrigue and mystery, but as he sat there watching Bogart as Sam Spade, the detective, being seduced by a beautiful woman who wanted him to find a black statue, he kept thinking of the Eyes of the World newsreel he'd seen before the movie. It had followed several cartoons—Woody Woodpecker, Bugs Bunny, and Mighty Mouse—which had put him in a good mood. The news, though, had wiped away any joy he had. Singapore had fallen months ago, America was battling Japan in and over the Pacific Ocean, and Russia and the Allies in Europe were trying to beat back Germany and Italy. There was film footage of a meeting of representatives of fourteen nations who said their pilots were ready to blast the alliance of Germany, Italy, and Japan. The announcer said in a gleeful tone, "Don't look now, Hitler and Hirohito, and what's the other guy's name?" Of course, he was referring to Mussolini, the prime minister of Italy, a fascist leader with an army of black-shirted soldiers. Shots of explosions and war planes whizzing through the grey skies filled the screen. Peter thought this type of newsreel footage was probably driving Johnny, his youngest brother, to consider joining the air force. As the projectionist at the movie theatre in Stony Mountain, he'd be watching film clips of planes soaring over battlefields repeatedly. Johnny had told him he couldn't wait until he turned eighteen.

Peter thought again of the letter he'd received from the government, asking him to join the armed forces, saying it was his duty and asking what his children would say after the war if he didn't serve. He guessed it was a mass mailing, because the government had to know he'd been rejected. The message suggested it would be embarrassing to have children and not protect them. He didn't have any yet, but he and Dolly had been talking about having a child. It had been four years since they married, and Egnat kept teasing his sister, asking her what was taking so long.

The second film was *A Yank in the R.A.F.,* with Tyrone Power and Betty Grable. Again, he thought of Johnny. Another movie that would stir his young brother to join. Peter was so tired he slept through some of it, and Dolly filled him in on the walk home. He was content to listen as they walked down deserted Main Street at midnight, but his thoughts kept drifting back to his brothers. Where were Bill and George now?

A Change of Heart

Now that Peter had steady employment, Lukia no longer thought of him as indolent or lacking initiative. She credited Dolly for finding a way for them to succeed in the city. Her thoughts drifted to Harry, who was planning to marry Marike Bartosh. Harry had a good job, and as long as Marike was willing to work in some position, they would manage. But with the war occupying everyone's mind and heart, the future looked uncertain. Already, the government had imposed rationing.

At the start of the year, Lukia could only buy eight ounces of sugar, the maximum amount allowed per person per week. She couldn't make enough cake or cookies to satisfy a family with that. Then, at the end of August, the government issued ration books for coffee, tea, butter, and meats of any kind. During the war years in the old country, Lukia had learned to do without, but those who'd had a softer life whined about the scarcity of the basics.

Harry and Marike set their wedding date for mid-October. Marike had hoped to wed in the summer, but Lukia explained her family would have difficulty making the arrangements because of the harvest. She told Marike that only after they had collected the grain and taken it to the elevators would they have enough peace of mind to celebrate.

Lukia hoped that would be true, that she would have peace of mind. But so much had changed. She was often alone. Mike would forget to come home, or was too drunk to drive. Lukia didn't understand her son's inability to handle liquor. Her family all drank; they did it to whet their appetite and then some. But Mike was different. His personality changed when he'd had too many shots. When he was sober, he showed a gentle spirit, but after drinking throughout the meal, he became argumentative, often after some perceived slight.

Oy, thought Lukia, what was to become of her farm and her life? She should have heeded her mother's warning in the old country. She said her children would grow up and leave and she'd be left to manage on her own. Lukia didn't listen. Even when Dmitro came calling after her sister-in-law's death. It was true she didn't love him, but he was a good man, and wealthy enough. She wouldn't have had to worry. But it was Mike who had complained the loudest about Dmitro's offer. She wondered what her brother-in-law was doing now. Had he survived the Polish occupation? And now that Hitler's troops had invaded Volhynia, was he safe?

Were the Poles still in charge? There was so little news.

And how long could she hold on to the farm? She had to nag Mike to do his chores. He grumbled every time. Egnat was right. She'd made too many excuses for her middle son over the years. Was he irresponsible because she kept forgiving him? She asked God for answers. She prayed for the strength to continue, and for Mike to change his ways.

With Harry's wedding only two months away, Lukia asked him to arrange a visit to Marike's parents' farm in Lorette, fifteen miles southeast of Winnipeg. Pan and Panye Bartosh ran their farm with the help of their four sons. Lukia noted that, like her, they were Slavic farmers who had immigrated to Canada. Because they had that in common, Lukia hoped they could work out marriage plans to the satisfaction of both families.

In their modest but comfortable home,

Pan and Panye Bartosh greeted Lukia, Harry, and Mike cordially. Lukia was pleased to find that even though their mother tongues were different, they had enough shared language to have a reasonable conversation. Marike, who was staying with her parents for the weekend, shyly embraced Lukia, then left the living room to prepare tea in the kitchen. When she brought out the china teapot, cups and saucers, and a plate of pastries, Lukia brought up the cost of the wedding to Marike's parents. She told Panye Bartosh, a plump woman with a kind, round face, that her side of the family would provide the hall and liquor and asked if she and her husband would provide the food for the guests. To sweeten the deal, Harry offered to pay for the bride's gown and veil. A nice offer, considering he'd already bought Marike a new coat and shoes.

"Of course," Panye Bartosh said, "we'll provide the food. I'll fry some chicken and I'll have my son kill a calf and a pig for the reception." Her husband, an unreadable man of narrow build, said little. Lukia couldn't tell if he agreed with the arrangement or not.

"Wonderful!" Lukia said. Satisfied they had divided the cost of the wedding equitably, she relaxed over a cup of tea and talked with Panye Bartosh about the challenges of farming, while Harry, Mike and Marike toured the farm with a young Bartosh boy.

The Bartosh family and the Mazurecs parted amicably, but on the drive home in their truck, Lukia—seated between her sons in the front seat—noticed Mike clenching the steering wheel. "What's the matter?"

"I don't think Marike's mother is going to do anything for the wedding."

Harry said, "Panye Bartosh says they're going to provide the food, so I expect they will."

Lukia murmured, "It's only right." The bride's parents were supposed to host the wedding, but with Mike having doubts, she fell asleep that night with an uneasy feeling.

In the morning, Lukia rose slowly. She examined herself in the bureau mirror as she combed her thinning hair back into a bun. The passing years had not been kind. The woman who stared back at her was overweight and suffering from rheumatism and high blood pressure. Where had the years gone? She was spending more and more nights alone, passing the time darning, or straining her failing eyes while sewing a new dress for the grandchildren, or working on some other handwork. She would need a new prescription for the gold-rimmed spectacles her daughter had insisted on buying for her.

Despite her deteriorating health, she took care of the garden, preserved the vegetables, cooked the meals, washed the clothes, milked the cows, collected the eggs, and fed the chickens. Taking care of the crops was Mike's responsibility, but with his poor work ethic, even two hired hands wouldn't be enough to bring in the harvest this year.

She stirred the porridge on the stove and thought of how Mike seemed bent on self-destruction. He used to be generous, but she'd stopped accepting cash gifts from him when she learned his money had come from selling homebrew.

"What will I do when they arrest you again?" she had said. "Egnat can't afford to keep bailing you out."

Mike looked at her like a little boy, with baleful eyes, and said, "Mama, don't say. Take it." And he pushed the money into her hands. Just as quickly, she pushed it back. The last time he had tried to force cash on her, she'd lost her balance and almost fell. She could have hurt herself.

Egnat and Dunya visited her not long after and shared their concerns for her wellbeing. Dunya asked her to come and live with her and Peter. She said, "Mama, it's no good, you living alone."

"I'm not alone," Lukia said.

"Mama, how many nights has he been out this week?" Egnat asked.

Lukia mumbled and shook her head.

"When he's not here to help," Dunya said, "you have to do the work. It's too much. I know you don't want to give up the farm, but you have to. Maybe Mike can find work in the city that suits him better."

"I don't know."

"What if you have a heart attack and he's not home? What then?"

Lukia rubbed her forefinger against her thumb. What her children said was true. A heart attack could happen, and then what? Or some unexpected accident. Over the years, there had been some close calls, especially with the chimney fires. Even if she could drive, she had no vehicle. Mike took the truck on his errands. She couldn't drive a tractor into the city to see the doctor or go to the hospital. She didn't have a phone, and even if she did, she wouldn't know how to use it. How had it come to this? She'd been so capable.

Her daughter was right. It was time to give up the farm. And yet, she couldn't imagine living with her daughter. Lukia was used to being the one who ran the house, the one who gave the orders on the farm. She and her daughter had their conflicts. Dunya was headstrong. Lukia would be underfoot. And what would Peter think? Nice as he was, would he welcome her, or resent her presence? All these questions caused her anxiety. Nothing was certain anymore. No matter how hard she tried, she couldn't change Mike, just like she couldn't stop the dust storms from happening. And yet, she kept trying.

On the Way

Dolly missed her monthly in late July. She thought it had to do with all the excitement of their new home and all the unpacking, but when her breasts became tender and swollen and a wave of nausea hit her in the morning, she realised she was pregnant.

Peter was in the kitchen buttering toast when she came up to him and put her arms around him. "Honey, ….," she said.

He turned around, the knife still in his hand.

She took the knife away from him and put it down on the counter. "You're going to be a father."

"What?" He held her shoulders. "You're kidding."

"No," she grinned, taking in his warm hazel eyes. "We're going to have a baby."

He took her in his arms, kissed her, then twirled her around the kitchen floor, singing, "Let me call you Sweetheart, I'm in love with you. Let me hear you whisper that you love me, too." He stopped dancing and said, "Are you feeling okay?"

"A little nauseous this morning, but I'm pregnant ... That's how it is."

He looked at her as if he couldn't get enough of her, and she thought no man could love a woman more. She pushed him gently. "Go. Get dressed. If we don't get going, we're going to be late for work."

He laughed and ran around acting so flustered he had trouble putting his socks on.

"One more thing," she said as they were leaving the house, "we'll have to save more. I want to have the baby in the hospital."

"Okay. We'll save more," he said and grinned again. Up to that moment, she hadn't realized how much he had wanted a child. She wasn't ready to have one; she wanted to wait until they owned their own home, but God had other ideas.

Her pregnancy had caught her by surprise, but she had long thought of where she wanted to birth her baby. She'd seen a movie showing a woman dressed in a beautiful nightgown in a pristine hospital bed, surrounded by vases of flowers. A pert young nurse in a starched white uniform brought her the baby, wrapped in a receiving blanket. Dolly wanted a birth just like the one she'd seen on the screen. And not one like the one her mother had, giving birth to her on the floor of a cold komora, with only the barrels of root vegetables for company.

Though a baby was on the way, life carried on as before. They rode the streetcar to work every day. After his bike accident, Dolly had convinced Peter there was too much traffic to cycle the streets safely. And since they now worked at the same meat-packing plant, it was nice to have his company there and back.

The ride was long, but it gave her time to think about their future. The rough patch in their marriage when he had drunk excessively had passed. He had grown more accommodating. And she had come to understand his pain. With the war on everyone's minds, it was no wonder he had suffered guilt and shame and had resorted to drink. Still, the possibility of Peter being conscripted and going to war preyed on her mind. With posters advertising war bonds displayed in storefront windows and war headlines on the front pages of newspapers, it was impossible to escape what was going on overseas.

Now, Peter fussed about her like she was a wounded bird. She had to keep reminding him that not much had changed and she could carry on like before. She thought his mother's story about losing her first three had caused him to worry his wife would have problems, too.

Dolly didn't worry about losing a child. Instead, she worried about how she'd manage once their child was born. She hoped to convince her mother to move in with them. It was the only way she and Peter could get ahead. They'd be helping her mother out of a difficult situation on the farm and she'd be helping them to care for their baby while they were at work. Dolly didn't expect any quarrel from Peter. Hopefully, her mother would want to live with them, too.

Peter surprised Dolly on her birthday. He gave her an engraved 14k gold heart-shaped locket with a filigreed design, and inside, her photo and his. It was a lovely romantic gift, but her first thought was, how had he paid for it when she watched every penny? Sheepishly, he told her he had been saving a little of his pay every week. Ordinarily, she would've scolded him for not telling her; she would've reminded him they were saving for a house and a hospital room for their baby's birth, but she said none of that. Later, when the time was right, she would remind him again of their need to save money. She guessed he had given her such a lovely gift to mark the fact she was carrying his child. He fastened the locket around her neck and went with her to admire it in the bureau mirror in their bedroom.

After supper, they sat down in the living room to listen to the radio; it had become their habit. While the radio was on, she ironed or darned his socks, and Peter tinkered with an appliance that needed attention. It was a pleasant and relaxing time, but she noticed one late August evening how solemn he had become after listening to another news broadcast.

Quebec had rejected conscription, but the other provinces were considering it if it proved necessary. The possibility of being made to fight for one's country no longer seemed so far away. She wished Peter could let go of his desire to do his duty, especially after hearing from his father that Johnny had joined the Royal Canadian Air Force immediately after his eighteenth birthday. With three brothers in the forces, his inability to join continued to grate on him.

She peeked at Peter over her ironing board. With his head buried in the newspaper, he said, "Listen to this. Dieppe casualties total 3,350 dead, wounded or missing."

"Awful," she said. So many young men—sons, fathers, brothers, husbands forever lost. She recalled a photo she'd seen in the *Winnipeg Tribune* of Canadian soldiers wearing helmets and carrying rifles on an open beach near a town called Dieppe. Peter had told her it was an all-assault attack with tanks and heavy weapons and air force support from three countries: Canada, Britain, and the United States. The newspaper reported that attack had ended badly. Now they had the details. Much worse than anyone had expected.

Peter folded the paper and put it down on the coffee table. "The war is everywhere," he said. "It's never been this bad. That's all there is on the front page. War stories from Moscow, Berlin, London, Australia, America and China. Will this war never end?"

They went to bed, each lost in their own thoughts. She expected Peter would stew about the war in his dreams, maybe churn in bed. How would she fare if he had to serve his country? Would she be left to care for a baby alone, like Anne, George's wife, not knowing if she'd ever see her husband alive again? Dolly cuddled closer to Peter in bed and stroked his thigh. He murmured something. She couldn't imagine such a future and prayed he would stay home.

Heartache

Lukia strolled through the fields that were so dear to her heart. She picked up a handful of dirt and let it sift through her fingers. Since she was a young girl, she'd toiled on the land and appreciated the gifts it had given her. Farming was in her blood, and it had served her family well.

She disliked being in a position where her children questioned her ability to take care of herself, where help was being forced upon her. She wasn't ready to give up control, but she also knew she'd never be ready. Her grit and determination had been the glue that had kept the family together, and now that glue had cracked.

Scenes from her life played out of sequence in her mind, as if the director of her story couldn't decide how to start it and how to end it. Her life on the farm was ending, and it was not the ending she would have chosen.

After Harry's wedding, she would move to Dunya and Peter's house in the city. At first, Lukia had resisted the idea of moving to the city. She complained about becoming useless, but her daughter and Egnat had said it was time to take care of herself. She harrumphed at that. Maybe it would be better. No more waking up at dawn to milk the cows. No more gazing at the sky, praying for rain. No more wondering where Mike was. And she could attend church every Sunday, no matter the weather. But before giving up the farm for good, Mike would have to bring in the harvest. Knowing he'd need help, Egnat had offered to bring Genya over. Her granddaughter knew how to drive a tractor and could pull the combine, while her uncle oversaw the operation with a couple of hired hands.

Lukia fondled the golden wheat, grown tall and ready to be cut. The bountiful yellow fields stretched in every direction, embracing the blue horizon, reminding her of the flag of Ukraine, with its equal horizontal parts of yellow and blue. Would her countrymen see freedom on their soil again? Would they be able to wave their flag proudly? She lifted her eyes to heaven and prayed they would. Then, trudging down each row, she said goodbye to all the strands of gold swaying in the light breeze and wept, knowing she would be leaving soon for the last time.

"No more," she muttered to the wind. "No more."

At Sobor, Lukia sat in a front pew, surrounded by her family, and watched Harry and Marike don gold crowns, then follow the priest around the altar three times. At least, she thought, her son had convinced Marike to get married in the Ukrainian Greek Orthodox church. Whether his bride would follow the traditions was yet to be determined. But marrying in his parish was a good omen for the future. She prayed for their happiness and also thanked God they'd had a successful harvest. Several days before, poor Genya had worked alongside her uncle Mike until two o'clock in the morning.

Lukia turned her attention back to Harry and Marike, kneeling in front of the priest. Harry appeared to be content in their relationship. What more could any mother want?

After the wedding ceremony, Harry and Marike left the church with their attendants to have their photographs taken at a studio on Selkirk Avenue. With the bridal party occupied, Egnat drove his mother and wife to the Ukrainian Reading Hall at Flora and McKenzie to set up the tables for the meal. But when Lukia and Elena met Mrs. Bartosh and her son, a tall pleasant-looking man, in the hall kitchen, Lukia noticed they had brought only a small chicken and a small pot of holupchi.

"Where's the rest of the food?" Elena asked.

Mrs. Bartosh said, "I brought enough for our guests. I expect you have food for yours."

Lukia's stomach dropped. "What are you saying?"

Elena frowned. "You only brought for your guests? What do you expect them to drink, then?"

"They'll drink the groom's drink. Harry's providing that." Mrs. Bartosh's son said, as if this had been the plan all along and Lukia had misunderstood.

Lukia stood there, dumbfounded. She realized Mike had been right. This was a family that either had nothing to give or didn't want to give anything. Seething, she considered complaining, but this was no time for confrontation.

Gnashing her teeth, Lukia looked around the hall in vain for Egnat and asked Elena if she'd seen him.

"Maybe he's outside smoking."

Sure enough, she found Egnat on the boulevard, smoke forming a white plume over his head. She quickly explained the crisis, then gave him the key to her house. "Bring me the big pot of holupchi from the pantry and go to the store and buy three big hams and three kybassa, also lettuce, cucumbers, and tomatoes." He pulled a piece of paper and a pencil from his jacket pocket and wrote the items down. She lamented having to serve her holupchi, as she'd made them for the propravyny, the after-wedding feast she'd planned, but she felt she had no choice.

Waiting for Egnat to return took all her emotional strength. She busied herself by fussing over the floral centrepiece made from flowers picked from her garden. She straightened the folds in the tablecloths with her hand too many times to count. The guests would show up within the next two hours, and nothing was ready. How embarrassing it would be to have her friends and family arrive to find a paltry table! Afterwards, she would not be able to show her face in church.

Egnat must have driven with excessive speed, as he was back sooner than Lukia expected. She and Elena helped Egnat unload the food from the cab of his truck and carry the dishes into the hall, past Harry and Marike, who had returned from the photographer's studio and were ushering Pan and Panye Bartosh to their positions in the reception line. Harry gave his mother an inquisitive look and said, "Mama, you have to join us."

"Not now, son, not now," Lukia said, as she rushed past his disappointed look to the kitchen, with Elena and Egnat close behind.

Lukia set to work with Elena and

Dunya, slicing the vegetables and meat and heating the holupchi for the buffet. Seeing the miracle of a bountiful meal unfold—they had prepared enough platters of food for their guests—Lukia crossed herself. "My God, I didn't think we could do it." She took her apron off and hugged Elena and Dunya. She'd missed the receiving line, but they'd averted the impending crisis.

Her relief was short-lived. There appeared to be enough to eat, but some folk went up to the table for second helpings, only to find there weren't any. This proved awkward, but there was nothing she could do except put on a pleasant face for Harry's sake. She hoped he hadn't noticed the fuss about the shortage. She would talk to him about the behind-the-scenes drama later.

When it came time to clear the buffet table, Lukia said to Elena, "I want to make sure I get my dishes back." She rose from her seat and approached the buffet table, where Anna Slipchenko was already stacking dirty plates. She was about to lift them when a drunken soldier, a guest of the Bartosh family, zigzagged his way to the table and threw a slice of ham on her back of her blue crepe custom-made dress. It dropped off, but left a large, greasy stain just above her waist.

Anna turned, her mouth open. "My God. What happened?"

Stunned, Lukia said to the drunken soldier, "Why did you do that? You dirtied that beautiful dress." Elena took Anna's arm and escorted her to the kitchen to clean the stain.

The soldier said, "I heard you were complaining there wasn't enough food. I thought I'd give you some back."

Lukia swore under her breath.

Mike, who'd been standing nearby talking to Peter and Dolly, barked at the soldier, "Are you going to clean that lady's dress?"

The soldier's head bobbed as he

narrowed his eyes. "Are you going to make me?"

Mike took off his jacket, handed it to Peter, then rolled up his sleeves.

"Mike," Lukia said, "leave it. He's drunk." Her son was, too. She knew how quickly a brawl could get out of hand.

Later, she couldn't remember who threw the first blow, but it didn't take long for Mike to be straddling the soldier on the floor and punching him in the face.

A man yelled, "Fair fight, fair fight!"

Mike looked up to see who was shouting, and that was when the soldier struck him in the eye. Mike keeled over backwards. The soldier dragged himself up and was about to go after Mike again, but two of the Bartosh sons pulled him away. "That's enough," one said.

Harry came over, with a distraught Marike behind him. He and Peter helped Mike up and guided him to a chair. Holding his eye, Mike slumped down on the seat.

"Dunya," Lukia said, "get a cold, wet cloth."

While Dunya ran to the kitchen, Harry said to Mike, "Why did you have to fight and spoil my wedding?"

Egnat, who had stepped outside to have a cigarette, pushed through the crowd that had gathered. He said to Mike, "When are you going to stop talking with your fists?"

"It wasn't my fault."

"It never is."

Ignoring his brother, Mike took the wet cloth from Dunya and dabbed his red and swollen right eye. Lukia regarded him with a pained expression. "You're lucky it wasn't worse."

"You're going to have a nasty bruise," said Peter, bending to get a better look.

A commotion at the front of the hall grabbed Lukia's attention. Two police officers were marching towards them. Harry stepped forward and assured them that the matter was now under control and there was no further risk to those attending.

Anna had also returned to the dance floor. The back of her dress bore a large wet mark. Lukia went over to her and said, "I'm so sorry, Anna."

"Don't worry, Lukia. It can be cleaned."

Lukia hugged Anna, thanking her for her help and understanding.

With the unfortunate fracas over, the band began playing the first waltz. Harry took Marike's hand and together, they glided around the floor. Halfway through the number, Victor, the bandleader, invited the attendants to join in. And for the second waltz, Mike put his arm around his mother. "Come, Mama." As they waltzed together, Peter and Dunya twirled past, laughing about something.

Then the band played the usual polkas, fox trots, kolomeyka, and schottische. Lukia sat on the sidelines with her friend Natasha and watched the dancers move across the floor. There were couples and children from both sides kicking up their heels in time to the music. She thanked God she had prepared dishes at home to bring. Though the reception had had a shaky start, and a fight had ensued, the celebration was now running without a hitch.

During presentation, Lukia clapped along with the others, but she noticed that the divide between the groom's and bride's families had grown even wider. Members of each side shot the other side cool looks, or turned their heads when their eyes met. For Lukia, the raucous incident was another layer of embarrassment added to what she already felt over the meagre food offering. And no matter how much her children said it wasn't her fault, the humiliation of what had transpired would haunt her for years, a humiliation she'd remind Harry of repeatedly.

A Dark Time

The biggest blow that fall came in a letter from Damien, Kolya's father. Kolya and his Polish naval unit had been en route to Halifax again, when the vessel went down and he was lost at sea. Damien wrote that Kolya had hoped to see his baba. Lukia collapsed when she heard the news and went to her bed. She remembered Kolya sitting on her lap, his chubby arms around her neck, and how excited he'd been when she gave him the sailor suit she'd sewed for his immigration to Argentina. Why hadn't she made the effort to meet him in Halifax when he'd asked her two years ago? Now she'd never see him again. He had perished not long after his nineteenth birthday. Her darling boy. Like his mother, he died too young. Her link to Hania was forever gone.

She wanted to scream at those who started the damn war and those who sent young men off to fight. But screaming about the madness would do nothing to stop this war or the ones that would follow. More people's lives would be snuffed out faster than a candle. *My God, my God, how to make sense of it all?* She fell asleep on a pillow wet from her tears, and didn't get up until late the following morning.

Family Matters

Dolly and Peter had never expected they'd have two brothers and her mother living with them. Harry and Marike had moved into a room upstairs the night of their wedding. It was a temporary arrangement, they said, and much appreciated. They hoped to find a larger room to rent before their first anniversary.

Dolly's mother and Mike moved in as well, not long after Harry's wedding. Dolly gave her mother a bed downstairs, just off the living room, and Mike took over a room on the second floor. Now that their mother had given up renting the farm, Mike planned to look for a steady job in the city. Dolly told her brother he could have free room and board until he found one.

Having her mother living with them meant Dolly had help in the kitchen, which was a godsend after working all day at Canada Packers. When she and Peter got home, there was a pot of borscht or kapusnyak simmering on the stove. Other days, her mother made varenyky with various fillings, or studenetz or kishka. Peter loved the blood sausage and smacked his lips, which was thanks enough for her mother.

So far, Dolly's pregnancy had gone well, and she could work and put aside several dollars from every week's paycheck to pay for a hospital birth. All seemed well, except for the evenings around the kitchen table, when her mother would bring up another sore point about Mike.

"Where's Mike?" she asked. "How come he's not here for supper?"

Peter sighed heavily, which wasn't lost

on the women. He normally ate in silence while they massaged their worries by talking endlessly about Mike.

"He's rung up an enormous debt at Dan Balacko's," Lukia said.

Dolly nodded. The fact her mother worried so much about her brother played on Dolly's nerves. Mike had taken advantage of Egnat on the farm. She did not want him to take advantage of her goodwill in the city. Wanting to avoid a blow-up on a workday, Dolly waited until the following Saturday afternoon to confront Mike. She caught him coming down the stairs, and, just as he had his hand on the doorknob to leave the house, she said, "Mike, I need to talk to you."

His face tightened. "I'm going to be late." She guessed it was the seriousness of her tone that had caused him to pause. His curly black hair had been side-parted and smoothed out with Brylcreem, and the lime scent of his aftershave was overwhelming. It was strong, but didn't fully hide the fact he'd had a drink of alcohol before coming downstairs. She guessed he was going out to meet some girl.

"This won't take long."

"What's your problem now?" he asked, shifting from one leg to the other.

"Mike, Peter and I have been happy to help you out, but Mama's worried you're not taking care of your debts. She said you owe a lot to Dan Balacko."

He shrugged. "I'll pay it. I just haven't had time."

"You never have time to pay what you owe. Peter and I can't keep supporting you if you're going to throw your money away."

His eyes darkened. "If Mama has a problem, she can talk to me directly."

"How many times has she already talked to you about this?"

He grabbed the doorknob again. "Are you finished?"

"No. I'm telling you, because it's not

fair to Mama. She's worked hard all her life—"

"I know she's worked hard all her life," he said, cutting her off.

"You're not listening. I know you're getting work. I've seen you come home drunk, so obviously you're getting paid. Are you still selling homebrew?"

"Why don't you mind your own business?"

"If you're staying here for free, it is my business."

"I'll get your money," he said, his voice rising.

"Pay your debts first."

He swore at her in Ukrainian and said, "I hope you lose your baby. You'd make a lousy mother."

Her heart pounded and her body shook. "You want me to lose my baby? That's what you want? Get out!"

He stared at her as if she might change her mind, then stormed out, slamming the door behind him. Upset, her body continued to tremble over the heated exchange. She took several deep breaths and leaned against the doorframe. What had happened to her dear brother, the one she went to for advice, the one who'd been so gentle with her nieces, and the one who had always taken her arm for the first dance at community affairs so local fellows could see how desirable she was? What had changed him into this man who could say something so cruel? For the rest of the day, she agonized over their quarrel. When she tried to tell Peter what had happened, she broke down sobbing. Her mother held her chest when she heard what Mike had done now.

Mike ended up at Harry and Marike's new place, sleeping on the floor. A week later, he knocked on Peter and Dolly's door, full of apologies. Peter said he'd go along with anything Dolly decided. She was grateful for his understanding.

Her mother, soft-hearted to a fault,

said, "Look at how beaten he looks. Does he have to beg before you take him back?"

"Mama, he wanted me to lose my baby. What kind of brother is that?"

"He didn't mean it. You know he didn't mean it. He was angry. It was the drink speaking."

They asked Mike to sit down in the living room, where they lectured him on his responsibilities. He listened, his eyes wet and glistening. He had apologized, but Dolly wasn't convinced he was contrite enough to change his ways. But like her mother, she relented. His room on the second floor was available and she let him have it, on condition he pay his debts and his rent. He promised he would.

The continuing rumours of layoffs at Canada Packers bothered Peter. He could see how it wore on Dolly, too. They couldn't tighten up anymore, she told him. Now that her mother lived with them, they had another mouth to feed. She helped some, because she had sold her farm equipment and animals, but how long would that money last? Yet Peter felt blessed to have his mother-in-law living with them. She was a soft-spoken woman who was willing to help any way she could, and the only arguments she had were with her daughter, not with him.

As for them having to tighten up, they weren't alone. All of Canada had to tighten up. Because of the war effort, the government announced that butter would be rationed. Only one-quarter pound a week.

Dolly said, "How can anyone cook with so little butter?" Fortunately, they had an acceptable substitute. They were lucky to get a box of bacon ends at the end of the week. Any bacon fat left over after frying was saved and reused.

Peter broke the monotony of his job by daydreaming. He wished he could allay some of Dolly's anxiety. His pay was as good as he could get anywhere else, as long as there were no layoffs. Enlisting could solve his uncertain job situation. So many dead and wounded had forced the armed forces to reconsider their requirements, and he was now eligible. He expected that any day, the government would call him up to serve. But with a baby on the way and the fact so many soldiers were dying, he wasn't sure how he felt about it anymore, and because of that, he got jumpy whenever there was mail to open.

One late afternoon in March, he came home and saw the mail his mother-in-law had brought into the house. It was sitting on the coffee table in the living room. He approached the letter with some trepidation and was relieved to discover it was another letter from Bill. He was replying to Peter's letter about Dolly's pregnancy and the fact the armed forces were now lowering the requirements to serve.

Bill wrote: *I talked to George and we both agree you're better off staying home. The damn forces have three of us, now that John has joined. That's enough of us Klewchuks. You're doing your duty by getting the meat cut and wrapped so we don't go hungry. Besides, Dolly's pregnant. You don't want your child coming into the world without a father there to greet him.*

Bill's words shook Peter. Even though what Bill said made sense, Peter couldn't forget how he felt about the war and the fact he wasn't in it. He also wondered why the army was so bent on recruiting more men when his brothers were still waiting to be deployed to some battlefield. It had been over three years since Bill and George had signed up, and yet, they were still sitting somewhere in England. Bill said higher-ups kept telling them they'd be setting out soon, but when his unit readied themselves to go, those in command inexplicably cancelled their orders to depart. Peter understood his brothers' disappointment. It seeped through Bill's words on the page. His brothers had been training in England since they'd first arrived on British shores. The war was happening, but they weren't part of it. With various countries supplying troops, Peter suspected that was part of the generals' challenges, figuring out who went where and when.

Dolly was relieved that Peter's brothers had recommended he stay home. And in a sense, so was Peter after he re-read Bill's letter. He stood taller now. Though no one had suggested he was a coward, he had counted on his younger brothers seeing it that way, too. And they were right. The forces had enough Klewchuks. No one could argue with that. Besides, after Dieppe's losses, more and more Canadians were questioning the merits of war. Too many shed tears over the loss of so many young men and women, and for what? They hadn't stopped Hitler or the other two monsters. He tucked the letter away and silently prayed his brothers would be spared the horrors of combat and come home safe.

A Glitch in Her Plans

One Sunday in early January, Peter's appendix acted up. He complained of constipation and pain in his belly. Dolly thought he had eaten something that hadn't agreed with him. But then she changed her mind. *It can't be that. I ate the same thing. And so did Mama.*

A few hours later, Peter said the pain had radiated to the lower right side of his stomach. Nausea followed. Since he'd had the same sharp ache a year before, they suspected it was his appendix. Back then, alcohol had calmed it down, so he tried a shot of horilka, hoping the pain would subside, but it became so acute that Dolly ran next door and asked her landlady to call their doctor.

Peter lived through an hour of agony before Dr. Novak arrived. He examined Peter's abdomen and reviewed his symptoms. Putting his stethoscope back into his black bag, he said, "You have to go to the hospital. Your appendix is likely inflamed, and it's not going to get any better on its own."

"Oy," Dolly said. "The hospital? How long will he have to be there?"

"I don't know. It depends on what they find."

Dolly groaned. They had the money, but they'd saved it so she wouldn't have to birth their baby at home. But what could she say? It wasn't his fault his appendix had acted up.

Peter must've sensed her disappointment, because he said, "I don't have to go. It's okay. The pain will die down."

The doctor gave Peter a concerned look. "No, it won't."

"Honey," she said, "don't be foolish. You have to go."

Fortunately, Mike was home and drove Peter and Dolly to St. Joseph's Hospital. He waited with her while the staff checked Peter in. When the nurse told Dolly nothing would happen until the morning, she went back to the house with Mike.

Dolly tossed in bed all night, agonizing about Peter and the upcoming birth of her baby. Her mother had birthed her children at home, but she'd also lost a few not long after they were born. Now, hospital deliveries were deemed safer than those at home, but Peter's health crisis had shattered her hope of delivering her baby there.

His operation took place in the morning. While she waited in the area designated for visitors, Dolly became so distressed she almost forgot to call their boss at Canada Packers to say they weren't coming into work that day. A staff member let her use the phone at the nurses' station.

After the call, to occupy her troubled mind, Dolly pulled out of her purse a large spool of heavy white thread and a steel crochet hook, and began to fashion a white bonnet for her baby. Time crawled in the waiting room. Periodically, Dolly would throw an anxious look at any medical staff who passed by, hoping for some word about Peter's surgery. She was afraid to go to the restroom, in case she missed the doctor with any news.

Hours later, the surgeon appeared and told Dolly in a serious tone, "His appendix ruptured, and we had to remove it. I did my best to clean up the infection."

"What does that mean you did your best?" she asked, her voice tense. "Will he be okay?"

"We hope so. We'll have to watch him."

"Can I see him?"

"He's sleeping now. Come back in the afternoon."

Assured that Peter was getting good care, Dolly went home to eat. While she and her mother were eating an egg sandwich for lunch, her sister-in-law Mary showed up. She had come to the city to shop, and decided to pop by to say hello.

After hearing what had happened, Mary accompanied Dolly back to the hospital for visiting hours. They found Peter lying in bed by the window in a room with three other patients in various stages of recovery. A nurse was taking Peter's temperature. When she took the thermometer out of his mouth and read the results, her eyes widened.

Dolly stepped forward and said, "How's Peter? I'm his wife."

"His temperature has climbed. I have to get the doctor." The nurse hurried out of the room.

Dolly took one look at Peter's pale face, the sweat beading near his hairline, and realized he was in trouble. Her body tightened. Placing her palm on his forehead, she said, "Honey, you're burning up." She glanced furtively at the door, expecting a doctor to rush in at any moment, but the seconds mounted to minutes and longer with no sign of any medical staff.

Mary patted Peter's arm. "You look like hell," she said jokingly.

Though weak, he grinned. "I bet."

Finally, the nurse returned, breathless, with a doctor. She raised Peter's head and gave him a pill with a glass of water, then placed a damp cloth on his forehead. She told Dolly, "I'm sorry, you'll have to wait in the waiting room."

Dolly cast an anxious glance at Peter. "I'll stay out of the way."

The doctor rolled back the sheet. "Mrs. Klewchuk, I need to examine his incision. You best go."

Reluctant to leave, Dolly bit her bottom lip and said to Peter. "I'll be back as soon as the doctor finishes."

In the waiting room, time moved as slowly as molasses. While Mary thumbed through a magazine she had found on a side table, Dolly rummaged through her memories. Had she had a bad dream recently? Had she overlooked some sign?

She said to Mary, "I don't want him to die."

Mary squeezed her hand. "Of course you don't."

"We're going to have a baby," Dolly said, her stomach in knots.

"Congratulations." Mary looked at Dolly's ample figure. "I noticed you got bigger, but I didn't want to say anything."

Dolly smiled. "No, not fat, Mary." She wrung her hands. "What would I do without him?"

"Don't jump ahead of yourself. He's not going to die."

Dolly gnashed her teeth, then opened her purse and pulled out the white baby bonnet she was crocheting. She had completed enough to show a flower design.

That's pretty," Mary said.

A child's crying caused them both to look up. Down the corridor, a nurse was comforting a girl of about ten.

Dolly stared at the child. "Poor girl. I hope she didn't lose her mother or her father." Immediately, Dolly thought about the baby she was carrying. She saw herself, pregnant and dressed in black, sobbing and walking behind a coffin. "Oy," she said, forgetting for a moment where she was sitting.

As if Mary had read her mind, she said, "No matter what happens, ...at least your baby will have a name."

"Oh, Mary," Dolly muttered. She knew her sister-in-law wished her daughter had a proper last name. Mary's remark didn't help Dolly feel less anxious, but she appreciated what her sister-in-law had gone through. The two women might never become close, but Dolly sensed the ice between them had melted.

While Mary went off to find a

payphone—so she could call her daughter and tell her she'd be late getting home—Dolly tried to calm her nerves. What was taking the doctor so long? Why couldn't she have stayed in the room? The nurse had looked alarmed when she raced off to find a doctor. What weren't they telling her? What were they hiding? Poor Peter. So pale and helpless lying in bed. She couldn't imagine having a baby without him. She closed her eyes and pushed the thought away. She recalled what Peter's mother had said regarding her son when he was a baby. She'd lost three infants before him and was afraid she'd lose him, too. Frantic, she'd taken him to a fortune teller, who tapped him on the forehead and said, "You can't kill this one. This one will live." Dolly hung on to that story. Still, she prayed: *Please, God, let Peter live.*

The week following Peter's surgery was an emotional roller coaster. Not knowing what was going on in the hospital kept

Dolly awake at night. Since they couldn't afford for her to be absent from work, she returned to the plant the following day, but begged the nurse on duty to call her if there was any problem. Lukia visited Peter every afternoon, and Dolly went every evening. Some days, Peter rallied, only to slip back into a listless state.

On the fifth evening, when Peter was still drifting in and out of sleep, Dolly raised her concerns with Dr. Novak, who had come by to check on Peter. "He's sleeping so much. Shouldn't he be better by now?"

He patted her arm. "He's doing what he has to do. His body's fighting the infection. That's why he's so tired."

At home, her mother reassured her as well. "Dunya, Peter is strong. He'll pull through.

When Dolly shook her head and groaned, her mother said, "Look, I almost died of typhus. They didn't give me treatment like the doctor is giving Peter.

God saved me. You have to pray. We'll pray together."

Later that evening, Dolly knelt down beside her mother's bed. Her mother was already there on her knees.

Her mother was right—Peter was strong. His infection cleared up, and the hospital discharged him eight days after his operation. Dr. Novak said Peter was very lucky. Dolly felt like crying with joy. He would miss more work, but at least he was on the mend.

One late January day, while he was still recovering at home, Dolly returned from work bubbling with excitement. "Peter!" she shouted as she came in the front entrance. "Big news at the plant."

He rose from the chair in the kitchen, where he'd been reading the previous night's newspaper, and walked to the hallway. She noticed he did it without grimacing and smiled. It meant he'd be back at work soon.

Placing her hands on his cheeks, she kissed him.

He shivered. "Brrr. You're ice cold." He took her hands in his, blew on her fingers to warm them, then rubbed them. "What's happening at work? What's the big news?"

"You remember Adam Borsk?" she said as she took off her snow-covered boots and put them on a rubber mat by the front door. "He used to work at Canada Packers. Now he lives in Toronto. He came to the plant today and told us we should all join the Packinghouse Workers Union. The union's strong in the United States, even in Ontario. He picked two Ukrainians, a meat-cutter and a canner, to sign up members." She took a folded pamphlet out of her fur coat pocket and gave it to Peter. "They stood outside the gates today and handed this out. Read it." She hung her coat in the tall wardrobe in the hallway, then followed him into the living room.

Peter sat down on the upholstered

chair by the floor lamp. The drapes were parted, showing the mounds of snow outside. Though bright white against the dark sky, they did little to brighten the room. He turned on the lamp to read the leaflet.

Dolly unbuttoned the heavy sweater she wore under her winter coat and settled on the chesterfield across from him. "What does it say?" she asked.

Peter read the pamphlet silently, then said, "The union organizers want us to join so we can talk with one voice to management. They say it shouldn't matter what race we are or religion we follow. There should be equal rights, fair treatment for all in the workplace." He put the pamphlet down.

"The time might be right for a union," she said. "If we had one, maybe you'd get paid for missing work because of your operation. And we'd get paid if we're sick."

"That would be nice."

"There are too many accidents, too."
She clicked her tongue. "You know how
the foreman plays favourites. And how
many times have they asked us to work
overtime with no extra pay? Then they
think nothing about laying us off in the
winter or whenever the hell they feel like
it."

Peter wrinkled his brow. "It may
sound good, but I've heard of this union
before. Some say the organizers are
Communist or Communist sympathizers.
You know all the trouble that can cause.
What if the foreman finds out who
signed? We could lose our jobs if he
thinks we're Communist or plotting
behind management's back."

"Honey, don't worry so much."

"Well," he said, "I don't think it'll hurt
to wait. See who else is signing."

She considered his suggestion, then
said, "I don't know. Maybe you're right."
Their discussion had taken the air out of
her balloon, but she had to agree. There

was no point in signing a paper that could cause them grief down the road.

Peter returned to work, but that wasn't the end of Dolly's worries, both at work and at home. There was continuing talk at the plant about possible strike action and potential layoffs. Mike hadn't paid his debt to Dan Balacko as promised and was becoming increasingly quarrelsome, especially when he was reminded of his obligations. And her mother obsessed about being a burden.

"What good am I?" she said to her daughter one evening, when they were sitting in the living room doing handwork.

"Mama," Dolly said, looking up from the white baby booties she was crocheting, "you've worked hard your whole life. You deserve to take it easy. And when the baby comes, you can stay home with her while I go to work. You'll be a big help to us."

"Nu, we'll see." Her mother picked a

blue rag from the bag by her feet and began braiding it into the rug she was making.

Dolly looked at her wristwatch. It was time for Lux Radio Theatre. She had been following the character Diane, who was waiting for her boyfriend to propose. It was too bad her mother couldn't follow the dialogue or understand the story. If she could, she wouldn't keep interrupting every time Dolly moaned about something or teared up.

Dolly left work at Canada Packers at the beginning of March, one month before her due date. She had hoped to earn enough to still pay for a hospital birth, but time had run out. The girls at work teased her about being as big as a house. She laughed and said, "Yes, a duplex." She told the foreman she hoped to return six or seven months after her baby was born. He made no promises there'd be a job waiting, but said to check in with him then. She was sad to leave, because the excitement of joining a union had grown since January. Over 560 workers had signed, which was a majority, and that list included Dolly's and Peter's signatures, too. Though the number of employees signing had increased, these were still early days. No one knew how management was going to react to a union making demands.

Not long after the signing, Peter attended a union meeting after work at Drewry's Hall by the Redwood Bridge. When he returned home, Dolly was waiting up for him in the living room. She put aside her crocheted handwork while he slumped down on the chesterfield beside her.

"Well, it's official," he said, bending down to massage his feet. "We have a union. We elected an executive. Jack Shewchuk is our president."

Dolly nodded approvingly. "He's good."

"Borsk was there, too. He's going to

write to Harris, the general manager of Canada Packers, and ask for a meeting to begin negotiations on wages, hours, and working conditions."

She clapped her hands. "That's wonderful. Maybe we'll finally get paid what we deserve."

"Maybe," Peter said.

Their elation was short-lived. Only days later, Peter walked into the house after work with gloom written plainly on his face. He said to Dolly, who had greeted him at the door, "Harris left for a vacation and won't be back until the end of the month. Everyone's sure he took off because he doesn't want to meet with the union. It's a stalling tactic. Jack was so angry. You should've heard him swear. He said that if he and Borsk can't arrange a meeting soon with the higher ups, we'll have to take action."

"That's serious. Does he mean a strike? You won't get paid." She rocked her head. "Oy, oy, oy."

"And what's more," Peter said, putting his wool tweed cap on the hallway hook, "the office manager said Canada Packers won't recognize the union, or Borsk any longer, and any negotiations for better conditions or pay have to go through the plant relations committee."

"What plant relations committee? They do nothing except parrot what the bosses say. What good is that?"

"Don't give up yet," he said, taking off his winter jacket. "Jack said Borsk is going to write the Department of Labour."

She grunted. "A lot of good that will do." She didn't trust the government to do anything but scratch wealthy people's backs. It was like that when she was growing up and as far as she could see, nothing had changed. When anyone campaigned for office, they promised they would improve the lot of the workers—the backbone of the country, they said—but after they were elected, they went back to their old ways of favouring the rich and powerful.

Unable to solve the workplace problem, they stopped talking. Dolly knocked on her mother's bedroom door to come and have supper.

As her pregnancy dragged on, Dolly worried about having a child when their future looked so uncertain. She continued to worry about giving birth at home, even though Dr. Novak had examined her and reassured her everything was fine.

Her mother tried to allay her fears. "The baby will come when she's ready." From the way Dolly was carrying the baby, her mother was sure she was having a girl.

Her due date came and went. She was so big now, she had difficulty sleeping. If she wasn't thinking about the upcoming birth, she was worrying about the ongoing labour issues at Canada Packers.

Then, like the lid blown off a steaming

kettle, an incident happened at the plant that galvanized the workers to do something more than just talk.

Push Comes to Shove

The last day of March turned out to be a fiery one at Canada Packers. As usual, Peter was working on the kill floor, lifting beef carcasses on and off the hooks. While he worked, he heard about the latest work conflict from Cameron, a burly Scotsman with a swarthy complexion. He was as tall as Peter, but twice as wide.

"Hey, Pete," Cameron said as he and Peter threw a side of beef on the steel table for butchering. "You heard what happened to Ross?"

"No, what?" Peter asked, turning towards Cameron. Ross was a senior employee, a jokester, and well-loved in the plant.

"After Harris came back from vacation, he was showing his brother around and saw a pile of empty cartons in the sausage kitchen. You know Harris, he hates messes. He told the foreman to do something about it. The foreman discovered it was Ross who'd left the cartons there and suspended him for two weeks without pay. Can you believe that?" Cameron's bushy eyebrows went up a notch.

"No kidding," Peter said, then grabbed the hose to wash some blood off the floor.

"Ross was so angry. You should've seen him. His face was beet red."

"He's a union member, right? Isn't he also on the plant relations committee?"

"That's the one," Cameron said. "Well, Ross went to see the plant superintendent, but the guy wouldn't talk to him. Ross was so upset I'm surprised he didn't punch the asshole."

Peter shook his head as he continued to spray water on the floor. "Good thing he didn't. He'd lose his job for sure."

"Ross went to see our union rep, Maurice. He's in canning. Do you know him?"

"No."

"Nice guy." Cameron wiped down the steel table after a couple of workers took the side of beef away. "Maurice told Ross to wait in the dressing room, then called Borsk. They're going to try to resolve the matter with management over lunchtime. If they can't, we'll refuse to go back to work after lunch."

"What? They want us to strike?"

Cameron grinned. "Just enough to make a point. Let's hope it doesn't come to that." He turned away, then turned back. "Oh, something else. I almost forgot. Borsk said not to leave any work unfinished. He doesn't want the bosses to accuse us of wartime sabotage."

"What? That's wartime sabotage?"

"Yeah." Cameron twisted his lips. "And we're not to leave the plant before our shift ends because that would flout wartime labour laws. They prohibit wildcat strikes." He leaned against the table and said, "Jesus Christ, they don't want much, do they? A pound of flesh, that's what they want. May as well hang us on a damn hook, too, the way they think."

When the whistle blew for lunch, Peter climbed the stairs to the dressing room. He was no rabble rouser. He hated conflict and had seen enough of that growing up, but there were some things worth fighting for. Still, with a baby on the way, he wished this wasn't the time to take a stand.

In the dressing room, he grabbed his black metal lunch pail from the bench under his clothes hook and sat down with Cameron and several others at a long wood table.

Across from him, Frenchy, a short guy with a wiry moustache, said, "This is bullshit. Ross said he tried six times to tell the superintendent there was no truck to put the cartons in. What was he supposed to do? Take them home with him?"

Peter laughed. He bit into his baloney sandwich, wondering whether they'd be returning to their stations after eating.

Just before one o'clock, Borsk came into the noisy dressing room. The men quieted down within minutes of noticing him.

Having their attention, Borsk said, "Sorry, men. Management wouldn't even see me. Are you with me?"

"Yes," shouted a few. Another said, "Hell, yes." And "You better believe it" was among the shouts resounding through the room. Peter looked around the table. There were a few others who were subdued like him; they were the ones who had children to raise.

Borsk was about to sit down when the plant superintendent roared into the room, yelling at the men to return to work or leave the building. "What the hell are you sitting here for? It's after one. Get back to work!"

The workers—having been warned earlier by the union not to leave the workplace—sat there and stared back at the bellicose boss. A few men grumbled to one another, but none of the workers moved. After glaring at the crowd, the plant superintendent stormed out.

Three-quarters of the men and a quarter of the women supported the sit-down strike—over 500 workers refused to go back to work that day. Though anxious about where this sit-down strike was headed, Peter was proud to be a member of a group standing up to management about unfair labour practices. For the rest of the afternoon, he sat with the other workers, playing cards or just shooting the breeze, until the plant buzzer sounded, signalling the end of the workday.

It was work as usual the next day, but the employees believed they were getting somewhere. The Packinghouse Workers

Union newspaper reported, "These timid, browbeaten souls had rebelled against the meat baron." They had rebelled, but the higher-ups were not about to give in that easily. Though management still refused to recognize the union, they made some concessions. And Ross had to admit to poor work practices in order to get his suspension reduced to one day.

On the killing floor, Cameron said to Peter, "It's not over. Ross is fed up. He's not taking this lying down."

Within days of the sit-down strike, Ross signed a statement saying he had been intimidated by his foreman. He wanted the higher-ups to know he had tried six times to contact the plant superintendent and the only reason he admitted to poor work practices was because he had no empty truck to put the cartons in. If there'd been a truck, as there had been in the past, he wouldn't have left the cartons in the sausage kitchen.

Peter didn't want to burden Dolly with the troubles at work, especially when she was already so anxious about being overdue. But she kept reminding him they were in this fight together, so he told her the union organizers wanted to threaten Canada Packers with a national strike.

"And then what?" Dolly asked. "Are they going to pay you if you can't work? And what if the bosses get fed up and hire new workers?"

Peter had no answer. Any day now, they would become parents. With the workplace so uncertain, their dream of having a home of their own seemed further and further away. With no solution at hand, he went to sleep wondering what changes the next few months would bring.

Like the Soap Opera

Dolly's water finally broke a week later, when she was doing the supper dishes. Peter ran next door to the landlady's house to call the doctor. Dr. Novak showed up a few hours later and coached Dolly through the night. She'd never experienced such excruciating pain; it radiated across her abdomen and lower back, causing her to scream as she gripped the metal bars of their headboard. After hours of mind-numbing pain, the doctor said, "Push, push."

She pushed, and the pain grew, becoming so torturous she wanted to die.

"Oy, Docha," Lukia said, as she soaked a small twisted cloth in horilka. "Bite down on this. It helped me." Dolly bit down but hollered and groaned in agony as she rocked her body in bed. Her mother mopped her brow and said, "Not long now."

When her labour reached its zenith, Dolly felt she could endure it no longer. "I want poison!" she said. "Give me poison!"

Lukia frowned. "Don't say. That's a sin."

The doctor coughed. "You're almost there. Your baby's crowning. It's coming. Keep pushing."

Dolly pushed harder than she'd ever pushed anything on the farm. She thought her insides would break, that everything would spill out with the baby.

When her baby finally emerged and gave her first cry, Dr. Novak grinned. "You have a big baby. She must be nine or ten pounds." Dolly looked at her infant in the doctor's arms. Covered in blood and white fluid, the infant looked healthy, but her head was malformed, axe-shaped.

"My God, a cripple!" Lukia said, moaning and holding her chin in both hands.

"A cripple or not, she's my cripple," Dolly said defiantly.

Dr. Novak placed the baby on Dolly's breast. "Don't worry. Her head will look normal soon."

Her mother shrugged—a wordless *maybe.*

"You're badly torn," Dr. Novak said. "I have to go back to the office to get some stitching supplies." Before Dolly could protest, he was gone. She felt chilled and was bleeding profusely. She was half aware of her mother doing her best to mop up the blood.

Exhausted from her ordeal, Dolly slept a little. She awoke when she heard the doctor talking to her mother. Their voices, a soft rumble in the background. Dr. Novak, seeing her eyes open, told Dolly, "I've sewn you up. Get lots of rest. You should stay in bed for five days until you've healed."

Her mother made a face. Dolly wanted to ask why she was frowning, but then she heard the doctor say, "You can go in now."

Peter came into their bedroom, grinning from ear to ear. He gazed upon their little girl and stroked her fine, dark hair as she sucked on her mother's nipple. "What a darling. Oh, sweetheart." He met Dolly's eyes. "You went through a lot. How are you feeling?"

"Sore. Tired. Hungry."

"That's my girl," he said, and kissed her. "Thank you for bringing our daughter into the world."

She gazed at her daughter and at Peter. There were three of them now.

Later, when Peter had gone to sleep and her baby needed another feeding, her mother said, "Are you going to do what the doctor said? Stay in bed for five days?"

"Why not?" Dolly said, taking her eyes off her baby and meeting her mother's gaze.

"Such nonsense. I was up after a few hours preparing food for your father in the tsar's army."

"Maybe your baby wasn't so big. Maybe you weren't torn like me."

Her mother tsked. She said no more, but Dolly realized she'd get little sympathy from her mother after what she'd been through in the old country.

What Peter feared came to be ten days after his daughter's birth. The union threatened national strike action because Canada Packers management refused to acknowledge the union and its demands for a meeting to discuss pay and working conditions. Faced with the threat of a national strike, the federal authorities became involved. It was the start of a very rocky road for all the workers.

Peter didn't know what would come of

it. He expected he and Dolly would face many troubled nights before Canada Packers finally recognized the union as the sole collective bargaining agent for the workers. Until then, he would keep his head down and hope there wouldn't be any layoffs.

With her daughter at home tending to her infant, Lukia felt useless. She helped as best she could. She cooked and baked and did her handwork, but it didn't satisfy her. She was used to following the pattern of many generations in farming families—rising with the sun to tend to the livestock and the fields and working until the sun dropped in the sky. Now she was living with her son-in-law and daughter in a rented house, no longer the head of her own household.

Egnat and Dunya had reminded her countless times that she should be a woman of leisure. *A woman of leisure! Ha!* She laughed, even though she agreed she'd earned it. But what did she care about leisure? She never hungered to be such a person. She had lived in Canada for fourteen years and what did she have to show for it? In two more years, she would be seventy, but still ineligible for the twenty-dollar monthly pension from the government. Only British subjects of twenty years were eligible.

Dunya had tried to comfort her. "Mama, you don't have to worry about rent anymore, or even food. Peter and I are so thankful you'll take care of Diane when I go back to work."

Lukia pondered going to work herself. Maybe she could set up a stall in the public market on Main Street, sell fruits and vegetables. It would be a help, especially when Peter and Dunya were so worried about their jobs. When they discussed the union problems at work, she said, "Look at what our family's been through. War, hunger, typhus, dust storms. We never gave up. You'll get through this. We always have."

She looked down at her granddaughter nestled in her arms. Thank God her head had straightened out shortly after birth. Her rosebud lips, hazel eyes, and oval-shaped face reminded Lukia of Hania, the daughter she'd lost. Father Mayewsky had christened her new granddaughter Domekia, because he didn't accept the name Dunya had given her. He said, "Diane is not a Christian name." Dunya had shrugged and told her mother she liked it. She had named her after a character on Lux Radio Theatre. Lukia regretted not learning the English language well enough to understand the stories and knew she annoyed her daughter when she kept interrupting the program with questions. No matter, thought Lukia, her daughter would understand one day, when her child got older and criticized her mother. Why is it, Lukia thought, we get wise too late?

Whenever she reviewed her life, she

couldn't believe all she had weathered. Was she better off than before? She thought so. It had been a sacrifice leaving behind what she knew in the old country, but her children had found a better future in Canada. It wouldn't be long before Dunya and Peter could afford to buy a rooming house of their own. Egnat had already shown some success. Last year's bumper crops meant he could get better farm equipment and a better car. And soon, he'd finish the house that Dunya and Peter had half-constructed.

Harry, her quiet son, had given her so little trouble in the past, but now erupted whenever she brought up the wedding fiasco. He said, "Every time we visit you, I have trouble with my wife at home."

Lukia couldn't help complaining about the Bartosh family, how they'd robbed her. But every time she complained, Dunya said, "Mama, you keep opening an old wound." And Lukia replied, "I can't help it. It stays in my chest."

But as much as she complained, she was proud of Harry. He and Marike, who called herself Mary now, had moved out of the room upstairs and found a three-room shanty to rent on Flora, near Salter Street. And Harry continued to run the service station that John Slipchenko had left behind. Lukia wasn't sure how far Harry would get in life, though, as Marike wasn't working and was pregnant with their first. Yet, they were content. Contentment itself was priceless.

But poor Anna. She still had no word from her husband. She didn't know if he was alive or dead. Her son, Walter, was now ten years old and hadn't seen his father in four years.

Mike was still the one giving Lukia too many sleepless nights. She continued to hope and pray he'd find some comfort in life. Many mothers knew the sorrow of raising a child who walked against the wind.

Peter had turned out to be a wonderful

son-in-law. He treated her as if she was his own mother. Noticing how she and Dunya shared the details of their dreams over breakfast, he had bought them a dream book from Dohanyk's store on Main Street. Peter said to Dunya, "This book explains in Ukrainian what some things we dream about mean."

Her daughter examined the book's contents and shared a few interpretations. Crying in a dream didn't mean that sadness would come. It meant the opposite, just as Lukia had always believed. She had also correctly interpreted many symbols in dreams. When she had dreamt about cows overflowing with milk, she knew this was a bad omen. Hadn't she warned her husband not to go into the woods that day? She told him she had a terrible dream. But he didn't listen. She was certain he'd be alive today if he had only listened.

It was unfortunate, she thought, that

Peter dwelt on the war as much as he did. It caused him so much grief. But who could blame him? He had three brothers in the service. Bill and George had recently landed in Sicily. From what she'd been told, they, along with the Allies, were about to begin the fight of their lives. Bill was now a sergeant major and George a sergeant. Up to their deployment to Sicily, they had joked the war would end before either of them got engaged in battle.

The war was on her mind, too. Volhynia was under siege, with various factions fighting for control. Thankfully, her brother Petro had returned to Toronto from the old country long before Hitler's troops set foot in Volhynia. Lukia groaned. Maybe one day, she'd ask Peter and Dunya to take her to Toronto. Though Lukia felt she'd been wronged by Petro, he was still her brother and if he couldn't see the error of his ways, well, she would forgive him.

As for her other brother, Pavlo, she

hadn't heard from him in a while. Egnat had written last, but hadn't heard back. With war raging in her homeland, she suspected mail in and out was a problem. She understood none of what was going on. But then, she'd never understood man's need to grab someone else's land and lose blood over it. She prayed for peace.

Diane had fallen asleep in her arms. Lukia put her in the carriage on the porch, and though the weather had warmed up some, it was still cool. She tucked a blanket around her granddaughter and sat down on the wooden chair beside the carriage. She looked out on the small fenced yard and thought again about how much had changed. She would never again have to worry about crops or livestock being fed, but she missed the land, with its smells and its promise. Thankfully, she could feed her need by visiting Egnat's farm. He had inherited her love for the treasures that hard work, sun, and rain could bring. He was his father's son through and through.

Gregory, you'd be proud of your children. She thought once more of his arms around her and smiled. There was so much she wanted to tell him. She wanted him to know she'd found a church in Canada, but he hated church. He'd mocked her beliefs. *Gregory,* she whispered, as a robin flew by. *How do you think I got through all these years without you?*

On Sunday, she would take the streetcar to Sobor with Peter, Dolly, and Diane. And come winter, she would go even after a heavy snowfall. No more worries about impassable roads. No more concerns about who would drive her.

Easter Sunday was a week away. She planned on wearing the new hat Dunya had bought her. It was black straw, with a pink cloth flower and a grosgrain ribbon around the brim. It seemed so long ago that she'd walked the streets of Warsaw, on her way to Canada, dreaming of trading in her babushka for one of the straw hats she saw on the ladies she passed. Now she had one of her own.

Glossary (Alphabetical)

Baba—grandmother

Babushka—headscarf

Boora—storm

Borscht—hearty soup made with beets, potatoes and cabbage

Daye Bozhe—"God willing," the toast given before drinking

Docha—daughter

Holupchi—cabbage roll

Horilka—vodka

Hrystyki—twisted sweet dough, fried and dipped in honey

Kapusnyak—sauerkraut soup

Kazshook—a sheepskin coat

Kishka—blood sausage

Kolomeyka—rousing Ukrainian folk dance

Komora—storehouse, pantry

Kutya—dish of cooked wheat with honey

and poppy seeds for Christmas Eve
Kybassa—ring of garlic sausage
Nalysnyky—cottage cheese-filled crepes,
    like blintzes
Oblast—region of the country, like a
    province or state
Pampushky—baked savoury or deep-fried
    sweet buns with fruit filling
Pan/Panye—Mr./Mrs.
Panahida—prayers for the deceased
Paska—a sweet yeast bread made with
    saffron and raisins
Perina—comforter, filled with feathers or
    down
Piyak—drunkard
Piroshky—yeast dumplings filled with
    either fruit or vegetables
Popravyny—the day after the wedding
    celebration for close friends and family
Rak—cancer
Rushnyk—a tea towel, often made from
    white cloth and embroidered
Shmata—rags, garments
Smachno—tasty

Smarkach—smarty-pants
Studenetz—jellied pigs' feet
Tato—father
Varenyky—filled dumplings that have been
    softly boiled
Vichnaya pamyat –eternal memory

Author's Note

When I first started writing *Sunflowers Under Fire,* the story of my baba's life in Russia during the Great War, I never expected I would write a sequel, let alone a trilogy. Prior to that, I had written two women's fiction novels and thought I would soon get back to writing more of that genre. But when readers of my baba Lukia Mazurets's story wanted to know what happened next, I wrote the sequel, *Lilacs in the Dust Bowl,* about her immigration to Canada with her family.

Though Lukia's Family Saga Series is fiction, it's biographical fiction, meaning it's based on the true stories of real people. My mother was a natural storyteller and I'm thankful I had the foresight to record her tales about life in the old country and in

Canada. I ended up with over 125 pages of notes, but there was much that had to be imagined. I was not privy to most of the conversations that took place between family members and I had to invent other characters and dialogue, not only to honour my mother's stories but also to bring them to life. As mentioned in my acknowledgements, I researched the place and time as well as the events that were happening during my family's life in the old country and in Manitoba, where they settled.

Now that I've come to the end of Lukia's Family Saga, I suspect readers may want to know what happened to the characters in my story.

My parents, Dolly and Peter, had a happy marriage, built on love and understanding. They ended up owning several rooming houses and a cottage on Lake Winnipeg. They had their moments of frustration, as we all do, but they managed to resolve their differences through dialogue. Egnat and Elena, with their three girls, were successful farmers; Harry and Mary also lived a contented life and had two beautiful daughters. Mike married, had three lovely girls, but his inordinate challenges kept him from achieving his dreams. I remember him fondly. He had an endearing personality. Unfortunately, there was little understanding of alcoholism as a disease in the 1930s and 1940s. If he'd had help, his journey might've been less volatile.

As for the Packinghouse Workers Union, the local in Canada Packers' Winnipeg plant was officially recognised as the sole collective bargaining agent for the workers in October 1943. That decision paved the way for a national union for the rest of the meatpacking industry in Canada.

The Klewchuk men—Bill, George, and John—survived the war, though the emotional scars of what they'd witnessed stayed with them. Shot in the throat during the Italian campaign, George had an especially tough time with frequent nightmares. He had one more child, a boy. John stayed in Northern Ireland, married, and had three boys. John kept the Klewchuk name, and when the Irish asked him about it, he said his name was Canadian. Mary married an Icelandic Canadian farmer and had three more children—two girls and a boy. Her youngest was a flower girl at our wedding.

John Slipchenko (my godmother's husband) returned from Hong Kong with some physical ailments, but his spirit remained intact. It hadn't been broken by his imprisonment and brutal torture in a prisoner-of-war camp.

My baba, Lukia, lived with my mother, father and me, until she was 84. In the bedroom she and I shared for the first fifteen years of my life, she told me she was ready to go. Not long after, she passed away peacefully in Winnipeg General Hospital. She left our lives physically, but her spirit and love of family continue to inspire those she left behind.

Acknowledgements

I feel blessed to have had my baba Lukia Mazurec, my mother Dolly Klewchuk, my father Peter Klewchuk, and my uncles Egnat, Harry, and Mike lodged in my memory, guiding me as I wrote the last book of Lukia's Family Saga. I'm thankful I recorded my mother's anecdotes, told over many cups of tea, which served as the foundation for the trilogy that formed this series.

My cousin, Jean Reid—who was just a baby when she immigrated to Canada with her father and mother, Egnat and Elena Mazurec—generously answered my endless questions, some about family, many about farming.

Cousin Eleanor, my Aunt Mary's daughter, gave me her blessing to write about the challenging time her mother had when she birthed her out of wedlock.

And my Uncle Bill Kendall (Klewchuk) gave me his diary, *Vignettes of Life in the Early Thirties* and *Army Memoirs,* years before he passed away. He was a colourful writer and I'm sure he'd be pleased that some of his entries made it into my story.

To discover more about life on the prairies of Manitoba, I researched weather, farming conditions, and news events in *The Winnipeg Free Press, The Winnipeg Tribune,* and *The Stonewall Argus.* Other helpful sources were: *Winnipeg Meat-Packing Workers' Path to Union Recognition,* a thesis by John Hanley Grover for the Department of History, University of Winnipeg (c) July, 1996; and *The Story of Stony Mountain and District* by Edward R. R. Mills, De Montfort Press 1960. The internet also gave me much to consider, from YouTube videos to articles on various historical sites. The story of the Martian Invasion,

"The War of the Worlds", a 1938 radio drama, aired by Columbia Broadcasting System radio network, is well-documented online.

As for what happened to Father Mayewsky, I had the benefit of examining the Supreme Court of Canada document—1940 CanLII 59 (SCC)—which gave the details of the case between the Appellants, The Ukrainian Greek Orthodox Church of Canada (Plaintiffs); and the Respondents, The Trustees of the Ukrainian Greek Orthodox Cathedral of St. Mary the Protectress and Peter Mayewsky (Defendants).

My editor, Doreen Martens, who edited *Lilacs in the Dust Bowl,* also combed this story for errors that needed to be addressed.

And my writers' critique group—authors Shari Green, Kristin Butcher, Jocelyn Reekie, Liezl Sullivan, and Sheena Gnos—read many chapters and gave me the encouragement to keep going. I'm thankful for my beta readers—Bob McClintock, Jo Nell Huff, Kathy Kostuck and Kaitlin Vitt—who read my unpublished draft and sent me their thoughts on the story. My family—Karen, John, Diego, Robyn, Michael, Chloe, and Mimi—cheered me on.

My daughter, Robyn, also acted as a beta reader and gave me invaluable comments, which I used in my revisions.

My dear husband, Robert, has read every word, sometimes twice. Without his love, care, and patience every step of the way, this series wouldn't have happened. I'm so grateful to have him at my side.

About the Author

Diana Stevan is the author of the award-winning novel *Sunflowers Under Fire,* historical fiction; the sequel, *Lilacs in the Dust Bowl*; debut novel, *A Cry from the Deep,* a time-slip romantic adventure; *The Rubber Fence,* women's fiction; and *The Blue Nightgown*, a coming-of-age novelette.

Her varied background includes work as a clinical social worker, teacher, professional actor, model, and freelance writer-broadcaster for *Sports Journal*, CBC Television. She's had poetry published in *DreamCatcher*, a United Kingdom publication, a short story in the anthology *Escape,* and articles in newspapers and an online magazine.

With two daughters grown, Diana lives with her husband, Robert, on Vancouver Island and in West Vancouver, British Columbia.

For more, visit her website:
https://www.dianastevan.com

www.ingramcontent.com/pod-product-compliance
Lightning Source LLC
Chambersburg PA
CBHW021244200726
48288CB00015B/1449